THE LATE ELEPHANT

BY

JANET SCRIVENS

Published in 2014 by

Valley Publishing Company

Copyright © Janet D. Scrivens
The author asserts the moral right, under Copyright Designs and
Patents Act 1988, to be identified as the author of this work.

All rights reserved. No parts of this publication may be reproduced,
stored in a retrieval system or transmitted, in any form or by any
means without the prior written consent of the publisher, nor be
otherwise circulated in any form of binding or cover other than that
in which it is published and without a similar condition being
imposed on the subsequent purchaser.

To my wonderful family who are always there
when I need them:-

William, Angela, Daniel, Harriet,
Michael, Leslie, Jamie, Sophie,
Lucy, Simon, Charlie and Tom.
A constant reminder that I have done something right in
this life.

§

"I thank the goodness and the grace
Which on my birth have smiled,
And made me in these Christian days
A happy English child"

Anne and Jane Taylor
1782 - 1866   1783 - 1827

Contents

Chapter 1 *Swepstone 1891* _____ 1

Chapter 2 *The Wedding* _____ 17

Chapter 3 *Farewell* _____ 39

Chapter 4 *The Honeymoon* _____ 53

Chapter 5 *Glenfield* _____ 65

Chapter 6 *Wash-day* _____ 89

Chapter 7 *Roosters* _____ 107

Chapter 8 *A Stranger* _____ 117

Chapter 9 *Après Sunday Dinner* _____ 127

Chapter 10 *The Dominoes Team* _____ 140

Chapter 11 *The Sale* _____ 151

Chapter 12 *Harvest* _____ 165

Chapter 13 *A Letter* _____ 180

Chapter 14	A Sighting	194
Chapter 15	The Black Maria	205
Chapter 16	Christmas	218
Chapter 17	Fullbrook 1892	224
Chapter 18	Master Henry 1894	245
Chapter 19	A New Hat 1895	256
Chapter 20	Parma Violets 1896	273
Chapter 21	Grief 1897	291
Chapter 22	A Wind of Change 1899	305
Chapter 23	Long Live the King 1901	321
Acknowledgements		339
The bibliography		341

Chapter 1

Swepstone 1891

Ada opened her eyes to the sounds of the dawn chorus and peered towards the open window. The sun's rays had yet to emerge from behind St. Peter's Church, so she indulged in a languorous stretch. Her first thought was for Duncan and just for once there was no question that she would see him. She turned over to clasp the pillow and, despite the importance of the day, spent a few minutes burying her nose in the clean linen. Her skin was fresh from last night's bath and she relished the pungent smell of the softening-butter.

The rooster added his discordant voice to the ensemble, so Ada Elverson swung her feet to the ground and, following the necessary use of the chamber pot, pulled on her bodice and skirt.

Leaving the dark tresses to tumble around her shoulders, she cautiously lifted the latch. Anxious not to awaken the rest of the family, she stepped out onto the landing, tip-toeing to avoid the creaking floorboard as she made her way to the stairs.

The stone floor felt hard and uneven beneath her feet but Ada was too impatient to bother putting on her boots. Embers in the fire-grate gave out a faint glow and smells from beer and tobacco lingered. She opened the windows before reaching into the bread bin in search of crusts. There were no sounds from above so she began her chores, grateful for the opportunity to ponder without interruption.

The back-door swung open allowing Moses, the black and white terrier, to struggle through the gap, desperate to cock his leg against the apple tree. Ada picked up the egg-basket, hitched up her skirts and followed him out into the fresh air. She relished the feel of her toes sinking into turf wet with dew. It was well worth navigating any stray droppings from the poultry.

Fruit trees hung laden with blossom and Ada noticed that the buds on the lilac bush were showing colour. Even at this early hour sweet perfume filled the air and it seemed certain that a hot day lay ahead. A hen emerged from its nest, with much clucking and fluttering of feathers and with the cockerel in hot pursuit. Moses barked furiously and, moments later, Ada saw the upstairs curtains being pulled back and Father's face peering down.

She carefully placed two brown eggs, still warm, into her basket, aware that with the family up and doing she could only spare enough time to empty the most obvious of nests. Any eggs laid away would have to wait until the morrow.

The boar began to urinate and a powerful mix of swill and manure rose from the pig-sty in a warm, comforting cloud. These everyday chores became all-important and the thought of leaving behind everything familiar brought a lump to Ada's throat. Initially she had been overwhelmed by excitement, but this morning doubts were appearing, raising questions for which there were, as yet, no answers.

Father called out to her as he hurried past on his way to the lavatory and Napoleon, tossing his mane and whinnying in expectation of a treat, startled her into action. Ada climbed onto the top of the gate, inhaling the horse's special scent and feeling the roughness of his coat on her cheek. She began to question her decision to leave home.

The whole of her life had been spent within the confines of the Leicestershire parish, comprising the three villages of Swepstone, Newton Burgoland and Snarestone. "Glenfield is about twenty miles from here," so Father had said. It sounded an awfully long way, but at almost fifteen years of age she was old enough to embark upon a career and would be doing the one thing in the world she loved best. At William's suggestion, a place had been secured for her at Glenfield Mill. She was to train as a cook, working with Mrs Ludlam. There had been a proper apprenticeship-agreement drawn up and Father was to pay towards her board and lodging.

Suppose they don't like me she thought, at the same time being aware that William would never recommend she be sent to an unkind family. Her biggest worry was bath-night. The thought of bathing in a house full of strangers filled her with dismay and she couldn't help fretting about what the arrangements would be.

She had dreamed for months about taking up her new position. William had portrayed a most genial household, and knowing how fascinated she was with the workings of machinery, had described the watermill in detail. Mother and Father informed anyone who would listen how, as a child, she had stood for hours before the grandfather clock with the door propped open watching the cogs turn, waiting for the tiny hammer to strike the hour.

Father nodded to her on his way back indoors. She heard him pumping up water into the sink in the scullery and could see through the window that he was filling the kettle.

With bare legs swinging, Ada closed her eyes to absorb the sounds and smells of home. She so wished Charles was there. It was such a comfort to talk to him. Napoleon's velvety nose nudged against her, anxious for his treat. She fed him the bread and looked up at the place where she had been born, the coaching-inn known officially as, 'The Late Elephant'.

"There you are, Ada!" Bess, her mother, spoke with some relief. "Good girl, you've collected the eggs. Will you cook breakfast so Jess and I can get on with the preparations?"

"I'll be there directly, Mother."

Ada lingered a few moments longer to peruse the thatched roof and eyebrow dormers of her home, but this was not a suitable time for lengthy deliberation as it was in fact her sister Jess's wedding day, and within a few hours she would be marrying William, so Ada put her negative thoughts to one side.

The question of Duncan was not so easily dismissed.

§

The kettle was already hissing. Father sat by the fireplace enjoying his pipe with Moses at his feet.

"Shall we make a start, Father?"

Billy, a man in his fifties, often described himself as pear-shaped, a firm fruit which, despite its sturdy appearance, was well-proportioned. Smoke escaped in a long, satisfying puff. He licked his lips and answered his daughter's question with a nod. Ada waited as he knocked the contents of his clay-pipe into the ashes of the fire and, on rising to face the day's demands, indulge in a sigh of resignation.

He bent down to poke the fire, and pumping a couple of times with the bellows, caused a cloud of fine ash to escape and settle onto the newly polished cast-iron. He became impatient. "This flippin' coal is no good. They've left us a bad load this time."

Ada sighed with annoyance. The previous afternoon had been spent black-leading the stove and although she appreciated that the mess he was making was nothing that a rub with a duster wouldn't put right, she began to feel anxious. It was all taking far too long. However, Ada knew better than to hurry him and stood back, allowing him space to pull the ash-tin out from beneath the grate. With a grunt he lifted it and took it outside to be emptied. Ada grabbed the brush and dust-pan and fell to her knees. She could see no point in wasting time.

It had been a busy period, leading up to the wedding. Extra beer had been brewed and Father hadn't seemed keen on bringing in help, apart from old Tom, of course, who worshipped the ground Father walked upon and would work his fingers to the bone for nothing. The problem was, that although Tom was willing, he was slow. Still, they had managed. The barrels were in place, mounted on trestles behind the counter, tapped and ready to pour. Flagons of elderflower wine stood on the shelf among the few remaining flagons of blackberry. Ada wondered how her parents would manage at the end of the year when harvest-time came around and both she and her sister Jess were away. She supposed they would recruit help from the village.

The fireplace had been put to rights and Father was carving rashers from a joint of bacon. Ada tied the long white pinafore around her waist, and not wishing to arrive at the church smelling of bacon fat, pulled the mob-cap well down over her ears. She took up her position at the black-leaded range with its many levels and ledges, each of the differently shaped pans becoming an extra appendage. Flames leapt erratically as fat sizzled and spat from the frying-pans, filling the room with smells from the bacon.

"Ada! Put on your boots. If a cinder falls from the grate, you'll burn yourself, and there'll be no wedding and no Glenfield Mill!"

Jumping half out of her skin at the unexpected chastisement, Ada apologised. "Sorry Mother, I didn't give it a thought."

"And put the guard into place, you'll have your skirts afire." Bess walked off, tutting as she went.

Ada pulled on the boots, not bothering to lace them. As she lifted the heavy fireguard, she saw Jess helping their younger brother Jarvis down the stairs. His blue eyes were still half closed, but he managed a sleepy smile as Jess placed him at the table. Ada ruffled his golden curls, and he removed his thumb from his mouth to give her a sloppy kiss.

"How are you feeling, Jess?" Ada was aware that this was the last time they would all breakfast together.

"I'll be a lot happier when I'm buttoned into the wedding gown. I just hope my hair behaves and there are no disasters between now and eleven o'clock."

The family were settling around the table, when Moses uttered a warning bark. A familiar figure filled the doorway. It was Duncan, the best man, and Ada's heart skipped a beat. She hastily removed the mob-cap. Jess, having uttered a cry of embarrassment at being discovered dressed only in her shift, made a hasty escape up the stairs, at the same time frantically pulling curling-rags from her hair.

Father rose to his feet, laughing, offering a hand to the newcomer, "Dear me Duncan, the ways o women. Come in and sit yer sen down. I didn't expect to see yer so early."

"It wasn't my intention to disrupt your meal, only I thought you may need an extra pair of hands. Perhaps I can make a couple of journeys with the trap to help transport the guests to church?"

Duncan placed his hat on the dresser, sending a nod to Bess and a wink to Ada, whose cheeks had turned pink. She'd never seen Duncan look so handsome. The black bowler suited him so much better than his usual cloth-cap and his unruly dark hair was combed and tidy.

"Can Duncan collect Grandma?" she suggested, while loading a plate with eggs and bacon, but the answer from the chair at the head of the table was loud and clear. "No need, she's coming wi John Thomas. He's bringing the stage coach and it holds twelve, so that should do."

"What about Mary and her family?" asked Duncan.

"They'll bring themselves. They're only over yonder in Sinope. Jack has gone down the pit yer know, he hopes to earn enough money to buy a few acres so he can farm."

Duncan took a slurp from the enamelled mug. "Shall I give Napoleon a good brushing and hitch him up to the trap?"

Billy nodded. "I'd be obliged to yer for that young man, it would be a great help." Father, apparently satisfied with the arrangement, excused himself and went outside to feed the pigs, only seconds after Jess returned, dressed and with her hair brushed.

"How's the bride feeling this morning?" Duncan asked with a grin, wiping egg yolk from his chin.

"Please," implored Jess, "don't tell William you caught me in my shift, and especially don't mention my hair was in rags."

"Of course not," Duncan assured her, "and I'll meet him off the train and have him at the church in plenty of time."

"When you've finished breakfast Jess, we need to make a start." Mother rose from the table, making her way back towards the tap-room. "Time is getting on."

Ada was grateful for the few moments alone with Duncan and waited until he had finished eating. "My word Ada, you'll make somebody a good wife. If I were ten years younger, I'd court you myself."

Ada turned away. That was not what she had wanted to hear. She was only too aware that being almost fifteen years of age did not make her marriageable, and she didn't expect a proposal, but his statement was a clear rejection and was painful.

She set about scraping bacon-rinds into Moses' dish. As she bent to rescue Father's recently polished boots, her heart was beating so fast, she wondered if Duncan could hear it and fervently wished she could add a few years to her age. Ada wished he hadn't shown up at all. His remark had taken the edge off her excitement.

She picked up a kettle of boiling water from the stove and made her way to the scullery, anything to avoid his eyes, and was relieved when, without another word, Duncan walked outside to join Father.

Pots and pans sat piled in the sink waiting to be washed. Hot water splashed into the enamelled bowl, dispersing the soda and soft soap. Ada glanced out of the window and saw the two men laughing together. Father had picked a red rose-bud from the garden and was trimming it, whittling away the thorns with his pen-knife, before inserting it into Duncan's button-hole. He handed him an extra one, presumably for William.

With a sigh Ada hung up the tea-towel and went to check that everything was in order in the public rooms. Today of all days, she couldn't afford to leave anything undone for wagging tongues to ridicule, Father would never forgive her

§

Time was fast disappearing and Jess was flustered. All her garments, including the new lace handkerchief and borrowed garter, lay on the bed, but she couldn't find her petticoats. She had searched through the linen-cupboard which was emptier than usual due to most of the contents being deployed downstairs.

The wedding dress, originally made for Mother, had been modelled on the one Queen Victoria had worn on her marriage to Prince Albert. It wasn't as ornate of course, but the skirt needed petticoats to fill it out and with the sash in place, Jess knew it made her waist look tiny.

Jess could feel butterflies in her stomach. Only yesterday she had agreed with Ada that finally leaving one's home, no matter how exciting the circumstances, was indeed a most perturbing prospect. Jess made a mental note to thank Ada for her hard work. Since leaving school a few weeks before she had set to with a will to help prepare for the wedding and there had been times when Jess had returned from working at the shop to find her sister looking decidedly weary.

Jess had been about to tell all of her family how much she appreciated them when Duncan had turned up. Ada had a soft spot for him and Jess couldn't see any harm in leaving them together for a minute or two. Ada would be leaving in just over a week, and would soon forget all about him.

In the meantime, the wedding grew closer. "Has anyone seen my petticoats?" Panic echoed in Jess's voice.

Mother answered. "I put them right at the back of the closet in our bedroom, away from the dust."

Once Jess had the white cotton undergarments, complete with tiny blue bows, safely laid on her bed, she flew back downstairs to fill a jug with warm water, anxious to complete her toilet.

The night before, the three women had taken a bath together, leaving Father to deal with things in the inn. As was usual on Friday nights, Father had carried in the tin bath whilst Ada heated water in any available pan. Jess went in first.

Mother had purchased a pot of softening butter containing honey and lemon juice to rub into their hands and feet. It was this simple yet somewhat intimate process which had made Jess aware of just how much she would miss the family.

She closed her eyes and thought of William, aware that her next bath night would be shared with him. The smile returned immediately to her lips and she uttered an audible sigh.

§

Billy stood at the sink in the scullery and slipped the braces down from his shoulders, leaving them to hang by his sides, recalling that once upon a time without their support, his trousers would have fallen down. He removed the serge work-shirt, pausing to give his hairy chest a comforting scratch. He first sharpened and stropped the razor before dipping the shaving brush into a pot of green soft soap. Lathering his skin more generously than usual he carefully dragged the blade upwards from the base of his neck, pausing to hold his breath before negotiating his Adam's apple. Bess had trimmed his side whiskers into a perfect set of 'mutton-chops' (a feature of which Billy was most proud), thus leaving only his neck and the very bottom of his chin to be shaved.

He held the mirror up to the light for inspection, pleased he hadn't missed a whisker. However, he did notice a rivulet of blood and after tearing a piece from the corner of a newspaper, licked it and stuck it firmly over the offending lesion.

Billy placed the pork-pie hat onto his head, more from habit than a need for shade, and sat down on the wooden bench outside, making time for a smoke. He gazed out over peaceful meadows, pondering on his situation. Jess would be gone by this evening and next week his beloved Ada would leave too. He shouldn't be sad, he should be relieved. The reality was that he could no longer support a family of five. The income from the Elephant had dropped considerably, but money for Ada's apprenticeship still had to be found.

The problems had started when the Bath House in Ashby closed down. It had caused John Thomas to rely heavily on the post office deliveries for his income. He had to fit in with the arrival and departure times of the railways, and the revised timetable did not allow an hour's stop for food and a pint of ale, neither for John nor his passengers. That had come as a shock to Billy.

There was talk of certain non-conformist preachers extolling the dangers of alcohol and Heaven forbid there were more than enough chapels around, indeed there were three in Newton Burgoland alone. It appeared that the members of some ladies' prayer-groups had taken these sermons to heart and threatened their men-folk with hell-fire and damnation if they dared to imbibe. It's a bit of a bugger, thought Billy, when a man is made to feel guilty cos he's partial to a drop o good ale. Then, as if that wasn't problematic enough, them at Measham Hall were asking for another rise in rent. All in all over the past year, takings had dropped so much that some weeks Billy hardly managed to break even. The time had come to contemplate moving out of the Elephant.

His biggest worry was Ada. It was obvious she was sweet on Duncan and try as he might, Billy couldn't take to the fellow. The lad was polite and hardworking, yet there was something about him which made Billy uncomfortable. He was too easy with the women for one thing. There was little chance of him taking Ada as a wife, as she was too young, but lately Billy had brooded on the attachment and prayed that nothing untoward had transpired. The sooner she left for Glenfield the better, but at some point she would have to be told about the ensuing changes. He couldn't tell her now and let her go to her new position full of worry and woe, so it would have to wait.

He dreaded the thought of telling his beloved wife, but knew his Bess would stand by him. He smiled on recalling his bath the night before. After the last customer had left, his daughters had retired upstairs and it was Billy's turn to step into the tub. He had relaxed as Bess washed his hair (what was left of it, there was more growing on his chin nowadays, than his head), and moaned appreciatively as she scrubbed his back, pausing to massage his shoulders. He recalled similar moments from their early marriage and a smile played on his lips.

"That feels good sweet'eart. What would I do wi out yer?" He had surreptitiously opened one eye and looked at his wife, gauging his chances. He could see the outline of her body through the voluminous cotton night-dress as she bent over and the wet patch clinging to her breast. She had kept her figure well and was still a good-looking woman. However, she appeared weary, perhaps tomorrow night after the guests had left and the house was quiet once more. She had dried him, given his toe-nails a trim and helped him into a clean pair of combinations, before leaving him to his usual supper of bread and cheese and a glass of rum.

Bess was a wife in a million and did not deserve the ensuing bad news, but it was not being delivered today, so he'd best get on. It was well past nine o'clock. With the dog shut safely in the wash-house and the cat not yet returned from his wanderings, Billy summoned a degree of determination and turned towards the stairs.

He found Bess busy in their bedroom, and already changed into her Sunday-best. He inhaled the perfume of her cologne as he stood watching her pull the brush through Jarvis's thick golden curls. His youngest son twisted and fidgeted until she was finished, and then placed under threat not to move until Father was dressed and could take him back downstairs.

Billy's frock-coat and waistcoat were carefully placed on the bed. It was lucky that his father before him had been a stocky man and the garments still fitted. The silk top hat sat on the chest of drawers, brushed and ready to wear. Bess reached out and gently removed the paper from Billy's chin, wiping away the dried blood with a blob of spittle on the end of her finger.

"To tell you the truth Billy, I'm worried to death that the milk will turn sour in this heat. If it does I'll not be able to offer them a cup of tea."

"Don't be daft woman, there's enough ale downstairs to keep em all going for a month. Failing that there's the pump, so don't go worrying yer sen over summat that may never happen. You should be enjoying today, its bin a long time since we had a weddin'."

Stretching out both arms he took Bess by the shoulders. "Come here, let me have a look at yer. Yer look as lovely as the bride. When did yer buy the new hat?"

"Do you like it? Our Mary trimmed my old summer one with ribbons. Made a good job of it, hasn't she?"

"Yer look grand, I can see I'll have to keep my eye on yer."

§

Ada, aware that guests from Measham would be arriving at any moment, and that she had only minutes left to get ready, made do with a quick swill under the pump in the scullery before dashing upstairs. Jarvis was audibly under orders from Mother, being threatened as to the consequences, should he dirty his clothes before arriving at the church.

"My word, you do look smart," encouraged Ada, watching him escaping down the stairs with Father in close pursuit.

Mother stood holding the primrose-coloured garment, ready to slip over Ada's head. She guided it carefully into place, before neatly tying the laces, then deftly coiled the thick dark hair into a chignon, braiding it with velvet ribbons which matched the colour of the dress.

"There Ada, you look just as beautiful as the bride." Bess gave her youngest daughter a kiss on the cheek.

"You'd best go down Mother. John Thomas will be here to collect Amy and Father at any moment and by the sounds of it a good many people have already arrived."

Ada pulled on her white gloves, inspecting them for any further signs of wear. She had made a good job of darning the hole and was content in the knowledge that the remaining seams had held together. At least her hands wouldn't be on show and by the time they returned from Church the softening butter should have calmed the soreness.

Ada relished the feel of the georgette dress-fabric on her body and preened a little before the mirror. She bent closer to scrutinize the braids, appreciating that their delicate colour accentuated her dark hair and skin, while the simple lines of the garment made her appear taller. She lingered just long enough to pinch her cheeks before finally closing the bedroom door.

Ada paused to take a peep into her sister's room. Jess was watching the comings and goings from the window. "Come and look, Ada, our Mary has just arrived with Jack and young Hannah. My, how she's grown, she's a little beauty."

"You look lovely our Jess," Ada enthused. "William will not be able to tear his eyes away from you."

Jess gave a nervous laugh. "Have you remembered your prayer book?"

This sent Ada scuttling back to her room, praying there was nothing else she had forgotten.

§

The void of silence created by the departure of the guests was swiftly filled by a whiff of lavender and the rustle of petticoats. On watching the bride descend the stairs, Billy Elverson suffered an unexpected moment of nostalgia. Both his daughters had inherited their mother's dark hair and smooth skin and were far from being pear-shaped. Jess was the epitome of his Bess on their wedding day.

Billy staved off a tear, almost lost for words and offered Jess his arm. "Daughter, yer make a beautiful bride. We'd best not keep that young man o yours waiting."

Chapter 2

The Wedding

Billy stood inside the church door with Jess on his arm. He could see Miss Johnson, the schoolmistress, positioned at the organ. The feathers on her hat pointed downwards, following the line of her nose as she peered over her spectacles and towards the south door. Her hands remained poised in mid-air and after a wave from the verger she plunged her fingers down onto the yellowing keys, flooding the church with the strains of a Bach Cantata, popularly known as 'Jesu Joy of Man's Desiring'. Members of the congregation either quickly rose or slowly struggled to their feet, many noticeably suffering the discomfort of a starched collar.

Billy caught a glimpse of a red-faced Jarvis, together with an older lad, taking a turn at the side of the organ, pumping for all they were worth. The choir stood to attention, a picture of saintliness in their white linen surpluses, holding the hymn-books open in readiness, while the curate, his ceremonial cope reflecting the green silk embroidery of the altar front, waited at the chancel steps.

The sun shone through stained-glass windows, marbling the ancient stone arches with vibrant colour as the bridegroom and his best-man stood waiting. Billy couldn't help noticing the look of undisguised love reflected in William's eyes as he turned to watch his bride approach.

Jess, wearing the crinoline wedding gown and a veil edged in lace, stepped forward to stand next to her intended. There had been talk of an expensive silk creation in the new fashion, with a slimmer skirt, complete with bustle and hat to match. She had seen it in the Girl's Own Paper, a lovely summer blue it was. Billy had been greatly relieved when Bess pointed out that it would look out of place in a country church. He was painfully aware that the homemade wedding-breakfast had already stretched the purse strings quite far enough.

Jess turned, handing her bouquet to Ada who flashed a half-wink of encouragement at their father. For one brief moment Billy wondered if his worries were beginning to show.

The final strains from the pipe-organ shuddered to a halt. A hush descended and the words echoed forth.

"Dearly beloved, we are gathered here to join together this man and this woman in Holy Matrimony."

Billy began to feel uncomfortable.

"William Osmond Chamberlain, wilt thou have this woman to thy wedded wife?"

"I will," echoed the gentle but dependable response.

Billy's throat was suddenly dry.

"Who giveth this woman to be married to this man?"

As he stepped forward into the silence, Billy felt the eyes of every person present burn into him.

"I do," he croaked.

He passed Jess's hand to the parson, only to watch it be placed elsewhere. He had given her away. Tears hovered as his bottom lip trembled. Billy appreciated that William was a good man and true, even owning his own house and business, but Billy had not liked that moment.

He pulled out his handkerchief and noisily blew his nose. He was resolved not to wipe his eyes in front of the villagers, so blinked several times before stepping back to join Bess in the pew. Billy took comfort from the squeeze of his wife's hand and, glancing briefly at the hymn book, allowed his rich baritone voice to join in with the words:-

"Rock of ages, cleft for me, let me hide myself in thee."

§

Bells pealed forth from the tower of St. Peter's as Duncan guided Napoleon along the lane, conveying the newlyweds to their reception. All able-bodied parishioners had witnessed the occasion and now spilled out onto the narrow path in anticipation of a good meal. A breeze filled the air with petals, fluttering and falling upon graves and headstones.

The jocular wedding party wended its way out of the village and down the hill back towards The Late Elephant, with Billy and Bess happily accepting compliments on behalf of the happy couple.

Ada looked around, but there was no sign of Charles. He should have returned from school by now for the

Whitsuntide holiday. She'd hoped to see him before her departure. She may have to leave a note at The Hall.

§

Guests inhaled aromas from the ancient hostelry as wafts from the ham, boiled with cloves, welcomed the ravenous throng. The uneven stone-floor had been scrubbed clean and sunshine filtered between an eclectic array of vases and gleaming copper buckets, all overflowing with wild roses and honeysuckle and intertwined with ivy. The assembly was ushered into the tap-room, an area not usually frequented by ladies but, being the largest available area, was being utilized for the occasion.

Trestle-tables, borrowed from the village school and draped with best white linen, groaned beneath the weight of dishes filled with slices of home-cured-ham and savoury pastries. Along the centre of the tables, in the fashion of Mrs Beeton, the girls had arranged tall dishes stacked with dessert. The choice wasn't vast as fruit hadn't yet ripened. However, crystallized ginger and glacé cherries were mixed with sultanas and nuts, all in all a satisfactory compromise.

"Come wi me, gentlemen," urged Billy as he led some of the menfolk, including the curate and the dominoes team, to the front of the building in order to escape the sun. They settled in silence around the pine table, holding down the cloth against the disruption of a stray breeze, while Ada placed a tray of food before them. Billy sat back, content in the knowledge that just for today his wife and daughters would deal with all matters of hospitality.

A peewit circled above, calling out its message. The hedges were in full leaf and filled with chirruping birds, busily maintaining their nests and feeding their young and the bleating of sheep echoed from the fields of Tempe House opposite. John Thomas had tethered his team of four to a nearby oak tree, affording shade and good grazing and with a bucket of fresh spring water placed beneath. Billy saw that all was in order and, on inhaling a whiff of sweet woodbine, peace descended upon him.

The curate, new to the village, had brought along a bottle of good brandy to share. "I really do have to say Mr Elverson, you certainly cut a dashing figure in Church this morning. Your frock-coat and silver watch-chain make a most sophisticated ensemble."

Billy was taken aback at this unexpected compliment. The man was obviously impressed and Billy glowed with pride. "Do yer think so Sir? It's most kind o' yer to say so. He drew deeply on his pipe before enquiring of the cleric, "How are yer settlin' in Sir? I trust our Reverend Townend is lookin' after yer?"

The young man was only too eager to reply. "Indeed yes. He is most generous. However, country-life will take some time to get used to, I fear. I am housed in The Lodge and the Reverend Townend has allocated an extra piece of garden from The Hall. I'm determined to be self-sufficient." He deliberated on the contents of a huge dish of what appeared to be savoury pastries.

"These are Bess's lamb and potato pies," explained Sam the Sexton, "they're a favourite round these parts."

"I say, this is most generous of you. Much obliged, I'm sure," expressed the cleric as he moved one onto his plate. "I don't know how long I shall stay at Swepstone.

I'm now qualified and so it's just a matter of completing my training. Three years is usual but the Bishop did say he will move me around, and as my experience so far has been of town livings, he feels I need to get a feel for the country." He thought for a moment before continuing. "I say, Mr Elverson, were you happy with the way I conducted the service? I expect you would most probably have preferred the Reverend Townend, but his absence was a good opportunity for me to make a start. I mean, it is the first time I have married anyone."

The dominoes team looked aghast at this, and all eyes turned towards Billy.

"Young man, I thought yer made an excellent job of it and no, we don't mind at all. Everyone has to start somewhere."

Billy picked up two jugs of ale, one in each hand. "If there's anything yer need help with, there'll be plenty to lend a hand. Yer only have to ask." He turned to his guests, "Now, which do yer prefer, hedgerow beer or stout?"

The villagers sank their teeth into Bess's pies, succulent ham and home-made bread with stilton cheese. Looking thoughtful the curate said, "There is one thing. I purchased some hens from one of the farmers, but they're not laying."

"Do yer have a cockerel running wi' em?" Billy raised his eyebrows, already knowing the answer.

"No! Should I have?"

The men chuckled. John Booton, owner of the general stores and post office and who, incidentally, lived in Church Lane, opposite to The Lodge and therefore The Hall, enlarged on the subject. "It'll help to speed things up and yer must make sure yer collect the eggs regular like and keep an eye on em. If they lay away, then it's likely they'll turn broody and sit on a batch and hatch em out. Before yer know where yer are you'll be surrounded wi chickens."

The curate looked confused.

"Don't worry," John assured him, "if yer do get chickens it dunna matter. They'll be grown in twelve months and yer'll be able to put em in the pot."

The curate was visibly agitated. "I couldn't kill them."

"Just gi' me the nod Sir, I'll do the job, nowt to it," John offered obligingly.

The clergyman, clearly uncomfortable with the subject, turned his eyes to the Elephant. "How come that building to the rear is built with so many different sizes of bricks?"

"He means yer lavatories," piped up the postmaster, yet again.

Billy chortled, causing his belly to move up and down. "Dunna tell me yer haven't heard of Joseph Wilkes?"

"Can't say that I have," replied the curate deeply quaffing, obviously relieved at having successfully steered the conversation away from his poor chickens.

Billy set down his tankard. "Wilks started a brickworks in Measham, years ago and then when they put a tax on building bricks, he made his twice the size so as to only pay half as much tax. Until they found out that is."

"Really?" Commented the clergyman, obviously believing he had been spun a yarn.

Billy continued. "Yer'll see em in most o the buildings hereabouts." He took a drink. "Jumb bricks they calls em. Round here we calls em gobs." He watched as the curate raised an eyebrow.

"And what happened when the authorities found out?"

The reply slipped comfortably from Billy's tongue. "They doubled the tax on the gobs. Shortly after that Wilks stopped making em and shut the place down."

The young man contemplated for a moment, not looking at all convinced. "So tell me, why is the pub called, The Late Elephant?"

Billy exhaled, pushing the tobacco down into his pipe with his forefinger. Lowering his voice a couple of decibels for effect, he leaned forward to look straight into the eyes of the curate. "Legend has it that, years ago, a monk travelled between Swepstone and Grace Dieu on an elephant." He chewed for a moment on the long slender stem of his pipe. "In fact, The British Archaeological Society came to the area and carried out a dig. In the process they unearthed not just elephant bones but those of a hyena."

"Mind yer, they wanna found at Swepstone," interrupted John Thomas, "they was in fact buried at Newton Nethercôte, just be'ind where I were born."

Feeling that last remark was totally unnecessary, and that in making it John Thomas had stolen his thunder, Billy sat back to view the reaction. At that very moment a wood pigeon fluttered by overhead and dropped an unwanted gift on John Thomas's best jacket. "Damn vermin!" shouted John as he sprang to his feet, "it's time yer shot some of the buggers."

"Here." Billy offered his handkerchief, smiling as he did so while at the same time thinking it was judgment on John Thomas for his interference and revelled in the fact that his swearing would not go down well with the curate.

"Humm," was the only sound from the clergy-man and Billy was delighted to see him reach down and pull the bottle of brandy from beneath the table, cordially announcing, "I rather think it's time we tried a drop of this."

§

Ada discovered Jarvis perched on a stool outside the back door, ravenously devouring a lamb and potato pie and with another one on his plate.

"You like my pies then?"

A nodding head was the only reply, his mouth too full of pastry to speak. He'd been playing 'tick' with some of the other children, but they had been taken off inside to be 'seen and not heard', whilst eating their food properly at the table.

"If Mother catches you with your mouth too full to speak, you'll be in trouble." Ada didn't have the heart to chastise him too much while he was so obviously enjoying his food.

A brown hen escaped from behind the makeshift fence which Billy had constructed especially for the day. Despite its screeching and fluttering, Ada pursued it, caught it by the tail, clamped both hands around its wings and threw it back into the enclosure.

The bell-ringers arrived.

"Wait until I fetch a blanket before you sit on the grass," Ada warned, "or else your clothes will be covered in hen-muck."

Satisfied that everyone was present she took advantage of the moment to check on the cake, her wedding gift to Jess and William. For safety's sake it sat resplendent in a corner of the snug which, despite its name, was the coolest room in the house. The aspidistra had been moved so the small table could be covered with Grandma's much admired and coveted linen cloth, hand-embroidered and with a deep crocheted edging. Her best silver vase, the one with the Georgian hallmark, had been filled with white rosebuds and myrtle and placed proudly on the top.

There had only been time to bake two tiers and Ada prayed that the bottom one would be large enough to go around, as of course the top one was, by tradition, to be carefully packed and stored for the christening.

She called Father inside. He stood proudly in front of the crowd, the large carving knife in his hand. Having scraped the stone from one end of the blade to the other several times, first on the front and then on the back, he gave it a ceremonial polish with a linen napkin until it shimmered. He handed the knife to Jess. With Williams's hand steadying, the couple plunged it deep into the fruit cake.

The applause was thunderous. Everyone joined in the celebration. "Well done," the crowd yelled, lifting their mugs, followed by a deafening, 'Hip, hip, hooray!'

Ada scanned the crowd for Duncan. He stood, tankard in hand, talking heartily to a group of men and, she observed, a couple of young ladies, both older than herself. In fact one, Ada had to admit, was quite attractive and wore a hat similar to the one Jess had bought for her honeymoon. She held an open fan before her, wafting it gently. It hid most of her face but not the fluttering of her eyelashes. Ada recognized her as Bella Bishop from Measham. Duncan didn't appear to be taking much heed and threw Ada a wink.

She smiled back, but was distracted by a familiar yet cutting voice. Jack Scarlett's widow stood scrutinizing. Ada could hear her commenting to her mother. "Yer wasting yer money sending Ada away to learn to cook Mrs Elverson, when she can already make cakes like these."

Trust her to spoil things. Ada could clearly see what it was about the woman that needled everyone. Bess tutted, but replied cautiously. "She'll be learning from a woman who knows everything there is to know about corn and flour. Mrs Ludlam is a miller's wife. She makes bread and pastries for many of the big houses thereabouts, or so my new son-in-law tells me."

Ada watched whilst Bess turned to William for support, leaving him to explain. "The thing is, Mrs Scarlett, Ada's father believes that if she is properly trained, it will stand her in good stead for the rest of her life. She'll be able to find a job anywhere, even choosing who she works for. It'll give her that extra degree of independence."

Ada was grateful for her brother-in-law's interventions, but wished the woman would mind her own business. There was a distinct note of something irksome in her voice and as she moved away could be heard muttering as to how her niece Maud had a sit down do, not this new idea of having to help yourself. Ada was affronted. There was an article in the Girls' Own Paper, clearly describing how to prepare for a wedding reception. There was even a picture. She wondered if she should show them to Mrs Scarlett, but doubted if she could read.

Father brought the mallet crashing down onto the wooden block. The crowd quietened. Members of the dominoes-team were present in full force. Having heard Billy's orations a few times before, they jostled for the front row in anticipation of a good story. Ada smiled, revelling in Father's ability to hold an audience with his tales.

"Ladies and Gentlemen, thank yer all for coming here today to celebrate the wedding o my daughter Jess and her husband William." Billy paused to look down at the familiar sea of faces but, instead of launching wholeheartedly into a robust speech, he began to stutter.

Ada took a sharp intake of breath as she watched the colour drain from his cheeks. "Father!" she called, "Father, are you not well?"

He regained control and, on raising his tankard, delivered the simplest of toasts. "To Jess and William. May God bless em."

Ada was offended by Father shaking her hand from his arm. "Stop fussing Ada, it's just the heat that's all. There's nowt wrong wi me," and was barely consoled by hearing her mother's intervention, "Alright love, leave him be, I'll keep an eye on him."

Welcome sounds of music lured just about everyone back into the tap-room. Miss Johnson played the harpsichord and some local men the fiddle and a concertina. They struck up first with the Lancers. Ada watched as Jess and William took to the floor and led the dance, when she felt a hand on her arm.

"Why are you not playing your mandolin, or do we have to wait until later for that?" Startled, she looked up into the serious eyes of Charles Townend.

"Charles, you are here! When did you arrive?"

Charles stood inches taller than Ada and, dressed in his school uniform, with his butterfly collar and waistcoat giving him a sombre air, Charles pulled himself up to his full height before replying. "Almost minutes ago. We left Repton immediately after breakfast. Papa sends his apologies at not returning in time to take the service for Miss Jessica."

Ada looked intently at him. "Charles, I have something serious to discuss with you. Perhaps we can slip away a little later." She smiled up at him, "And the answer to your question about the mandolin is that I have broken a string *and* the bridge, so for the moment it is out of commission."

"In that case please do me the honour of dancing with me." He offered his arm.

"Thank you, Charles."

Ada's eyes filled with tears. She was overcome by the stark reality that, within the week, she would sever herself from everything safe and familiar.

"What's wrong? Ada, please tell me." Charles Townend, son of the rector, followed the slight figure outside, through the gate and into the paddock beyond, taking her hand as they sat down together behind the hedge.

"Don't cry dearest. What is it?"

"You have no idea how relieved I am to see you. In one week from now, I'm to take up a position in Glenfield. Do you know where that is?"

"Of course. I have cousins living there."

"Really, whereabouts?" Ada's eyes glowed with anticipation.

He hesitated. "At Glenfield Hall."

The glow quickly faded. She was to be a servant at the Mill, a very different position even from that of a landlord's daughter. There was no possibility of an invitation to visit there.

His eyes held hers. "Ada, we can meet, we will still see each other." His arms wrapped around her, holding her tightly, his lips kissing the top of her head.

She struggled. "Charles, whatever are you doing?"

He sprang away. "Ada, I am so sorry. I was just..." he coughed, holding his hand to his mouth, "...trying to comfort you. Please forgive me. I see now my behaviour was inappropriate. It will not happen again."

Ada was flabbergasted by what had just taken place and struggled to know what to do next, when she heard the musicians strike up with a polka.

"Charles, it seems such a pity not to take advantage of the music."

Ada was thankful to see him make an immediate recovery, jump up and offer his arm.

§

Jarvis felt sick. His last piece of cake had been thickly spread with butter. His mouth was horribly dry and the music had begun to get on his nerves. He had a suck of his thumb before peering around, desperately needing a drink. The bell-ringers were taking a turn in the dance, having left their pewter mugs perched close to the edge of the table, just about level with his nose. He reached one down and drank deeply. Within seconds his body began to feel heavy. He became uncontrollably sleepy.

Searching for his mother, Jarvis forced himself through the crowd of silk skirts and serge trousers, aware that some of the boots appeared a little hazy. He managed to open the door of the snug, but there was someone in there making a noise like they were in pain.

"Are you ill?" he asked, "Do you want me to fetch someone?"

But it was only Duncan fiddling with his trousers. He continued to stand with his back to him, not even bothering to turn round. He said, "No, Jarvis, I'm quite alright, just letting out my belt. I've eaten too much."

"I'm looking for Mother." Jarvis informed him.

"Well she's not in here, try the living room."

There was a woman sitting in a chair, with a silly smile on her face, watching Duncan. She opened her fan and hid behind it, but Jarvis didn't know who she was and he was too tired and irritable to care so he turned towards the living-room.

Thankfully he heard Mother's voice, but was most put out on seeing her deep in conversation with Mrs Scarlett. He had hoped to be cuddled, but it was rude to interrupt ladies when they were talking. A tear came dangerously close to escaping. He looked around for Ada, but by the sound of it she was in the scullery, washing pots.

Grandma sat in a chair by the fire. He was far too tired to bother with her. The first to acknowledge his entrance however, was Mrs Scarlett.

"Hello Jarvis, yer did well today to pump the organ, it's hard work. How old are yer duck?"

"Four and a half, Missus." He pulled down his comforter from the hook next to the fireplace and sucked harder on his thumb.

"It'll be a few years yet then afore yer'll be going to school." She looked towards Bess for endorsement, before turning her gaze back in the direction of the young man. "Have yer enjoyed today?"

There was no reply. He had curled up on the rug and was sound asleep.

§

Ada observed Father. He was back outside with the dominoes team, and apart from being quieter than usual, did appear to be back to normal. His colour had returned and so she withdrew, afraid to question him.

Charles hadn't eaten since his return, so Ada placed him at a table in the snug, leaving him to eat alone. Someone had left a fan behind. Ada decided to leave it be. Whoever it belonged to would more than likely remember where she had last used it.

Grandma Elverson was complementing Bess on her hard work and delicious food. She had a soft spot for her daughter-in-law, as indeed for her grand-daughters. She was seated by the fireplace in Father's chair, a faded lace bonnet tied beneath her chin. There was a cameo brooch pinned onto the high-necked collar of her dress and a heavy shawl sat on her shoulders. Ada thought how uncomfortable it must be in this hot weather. Everyone else was fanning the air, but she appeared quite content. Grandma had only one tooth. It was at the bottom, a little yellow, and she took ages to chew food. Children watched in awe. She began to speak, her full slightly throaty voice filling the room. "Ada my dear, come and say hello to your grandmother." Ada embraced the frail body. A fusion of moth-balls and peppermint surrounded her and the silk of her dress felt soft against Ada's cheek.

"I hear you're about to leave home. Now, I know that you're a young lady who conducts herself well and I know you would never let yourself or your father down, but there is something you should know."

Ada sent a questioning look at her mother, anxious to hear Grandma's words. "If a young man says to you that he wants to touch your knee, then you're not to believe him, because my dear, it's not your knee he's after."

Ada was astounded, struggling to take in the words. "Grandma, you cannot be serious. I know about boys. Jess told me when I was nine."

"I hope she did no such thing!" retorted Grandma, obviously furious.

"I asked her! I needed to know where babies came from. Everyone else but me seemed to know."

"What did she say?"

There was an expectant silence and Ada said, "Watch what the cockerels do. That's how the chickens get into the egg."

The expression on Grandma's face caused Ada to collapse into uncontrollable giggling. "Just wait 'till I tell Jess."

Bess pulled a handkerchief from her sleeve, wiped her eyes and tried, unsuccessfully, to remove the smile from her lips.

Seemingly unperturbed by the occurrence, Grandma held out a small pouch. "As I don't expect to see you again before you leave, I've brought you a little something to help you along and I would also like you to have this. I no longer need it and I think you may find it useful."

There was a spontaneous intake of breath. Ada looked askance at the gift. It was Grandma's precious copy of Mrs Beeton's Household Management.

"Grandma, this is most generous," Ada enthused, before pulling open the strings of the small bag to count out four one-shilling-pieces and four thrupenny-bits, making five shillings in all.

"Thank you for both your gifts and the advice," a grin played, not only on Ada's lips, but also in her eyes. "I will indeed take it into account, should the need arise."

Grandma, affable as always when being fussed over, nodded her head. "The cookery book is of no use to me now dear. I can't see well enough to read it."

Mary made an entrance with cheeks glowing from the strenuous demands of a reel. She picked up a fan from the table and plonked herself down, wafting briskly, lost for a moment in the need to regain her breath.

"Mary," called Grandma, "come and have a word. I haven't seen you since Christmas."

Mary took her hand and lightly placed a kiss on the wrinkled cheek.

"My dear, I have to congratulate you on your dressmaking. Ada's frock is beautiful and your remodelling of the bridal gown is perfection."

Mary, somewhat calmer now, was obviously thrilled at the compliment. "Thank you my duck," she replied, "most kind of you to say so, I'm sure."

"Mary!" retorted Grandma, shocked at the words. "My duck, indeed! Mrs. Abney would never have allowed such a word to be spoken in The Hall. Whatever are you thinking?"

Ada dissolved into yet another fit of giggles. 'My duck' had come from Mary as naturally as the kiss, but was most frowned upon by Grandma, who had once held the position of Lady's maid for Mrs Abney, at Measham Hall. Woe betide any female member of the Elverson family caught voicing such words. This principle was not, however, applied to the menfolk.

"I remember when you left to go to Normanton-le-Heath to take up the position of milk maid. I told your Father that with your skills, you should have been apprenticed as a seamstress." Grandma tut-tutted.

Mary had left home at thirteen, just one year after Ada was born and so there hadn't been a close bonding, but Ada recalled overhearing Father tell someone in the pub how different Mary was from his other children. He reckoned she should have been born a boy.

A deep male voice pierced the female dominion. "There you are Ada." The words were nectar to Ada's ears, being spoken by the voice she most wanted to hear in the whole world.

"Come and have this dance with me. We can't have Master Charles stealing them all."

§

Jess clutched William's hand as he helped her into the trap. She had changed into a smart grey suit with a hat to match. Ada loved the hat. The brim was decorated with pink and mauve ribbons and Ada thought how truly beautiful her sister looked.

Duncan once more held the reins. The whooping and hollering was merciless, but before they left Jess threw her bouquet into the crowd. She aimed it directly at Ada but as Napoleon stepped forward, the wheel hit a pot-hole and the flowers landed straight into the arms of a choir boy of about seven years old. This caused the utmost hilarity. The child, whose name was Ernest Forrester, was too young to understand the implications. He laughed good naturedly with the rest of them, both arms clutching the enormous bunch of white blossom and trailing fern.

Ada stood, nursing a sudden and unexpected ache in her heart, as she watched the trap disappear around the bend until the last of the dust had settled.

§

Ada sank down onto a chair in the living room, allowing her head to rest on the table. She watched wearily as the flame from the oil-lamp cast patterns onto the walls. The silence was broken only by the ticking of the grandfather clock and Father's breathing, as he nodded in his chair by the fire. Mother descended the stairs, having settled Jarvis for the night.

"Today went well, Mother."

"Yes," replied Bess, "you made a wonderful job of the cake Ada, moist and rich it was. I thought Mary looked well. Little Hannah is beginning to look just like her." Bess laughed. "Mind you, she's a little madam, just like our Mary used to be."

Billy opened one eye. "And despite the weather the milk didna turn sour, so all that whittling were for nowt." He took one look his wife's scathing glance and allowed the eyelid to close.

"What did you think to Mrs Scarlett?" asked Ada. "She does like to make trouble."

Bess pursed her lips. "I don't think she means any harm. I noticed her looking at Jarvis fast asleep in front of the fire and there was a look of wistfulness about her. Mind you, she was telling Grandma how bad luck will befall the Elephant, because we've brought wild roses inside."

Ada was confused by this. "I thought that was about hips and haws, not flowers."

"Yes, well her argument is that the roses turn into hips when the petals fall off."

"Dunna take no notice," Billy risked another comment, "everybody knows her's been like that since both her lads were lost in that pit accident. It must o been a terrible time for her, knowing they couldna get out."

"Thank goodness our George saw sense and joined the army. He's the same age as her eldest." Bess observed.

Ada sighed. "If only George could have come today, we would have been a complete family."

"You canna disrupt the British Army for a weddin'," pointed out Father.

Bess turned to her daughter. "What did Master Charles say about your move to Glenfield? They'll miss you at the tennis afternoons."

"He didn't say much about it, except that he has cousins living there."

"Whereabouts?" Billy asked..

"In Glenfield Hall, no less. I can't see *them* issuing invitations to Mrs Ludlam's servant."

"Why not?" her mother retorted, "His parents made you welcome."

"I'll get Sunday afternoons off, but Jess has invited me to her house. I'm to take the stage-coach as far as Wellington Street and Jess will meet me there." Ada's eyes lit up. "You could come too, you could take the train. The house is really close to the station, William said so."

Bess's face was a picture. "What a good idea. I wonder if they've arrived yet."

Billy pulled the fob-watch from his waistcoat pocket, checking the time against the grandfather clock. "I should think so, they left Ashby at a quarter past nine and it's now just past midnight."

Ada lit a candle and trudged up the stairs. She was disappointed that Duncan had only danced with her once, but she no longer believed that he really thought her too young to be taken seriously. He had in fact, told her how fetching she looked, and that he had indeed tried to claim her for the first dance, but she had already paired with Charles.

Ada was too tired to offer up to God a proper prayer, so she simply thanked him for the success of the day and the lovely dance with Duncan. Ada sank into the softness of her feather-pillow, knowing that she would see him again the following morning. He had to return Napoleon and the trap and Ada would have an opportunity to take the reins and return him back home to Measham, spending the best part of an hour alone with him.

Chapter 3

Farewell

There was something so wonderfully peaceful about Sundays, with the Elephant being closed for the Sabbath. Ada was happily marking time until Duncan's arrival. The last of the potatoes and a few carrots from the winter camp, sat peeled and ready in a saucepan with crisp spring-greens nestling in another. Ada had placed the meat pies left over from the wedding into the oven to warm and there was ham waiting to be carved. Father had brought the last of the Bramley apples down from the loft. Their skins were somewhat wizened, but Ada had found enough flesh to make apple sauce. It would go nicely with the ham.

She was wearing her best blue Sunday dress and mother had coiled her hair into a cottage loaf before going to church. The service had been shorter this morning, as there were no banns to be read so Ada had been able to take a closer look at the altar flowers. Mrs Scarlett had arranged them especially for Jess and white lilac sat well with sprigs of laurel and the carefully selected twigs of woodbine. Ada had paused at the chancel steps imagining how it would feel to stand there next to the man she loved.

The only one who held even a smidgen of a chance in her affections would be with her very shortly. She sometimes felt the twinkle in his eye held a naughty secret, or was it perhaps, a naughty promise? Since they'd played Postman's Knock last Christmas, he had kept her at a distance. She recalled how it felt when his arm had slipped around her waist and he pulled her to him. Their lips had met and Ada had practically swooned with the force of her feelings. He had smelled of rum, and on remembering his tongue invading her mouth, she was in little doubt that he had shared her passion. She blushed with embarrassment at the recollection of not knowing what to do with that tongue.

Ada heard the sound of wheels crunching on cinders. She quickly wiped her hands and removed the apron. She foraged in the bread-bin on the way out, her cheeks burning.

"Good morning, Duncan." She hesitated on seeing both he and Father scrutinizing Napoleon's hoof. "Is there a problem?"

Duncan looked decidedly guilty. "I am really sorry Ada, but Napoleon has lost a shoe. My fault, I gave a couple of guests a lift home last night and I think it was a bit too much for him, especially when we came to the slope towards the tan-yard"

Napoleon whinnied and tossed his head. The two men stepped quickly back as the horse flashed his eyes and removed his fetlock. Ada stroked the velvety neck, speaking gently to him and feeding him crusts, watching with concern as he limped through the gateway and onto the soft springy grass of the paddock.

"I let him take his time this morning and kept him on the grass. I can walk back to Measham, it's not a problem."

Ada's heart sank.

Mother joined them and Duncan briefly explained.

"Oh dear," sympathised Bess. "Never mind, as Ada's not leaving for a day or two, she can take him to Snarestone to have him reshod. You must stay and join us for dinner."

"No, thank you kindly Mrs Elverson, I have to get back."

Duncan held out a sovereign. "Take this Ada, it should cover the smithy's costs and please accept my sincere apologies." He shuffled his feet in the cinders, looking somewhat shamefaced and, with a repentant glance in Ada's direction, took his leave. She observed with irritation that the twinkle had returned. He doffed his cap and with a jaunty gait, strode off towards Measham. Ada noticed his hair had returned to its usual ruffled state.

She was most disgruntled, having a pretty good idea who had generated the new spring in his step, and wondered if that same person would be cooking his Sunday dinner.

§

The aspidistra had finally been reinstated and the extra linen used at the wedding was successfully washed, ironed and either put away or returned to whoever had loaned it.

It was Friday before Ada was free to make the journey to the blacksmith. Her anger at Duncan had reached boiling point. He knew full-well that the trap was designed to take two people, three if they were all relatively small and the horse was fresh, but to take yet another extra person, when the animal had been worked for much of the day, was monstrous.

Had the passengers been sober, it was odds on that at least one of them would have seen sense in disembarking whilst the animal was still on the flat.

Ada tied the ribbons under her chin, making sure that the straw boater stayed in place, and climbed up onto the trap. Taking the reins, she gently persuaded Napoleon forwards. She coaxed him along Quarry Lane, towards the village of Snarestone, then along the main street and into the blacksmith's yard. Mr. Clamp was nowhere in sight so Ada was forced to enter the building.

She ducked her head around wheels and horse-shoes hanging from soot-clogged walls, whilst at the same time negotiating a tangled conglomeration of railings and tools heaped on all sides. The air was thick with smoke. She covered her ears against the commotion of thudding implements and struggled with the intense heat permeating from the forge. The orange glow was kept at optimum by blasts from huge bellows, and it reflected on the sweaty muscles of the smithies, giving them a look of well-oiled leather. Having stripped down to a singlet, every ounce of their strength was channelled into slamming down hammers in a constant pounding, beating the stubborn metal into submission. They barely had time to acknowledge her with a nod. She could taste the acrid contamination and found the heat and clamour unbearable.

Mr Clamp left his position at the bellows and steered her back outside. He removed his cap and wiped the black sweat from his forehead with the back of his hand. "What's up?"

Ada explained the problem.

"Leave him wi me duck. Frank's almost finished, so he'll have a look at him. Go and sit by the cut for a bit and watch the boats."

Ada took the path along-side the Globe Inn towards the canal. It was busier than usual as the waterway-traffic made its way towards Measham and the Friday market. Ada wondered if William would be there. The family had expected to see him before now and were hungry for news. Colourful narrow-boats were arriving, pulled along the water by horses, mostly shires and the odd Suffolk Punch. The animals ambled along the towpath, their ropes attached to a harness, until they arrived at the cut. There the rope would be disconnected and the boats would have to wait their turn before continuing on.

Ada could hear the rattling of dog chains on the decks and the incessant barking as they competed with the issuing of commands and laughter from the boat-children. She waved her handkerchief and the children responded, excited at being about to pass through the narrow passage-way. Almost all of the boats were hung with lace-curtains and displayed collections of large buckets and jugs, painted in the brightest of colours, creating an aura of festivity which, Ada considered, reflected the mood of the hullabaloo. Perhaps she should join one of the boat families and cheer herself up.

Ada sat down on a grassy bank and thought of Duncan. She was disappointed about Sunday, having wanted so badly to say a proper goodbye. She longed for him to kiss her again, but there would no opportunity, so how was she to deal with her feelings for him? The magnetism she felt was intense, yet within in a few days she would be miles away without a chance of catching even a glimpse of him. She recalled their dancing together at the wedding. He had held her and touched her, so lightly and gently, meeting her eyes and returning her smiles. He had flirted with her and she had responded. How could she not? Ada had been aware of the Bishop girl, the one with the hat, watching them with a frown and had seen her lips tighten with jealousy.

Tears spilled out as she clutched her knees, splashing onto the skirt of her dress. She wiped them quickly away, concerned that someone would discover her. Common sense dictated that she wouldn't be too young for ever. In just over a year she would be sixteen. It was simply a matter of waiting.

Ada walked back towards the boats and the carefree sounds of the children. The tow-path ended at the tunnel entrance and she watched the boat-men propel the vessels forward by bracing their shoulders against the cabin rooves, whilst at the same time pushing their feet against the curved brick structure of the tunnel. It was almost like walking upside-down.

At this point the horses had to cross over the road. Ada moved hastily out of the way, whilst a Suffolk Punch gelding, his chestnut coat contrasting magnificently with blonde mane, tail and fetlocks, was coaxed into scaling the hillock. The animal rolled his eyes and whinnied, but without too much resistance, did as he was bid, flexing his powerful withers against this unfamiliar situation. Once over the other side he would be re-hitched and the towing process be continued.

Ada raised her skirts and followed in the animal's wake, picking her way through the piles of horse dung, anxious to check on her own horse and settle the account. Napoleon had been returned to the hitching rail. He shook his head and nuzzled Ada as she stroked him. Mr Clamp persuaded him to raise his hoof and pointed out where the problem had been. A shiny new shoe had been fitted. He handed the old one to Ada and she slipped it into one of her shopping bags with the intention of giving it to Jess and William to place over their back-door for luck.

§

Ada guided Napoleon into Measham's High Street, slowing him down to a walk, in order to ensure the safety of the crowd, many of whom were children. Having tethered the horse next to the water-trough outside the tan-yard, Ada looked around. There was no sign of either William or Duncan.

A group of noisy youngsters leaned over the canal bridge and Ada couldn't resist joining them. Narrowboats were moored all along the west side and there was much cheerful bartering. She waved to a cousin before taking a look through Mrs Bonus's shop window next door, it being full of Measham pottery and the famous tea-pots. Grandma Elverson had one. It stood over two feet high.

Ada called at Fletcher's shop to buy some humbugs for Jarvis, but her next priority had to be new ribbons and tape for her working bonnets and so she made her way to the top of the hill. The bell over the door of Wade's shop clanged as she entered and Ada was immediately set upon by relatives and friends, all anxious to discuss the wedding.

"Hello Ada, we were just saying, it doesn't seem long since your Jess met William, just over there at that counter." Ada laughed and nodded in agreement.

"He asked her to choose a neck-a-chief, if I remember correctly," stated the woman, retelling the tale of how William had boldly walked over to Jess and asked her advice. The problem was that the shop had a gentleman's side and a lady's side and although William had selected a box of cravats from the gentleman's side, he had trespassed in crossing the line to speak with Jess. Mr Wade had coughed loudly and tutted at him, apparently, but being a gentleman with sense of humour, had simply looked over the top of his spectacles and grinned.

Ada rummaged in her bag to retrieve her fan. The shop was crowded and stuffy. The door-bell rang again and Bella Bishop, together with her friend from the wedding, joined the queue. Between snatches of gossip, Ada overheard scraps of a whispered exchange between the two young women, both of whom lived in tan-yard row. They giggled and sniggered and among the words Ada caught 'Duncan' and 'horse went lame'. Ada recalled that look of jealousy when she and Duncan had danced together, and remembered that Duncan rented a room in a cottage just a few doors away from where Bella lived with her family.

Ada doubled back to the market, furious now on believing that indeed there could have been as many as four passengers in the trap on the night of Napoleon's accident. The girl with Bella had a follower from Measham, so it was more than likely that he would have been included. In fact, there was no telling how many people had ridden home that night. Ada left the shop, carrying with her an image of drunken, marauding passengers riding in her trap with poor Napoleon dragging them through the steep tunnel of trees and all the way to Measham.

She turned the corner into the square where the market was held. Mother needed potatoes and on passing the largest shopping-bag to the stall-holder, requested that he half fill it. Struggling under the weight, she was startled by a familiar voice.

"Ada, give that here, I can't have my favourite girl carrying heavy bags."

There was something in the timbre which dissolved her anger and at the same time caused her to blush. She desperately wanted to ask him if what she had overheard was true, but he had disarmed her simply by his presence.

"Good morning, Duncan." She willingly handed over the bags, "Is William here?"

"No, you'll not be seeing him until at least Monday. He's taken Jess to Skegness for a few days. Did he not tell you?"

Ada's face fell. "I had no idea. It is strange Jess didn't mention it. I'm leaving on Monday and was hoping to speak to one of them before then."

Duncan seized her arm to prevent her crossing the road, taking hold of her hand as they stood, and she felt the familiar burning sensation flooding her body. They waited for the stage coach to make its way through, the driver cracking his whip on the cobbles, shouting for people to move back so he could pass. Duncan looked down at her. "Jess didn't know anything about it. He wanted to surprise her. They should be back at Albion Street sometime today." He steered her through the crowd, holding her hand for the whole time it took to make their way down the hill and into the tan yard, but the short walk didn't give Ada nearly enough time to properly collect herself.

"I'll tell William I've seen you and I wish you the best of luck in your new position." Duncan placed her bags in the trap before stroking Napoleon. "I see you've had him reshod. Thank you." He reached out and gently wiped his finger across the end of her nose. He grinned, his eyes holding hers, "A speck of soot from Mr Clamp's, I shouldn't wonder."

She remembered the change from the blacksmith. She took it out of her pocket and held it out to him, but he refused to take it, so she slipped it into his jacket pocket. "I don't want it, thank you. It belongs to you." His familiarity had rekindled her anger. She tossed her head in the air, annoyed because Duncan was treating her like a child and was hurt by his condescending attitude. The last thing she wanted was his charity and certainly not in the form of money.

Ada jumped up onto the trap, flicked the reins and Napoleon trotted away. Her feelings were out of control and she ached for just the slightest sign of encouragement from him.

Halfway down the hill she turned and looked back. He stood in the middle of the High Street, hands on hips, shaking his head. She waved to him. He blew her a kiss. She knew there would be a smile on his face and his eyes would be twinkling, but as sure as her heart was breaking, Ada knew he had no intention of asking her to stay. Ada had never before felt so miserable. Why, oh why did he not feel the same? Tears fell as Napoleon trotted along, keeping a gentle pace. It was only when he turned left at the cross-roads, that Ada became aware of her plight. There she was, perched several feet above the crowd, crying like a baby for all to see. She pulled her handkerchief from her sleeve and composed herself.

Focusing on hedges, heavy with the perfume of May blossom and honeysuckle, Ada made her way along the road busy with both pedestrians and vehicles. She looked for a familiar face, but most of the folk taking this particular stretch of road were returning to Snarestone.

She inhaled the sweet smell of clover. Cow-parsley was beginning to show creamy-white, festooning the hedgerows with lace-curtains. Cowslips peeped through the grass, tinging the road-side with hints of palest yellow. Ada wondered if Glenfield Mill was surrounded by fields and felt her stomach turn over at the thought.

Instead of heading for the cross-roads and home, on a whim she steered Napoleon towards Bosworth Road. Grandma Elverson's cottage stood close to the canal in Horses' Lane. Leaving Napoleon to champ on cow parsley, Ada walked across to the front door. The smell of baking and coffee welcomed her inside.

"Ada! What a lovely surprise. I thought you'd already left." Grandma manoeuvred her full-skirt around the table and across the red quarry-tiled floor, to take her grand-daughter into her arms.

"No Grandma, I couldn't leave without saying goodbye. I've just been to the market."

"Come and sit down. I've just taken these scones out of the oven. You can try them for me."

Ada settled down at the table and Grandma placed before her a large china cup full to overflowing and two cheese scones spread with best-butter and home-made gooseberry chutney. Ada looked around her with a loving eye. There was a special smell about the house, like memories which have deliberately lingered to leave behind reminders of themselves. Ada absorbed the ambience like a sponge. The coffee grinder was in place on top of a cupboard. Everywhere was, as usual, in exceptionally good order, with the Measham tea pot placed on the dresser and the faded green curtains pulled back exactly the same amount on either side of the window. Ada took comfort, not knowing when she would be able to visit again, and with a sigh, followed Grandma out into the garden.

"I am glad you came, there's something I would like to say to you."

They sat together on the wooden bench, surrounded by purple toad-flax and lilac blossoms. Ada anticipated the little pearls of wisdom which were about to be dispensed.

"Now, young lady, it's time to begin collecting for your bottom drawer. At some point in the future, you'll meet a nice young man and be married. You can never have enough linen, so perhaps now is a good time for you to take up sewing. I know your life at the Elephant has been a little different, but most ladies sit after dinner with their embroidery or they sew seams, making towels and tablecloths."

The words took Ada by surprise. She experienced a fleeting picture of herself, surrounded by white linen, about to climb into a very large bed with Duncan.

"How will I know when I have found the right man?"

Grandma took her hand. "My dear, the Bible teaches us that the eyes are the window of the soul. Look deeply into the young man's eyes and your heart will tell you if he is the one. Your unease will tell you if he is not."

Ada left the cottage, swathed in an aura of baking, coffee and peppermint, all spiced with the unmistakable aroma of camphor from the moth balls. She held this special combination to her, and mulled over Grandmother's words. She promised to write at the first opportunity and turned for one last glance as Grandma waved her off.

Back on the road Ada's thoughts turned to Charles and his sudden and unexpected reaction at the wedding. She had relished the summer tennis parties at Swepstone Hall. His parents had sat on the terrace, encouraging the players, even supplying refreshments. A selection of youngsters had attended and Ada found them pleasurable occasions. Afterwards, Charles would walk her home. It was perfect. He was her best friend. All of that was gone now. She had become awkward with him. Most of the time Charles was terribly serious and Ada didn't always understand what he talked about and anyway, she simply was not romantically disposed towards him. Duncan on the other hand was always so cheerful, his twinkling eyes happy and inviting. If she felt about Charles the way she did about Duncan, life would be perfect. With all these complicated problems of the heart, perhaps it was just as well she was leaving.

Ada steered the trap into the yard, surprised to see Charles waiting for her. Instead of standing, stiff and starchy in his school uniform, he was wearing cricket whites. He rushed forward to carry her bags.

"Good afternoon Ada, I came to say goodbye. Mama thought I shouldn't leave it until the very last minute, as you must be frightfully busy."

Not quite sure how to approach him, Ada summoned a smile. "What a lovely surprise Charles, have you been playing cricket?"

"No, but I'm about to. Ashby has a friendly match against Melbourne this afternoon, and so Papa has offered my services." He seemed at ease and Ada, after removing her hat, prepared a tray with lemonade and fruit cake.

"There you are," offered Charles, passing across the table a brown paper bag, "a set of strings for your mandolin and a new bridge. I had some spare," but before Ada could thank him, he said, "and I have brought this for you, too." He coughed nervously and held out a small package. "I hope it's to your liking. It's a farewell gift."

Ada took the package and untied the string. Folding back the brown paper, she revealed a book of poetry by Elizabeth Barrett Browning. "Charles, this is truly lovely and so generous of you. Thank you so very much." She was blushing.

"Look," he said, reaching forward to open the anthology, "I have written in it."

She read, 'To Ada, my friend. With fondest thoughts and good wishes'.

Chapter 4

The Honeymoon

William signalled a cab from the rank at Leicester Railway Station, generously tipping a porter to help with the luggage. The house was just a stone's throw away, so within minutes of the crates and bags being loaded, the horse-drawn vehicle came to a halt outside No 21 Albion Street and William and the driver began to unload them onto the pavement.

Jess had only visited once before. It had been during the daytime, over a year ago and she had taken Jarvis along as chaperone. This was the first time she had seen gas-lamps lit in the street. There was one directly outside No 21. Jess observed for a moment, impressed by its ornate wrought iron casing and the flickering of the light, when she was startled by a movement overhead. An owl flew silently by, its huge wings soaring around the side of the house and out of sight. "Goodness me, I didn't expect to see an owl here in the city."

William explained. "Yes. They nest in the park,"

Laden with bags and parcels, he showed Jess into the parlour. She removed her hat, straightening her hair as best she could, before looking around. She felt a little lost, relying only on borrowed light from outside. There was a smell of furniture polish and a fire was laid in the grate.

William took her hand, but she was somewhat reticent, and was greatly relieved on hearing his comment, "It feels a little chilly in here." He took a box of matches from the drawer of the chiffonier. Jess inhaled the smell of sulphur and watched the flames light up the colourful tiles surrounding the parlour fireplace. Taking a spill from a container in the hearth, William poked it through the bars of the fire. It caught almost immediately and shielding it with his hand, he took it over to where the oil-lamp stood. Silence hung somewhat awkwardly between them, as they both waited for the flame to settle. He replaced the glass and turned down the wick before putting it on a table next to Jess. She removed her jacket and sat down on the couch, feeling nervous and somewhat uncomfortable. She was still a little chilled, but was wearing the new silk blouse with pin-tucks on the front. Tonight she wanted to look her best.

William carried over a silver tray and poured them both a glass of port. "This will warm us until the fire gets going." He raised his glass. "Well, my love, this is your new home. Let us drink to it."

Fire-light reflected on the furniture and Jess noticed that the parlour was neat and tidy. The wood had been recently polished and the tray and decanter looked new.

"The parlour looks very smart, William." Jess felt compelled to say something, in spite of her awkwardness.

"I asked Mrs Finney to come in. She cleans at the warehouse. Not made too bad a job of it. What do you think?"

"I agree. It looks lovely."

"I couldn't have you coming into a mess, now could I? Not on our wedding night."

Jess blushed and took another sip. On their way to the reception William had told her how beautiful she looked. It had all seemed fine then, out in the open air, but suddenly she felt bashful and most apprehensive about the very moment she had longed for.

William had looked so handsome in Church, waiting for her in his best Sunday suit, holding his leather gloves and with a well-tied cravat at his neck. His smartness of dress was one of the things which had first attracted her.

He jumped to his feet. "I've left the crates in the scullery. We'll see to them in the morning. Now, which bags will you need upstairs, my love?"

He carried them up to the bedroom and Jess wondered if she should follow, but noticed that his glass was still half-full. They both sat quietly and watched the firelight weave its magic. She turned to him, her cheeks flushed.

William made sure the fire was safe and having extinguished the lamp took her hand, but did not lead in the direction she was expecting. Once outside the front-door however, he scooped her into his arms.

"We have to do this properly," he uttered. Back over the threshold he had great difficulty in turning the huge door-key. Left with little choice, he lowered her back down to stand on the floor for a moment. They both burst into laughter as he scooped her once more and carried her up the stairs to bed.

The door stood wide open and a candle had been lit. As William closed the drapes, a seductive call of twit-twooo drifted in on the still night air.

§

Jess was wide awake. Husband faced her with his hair tousled. She watched for a moment, fascinated by the way his lips fluttered as he exhaled, not quite a full-blown snore, she observed. He looked like a small boy, innocent and vulnerable.

She hugged the lace-edged pillow and sighed with contentment, stretching out her hand to look at the shiny gold band on her finger, before slipping out of bed to use the chamber-pot. He had purchased a new one especially for her, a cream vessel with a handle and violets painted all around, whilst his was a taller affair with no embellishments and no handle.

She noticed the blood in the chamber-pot, just as Mother had described, and reached into her bag to pull out the prepared rags. As she slipped back between the sheets, William opened his eyes and pulled her towards him.

§

Jess busied herself in the scullery, unpacking the hamper of food and arranging its contents on the thrawl in the larder. There were ham and pies from the wedding plus two loaves of bread, each wrapped in a linen towel. She was delighted to discover the joint of home-cured bacon and a dish of eggs, together with jars of relish and preserves. There was so much to do, Jess hardly knew which direction to take first. Her cheeks still glowed from their wedding night. She had never before felt such excitement at the thought of cooking breakfast. She felt an arm steal around her waist, threw back her head and laughed with joy.

"I can't quite believe that you are my wife and you are here," he declared, nibbling her ear.

She turned to face him." My dearest William, please believe it and be assured that I'll do everything in my power to be the best wife ever. If you'll light a fire in the range I'll cook bacon and eggs for breakfast. How does that sound?"

"I rather thought something cold would do for now, because I would like us to go away for a few days to the sea-side, a fitting honeymoon for my beautiful bride. Now how do you feel about that?"

Jess was overwhelmed by his generosity, yet torn between his unexpected offer and her sudden urge to take charge of the house. William made an alternative suggestion.

"How about we stay here today and leave first thing in the morning?"

"Perfect!" Was the joyous response, as she promptly set about planning a meal fit for a king.

§

Jess had somewhat reluctantly left her new home for the railway station. However, it was only the second time she had travelled by rail and she boarded the train with great excitement. She waited in the corridor, whilst William visited the newspaper stall, and revelled in the noise of the railway station and the smells of steam and axle-grease. People jostled for seats and to obtain publications from a stall on the platform. Her husband returned, handing her the latest edition of The Girls' Own Paper and with a copy of The Manchester Guardian tucked beneath his arm. William had deposited their bags in the luggage compartment and the couple settled into their seats. Jess sat next to the window with her husband beside her. Already opposite sat a middle-aged couple with a son of some eleven or so years. The two adults nodded, showing only the barest signs of acknowledgement. The family was smartly dressed and all three had their noses firmly fixed in a book. Jess noticed the woman's hat. It was almost identical to the one Miss Johnson had worn at the wedding.

The boy was seemingly uninterested in the goings-on of the station. This surprised Jess. Were it Jarvis sitting there, she mused, he would be mesmerised by it all, and asking copious questions, which they would, no doubt, be unable to answer. For just one fleeting moment, Jess experienced a twinge of home-sickness.

A lady, together with an elderly man wearing a dog-collar, entered the carriage and seated themselves, after first politely enquiring as to whether the places were taken. They greeted their fellow passengers in a most pleasant manner. The woman commandeered the seat opposite, leaving her husband to take his position by William, but only after pulling the door across, in what appeared to Jess to be a signal that the compartment was now full.

The corridor had become dense with people, and in less than a minute, the aperture slid back, admitting a woman of ample proportions, clutching a covered bird-cage. Perspiring profusely, she plonked heavily down next to the clergyman. There was some adjustment of space as the parson moved nearer to William, who in turn moved closer to Jess. Somehow or other, this shift appeared to cause an imbalance, resulting in the cover falling from the cage. The poor creature, obviously terrified, let out a deafening screech and began to flap its wings in a wild fashion, sending showers of green and yellow feathers and corn-husks to fly everywhere. Peace was quickly restored however, on replacement of the cover, but consternation among the passengers loitered.

"I am sorry about the parrot, but he'll soon get used to it." The woman appeared almost as flustered as the bird, but sat resolutely clutching the cage which was firmly placed on her knee.

The Reverend's wife, attempting to dislodge the offending detritus from her clothes, looked most disapprovingly, first at the woman and then back at her husband, raising her eyebrows, as if expecting him to do something to improve the situation.

"My dear Madam," he began, straining to turn and face the woman directly, "do you think a railway-carriage an appropriate means of transport for a bird? Would it not be better off in the luggage compartment where it is a little less crowded and certainly quieter?"

"Oh no, he'd miss me. The one I had afore died when I went on holiday and left him. I'm going to my daughter's on the East coast, see, and I have to have him with me. I can't face losing another one."

The whistle sounded, doors closed with a thud and the shriek of the warning contraption signalled that the train was about to depart. The parson's wife pulled a fan from her bag and wafted furiously. Slowly the carriage moved forward. Jess could scarcely contain her excitement and gave William's hand a squeeze. The diverse mixture of passengers continued without conversation, rocking to and fro with the train's movements. The newly-weds withdrew behind William's broad-sheet, escaping the somewhat awkward atmosphere, until it was time for lunch.

Mid-day arrived and William folded away his newspaper, before reaching down Jess's shopping basket from the over-head rack. She carefully peeled back the linen napkins to reveal ham sandwiches spread with mustard, just the way William liked them, together with the last of Ada's pies.

The family opposite retired to the restaurant-car followed, after an appropriate interval, by the clergyman and his wife. Jess noticed fluff and seeds still sticking to the ladies' hats, and wondered if she should inform them. Instead she offered sandwiches to the woman with the bird-cage, who gratefully accepted, introducing herself as Mrs Turner from Glenfield. She eagerly informed the newly-weds that she certainly did know the Ludlam family, and that not only did her son Eli work for them, but in fact she herself sometimes helped Mrs Ludlam with the laundry and the bread-making.

"I'll tell our Eli I've met yer when I get back, he's living-in while I visit my daughter, only she's expecting her first baby, and she wants me with her." She preened a little. "My son-in-law paid for my ticket. He insisted I travel first class."

"Salt of the earth," was how she described the Ludlam family, assuring Jess that her sister would be well treated.

Taking comfort from the unexpected but welcome information, Jess turned her thoughts to the few days ahead and their stay in Skegness. Suddenly a thought came into her mind.

"William, what did you do with the rest of the loaves Mother sent?"

"I gave them to a neighbour, one who's not very well off and who will appreciate them."

"Good." Jess settled back again, thanking the good Lord for giving her such a wonderful and thoughtful husband.

§

The smell of seaweed filled the air as gulls squawked loudly, swooping and diving. The tide was receding, leaving the sand patterned with dark wavy ridges. Roars of the ebb and flow reverberated with a thunderous crashing of waves on sand and shingle, before retreating into a whisper. Holding onto her hat, Jess looked up as clouds passed intermittently over the sun, creating their own luminous impressions on the beach.

They settled themselves at the table in the tearooms, William pausing just long enough to hang his hat on the stand. It was three-thirty in the afternoon. There was a perfect view of the sea and they had the place to themselves, apart that is, from the young waitress who politely took their order and gave a small curtsey. They ordered a pot of tea and two chocolate éclairs. It was warm by the window, sheltered at last from the wind and Jess searched in her bag for a fan.

"Our last day." William sighed wistfully, interrupting her observations.

Jess's eyes gazed into his, radiant and full of love. "It's been perfect. Sharing my first visit to the sea-side with you could not have been better. Your generosity is appreciated." Jess hesitated, lowering her eyes to look at the table cloth. "But to tell the truth I'm ready to go back home and start on the house."

He feigned mischievous surprise. "Really! Whatever do you have in mind?"

Jess noticed his effort to conceal a grin, and knew he was happy with whatever she did to the house, but despite this, couldn't help feeling a little guilty at having displayed her obvious desire to rearrange his belongings.

He reached for her hand. "Surely you're not fed-up with me already, Mrs Jessica Chamberlain. Here am I wishing we could have more time alone together".

She could hardly tell him the truth that, despite his and Mrs Finney's efforts, number twenty-one was in need of a thorough clean and Jess would not settle until it was done. Instead she playfully tapped his hand with her fan. "You know differently. I'm anxious to properly acquaint myself with the oven, and I'm looking forward to unpacking our wedding gifts."

"I wonder how your Ada is getting on at Glenfield. She should have started there by now, should she not?" He took a bite from the end of his chocolate-éclair, whilst Jess poured the tea.

"No, not until Monday. What made you say that?" Jess approached her éclair with a fork.

"It was you saying about wanting to bake. It jogged my memory." He stopped to suck the cream from his fingers.

Jess nodded. "It is going to be a shock for her, moving so far away from home and being among strangers. I pray they are kind to her. I wonder how long it will be before she can visit the Elephant. She loves the inn and I worry that she'll be lost without Napoleon."

William wiped his fingers onto the starched white napkin, the chocolate forming impromptu configurations on the unsuspecting damask. He summoned every ounce of courage before looking across at Jess, and with a most serious look on his face, began, ever so gently. "You heard from the lady on the train that Mrs Ludlam is a good woman, in fact the whole family is. Even the children are well-behaved and sociable." He took her hand. "I'm not at all sure that Ada will ever go back to the Elephant. I know this will come as a shock, my dear, but I think your mother and father may move, now that you have both left home."

Jess was aghast, hardly able to comprehend his words. She pulled her hand away.

"Never! Father will never leave! It's his whole life, and Mother's. Why do you say such a thing?"

"My dear, things are not the same as they were when you and I first met. Think carefully about it. Trade has dropped dramatically. He can't be making a living."

Jess put her hand over her eyes. "Oh Good Lord in Heaven, do you really think there's a problem?"

"I'm afraid I do."

Jess groaned. "Fancy him allowing us to go ahead with the wedding reception. It must have cost a fortune. I would have kept it just for family if I'd known. Why did he not say something?" She removed her hand from his, dabbing at her eyes with her handkerchief.

William's answer was immediate. "I'll pay them a visit as soon as we are back and offer help, and then we'll see." He finished off the remains of his éclair.

"I can tell you now, William, Father will never accept financial help from you. He's far too proud. It's most generous of you and I do appreciate it, but please, be very careful what you say to him." Jess held her napkin to her mouth, whilst absorbing the reality of William's words. It was bad enough knowing that she herself might soon lose the security of the Elephant, but she was horrified at imagining how Ada was going to feel. Jess, during a rare moment of disclosure, had been made aware of Ada's misgivings on pursuing her passion for cooking, and recalled her own words of comfort to her sister. "It's not that you are leaving for ever, we shall all come back and visit from time to time, and be together again."

Jess had thought it would give Ada something to hold on to. Never in her wildest dreams had she anticipated this situation. She raised her eyes to William. "How selfish I have been, not recognising how Father must have felt. I should have been aware. I was too involved with the wedding. Now I understand why he nearly broke down whilst making his speech. I just thought he was sad because I was leaving home."

Jess was all-consumed with an acute urgency to leave Skegness and return to safe and familiar surroundings, not that Albion Street was that just yet, but it was the nearest thing she had, and William would be there with her.

Chapter 5

Glenfield

Ada stood in the corridor of the train. Father, with head down and hat in hand, made a still figure among the bustling throng. Shuffling his feet and looking anywhere but at his daughter, he reminded her of Jarvis after a telling off and Ada wanted to leap out and put her arms around him and tell him it wouldn't be long before she would return home for a visit.

She jumped at the sound of a whistle. Steam spilled out, engulfing everything and a loud screech echoed over the length and breadth of the platform. As the train lurched, Ada grabbed hold of a leather strap, having difficulty now in keeping her balance. It took a moment or two to become accustomed to the jolting movements and the harsh sounds of metal on metal. As it dawned on her that the train was leaving, Ada waved frantically, only to see tears escape uncontrollably down Father's cheeks. She automatically reached out an arm towards him, but her attention was taken by the huge sign saying Ashby-de-la-Zouch and her attempts to stay upright, and by the time the train had crept onto the bridge, he was lost from sight.

Ada stumbled back into the carriage where her carpet bag lay. She sank down onto the seat, upset at having seen Father crying, but was startled by a man staring at her from the compartment entrance, his frame almost filling the aperture. The uniformed ticket-inspector stepped inside. She was relieved on discovering who he was and astonished to see him place her tiny ticket into his hand-held machine and make holes in it before handing it back.

"Excuse me Sir," she timidly approached him, "but how will I know when I arrive at Glenfield station?"

"You'll see the name written in big letters on the platform and the porters will announce it. Watch out for the name, Desford. That's the stop directly before Glenfield."

"Thank you." She suffered a surge of panic. "Sorry, what did you say that name was?"

"Desford, Miss."

Ada detected a certain irritation. His left eye was twitching and his lips had clamped together. Nevertheless she was compelled to continue. "What will I do then?"

"There'll be porters on the platform. Someone will show you where to go." With that he stepped back into the corridor, pulling a door from out of the wall as he did so and shutting her inside. Ada watched in amazement as it clunked into place. She immediately jumped up and took hold of the round brass handle. She turned it and it disengaged, gliding easily back. Ada hauled it once more into the closed position and sat down on the chenille covered seat, relieved that the stranger in the dark blue hat and jacket hadn't locked her inside.

Ada saw her reflection in the glass and pulled a face. She had been wearing the same straw boater since she was twelve. It had been handed down from Jess and Mother said there was nothing wrong with it and it suited her. Ada simply didn't like straw boaters. They were more suited to little girls, she thought, not a young woman embarking on a new position in life. Nevertheless, she straightened it and removed her shawl, folding it neatly and placing it by her side.

The look on Father's face continued to bother her. Common sense dictated that he would be halfway home by now and Mother would comfort him immediately on his return. It wasn't often he cried and Ada was somewhat baffled as to why he felt the need to do so today. It stood to reason that he would miss both her and Jess, yet it was out of character and most unexpected.

The train passed by the backs of some terraced houses. She could see washing hanging on a line, blowing for all it was worth. Ada remembered it was Monday and wondered how Mother was coping, having to deal with the laundry by herself. She saw someone kneeling at the side of an upturned perambulator, surrounded by greasy rags, obviously attempting a repair. There was a row of lavatories, one with the door wide open. She could see the wooden seats, three in a line, and felt quite wicked at having such a clear view of someone else's back yard.

Ada's stomach began to churn. She was split between nostalgia for the home she was leaving behind and trepidation about the place she was going to. There was no turning back, and she was beginning to feel most unsure about it all.

The train began to slow down and she read a sign, 'Swannington'. The carriage door slid back and a voice enquired, "Do you mind if I join you? I do so hate travelling alone."

"Not at all Ma'am," Ada answered enthusiastically, glad of the company. The lady, about her mother's age, was well-dressed and wearing a new-style hat with feathers. Ada thought it a little austere. However, she did admire the elegant skirt and jacket, fashioned in the Russian style. The woman was friendly enough, introducing herself as Mrs Bullen.

"Are you travelling far?" she asked and, whilst at the same time fanning herself profusely, explained that she herself was indeed travelling into Leicester to collect a pair of new boots which she had ordered to be made weeks ago. She chattered on endlessly about her children and how she had recently become a grandmother. She appeared uninterested in anything else.

They continued on into open countryside and all that could be seen were herds of cows grazing sedately and the odd flock of sheep. Lambs either cavorted in the sunshine or suckled, their back legs flexed and tails jiggling as they fed. Ada noticed how high the grass had grown in the meadows. It would soon be time for haymaking and next week would be Whitsuntide and she wondered how it would be spent and what the people at The Mill would be like. She felt safer now there was company and as her nerves began to settle, the motion of the locomotive made her sleepy.

§

Ada's eyes burst open to a horrifying situation. A terrible noise filled her head and everywhere was in darkness.

"Don't worry my dear, we're in the tunnel." The woman leaned forward and took her hands. "It'll soon be over and we'll come out at the other end."

Ada could hardly take in the words. She sat petrified.

"My dear, it really is alright, you're quite safe." The woman laughed and it was this which penetrated Ada's psyche, finally allowing her lips to dispel a large amount of breath.

"Someone should have warned me!"

"Yes dear they should, only I expect no-one thought about it. I hadn't realized you were unaware of the tunnel."

"Thank you!" With that Ada pulled her hands away, angry now at not having been prepared for what she could only describe as a terrifying situation. The noise of metal jangled in her ears. She had to shout to make herself heared. "How much further?"

In answer to her plea, the train exited the earth to escape once more into sunshine, and to Ada's relief, the contraption slowed down. Within minutes she spotted the name, Glenfield.

Turning to the woman, she asked, "What happened to Desford?"

"I think you were taking a nap, dear."

The steam train lurched to a halt. Ada was disoriented, her heart beating rapidly. She struggled to lift the bag. She had packed last year's copy of the Girls' Own Annual, which Charles' mother had given her. It was a whole year's supply of the Girls' Own Paper, bound into one large book. There was so much to read that Ada had barely managed to get past the first month, and there was of course, Mrs Beeton's book of Household Management. It was just as well she had decided to leave the mandolin at home.

She dragged her heavy load through the doorway and into the corridor. The clattering and banging as doors opened and closed was deafening, with hand-carts scurrying to and fro. On negotiation of the steps leading down onto the platform, she was rescued by a young porter.

"Allow me, Miss." The young man touched the peak of his cap before lifting the bag down onto a wooden trolley. Clutching the handles as if his life depended on it, he took off at almost a run, metal wheels scraping along the hard surface of the platform. Ada struggled to keep up. Her new boots were beginning to pinch.

"Where are you headed, Miss?" He inclined his head to catch her reply.

"To Glenfield Mill."

The young man came to an abrupt halt and pointed to a horse and dray. "Just you wait here and I'll go and find Mr Ludlam," but instead of moving, he stood before her with his hand held out.

"Sorry?" Ada was confused, wondering what on earth was going on, when suddenly she realized that a tip was expected. She pulled the purse from the pocket of her skirt and looked at the four separate shillings and the four thrupenny bits. Surely a whole silver thrupence was too much to give. It didn't seem appropriate to ask for change, so as she had nothing less, begrudgingly placed the coin in his upturned palm.

"Thank you, Miss." The boy was obviously delighted. He removed Ada's bag from the trolley, before dashing off to complete his errand. Ada was mesmerized by the steam train and suffered a pang of disappointment on watching the monstrous creature move out of sight.

The horse, attached to a hitching post, whinnied and shook his head in alarm, its eyes showing panic, but almost immediately a gentleman strode into view. He was a lean figure, tidily dressed with a collar and tie. Ada thought he looked dusty, as if a good brushing was in order. He took the reins and calmed the animal.

"So you'll be Ada Elverson then?"

"Yes Sir."

He held out his hand. "I'm Alfred Ludlam. Is this your luggage?" He placed the bag on the back of the dray and with a nod signalled her to follow. On answering his question as to how she found the journey, Ada thought twice about describing the row of lavatories and simply answered, "Very good thank you, but I had no idea about the tunnel."

"Oh did you not? Glenfield is extremely proud of that tunnel. A wonderful piece of engineering, don't you think?"

Ada was lost for words.

The man continued. "It was designed by George Stevenson. He lives not too far from Swepstone, on the Alton's Hill near Ashby-de-la-Zouch. My wife has relatives living in Ravenstone, so we know the area quite well." He put a finger and a thumb in his mouth and whistled. Within seconds, a black and white border-collie dog rounded the end of the building at lightning speed, sliding to an ungainly and dusty halt in front of them.

"Good boy, Clipper," he addressed the dog, who sprung up onto the seat, with pink tongue lolling and tail beating dust out of the leather. Ada felt the roughness of Mr Ludlam's hand as he helped her up, before taking his place on the other side.

"Walk on, Homer."

Ada grabbed the arm-rest as the horse's ebony flanks rippled and dimpled, sending the dray hurtling forwards. She was intrigued to see Station Road busy with people. The place had a similar atmosphere to that of Measham on market day. They passed a boot and shoe factory with a baker and confectioner just next door. Ada thought how convenient it was for the workers and wondered if the shop sold Mrs Ludlam's bread. A large grocer's shop dominated the square with a hanging sign above the door announcing, 'Henry Heames', but the one which most delighted Ada, was the one indicating the post office. That was where she would post her letters. The village was much bigger than she had expected and was busy with traffic. Almost everywhere washing lines bore garments, billowing out into the fresh, dry air.

A few yards into Kirby Road and the black horse trotted into a farmyard. The church sat almost opposite, so she wouldn't have far to walk on Sunday mornings. A great fluttering of hens caused a din as the wagon interrupted their pecking and a cloud of feathers pothered into the air. A cockerel came to the aid of his hens, running with head down, dispersing dust and cinders in his wake.

Ada took a side-long look at her new master. His black fedora had seen better days and a film of flour clung to the brim, but he was a handsome man, not much older than Duncan she deduced, but her observations were short-lived.

Unable to put an exact direction to it, Ada experienced her first sound of the mill-race, the enigmatic voice of rushing water, and felt a thrill of excitement. She was somewhat put out, however, on realizing that the Mill was in fact a separate building, nestling next to the brook, at the bottom of a small field.

The double-fronted building known as Mill House stood at right-angles to the road. Several lines of washing blew in the wind, gentlemen's combinations and singlets flapped next to ladies' cotton nightgowns, with bed sheets and towels spread over a thorn hedge. The access road leading to the Mill was a little further along, but was clearly spotted, as a line of horse-drawn vehicles, some loaded with sacks, were either parked or in the process of leaving.

If she stayed still, she could hear the huge wooden mill-wheel turning, water gushing from the mighty paddles, producing what Ada realized would be an almost deafening sound by the time one came level with it.

Alfred Ludlam turned to inform her, "That's Fullbrook!"

"Sorry?" Ada looked back at him.

"The water, the mill race, it's called Fullbrook," he repeated as he pulled her bag from the dray.

"Oh, is it? Thank you, I shall remember."

Ada followed him. The back door stood open and a tall, slim lady wearing a worried frown and with hair escaping from a large tortoiseshell hair-comb, stood waiting. She heaved an audible sigh, stepped outside and looked the newcomer up and down. "So, you'll be Ada, then."

Hardly having time to wipe her feet, Ada was ushered through what was clearly the scullery and into the living room, the lady seemingly flustered. "Sit yourself down. I dare say you could do with a drink." She returned from the pantry with a slice of beestings pie in a dish, before filling a white enamelled mug with milk from a jug and setting it down onto the well-scrubbed table.

"You found her alright then, Mr Ludlam?" She called after her husband, as he disappeared through a door, carrying Ada's bag.

"Give me your shawl and take off your hat, it's warm in here. Is this your everyday shawl?"

"Yes," replied Ada.

"Very well, it can hang here by the door, look. No point in keep carrying it up and down the stairs every time you take it off."

Ada contemplated the black range as she ate, thinking that it wasn't too different from the one at home, but there was no sign anywhere of a bread-oven. She counted eight dining chairs and wondered if they were filled at every meal-time and by whom. There were two rocking chairs, one either side of the fireplace, the fire being well-damped down with coal-slack and a line stretched over, with tea-cloths drying. Cupboards spanned both alcoves, reaching almost from floor to ceiling. Mother would give her eye teeth for those. A huge dresser running along the back wall was packed with crockery, a basket of cutlery and with all sorts of bits and pieces stuffed between. Ada caught sight of a needle and thread, a sock with a darning mushroom and several small butts of used candles.

"We have a daughter called Ada."

"Sorry?" Ada turned back abruptly, hoping Mrs Ludlam didn't think her nosey.

"Our Ada, she's at school and Allen the little one is asleep, he's just turned two." As she spoke, Mrs Ludlam sprinkled water from a white enamelled bowl onto dry linen before rolling each piece to add to the already substantial pile on the end of the table.

"How are you at ironing?"

Ada was beginning to feel under pressure. It was looking as if work was about to commence immediately and in earnest. "Quite alright, I think. Mother didn't often complain." She quickly consumed the remains of the pie and stood up.

"Shall I start now?"

"Oh dear me no, I'm not even half way through the washing." Mrs Ludlam's face broke into a smile, accentuating her high cheek-bones, and Ada saw how beautiful she really was. "I'll take you to your room first, then when you're settled, come down and I'll show you what needs doing."

Ada's room was situated at the end of the upstairs corridor. She was enthralled. A lovely wash-bowl and jug sat on a wash stand. Some of the rims were chipped and the surface a little crazed, but the cream pottery was decorated with deep pink roses. Ada fell instantly in love with them. There was a cast-iron bed with a pretty eiderdown. She squeezed the soft feather pillow, covered by a plain white pillow-sham, starched and perfectly ironed. A chest of drawers stood next to the bed and there was a closet with clothes hooks and a rail with hangers, each one bearing a small bag of lavender. The room smelled fresh and inviting. However, despite the window being wide open, it was warm.

Her bag had been placed on the floor and Ada took no time at all in unpacking it. Her toothbrush and a brand new tin of toothpowder sat on the top. She looked around for something in which to house the brush, but there wasn't a tin or a mug or anything, so she laid it directly onto the wash-stand next to a towel and face-flannel.

There was one pair of brown leather boots and her best dark blue day-dress, the one she would wear to Church. Ada looked down at the brown boots and quickly unlaced the new ones she was wearing which mother had bought especially. It was a great relief to feel her old ones back in place.

There were underclothes of course. Mother had made sure she had two liberty-bodices for the winter and two new pairs of pantaloons, plus petticoats. Lastly there was the new hand-crocheted shawl, with dark blue worked into the pattern, which Mary had given to her, together with a beautifully embroidered pair of velvet slippers. What a lovely thing to do, Ada thought, knowing that Mary had little time to spare. She set the slippers by the side of the bed, before placing a night-gown under the pillow.

A thick bundle of rags lay at the bottom, which she wouldn't need for at least another two weeks or so. At some point she would find time to cut them into the required size, ready for her woman's days. On moving them slightly she noticed an extra item and lifted out a beautifully decorated box. On one corner of the lid was written, 'To Ada, be happy in your new position. God bless you, Mother and Father'.

She recalled Father's face as the train pulled away and resolved to write at the first opportunity. Ada lifted the lid and almost as if it had read her mind, discovered writing paper, envelopes and four postage stamps. A familiar perfume wafted upwards and she knew that Mother had put a spot of cologne somewhere inside.

Charles' book, together with her Bible and Book of Common Prayer, were placed on the chest of drawers at the side of the bed and Ada stood back to take stock. She had at last arrived at Glenfield and it was most pleasant so far. In fact, she had to admit to feeling more than a little elated, and couldn't resist a quick peek through the window.

The mill was visible and the sounds were clearer from upstairs, but the wheel was at the far side and only partially visible. Nevertheless, she watched in awe as it rotated, fascinated by the constant sheet of cascading water and hoped it wouldn't be too long before she could visit.

Someone whistled and Ada was startled to see a young man looking up at her, laughing. She pulled back, but not before taking note of his dark hair and the red spotted kerchief round his neck.

She pushed the bag under the bed with her foot, only to hear a sharp ping as it intercepted the chamber pot. On peering beneath, she was delighted to find that the pattern on the pot matched that of the jug and bowl and suddenly felt an urgent need to use it.

§

Ada was back down stairs, but Mrs Ludlam was nowhere to be seen. Smells of wet washing and starch filled the room. Despite being desperate for the lavatory, Ada couldn't resist reaching up to touch the brass oil lamp suspended by chains over the table. It was magnificent, measuring almost a yard across. The three brackets forming the mountings for the bowl were fashioned in the shape of peacocks and above the bowl sat a milky-white glass shade. It appeared that, with the help of chains and weights, the contraption could be raised or lowered as necessary.

From the beamed ceiling hung baskets and copper bowls, a few bunches of dried herbs including lavender and if Ada stood on tip-toe she could almost reach the row of white pottery jugs, sizes ranging from a gill right up to a quart.

Mrs Ludlam entered through the hall door, carrying a small boy in her arms. His head lay on her shoulder and he was sound asleep. "One thing I do need to tell you. We have two mill-hands living in. Their room is on the other side of the wall from yours, but they have a separate staircase, so you'll not be bothered by them," she paused to reposition the child, "but first I want to show you the bakery."

"Please Ma'am, do you mind if I pay a visit first?" Ada hopped from one foot to the other. With a nod from the lady, followed by a short instruction, she ran to the very last building, catching only the merest glance of the farm-yard and cowsheds. Having closed the wooden door firmly behind her, there was barely time to bring down the catch and not a second to lose or to agonize about the quick sighting of a red neckerchief. Ada selected the children's seat. It was much more her height.

Sweet relief finally allowed an opportunity to take stock of the Ludlam's lavatory and she could see through the gloom that all three seats had been well scrubbed, and there was an adequate supply of newspaper, properly torn and threaded onto string.

She thought wistfully of the lavvy at Swepstone. There she had sat with the door wide open and all the time in the world to cogitate. It was there that she had put her world to rights while looking out onto open fields and with not a single person in sight. There was no chance of that here. In fact Ada looked with some trepidation at places where the odd knot or two had disappeared from the panels in the wooden door, leaving holes large enough for someone to peep through.

§

A loaf of bread had been placed on the table, and a fresh pot of chutney opened. Mr Ludlam pulled the horse to a halt outside the back door. He removed and shook his jacket, stooping to

bash his trousers and shirt with his hat. Gusts of flour rose from him and his face showed rivulets of sweat trickling down through the white powder. He doused his head beneath the pump in the scullery, and with towel in hand, nodded towards the bakery door. "How's she getting on? I've just watched her pour the washing water over the causeway. She gave the bricks a good scrub!"

His wife beckoned him to follow. She threw open the bakery door to reveal Ada at the mangle, both hands firmly grasping the handle. Struggling to turn the heavy wheel, she was forcing the folded linen to squeeze between the huge rollers.

"Good Heavens child, you've done marvels."

Somewhat out of breath, Ada broke into a radiant smile. "It's good of you to say so, Ma'am."

"Come and have something to eat."

"Can I just finish rinsing these first, and then the coppers can be emptied, ready for the starch?"

The miller pulled a brush through his hair before taking his place at the table. He looked across at his wife as he carved slices from the bacon joint, "Let's hope she keeps it up."

His wife nodded. "When I first set eyes on her, I thought, she's just a child, I'll never get any work out of her. She's very small, yet I think we've struck gold, but there's a job I think you should attend to."

"What's that?"

"I think you should put some bolts on the stairs' door leading down from the boys' room. She seems anxious about taking a bath."

"A good thought, Mrs Ludlam. No point in asking for trouble. I've been wondering what young Eli will make of her. She's quite a pretty little thing, don't you think?"

"Yes I do and if anything were to go wrong I daren't imagine what William Chamberlain would say." She paused, spooning chutney into a dish. "He's a good man, but I wouldn't like to be on the wrong side of him."

§

"Now, do you like to use a trough or are you more comfortable kneading on the table?" Mrs Ludlam inclined her head towards the wooden contraption sitting in a corner of the bakery, obviously unused for some time. "For myself I prefer the table, can't be doing with bending down, it gives me a stiff back. If I put the trough onto the table, as tall as I am, I struggle to reach into it."

Ada pondered but, as she had always mixed and kneaded on the table at home, opted for that. Mrs Ludlam walked into the pantry, the shelves of which were lined with small white sacks of flour, all labelled with their contents. She emerged with one under each arm. Enveloped in pinafore and mob-cap, Ada emptied the contents of her bag as gently as she could, relishing the sight of the speckled shades of brown as the flour settled into a heap. Her hands entered the pile, to feel the soft, silkiness between her fingers as she formed a well in the centre.

Inhaling from a bowl of warm, foaming yeast, Ada half-filled a small jug, adding sugar, well-refined oil and a small amount of milk, fresh from the cow, just as Mrs Beeton advocated. She allowed the yeast mixture to trickle into the centre and began to weave it around in a circular motion, pulling in flour from the edges as she did so. She wound the mixture through her fingers, the blend of warm dough enveloping her, bringing a sense of peace and tranquillity to her soul.

Ada had been most impressed to learn that the bakery had its own sink, and had been much relieved on finding out about the bathing arrangements, especially on seeing two hefty bolts on the door and the two tin baths hanging from hooks on the wall. Mrs Ludlam had explained how the room never really had time to cool down, even in winter, and that Ada would be comfortable taking her bath in there.

The kneading continued and the warm mixture morphed into dough. It ceased clinging to the rough surface of the wood and adhered only to itself, almost as if a new life had been created. The whole process took only minutes and Mrs Ludlam placed Ada's masterpiece in a large enamelled bowl, covered it with a piece of warm, damp linen and placed it safely onto the proving shelf above the bread oven. Ada calculated that the mixture would be enough for about four good loaves or maybe six cottage loaves.

Mrs Ludlam seemed content with her performance. "It doesn't take long once you get started." The whole process was repeated several times, just enough to supply Tuesday's orders.

"So when shall we actually bake the bread?" Ada felt compelled to ask the question.

"Tomorrow morning. We don't bake on Mondays, because with both of the coppers and the oven going at the same time, we would end up cooking ourselves. We should have time to knock back later, but if not, then that too can wait until the morning."

Ada glanced at the monstrous bread oven, hoping she would be able to deal with it. She had watched in awe as Mrs Ludlam lifted the latches on the cast-iron door, to reveal the large cavity.

"I used to have a woman from the village come to help, but she left last week. She's gone to Lincolnshire to visit her daughter for a while. She's expecting her first child. If we can't manage I'll find someone else from the village."

Ada vowed to do her very best to see it would not be necessary and proceeded to clean the table.

She was about to ask where the extra doorway led, the one situated on the wall between the two coppers, when the door burst open and in dashed a young girl, red-faced and breathless.

"Here comes our Ada," welcomed her mother. "Leave the door open, there's a good girl, it's getting stuffy in here." The girl took a fleeting look at Ada.

"How do?" said the youngster, slightly off balance on finding a stranger already settled into the household routine.

"How do you do?" responded Ada, scrubbing brush in hand. She smiled at the girl, not quite sure as to how formal she needed to be and wondered if, now there were two Adas living in the house, that maybe they would change her name to Mary. She would hate that, but knew it was almost certain to happen.

§

Mrs Ludlam selected some potatoes from a trug in the scullery. "There are enough potatoes here to make a shepherd's pie. You can mince what's left of the leg of lamb from yesterday's dinner."

Bacon joints hung from beams in the larder and a huge thrawl was stacked with dairy produce. In addition to butter, there were dishes and puncheons of varying sizes, full of dripping and lard. The mincing machine was already fixed to a table top and the remains of a leg of lamb could be seen through the thin wire mesh of the meat-safe.

Ada began peeling potatoes. She was beginning to feel the effects of the day, but as long as she was cooking, she would find the energy to keep going. Mrs Ludlam returned from the garden with fresh shoots from the Brussels sprouts and cabbage plants, taking them into the scullery to be washed.

"Shall I fry the onions first?" Ada called out, anxious not to overstep the mark and do things without asking.

"If you like and there's a jam pasty on the thrawl which will do for pudding."

Ada fetched eggs and milk from the larder and set about making custard.

"Before you do anything else, start off a rice-pudding in the bottom oven. I usually do one in case the men are still hungry after finishing their meal."

Allen, who had been happily playing on the rug at Ada's feet, suddenly let out a yell, pushing a clenched fist into his mouth. Mrs Ludlam rushed to pick him up. "Oh dear, he's teething again. Just look at his colour, he's burning. Can you manage on your own, while I take him upstairs and rock him in the cradle? It seems to be the only thing which comforts him."

§

A tall, strapping ginger-haired youth of around sixteen years old, with cheeks the colour of beetroot, shuffled in through the doorway. He nodded in Ada's direction, his face glowing more brightly with each step. Following behind was the slightly shorter and skinnier, dark-haired young man with the whistle, noisily dragging his feet.

After blatantly looking her up and down, he said, "This here is Ben and I'm Eli." His eyes continued to linger, staring unashamedly at where her breasts were beginning to form. "You'll be Ada, then."

The hairs on the back of Ada's neck began to prickle and colour flooded into her cheeks and she felt painfully self-conscious. She turned away, wiping an arm across her brow, as much to escape his stare as remove the moisture.

The girl ran in from the farm-yard and began setting the table. She tried in vain to spread out the table-cloth and Ben went to her aid, gently instructing her to pull and smooth where necessary. Ada thought what a gentle giant he was and saw that he had washed his hands and face before coming to the table. Ada was close enough to notice that the red spotted kerchief tied around Eli's neck was not just scruffy, but heavily soiled and his hands were still dirty.

It was a relief when the mashed potato was safely ladled onto the shepherd's pie and placed in the oven. Mrs Ludlam came in with Allen half-asleep and mizzling on her shoulder. "I see you've met the lads."

"Here you are, Miss Ada," said Ben as he passed the basket of cutlery. Ada smiled across at him and held out a hand, only to find that he was referring to the daughter.

"I think we're going to have to call one of you something else," laughed Mrs Ludlam. Ada's heart sank. However, before anyone had a chance to comment, Allen removed his thumb and attempted to repeat Miss Ada, but it came out as Missy. He reached out his arms in the direction of his sister and repeated it, but she was busy lugging a three-legged-milking-stool from a collection in the corner. Placing it near the table, she climbed up onto it, grinning at her brother.

"Missy, will you help Ada while I take Allen back to his cradle?"

"Yes Mother," giggled the girl, obviously happy with her new name, and with a toss of her fair curls and a knowing smile at Ben, continued with her preparations.

Ada offered a silent prayer of thanks.

Mr Ludlam was last to arrive. It seemed to Ada that the room, large though it was, had filled to overflowing. The lads teased Missy about her new name. Mr Ludlam settled into the chair at the farthest end of the table, with a pair of spectacles balanced on the end of his nose and peered over the top of the newspaper. "What's up with your feet, Eli? You seem to be having trouble walking."

"My boot-lace has snapped. I'll have to get some new ones from the village."

Mr Ludlam walked over to the dresser, opened a drawer, and after a short search handed Eli a pair of new black leather laces. "Here, they don't match your brown boots but they'll do for now."

They waited for Mrs Ludlam to return before sitting, heads bowed, as Alfred Ludlam said the Grace, "For what we are about to receive, may the Lord make us truly thankful. Amen."

Ada watched as he spooned out the portions from the pie dish and handed around the plates, first to Mrs Ludlam and next to Missy. Then it was the turn of Ada the servant, next the two mill hands and lastly he served himself. Ada appreciated just how lucky she was to be in such a place. Father had warned her there was a possibility she would be expected to eat alone in the scullery, maybe even expected to eat what no-one else wanted, but it wasn't happening and for now at least, she had kept her name.

They continued in silence. Ada glanced around, wondering if the meal was enough for growing men. George would have devoured twice of what was on these plates and she worried that she hadn't prepared enough. There was a mountain of bread with good butter and the two puddings, so no-one needed to go hungry. They all seemed appreciative of her efforts but Ada wondered if they were just being kind.

With the tablecloth folded and returned to the drawer, Ada made a start on washing the pots, finding a willing supporter in Missy. She stood beside her on the milking stool, drying the dishes and stacking them in neat piles ready to be placed back on the dresser.

"Which of your jobs do you like best, Missy?"

The girl grinned. "I like ironing much better. We'll be doing that tomorrow. I usually press the tea-towels and the handkerchieves."

Ada frowned. "I sometimes think it unfair that the men don't help with this."

The reply from the girl with the blue eyes was not what she had expected. "But they haven't finished work yet. They have to cool the milk before it goes into the churn, and roll it out to the gate, ready for the dairy dray calling in the morning. The yard needs cleaning up, the cows make a terrible mess when they come in for milking and Father insists that the cow pats are removed and sometimes they have to chop logs."

"Oh, I see," replied Ada, thinking that she must make sure of her facts in future.

§

Ada had removed her tired aching feet from the bowl of warm water and dried them on the towel. She knelt down by the side of the bed, her elbows sinking into the eiderdown. With hands together she gave thanks to God for bringing her to such a place, and asked him to bless her parents and Jarvis and keep them safe.

She lay in bed relishing the smells of starch and lavender, but despite her tiredness, sleep was evasive. Instead of blowing out the candle, she reached for Charles' book. A thin red ribbon marked the page and she opened it to read the words:-

'How do I love thee?Let me count the ways'.

It didn't seem appropriate to apply those beautiful words to one man, when another had given her the anthology in good faith, but she couldn't help admitting that those same words would sound most discordant if spoken by the wrong person. Ada gave the beautifully sculpted cover an appreciative stroke, and returned it to the chest of drawers. The cool night air blew gently in and she could hear the distant gurgling of the brook, as the huge mill wheel sat still and silent.

Swepstone and Duncan seemed a long way away.

Chapter 6

Wash-day

Jess struggled to lift the heavy wooden lid from the copper. It had been covered in various tins and boxes containing nails and tacks and goodness only knows what else. William had been using the out-building as a stores rather than a wash-house.

She had been up since before five o'clock, and was already beginning to feel as if she'd lost the battle. This was the first time she'd approached wash-day alone and, anxious to make an early start, had left William in the house to eat breakfast and prepare for his day at the tannery. She had already cut her fingers on rust whilst trundling out the mangle, it having stood for ages covered in cobwebs and like everything else, had needed to be scrubbed and oiled before use.

She gave a determined tug and the copper lid flew off. To her horror, she saw inside the skeletal remains of several dead mice, all in various stages of decay, mixed with debris from past years. Jess let out a moan.

The water had eventually reached a rolling-boil and the first load was bubbling and almost ready to rinse.

Fretting at being so behind, she vowed not to stop again until all of the whites had been dollied, boiled and put through the wringer. She clasped the copper-stick firmly in both hands and plunged it right into the centre of the boiling mass of white cotton, stirring until a bed-sheet became caught on the end. She twisted the stick round, again and again, until the linen formed a large bundle, only to find the weight on the end too heavy for her to lift. She had never before had to do this. Indeed, Mother and Ada had taken care of the washing while she was out at work.

Clutching the copper-stick, Jess was at a loss to know how to move the load from the copper-top and into the basket. She wondered how long it would take to cool down enough so she could take hold of it with her bare hands, but the heat from the fire beneath was fierce and beginning to burn her ankles. She couldn't stay in this position much longer and as she was alone in an outside wash-house, there was little point in calling for help.

There was only one thing for it. She placed both feet a small space apart and braced herself. Having positioned her hands as close as possible to the steaming load, Jess flexed her shoulders and gave an almighty heave. The bundle responded and with a resounding slap, landed on the narrow area at the top. A deluge of boiling water flooded the old bricks, flushing out ancient detritus from between them and swamping Jess's right wrist and fore-arm, causing excruciating pain. She yelled, and at the same time sent a silent plea to Heaven, praying that indeed she had cleaned the surrounding bricks sufficiently enough not to have marked the sheets. She couldn't possibly go through all this again.

Jess rushed out to the water pump and frantically thrusting the handle with her left hand, held her reddening flesh beneath the spout of cold water. The relief was instantaneous but it was impossible to continue the action indefinitely. Jess's heart sank. It hadn't been in her mind to prepare for illness or injury. She was dripping in sweat and her hair was sticking unpleasantly to her head. She pulled off the mob-cap only to feel the hair-comb become dislodged and hear it drop into the muddy slops on the ground. Her apron and skirts were drenched and beginning to feel cold against her legs so she wrung out as much water as she could, and with a reluctant sigh and a throbbing arm, returned to the house.

"My love, what has happened? It that a scald?" William rushed from his seat to open the cupboard door at the side of the fireplace. Setting a large tin box onto the table, he cut a piece of lint from the roll. He picked up a small bottle which he shook before removing the cork and Jess smelled witch-hazel as the cooling liquid brought sweet release to her reddened skin.

"How did it happen?" William asked, stroking back her rebellious hair.

"I was lifting the whites from the copper and the top flooded. It was stupid of me."

"You should have fetched me, I would have lifted it for you," he told her sternly.

Jess sighed and looked helplessly up at him.

William held the lint gently but firmly in place before applying a bandage. He put his arms around her and she rested her head on his shoulder.

"Would you like a drop of brandy?" he asked, placing a kiss onto the top of her head and smoothing the stray hair from her brow.

"Oh no, for goodness sake, I still have to finish the washing."

"A cup of tea, perhaps? There's one left in the pot."

She nodded. "Where did you learn nursing skills?"

"Father taught me. We have to treat the men at the warehouse. Sometimes injuries occur when they cut the leather."

Jess realized just how little she knew about her husband's business. He hadn't offered much information, but now was not the time to ask. She was recovered and anxious now to continue with her chores. Having persuaded William that she wasn't in mortal danger, Jess was relieved to see him slurp the last of his tea. As she had hoped, he delivered a quick kiss on her cheek and took his leave.

She re-pinned her hair into some semblance of neatness before returning once more to tackle the laundry. She admitted to pangs of disappointment that the property didn't have a garden, just a back-yard. However, at the far end of the street there was only one wash-house and lavatory to every four houses, although those were rented properties. At least she didn't have to share hers with strangers. The bread oven had almost fallen down, it hadn't been used in so long, but the range in the house was more than adequate to cope with bread-making. William had said he didn't mind her going to the baker, instead of spending hours kneading and proving. It was certainly an advantage, Jess mused, to have married a man who was used to fending for himself.

The lavatory was easy to deal with. It was a pan, with a wooden seat above, and once a week the council came around to empty it. It was far nicer than the one at home, where Father had to shovel the effluent onto the midden. Jess shuddered on recalling the stench and the sound of escaping rats.

It was different here in Albion Street. Once a week the night-soil men emptied the contents into a cart and the following morning, all Jess needed to do was douse the pan with water and Jeye's Fluid, and scrub the seat. That, and tear the newspaper into squares of course, to hang on the nail.

Pulling on the mob-cap, Jess stepped back into the wash house. The bundle of wet sheets wasn't too badly soiled and she decided it would make do with a rinse. She'd managed to complete the washing and boiling of the whites, but before the coloureds could go in, she rubbed carbolic-soap directly onto any obvious stains, including shirt collars, cuffs and of course, William's underwear. Men were not as adept with the lavatory as women, and the offending streaks had to be dealt with.

Jess added an extra cup of soft soap to the dolly-tub took hold of the dolly-pegs and began the punching of the coloureds. She had intended to complete the ironing before the end of the day, but time was getting on and she hadn't yet attended to the starching. Before the end of the week she was hoping to distemper the scullery. There had been black finger-marks all over the white tiles around the thrawl in the pantry and on the sink in the scullery. Scrubbing them clean had merely resulted in making the distempered walls look grubby.

Finally she was in a position to peg out the sheets and manoeuvred the line-prop into place. Jessica

Chamberlain stood admiring her first line of whites, billowing triumphantly in the wind, when she heard the back-gate close with a bang.

"Hello wife." A cheerful husband gave her bottom a friendly pat.

She blushed, wondering why he had returned, surely not to check on her well-being. "What brings you back so soon?"

"I need to go over to the Tan-Yard at Measham. There's a problem with some of the hides. I'm thinking you will join me and spend the rest of the day at the Elephant. Depending on what the problem is, I may have to stay over until tomorrow."

"Certainly not! I haven't finished the washing, not to mention cleaning the wash-house floor and the bed still needs re-making and I do so want to distemper the scullery. I have no choice but to say no."

Jess was totally put out. She felt the colour come to her cheeks on remembering that she had completely forgotten to deal with the slops, so the two chamber pots in the bedroom were still full. She crossed her fingers, hoping that there would be no need for him to go up there.

"But you shouldn't be lifting, with your arm the way it is and I thought you would want to see the family. I'll put the kettle on and mash a pot of tea."

Facing him across the table, Jess sensed his disappointment. "Considering what we discussed on holiday, I think it would be fitting if you came too, in case they need to talk to you and I'm not at all happy to leave you here alone, especially not with that scald. In the morning the dressing will need to be changed, and then by tomorrow night you'll need to spread butter on it."

Jess longed to see Father for herself, and to speak with him about the troubles but how on earth could she just walk out and leave, half way through wash-day? She was near to tears and in desperation made an alternative suggestion.

"Why not invite them over on Sunday like we discussed? It'll be even better if Ada can come too. Do you think the Ludlams will allow it? She only started work today."

William sighed, having little choice but to accept his wife's unexpected refusal. "Very well I'll call in at Glenfield, between now and the weekend, and explain. Is that decided then? I'll ask your parents, together with Jarvis and Ada, to come to dinner on Sunday?" He leaned back, seemingly resigned.

Jess's smile vanished on looking out of the window. "Oh look! It's started raining."

The couple dashed out together to rescue her mornings work.

§

Bess bent down to retrieve the last pillowcase from the wash basket and pegged it firmly onto the washing line. It had been a busy morning. She had dealt with the beer wagon, feeling embarrassed on only ordering the one small barrel of stout. The draymen had looked at her with some concern. It must have been obvious for some time that business at the Elephant was not good and another pub closure would not bode well. However, Bess had dealt with it, knowing that, as soon as the draymen had turned the shire-horses around and manoeuvred the dray back in the direction of the brewery, they would gossip about the predicament, no doubt passing on the news at the next pub they called at.

She had been up since dawn and after dealing with the washing, little though it was now both girls had left, had cleaned out the copper and set down some hedgerow beer. It would help out until they finally closed the doors and, although it was lively, particularly in this warm, thundery weather, it was a great deal cheaper than buying from the brewery. She just had to wait for it to cool, so it could be sieved and ladled into the barrel.

With the last of the washing blowing on the line, Bess walked through the inn and out of the front door. A breeze was getting up, and branches from the mighty oaks brandished their anger against a darkening sky. It looked like rain. She sat down on the bench, taking time to mull over Billy's declaration. He'd painted a grim picture. The thought of moving into a two-up-two-down-cottage, after the spaciousness of the pub, was daunting to say the least, but there didn't appear to be much choice. Thankfully, as it had turned out, there was only Jarvis to consider, but what if Ada needed to come back home?

Bess heard the clip-clop of hooves. That must be Billy about level with Clock Mill, by the sound of it, and she was anxious to hear how Ada had seemed when she left, travelling for the first time by rail. She crossed her fingers for the outcome of his meeting with the farm bailiff at The Hall, and prayed for an agreed reduction in rent.

The Late Elephant

Bess walked over to the drive leading to Tempe House where the woodbine grew. It was Billy's favourite flower. She picked half a dozen or so sprigs, pressing them to her nose, losing herself for a moment in their intoxicating perfume, before stepping back into the Elephant and placing them in a jar.

She heard the sound of boots on cinders but didn't dare to look up.

"Is anyone at home?"

The voice was not the one Bess had anticipated. She spun round, delighted to see the tall figure filling the doorway. "Come in William, how good to see you. You must have smelled the tea-pot."

William removed his hat and shook her hand warmly.

"I was expecting Billy. I'm anxious to hear how Ada was at leaving us."

"Is he not back yet? He wasn't on the platform when I arrived."

"No, he has other business." Bess shrugged her shoulders. "I may as well tell you what has been going on."

After a few tears, she began the tale. Her son-in-law sat patiently as she recalled the early days of toil. How life at the Elephant had quickly developed into a lucrative and gratifying business. Even with the arrival of the babies, there had been ample funds to pay for extra help and no shortage of willing candidates. She described how helpful Billy's mother had been in looking after the children, and with her own mother dead and gone, how much she had appreciated the help.

"But you're on the stage coach route?" said William.

"Oh indeed yes, we're about half way between Ashby and Market Bosworth, but of course John only stops now to deliver papers." She sighed. "Everything changed when the railways came. People don't travel long distances by coach any more. It was that regular trade which kept us ticking over. I've known the time when a dozen or more folk stayed overnight and the place was always full in the middle of the day, with John's passengers breaking their journey to eat.

"The only time we're busy now is at harvest when the tap-room is heaving with thirsty labourers. Even if you take into account lambing time and hay-making, it's not enough to pay our way.

"Tempe Farm opposite breeds a good strain of mutton and it's from there that our supply is purchased." Bess couldn't help but smile. "If anyone complained, Billy had his answer, 'Well, if the meat is tough yer'd better complain to them across the road. They reared em.'"

William laughed. "I can just hear him saying that."

Pulling a handkerchief from the pocket of her pinafore, Bess wiped her eyes, "I've been aware for some time things have changed, and I haven't dared to admit it, but I have to face the truth. Enough businesses in Measham have been forced to close, and once work dries up money disappears with it. No wonder so many local men have resorted to working in the coalmines, but it's unpleasant and dangerous work. The pit closed following a bad fall in which several died. It's impossible to say which is the worst, a dangerous job or no money to live on." She paused for a moment. "Did you know there's talk of sinking a new shaft? Even so it'll not be ready to mine for some years yet. God forbid that Jarvis or you, for that matter, will ever have to resort to that life."

She was halted by the unmistakable sound of hooves and wheels on cinders. She looked at her son-in-law and sighed. William jumped to his feet on seeing Moses enter, tail wagging, with Billy just a step behind.

It was Bess who spoke first. "How did you get on?" She felt the tension in his silence, but carried on raking the fire, not daring to face him.

After removing his hat, Billy nodded in the direction of William. "We have to be out in three weeks. Farmer Wragg at Minorca Farm has shown an interest in buying it. He's going to turn it into two dwellings to house his labourers."

"Oh!" Bess turned to face him.

William shook hands with his father-in-law, before sinking down beside him. Billy sat with his head in his hands. Bess placed the tea-pot on the table, giving his shoulder a squeeze. "Something will come up."

"Yer've caught us at a bad time, young man."

"So it would seem, Sir."

"I'm off to the village in search of a cottage to rent. Once that's sorted out things won't seem quite so grim. Mind yer, I'm not at all hopeful. There isn't a one standing empty and I canna think of anybody about to move. I'll call in at The Manor, and see what's what. If there is a cottage vacant, somebody there will know."

"I am sorry to hear all this, Sir, but I was half expecting it. It's obvious the Elephant can't be paying its way. Now, I would like to pay my share of the wedding expenses, I…," but he wasn't allowed to finish.

Billy rose to his feet. "Thank yer, but we'll manage. I'm not so flippin' destitute that I canna afford to pay for mi daughter's wedding, or to support mi wife and child." Billy's embarrassment brought an angry colour to his cheeks, and Bess felt uncomfortable for them both. She turned to her husband. "It'll be alright, Billy, we'll work it out together."

Billy moved towards the door. "I'll be off to the village then, before I lose mi nerve. Stay a while, William and keep Bess company."

The young man was determined not to be put off. "Actually, I was rather hoping you will put me up for the night. I have further business at the tan-yard tomorrow."

Bess was delighted to hear this. "Of course! You can have Jess's old room."

"I'll see yer directly, then."

"He's not taking this well," commented William, "can't say I blame him."

"No," was Bess' sorrowful reply. "It's Ada I'm most worried about. Even if she settles well at The Mill, she'll be heartbroken, and I cannot conceive of a situation where I can't offer my daughter a roof and a bed."

"What will you do with Napoleon and the trap?"

"Oh my goodness," retorted Bess, "I haven't given it a thought. We'll have to sell them I suppose. How can we tell Ada? It'll break her heart when she hears that both her home and her horse are gone."

"I think I may be able to help with that. Jess and I would like you to take the train to Leicester next Sunday and I'll ask Mrs Ludlam if Ada can come too, and we can all explain together. What do you think?"

"Well, I do declare, William, before any of this happened, our Ada suggested we do just that. She sat where you are now and said it, on the evening of your wedding day to be exact."

"You shouldn't worry too much about Ada. She's bound to have some reservations at leaving home, anyone would, but she needs to stretch her mind. Swepstone will not do that for her."

"I know that," nodded Bess, "she was becoming restless and I feared that if she didn't branch out, she might settle for a follower instead, and I don't think for one moment she's ready for that. I remember once after she'd seen a lantern-light show at the Sunday-school, I caught her lost in her own little world. She said, 'Mother wouldn't you just love to travel the world and see how other people live their lives?'"

"Perhaps she will eventually," William said.

"Goodness me," Bess declared, jumping to her feet. "I'm forgetting my manners. Let me offer you something to eat."

"Food can wait until Mr Elverson gets back. I'm eating far too much as it is."

"Can you ever eat too much?" asked Bess, questioning his logic.

"Well I'm having difficulty fastening my trousers. We can't have that now."

Bess turned immediately away, somewhat put out by his reference to the fastening of trousers. It was not something a gentleman usually said in front of a lady, other perhaps than his own wife.

"Well now, tell me about Jess. Has she settled in Leicester?"

Making a start on the preparations for supper, Bess poked life into the fire and replenished the wood.

"I asked if she would like to come and spend the day with you, but being Monday, she was half-way through doing the washing and, as I'll not be returning home tonight, tomorrow she intends to distemper the scullery." His face broke into a smile. "I expect supper to be late tomorrow, but she insisted, and I know better than to argue with the lady of the house."

Bess laughed with him, content in the fact that all seemed well with the couple. William described the trip to Skegness and painted a happy and lively picture of Jess rearranging the house. He told about how quickly she came to terms with his range, how the back-draught was much more rapid than the one here, and how wonderful her cooking was. Bess appreciated his attempts to alleviate the atmosphere.

They both contemplated the fire as flames began to rise and enjoyed a moment of quiet reflection.

William looked around him. "I've just realized there's something missing. Where's Jarvis?"

"He's with Violet Bentley from the village. She often takes him out for the afternoon. He'll come back with Billy." No sooner had she spoken the words, than the child ran in through the door, to climb onto the chair opposite, and stare in gleeful wonderment at William.

"Hello, young man," William addressed him, ruffling his blonde curls, "have you had a good time with your friend?"

"Yes fanks. Are you staying for tea? Can I sit next to you?"

William moved round to the other side. "Now, I have something to tell you."

"What? Tell me, tell me!" The child's spontaneity was infectious.

"Sometime very soon, you and your mother and father are going to ride on a train from Ashby station and you're going to visit Jess and me. Do you remember coming once before?"

Jarvis nodded his head. "When, tomorrow?"

"No, but very soon."

"Will Ada be there?"

William smiled at him. "Would you like her to be?"

Jarvis jumped up and down with excitement. "Yes please. Can she come?"

"Being as you asked so nicely, and have remembered to say 'please,' then yes, she can."

They all started as the unusually gruff voice intercepted. "There'll be no money for flippin' train tickets."

"Oh yes there will." William jumped up to give his words potency. "Instead of paying for tonight's meal and my lodging, I shall purchase the tickets. Jess is looking forward to seeing you all." William looked sternly at the older man, and Bess guessed he was trying to appear more heroic than he felt.

"We'll see!"

"How did you get on with the farmer?" Bess was hoping against hope there would be positive news.

Billy shook his head. "Nothin!" He pulled a face. "Mrs Scarlett was there, ears cocked. I expect it'll be all over the village by tonight."

"And did Ada get off alright?"

The look of dismay in Billy's eyes almost made Bess wish she hadn't asked the question.

§

Puffing heavily on his pipe and with a glass of rum in his hand, Billy placed the pork-pie hat on his head and sat down on the wooden bench outside. Bess and William had stayed with him until the sun disappeared below the horizon. The atmosphere had been uncomfortable and the conversation stilted, with no-one knowing what to say. He'd been relieved on seeing them retire to bed.

As on most Monday evenings of late, there hadn't been any customers. The dominoes team wasn't due to meet until Wednesday and Tom, who hardly ever missed a night, was helping with the hay-making up at Swepstone Fields, and didn't finish work until well after dusk. Billy wasn't bothered by this, in fact as things were, it was a blessing.

Stars were already visible in the twilight, but there was still enough light left to gaze around the vast panoply of fields, thick with groups of oak trees and watched over by St. Peter's, sitting on the hill. It was with this, his favourite view before him, that Billy slowly began the painful process of acceptance.

How many years had he spent gazing out, nodding benignly as the seasons dictated the time to plough the land, pre-empting custom from the agricultural calendar? Instead of watching in wonderment at the rippling flanks of the shire-horses, as they pulled the ploughs, he would soon be taking up an implement and doing some of the jobs himself, or even walking behind them.

It wasn't hard work which bothered Billy, but losing face, sensing the unasked questions as to what had gone amiss. There would be endless squeezes of his shoulder, unspoken pity emanating from his neighbours' eyes and, come what may, he would have to grin and bear it.

Words from his father came back to him. "You can't stop change, no matter which direction it takes, nor should you, in my opinion." His long departed parent would have been a tower of strength, just at this moment. Despite his family's support, particularly Bess's, whose love and devotion had never failed him, Billy suddenly felt incredibly lonely.

Ada and Jess were now out of his protection. William would look after Jess, of that he had no doubt, but Ada was alone and vulnerable. Up until now all he'd wanted was to remove her from Duncan. Billy couldn't bear the thought of that womaniser touching his Ada. She had her mother's eyes, like those of a fallow deer, and the same soft golden skin. Until Duncan had come sniffing around, she had never caused him even as much as a modicum of concern. He missed both of his daughters. The place was flat and lifeless without them, and Ada still had to be told about the move. He was dreading the moment, but it didn't have to be done right now.

Sometime tomorrow he would take a pen and ink and list his chattels. There was the horse and trap, three good Tamworth sows in the sty and maybe he could sell the tap-room furniture to some of the new establishments in Measham. Then there was the linen, cutlery and plates and the trays and all those tea towels. Perhaps they should have a sale. Yes, he would make the list tomorrow in daylight and he would have a good look around. When they were settled Ada would visit.

There was no need to go into a fluster at this stage, as he had assets. Billy took another swig of his rum and sucked heavily on his pipe only to find it had gone out. He rose unsteadily, returning inside to reach down a spill from the mantle shelf and after dipping it into the glowing embers, directed it towards the tobacco. He replenished his glass. He would concentrate a little longer on his plans for the sale. Perhaps Bess would make some pies and cakes and they could sell them. He needed to calculate how much he could expect to make. Then he would plan.

Chapter 7

Roosters

Ada awoke to the sound of a rooster. She jumped out of bed and crossed straight to the open window. A light mist blanketed the fields and hedges. Below her window cockerels were fighting and a raucous squawking carried clearly through the fresh morning air.

To her horror, Ada heard a step on the landing and panicked into action. After a hurried wash in last night's water, she twisted her hair into a bun, positioning hairpins for all she was worth and pulled on her boots.

Only Mr Ludlam was in the living room, riddling out the ashes and poking life into the fire. "Good morning, Sir. Sorry I'm late, Sir."

"Morning, Ada. Take your time."

Ada grabbed the kettle, rushing to the pump in the scullery, wondering what on earth he thought of her. He didn't seem overly concerned. Fancy not waking on her first morning! If Father were to get wind of it, she'd get a telling off.

The master stood behind her, waiting to take his turn at the sink, braces already hanging by his sides. Ada blushed and scuttled out of his way, but by the time the kettle had boiled and Ada had set the table, his wife arrived downstairs to find him suitably washed and shaved with his shirt-collar and tie properly in place.

"Good morning, wife." He stood up. "I'll give the lads a shout."

"Good morning, Ada. How did you sleep?" Mrs Ludlam yawned. "Mornings are not my best time."

"I slept very well, thank you." Ada placed a cup of tea before her. "How's Allen?"

"Settled at the moment, but not for long, I suspect. It was very late when I finally managed to get him off."

Ada noticed the dark shadows beneath her mistress's eyes as she wearily picked up the spoon from the saucer. She yawned, then yelled, "Mr Ludlam have you lit the faggots in the bread oven?"

"I have Mrs Ludlam, yes."

Footsteps sounded on the stone floor and Ada was surprised to see Ben and Eli enter from the bakery. It was then she realized that the extra door on the wall between the coppers, must lead to their room. There was no lock on that door.

The boys took it in turns at the pump and settled at the table to enjoy a drink of milk. Ben's eyes were focused on his and Ada watched his Adam's apple rise and fall as he drank, but Eli was fixing Ada with a stare. His eyes held hers as he lifted the mug to his lips to noisily slurp and she looked back in revulsion, taking in his filthy clothes and black fingernails. His face had a greasy film about it and the dark stubble gave him an unpalatable look. She was praying for the moment when they would leave to begin the milking.

"It takes one and a half hours at least, to bring the oven to temperature, so we have plenty of time." Mrs Ludlam's voice interrupted the uneasiness. It was a relief to hear her continue with the instructions.

Missy quietly joined them at the table, dressed ready for school, wearing a starched white apron with pretty broderie-anglais frills on the bib. "Good morning, Missy. You do look smart."

"Would you mind brushing my hair?" The girl pulled up a stool. Ada saw the look that Eli sent in the girl's direction and wondered if anyone else noticed.

§

"We'd best get on. Allen has developed a cough and it's beginning to sound like croup."

Ada and Mrs Ludlam began knocking back in earnest. The sounds were faint, but unmistakably those of a child whimpering and puking. Mrs Ludlam lingered only long enough to wipe her hands before scurrying upstairs, but she was back down within minutes, holding the child in her arms, seriously worried about his condition.

"We'll have to steam him. We can't do it in here, or the bread will taste of eucalyptus, so we'll have to bring the bath into the living-room."

Ada dragged it in, placing it in front of the fireplace and began transferring hot water, a jug-full at a time, from the boiler. It seemed to take forever and Ada was aware of the cough becoming worse.

The women hung sheets from the beams, draping them in a wigwam-like arrangement. Mrs Ludlam sprinkled eucalyptus oil and cloves into the water, before finally sitting beside it with the child fidgeting fretfully on her knee. She dipped her fingers into a pot of goose-grease, scooped out a generous finger-full and rubbed it onto his chest and back before feeding him a tiny amount from the end of a spoon. "Just help me put this on him, Ada." She held up a piece of brown paper and a simple vest made from a piece of flannel. "Hold the paper in place while I slip the vest over it."

Ada did as she was bid.

"There, that should keep the heat in."

The boy continued to struggle for breath, every intake sounding is if it was being dragged through vibrating cinders. His skin was ashen except for two bright red cheeks. Ada looked on helplessly, but Mrs Ludlam was adamant. "Don't worry about me, I'll manage here. You carry on with the dough or else we'll lose the heat in the oven, and wash your hands well before you start, in case any there's any eucalyptus oil on them."

Ada pulled the sheets around the two, eliminating draughts as much as possible and returned to the bakery. The bread oven was drawing well and Ada flagged as the temperature continued to soar. The child looked really sick and Ada was worried. She had known of youngsters expiring from weaknesses of the lungs.

She worked, bringing the mixes to a point where they could be left for the final proving, listening to heartrending sounds of coughing from the room next door. The child's rasping was considerably worse. Ada whispered a prayer, pleading for the child's recovery.

She took hold of the paddle and began to place loaves into the oven, the heat burning the skin on her face and arms. She paused long enough to make a note of the time. The last thing they needed his morning was for her to burn the bread.

Anxious to check on the patient, Ada closed the door behind her, breathing in air heavy with medication and coughed politely before parting the sheets just enough to peer inside.

"There you are, Ada." Mrs Ludlam was nursing the child on her lap. She held him upright, but he was struggling, irregular short breaths coming in rasps.

"He's no better, look." Her face was a picture of distress and Ada felt utterly helpless, not knowing what to say. The next moment, Allen coughed for all he was worth. His face turned to purple as he wheezed and spluttered, seemingly unable to take the next breath. His eyes began to bulge. His mother jumped to her feet, held him to her shoulder and administered a slap on his back. The child gasped and, after holding his breath for what seemed to be an inordinate amount of time, coughed up a ball of green phlegm which burst forth from his mouth, spattering his cheeks. Mrs Ludlam cried out with relief before lying him gently back onto her knee and rubbing his back.

As if to pacify her that all was well once more, he took a deep, shuddering breath and it was clear that, for this time at least, he had successfully removed the obstruction.

§

Mrs Ludlam struggled through the back door. Using elbows and hips she entered the scullery back-side first. Clutched in her hands were the feet of two dead cockerels, their red combs hanging down below lifeless eyes.

"You'll have to pluck these. Have you done it before?"

Ada nodded.

"How do you prefer, with hot water or without?"

"I'd rather do it with. It stops the feathers going up my nose."

"Better put the kettle on." Mrs Ludlam deposited the birds in the scullery sink. "I'll leave you to it then. I prefer to do them dry. I can't abide the smell of wet feathers!"

Before Ada had time to roll up her sleeves, Mrs Ludlam bustled back in. "Ada, I almost forget to tell you. While Mr Ludlam was dealing with the cockerels, Mr. Chamberlain called. He didn't have enough time to come across and speak with you directly, but he wants you to go to his house on Sunday, for dinner. I said yes, of course, and so you're to take the stage and he will meet you there."

Ada was thrilled. "I am obliged to you, Ma'am. Did he say what it was about?"

"No, and he was in such a hurry there was no time to ask. Not that it's any of my business, of course, but your parents are to attend."

Ada set to work with gusto. Before dousing the birds, she first removed all tail quills, and any others which may be useful. After the plucking, she hacked off the wings, together with the birds' heads and feet. Then, with sleeves rolled up as far as possible, and entering through its rear end, pushed her hand into a carcass, until she felt the gritty squelch of the gizzard in the lower part of the neck. She grasped it firmly, and on opening her fingers slightly, she pulled hard, raking out the remaining innards, feeling the smooth, wet organs and intestines slither out and glide onto the wooden draining-board. This, Ada felt, was far more enjoyable than plucking feathers, and stepped back to relish the satisfaction of a job well done. It was obvious to Ada that the birds were young so there would be no need to boil them first before putting them in the roasting tin. She resolved to ask Mrs Ludlam if she could take some tail feathers to Jess. They always come in handy for oiling clocks or cleaning the places on a piece of good china which are too tiny for the cloth.

Selecting the liver, kidneys and neck for the gravy, she removed the rest of the giblets, throwing them into the bucket already full of feathers. She grasped the leaden handle of the water pump, plunging for all she was worth, to see the clear fresh liquid gush forth in an arc, washing away blood and guts firstly from her arms and then from the wide clay sink. Ada gave the skins a good rub with a towel, took the carcasses and a burning taper outside, and singed the downy residue from the cockerels' skin. The smell of burning feathers was not something one needed inside a house, especially where there was a sick child. A good potage of meat from the birds together with a little mashed potato was just the thing to give strength back to an ailing child.

§

The vegetables scarcely had time to boil, before sounds from the scullery announced the arrival of the men. Ben was goading Eli about the colour of his boot-laces.

"Something smells good," Mr Ludlam commented, settling at the table, promptly absorbing himself in yesterday's Telegraph and dutifully lifting his elbows to allow Missy to spread the cloth. As usual the wash under the pump hadn't achieved much for Eli.

The fat in the roasting tins sizzled and spat as Ada lifted the golden carcasses from the oven, laying them on the hob to rest. Aromatic smells exuded from the thyme and parsley stuffing and the three men began to shuffle in anticipation.

"Ada, do you need any help?" called Mrs Ludlam. "How about thickening for the gravy? Do you know how to do it?"

"Yes Ma'am, I can manage thank you. Ada already had the flour to hand so, trying her best to keep calm whilst aware of eyes following her every move, she continued wielding the wooden spoon around the cast-iron pan, anxiously beating out every lump into a smooth paste. It seemed to Ada that the next few minutes took forever, but the gravy finally bubbled to a golden savoury concoction and lips were being licked in anticipation.

Alfred Ludlam began the knife sharpening ritual. Allen was tucked safely in his cot and Mrs Ludlam settled herself beside her husband.

Ada hardly tasted the tender flesh or the rich gravy, so intent was she to see how her first proper dinner was received. The only thing left was a heap of well-chewed bones sticking out from an ungainly heap on a dish in the middle of the table. Ada wondered what Grandma would have thought to that. Mr Ludlam devoured his final morsel of gravy-soaked bread and with a groan of satisfaction turned towards their new cook. "Ada that was delicious. You did well."

Eli had a finger in his mouth, picking his teeth, so she kept her eyes diverted in other directions, but not before she had registered his nod of appreciation.

Her rhubarb crumble generated similar results, so she no longer felt a need to worry. Tonight the rice-pudding would be placed, untouched, on the thrawl in the larder. Ada's face beamed in delight at having assured herself that she was indeed going to make a success of her new position here at Glenfield.

With the men back outside, Ada set about clearing the pots from the table. Mrs Ludlam followed her into the scullery. "I've been thinking, Ada. Why don't you take your bath on Saturday morning, after I've delivered the bread? There'll be no men about until at least midday."

Ada's eyes lit up. She'd been wondering about this. Mr Ludlam had put a bolt on the door, but it could be awkward if one of the boys needed to come downstairs.

"Yes please, Ma'am. I would be most grateful." It would mean taking her bath and washing her hair after the last bake. That way there would be fewer cooking smells to attach themselves before the visit to Jess's house.

"There's one thing certain, tomorrow morning will be somewhat quieter. There are only two roosters left to fight it out." Mrs Ludlam sighed. She reached down the darning mushroom and a basket containing several balls of wool and began matching them, as best she could, to various socks which needed attention. "This is not my favourite occupation, but needs must."

Ada pulled the cloth from table and shook it outside where hens were waiting to peck the crumbs.

On Saturday she would be with her family.

Chapter 8

A Stranger

Jess paused to reposition her hat-pin, before closing the front door. She was wearing her new grey hat, the one she had bought for the honeymoon. She thought it prudent to make a good impression on her first outing into the city.

To her astonishment, a rather scruffy woman was peering straight at her through the railings. She had with her a child of about six or seven years old. His clothes were filthy and his face looked as if it had not been washed in days. The large and somewhat grubby-looking laundry basket the woman was carrying under one arm appeared to be full. A soiled sheet had been placed over the top, making it impossible to view the contents. The buttons of her shift were open, revealing a little too much breast and hair escaped from beneath a roughly placed turban of grimy cotton. It was obvious from her expression that she had something to say.

"It's Mrs Chamberlain, ain't it?"

"Yes," replied Jess somewhat taken aback.

"How do you do? I'm Rose Finney. I hope you found the parlour to your liking, only Mr Chamberlain asked me to see to it for you."

Jess shuddered at the thought of this woman touching her things. It certainly accounted for the dirty finger marks.

"Yes, thank you," Jess stuttered, embarrassed and uneasy. "Did you... I mean...did you just do the parlour or did he ask you to clean the rest of the house?" Jess took a step backwards, she was getting a whiff of something decidedly unpleasant.

"Well, I did all a downstairs, I did, and changed the sheets on your bed. Might as well, he paid me for the whole afternoon." She was almost crowing. "Wedding went well did it?"

"Yes, thank you," replied Jess.

"Well, nice ter make your acquaintance, taraar." An insolent grin exposed a set of discoloured teeth, after which she took her leave, instructing the child to follow. "Come on, Osmond."

Jess watched as the woman tossed her head in the air, transporting her ample rear-end post-haste up the hill. Jess did not at all like her attitude and wondered how to broach the subject with William. The woman was inordinately familiar, certainly for a first meeting, in fact Jess felt she was bordering on being rude. What on earth was William doing allowing such an individual to go into their house? Surely he could have found someone more presentable, and apparently she cleaned for him at the warehouse.

Thank goodness I made the effort and distempered both the scullery and the pantry, Jess deliberated, it was enough to send a shudder of horror through a decent woman, imagining those hands touching her things.

Jess put down her basket and turned the heavy key in the lock of the front door ready to head off into town. A hydrangea bush growing beneath the window was about to break into flower. Jess thought how pleasant it would look. However, some shoots had grown up almost higher than the window and it needed cutting back. She must remember to mention it.

Still mulling over her unpleasant encounter Jess closed the gate behind her. The anticipation of being reunited with her family was enough to cancel any effects of Mrs Finney and she needed to make haste. William had agreed to come home early, for it was Friday and bath-night. A fire was already laid beneath the copper. They had agreed that, as the weather was warm, they would in fact take their bath in the washhouse, thus avoiding having to mess up the house which was now in good order.

She proceeded first to the market, still undecided whether to purchase lamb or beef. William had said he would like her to cook roast beef and Yorkshire pudding. He had read that it was the favourite Sunday dinner of Prince Edward, but Jess thought it a bit extravagant, the price of beef being what it was. She spotted the butcher's in the market square. Game birds were out of season, but hanging in front of the shop were rabbits. Jess resolved to purchase one, so in place of his favourite roast pheasant William would enjoy a rabbit pie.

The butcher emerged from the shop. He had removed his straw boater and was giving his head a scratch. On seeing Jess he replaced it and with his plump hands smoothed the blue and white striped apron, giving Jess a smile and a nod.

"Have these rabbits been hand-reared?" Jess enquired.

"Indeed they have, Madam."

"And have they been fed cabbage?"

"Certainly not, Madam, I rears em miself! Tender as a lady's heart they are."

Jess could see from the pale colour of their flesh that they had never been near a cabbage, but it didn't hurt to make sure the butcher knew she was serious about her cooking and not prepared to accept anything less than the best.

"I don't believe I've had the pleasure, Madam?"

"Jessica Chamberlain, Mr William Chamberlain's wife." She lingered over the words, relishing the thrill on using her new name.

"Ah yes, I am indeed acquainted with the gentleman. Please convey my congratulations to Mr Chamberlain and my best wishes go to you, my dear. I'm sure you'll both be very happy. Might I say Madam that he is partial to a loin of pork?"

"Is he indeed, but is the weather not a little too warm for pork?"

"And pork pies, Madam, will you be requiring a couple of those?"

William had been quite adamant that the pork pies were to be purchased only from Walkers pork butchers.

"Not today, thank you, but I'll take a rabbit, if I may, and if you can furnish me with a rib of beef, enough to feed six, I will be obliged."

The butcher wiped his cleaver on his apron and, with the help of a pulley fixed to a beam on the ceiling, lowered down a whole side of beef. Jess patiently waited while he chopped and sawed a piece to the size she had requested.

"Will you make the Yorkshire pudding to go with it, Madam? It's become very popular since The Prince of Wales promoted it."

"I do intend to do that, yes. I haven't made it before, although I believe it is in fact, just a simple batter pudding."

The butcher weighed the beef, putting the brass scales into place as necessary. "My wife tells me that, as long as you leave it in a very hot oven for the full half of an hour, without opening the door once, you can't go wrong."

"Thank you, I shall heed your suggestion, and inform you as to how it turns out when I'm next in town." With the beef duly wrapped in brown paper, Jess managed to fit it into her shopping bag. "Much obliged, I'm sure. Now, please tell me, how much do I owe you?"

§

Ada was up and doing even before the remaining roosters began their crowing. She felt wonderful after her bath yesterday and didn't really want to have to cook breakfast and end up stinking of fat.

Her hair was behaving well and it shone beautifully. She had taken the trouble to wash it in rainwater, collected from the butt. In the meantime, the mob-cap would afford protection.

The whole of bath-time had taken no more than a quarter of an hour, so concerned was she at a possible interruption, but she did feel so much fresher. Mrs

Ludlam had stood guard in case the men had reappeared sooner than expected and she hadn't even needed to lift the bath back on the hook as Mr and Mrs Ludlam had taken their turn almost straight afterwards.

The breakfast table was laid and at least half the vegetables prepared before Mr Ludlam made his way down the stairs. "My word, someone is eager this morning."

"Yes Sir, I can't wait to see our Jess's house." She began cutting the bread ready for frying, when Mrs Ludlam appeared.

"Good morning, Ada, it looks like being a hot one again." She was obviously having trouble with her hair. Despite her attempts to push it back in place, it kept escaping from the pins. "It's always the same after it's been washed, it'll take it a good two days to settle."

The lads arrived just as Ada was placing the frying pan on the fire. "You were up early," Eli commented. Ada kept her eyes lowered, she was not going to let anything unpleasant interfere with her day.

"Ada is paying a visit to her sister's house in Leicester," explained Mr Ludlam, "so we need to get a move on. As soon as we're back from church, she will catch the stage-coach into town and she needs to complete her jobs before then, so perhaps just for today, we can all help to clear the things away?"

"Do we have to have eggs and bacon, Mr Ludlam?" asked his wife, "I think the weather is too close, can we not manage on oatcakes and toast? After all, we'll be having a roast dinner straight after church. If you're really hungry we can always boil some eggs."

"Very true, wife. Ada put the pan away."

The Late Elephant

§

It was obvious that the day was to be hot, and Jess was anxious to complete as much preparation as possible before the sun made its way round to the living-room window. She didn't need to worry too much about having the meal ready early, as Ada's stage coach wouldn't get in until around two o'clock, but she was aware that the rib of beef would need to be cooked in a gentle heat over a long period. Cooking the Yorkshire pudding would be the worst job, having to fire the oven to its hottest right in the middle of the day. The recipe had been printed in the Girls' Own Paper and Jess was anxious to try it out. Still, they would be eating in the parlour and if William managed to release the window sashes, at least they would have a cool haven in which to enjoy the meal.

Jess had dressed the table with Mrs Wade's wedding gift, a white damask table-cloth. She had even found some napkins in the chiffonier left behind by William's Mother. She felt a twinge of sadness, knowing that his parents were no longer there and that she had inherited a home which belonged to someone she had never met. Except for once, ages ago, William had never spoken of them. Even then he'd only briefly explained that there had been an accident with some chemicals which his father had used to tan the hides. She wondered why this had affected his mother and wondered if they had both died in the incident, but it was a sensitive topic and there never seemed to be a right time to ask the questions. William was obviously not prepared to discuss the affair in any more detail and Jess felt it inappropriate to enquire further.

William told her that when he inherited the leather warehouse, he had discovered there was money owed, and he'd been forced to take on a partner, hence Duncan. Soon after that, they had the opportunity to buy a business in the tan-yard at Measham for very little money. It was too much of a bargain to miss, so now William handled the warehouse in Leicester, whilst Duncan supervised the one in Measham. Jess was aware that they needed to repay the loan and that meant working long hours.

Jess was at the sink in the scullery when she felt his arm creep around her and his warm mouth on the nape of her neck. "I missed you. I woke up and you were gone."

Yesterday's encounter came to mind. Instead, she made to put the knife down and return his embrace, but he gave her a quick hug and turned away. "You carry on, I can make the tea. I know how important today is."

This unexpected withdrawal somehow provided Jess with the impetus she needed. "I met your Mrs Finney the other day."

"Did you, where?" He seemed surprised, but not overly interested. Jess briefly explained about the woman introducing herself, but William chose to see to the bush at the front of the house and she didn't gain any further information, not that she knew precisely what it was she needed to know, if indeed, anything. Then a thought stuck her and she wondered if it was Rose Finney to whom William had given the loaves of bread.

Time was fast approaching for William to meet the train. However, there was much banging and muttering under breath as he tried to free the sash-windows in the parlour. They had been closed for many a year and were proving obstinate. She was hoping he was not making a mess. The last thing she needed was to find the table-linen covered in dust. She could not complain, however, as he had duly pruned the hydrangea bush and swept up the front causeway, making the house look most neat and tidy. Unfortunately, however, not being a gardener, there wasn't one single flower-bud left to open up its splendour to the world. Jess put the thought behind her, telling herself that it would certainly help towards producing more blossoms for next year.

On finally hearing the front door close, Jess ran into the parlour, but found that all was well. Returning to the scullery, she pumped furiously until the bowl was full, slipped off her bodice and spent a few precious minutes delighting in the fresh cool spring-water on her flesh, before re-stoking the fire and opening the back-draft. She ran quickly upstairs and put on the new blouse she had purchased in town. It was a slub-satin, with stripes in cream and brown.

Within minutes the Yorkshire-pudding would go into the oven together with the roast potatoes and, with the vegetables already set over the fire, the last stage of the food cooking would be under way. Once the rhubarb and ginger pie had warmed through, her meal would be complete, so she donned a clean pinafore, the new one with the frills.

If everyone arrived as planned, there would be time to discuss how they were to approach Ada about the closing of The Late Elephant. It had to be done, but Jess had an uneasy feeling as to Ada's reaction. She was still a child, despite the new position and Jess was dreading the moment they told her she was to lose Napoleon.

The front door burst open and voices resonated through the house, bringing a familiarity and warmth which was more than welcome, but which hung somewhat strangely in this new environment. Jarvis entered the room like a fresh spring breeze, his big blue eyes sparkling and flung his arms around his sister.

William would be meeting the stage-coach and Ada within the hour.

Chapter 9

Après Sunday Dinner

Ada was raging. William had no right, absolutely no right whatsoever in allowing her to walk unprepared into such an awkward situation! Who did he think he was? She shuddered on recalling the moment when Father had attempted to explain that there was a problem. He had struggled to find the words and stuttered to an uncomfortable silence, allowing William to take over and complete the announcement.

Ada neared the brook, its perpetual gurgling offering a promise of comfort, a salve to quieten both her turbulence and feelings of desolation. It was Sunday evening and the sun had almost set. Shielded on two sides by trees and bushes, and ensuring the chosen spot was hidden from the house, she sank to the ground, needing to give vent to her demons.

With head in hands she closed her eyes and was back there sitting at the table, feeling happy and contented, relishing a mouthful of Jess's wonderful roast beef and the new addition of the Yorkshire pudding.

Those frightful words had floated around in mid-air before solidifying into fact. As the dreadful truth had suddenly become clear, her world had entered a state of slow-motion. Her eyes had opened so widely that they hurt and her jaws had clamped together, unable to deal with the food. Only her ears functioned as the facts poured relentlessly in, her brain struggling to process their meaning. They were to leave The Late Elephant. In three weeks from now her home would be gone. She would have nowhere to belong.

A reaction manifested itself in an overwhelming flood of nausea and as her metabolism visibly registered the shock and horror, the family had become quiet. They looked guardedly at each other. She swallowed, but the effort had simply made her choke. After several gulps of water and a racking cough, everyone had begun to speak, at first together then more slowly, one by one, in attempts to placate her and soften the blow.

William had increased the drama by telling her that Napoleon would have to be sold. If that wasn't enough, he embarked on a lecture about how, at this difficult time, she should be putting her parents first and how Father had been struggling to make ends meet.

Did he think for one moment that she wasn't concerned for them both? Of course she was, but the news hardly had time to settle in her mind and he hadn't given her any time at all to recover. Who was he to tell her what to think? He was not her father! It was a miracle she hadn't shouted at him, told him to mind his own business, but the look on Mother's face had been more than enough to make Ada bite her tongue. She had withdrawn from them all, not wishing to hear for the umpteenth time, "It'll be alright once we're settled."

Ada had carried her pent-up feelings out of harm's way and back here to the safety and privacy of the brook. She felt let down, knowing they had conspired behind her back. Why had Father not told her? They had always been so close. No wonder he was crying at the station. They must all have known about this before she left for the Mill, so why had they not warned her? It was too unbearable to contemplate.

The deluge of tears flowed uninterrupted, but on opening her eyes for a second in search of a handkerchief, Ada saw the pair of scruffy boots with laces which did not match. She was not alone. Startled, she looked up at him towering over her, just seconds before she heard the voice.

"What's up, Ada? You look as if you've lost a pound and found a penny." He dropped down beside her, draping his arm around her shoulders.

"It is nothing Eli. I just need to be alone that's all." Ada was annoyed, her body recoiling. "Eli, can I ask you to leave me be?" She was shouting.

His eyes devoured her. "Why? I can make you feel better."

Ada could smell his unwashed flesh and his fetid breath was warm on her cheek. "No, you can't. Please believe me, I need to be alone." She attempted to stand up. "Let's walk back to the house."

"What's up? You're sweetheart gone off with another? Come here, I'll be your lover."

Ada pushed him away, "Don't talk such rubbish."

He pulled her down onto the grass. "Come on, give us a kiss." He took her face between his hands, knocking off her hat, and kissed her full on the mouth, trying to force his tongue between her lips. The strings of the boater were still knotted and they were cutting into her neck, and as she twisted and turned, pain burned into her skin. She was frantic, kicking and yelling at him to leave her alone. She scratched his face, feeling his flesh beneath her finger nails, but he threw her backwards, flinging himself on top of her.

"Get off me, you brute" she screamed at him, but he took no notice. "Eli, get off."

She struggled, anger and revulsion driving her, yet despite her frenzied attempts to escape, it became sickeningly obvious that her small frame was no match for his. Ada felt his knee push between her legs and his hands groping her breasts, but struggle as she might, she couldn't move him. She took a deep breath and screamed, "Help!" He placed a hand over her mouth. She made the most of his only having one arm free and beat him with her fists, but he grabbed both of her tiny wrists with only one of his huge hands, pinning her arms above her head and with the other one took hold of her breast. With horror she looked back at him, sickened by the leer on his face. The stink of him was choking her. She threatened to tell Mr Ludlam, so he returned his hand to her mouth, straddling her and pulling off his belt before unbuttoning his trousers. She fought him as best she could, calling him a beast and a brute, as her small fists pounded him, but he laughed down at her. His face was set in a sneer and his eyes glistened with absolute power, conveying the message of what he intended. The horror of what was about to happen gripped Ada like a nightmare.

She heard a yelp and felt the soft coat of the dog on her cheek and the saliva as he snarled and she screamed as he scratched at her face, trying to remove Eli's hand.

A thunderous yell filled her ears as she felt Eli's body fall from her. She was free. On struggling to sit up, she saw Ben astride Eli, holding him by the ears, yelling at him and banging his head against the ground. He made fists and pummelled them into Eli's face, blood bursting from his nose.

It took a moment for Ada to recover sufficiently in order to function. "Ben, stop! You'll kill him." Her pleas merged with the frantic barking of the dog, but still Ben continued.

Recognizing the impossibility of her ending the onslaught, Ada ran towards the house, arms flailing, screaming for help. She staggered and fell, but Mr Ludlam was already flying across the field as though the devil was after him. All Ada could do was point towards the trees. Clipper stood barking for all he was worth, positioned between the two adversaries, threatening both and baring his teeth.

On returning to the vicious scene, Ada registered Mr Ludlam's shock on seeing Eli's face, swollen and with blood pouring from his nose. Then he looked across at Ben standing, with face as white as a sheet, his blooded fists still clenched. Ada's knees give way and she sank to the ground.

"He's alive, thank God." Mr Ludlam's voice was clipped and angry. "Go and fetch the cart Ben, we need to get him back to the house."

He turned towards Ada, his eyes furious. "What happened? How did this come about?"

Eli stirred, a long painful moan emanating from somewhere within. It prompted Clipper to resume barking and Ada's answer was postponed.

§

"Are you hurt, Ada?"

"Only my neck, Ma'am. It's where the strings of my hat cut into my skin."

"Dear, dear, just look at that." Mrs Ludlam offered a clean handkerchief. "Here, take this and come and sit down. Whatever has happened?"

Ada struggled to control her sobs but, anxious that Ben be absolved from any blame, choked out the words. "Ben came to help me. It was dreadful. I didn't know Eli was there. He started kissing me. I told him to stop, but he carried on."

Mrs Ludlam raised an eyebrow. "Eli? But what on earth were you doing down at the brook with him at this time of night? We were waiting for you to come home from your sister's. In fact we were looking forward to hearing all about it. Dear me, you are in a state."

Ada looked down to discover her bodice was torn and instinctively covered it with her hand. Again the tears began to flow. In between sobs she attempted to explain, but was taken aback when Mr Ludlam strode in and stood before her looking ominous, his eyes burning into her's. "Well, young lady, I think you owe us an explanation."

Ada was mortified at his accusing stare, but his wife interrupted, "By the sound of things it's a long story. Perhaps it could wait until tomorrow."

He frowned, obviously unhappy with this suggestion.

"Oh please, let me explain if you don't mind Ma'am, I need to." Ada was pleading, unable to endure the look of contempt on his face.

Mr Ludlam pursed his lips. "Right, go ahead and begin at the beginning. I want to hear it all."

Ada twisted the wet handkerchief in her hands, searching for a place to start. "Well Sir, William met me off the stage and took me to their house. It was lovely, seeing everyone." She paused, her bottom lip threatening to quiver.

Mr Ludlam stood before her. She was aware of his eyes taking in the grass stains on her dress and the buttons missing from her bodice, but as she tried to cover herself with her hands, he spoke more gently. "Take your time," he said and pulled up a chair.

Ada began again. "It made it difficult for Jess cooking the dinner, because I didn't get there until two o'clock, so we sat down to eat straight away, as soon as I walked in. I was so happy, looking forward to telling them all about being here, but they told me that they're leaving the Elephant and selling Napoleon." She stopped, feeling the anger flooding back. "It was William who said it." She turned to Mrs Ludlam. "Did you know?"

Ada was relieved to see the older woman shake her head. "No Ada, he said it was a family matter and would I agree to you attending."

Tears welled up once more. "He should have told me before we went into the house. He should have warned me. It was horrible. I had so looked forward to seeing them all and Jarvis is missing me and he wanted to tell me all about his journey on the train, but William wouldn't let him. He snapped at him, told him to be quiet."

"But it doesn't explain what you were doing down at the brook." Mr Ludlam persisted.

Ada was anxious now to defend herself. "I was too upset to come in and face you. I didn't want you to see me crying. I needed time to think about it, to get used to it. I'm worried as to how Mother will cope. I think she'll be unhappy away from the Elephant, no matter where she goes and I can't bear the fact I'll never see Napoleon again."

She sat red-faced, with tears still trickling over her cheeks, but held her head high, and, fired by the injustice of it all, nursed a stubborn resolve to make them understand. "I thought I would be alone down there, when Eli appeared. I tried to fight him, but he was too strong. I begged him to stop, but he wouldn't."

Ada watched Mr Ludlam scratch his head and she wondered why he hadn't taken her word for what had happened. Surely they could see how upset she was.

"Well Ada, I have to admit I have never seen you behave improperly in front of the boys, or come to that, in front of anyone here. I know Mrs Ludlam agrees with me on that." He cleared his throat, obviously uncomfortable with the subject. "Ben is also adamant in your defence, assuring me you have not at any time encouraged Eli."

Ada waited, relieved at his words, expecting an imminent verdict, but she was disappointed.

"However, I still need to speak with Eli and for the moment he's sleeping. We'll resolve this as soon as he's able to talk."

The miller's wife rose to her feet. "Go and change your dress Ada, then come and help me set the table for supper. It'll take your mind off it."

Ada was suddenly aware that Ben was in the room and wondered how much of the conversation he'd overheard. His head was down as usual.

"Here's your shawl." He passed the soiled garment to Ada. Tears once more threatened as she saw the sorry condition of one of her most treasured possessions.

Ben turned to his master. "Sir, I've moved my things from the room. I'll sleep in the barn tonight. However this is resolved, I can't share a room with him, not after what he's done. He were like somebody demented, the way he were with Ada, Sir."

Ada dabbed her eyes, noticing the Ludlams exchange glances, wife raising an eyebrow, leaving husband to respond. "We'll find you some blankets then, but just for tonight. He can't be moved at the moment and I feel duty bound to speak to him before judging him, so bear with me." His voice was firm but no longer accusing.

Ada sat very straight. "Please, I need to ask a favour."

"Go on."

"Please Sir, Ma'am don't tell anyone what has happened here this night. My father and mother have enough problems without having to worry about me."

"You have my word, and I'm certain that you can trust both my wife and Ben to keep your confidence."

Ada turned towards her mistress. "You'll not speak of this to William, will you Ma'am?"

Sarah Ludlam put her hand on her heart. "You have my word."

"Please Sir, there's something else." Ada turned to Ben, "I have to say thank you to Ben. I'll never be out of his debt. He saved me from a fate worse than death… Sir!"

She threw Ben a shy smile, aware that her attempt at an accolade was totally inadequate, but couldn't let the moment pass without some recognition of his gallantry.

§

It was still dark, and she had no means of lighting the candle. Ada drew back the curtains before brushing her hair and pulling on a clean pair of stockings, flinching as her garters caught against the bruises. As her eyes became accustomed to the gloom, she peered into the mirror. Was this the same person who, only yesterday, had twisted her locks into a smart bun in anticipation of attending a family party? Her face was scratched and bruised from the assault and her eyes reflected the sadness in her soul. She rubbed some softening butter into her neck and resolved to keep her head down to hide the abrasions.

A lifetime's expectation 'to do her duty', automatically directed her towards the stairs. Very soon now she would be facing her assailant and the raging emotions were so strong, she had no idea how she would handle it. From somewhere deep in her heart she believed that her employer would do the right thing by her. She prayed that her instincts were accurate.

Having lit two candles and having made sure no-one was lurking in the shadows, Ada began the morning's tasks. There was no sign of Ben. A quick look up at the staircase assured her that the door to the back bedroom was firmly closed and as there was no obvious movement coming from that direction, she felt confident that Eli was not about to make an immediate entrance.

Ada filled both coppers ready to begin the boil. The fires were pulling well before muffled sounds from above signalled the master's imminent arrival. Her whole body stiffened. The kettle's hiss and the cockerel's crow were welcome intrusions on the oppressive quietness of the house.

Ada's insides screwed up into knots as Mr Ludlam paused barely long enough to mutter, "Morning," before striding with serious face towards the scullery. Completely ignoring the cup and saucer, filled ready for him to drink, he declared, "I will speak with Eli first. I need to deal with this once and for all, but before I go up to him, I need to know if he hurt you." His eyes were directed to the floor and his face was scarlet. The delicacy of the situation was palpable. "You know what I mean."

"No Sir. I'm only bruised."

Ada stood in the early morning stillness and registered each and every footstep mounting the staircase, culminating in the inevitable raising of the door-latch. There was a long silence. She counted the steps as he walked back down, through the bakery and into the room. Ada's heart was pounding as he looked directly at her, before announcing. "He's gone, taken his things and left, so unless you wish me to take this further it's the end of the matter."

Implementing his usual custom of thrift, he blew out one of the candles, before lifting the tea-spoon from the saucer to noisily stir his tea.

His wife entered the room. "Well thank goodness for that. At least he did the decent thing. We can all heave a sigh of relief and Ben can return to his bed."

The miller jumped to his feet. "Where is Ben? Ada, have you seen him?"

On a sudden realization that this might not be the end of the troubles, the two women watched aghast as he flung open the back door and ran towards the barn. Within minutes they saw him emerge with Ben, looking somewhat bewildered, but obviously unhurt.

§

Ada hitched up her skirts before mounting the narrow staircase to the boys' room. She set down the bucket and propped the mop beside the window. On looking around she was amazed to see how tidy it was. Eli had a reputation for being disorganized and Mr Ludlam had often chided him on his untidiness. She had never before known him to make his bed. She stripped off the sheets, noticing the blood-stained pillow-cases and made a mental note that they could do with a soak before being put into the wash. His injuries must have been more insignificant than they had appeared for him to pack his things and leave. Still, his departure had come as a sweet relief.

Glancing down through the window Ada caught site of Ben staring up at her. She nodded in acknowledgement, but he quickly lowered his eyes. He seemed a little taken aback, but Ada thought no more of it, knowing how shy he was. Obviously he would not have expected to see movement coming from the room.

Ada wondered where Eli had gone, perhaps to the east-coast to his sister. It would be difficult for him to explain why he had left Mill House. Still, that was his concern, not hers. Her one misgiving was that he may return one day and finish what he started.

The thought terrified her.

Chapter 10

The Dominoes Team

It was Tuesday evening, and the grandfather clock struck six. Tom walked into The Late Elephant on time, exactly as he had done for almost as many years as Billy has been landlord.

"Is it true," he stuttered, "are yer leaving? She'll send mi to the workhouse if yer leave."

Billy was shocked. He hadn't given Tom a thought. "Oh mi old friend, don't take on so. We'll sort summat out."

Billy, near to tears, handed Tom his ale. "Here, get that inside yer. In fact I'll have one miself,"

He was more than a little relieved to see Bess walk in and watched while she placed an oil-lamp onto the bar. The flame soon settled to give a warm glow to the room and she turned to Tom. "Good evening, Thomas. How are you this evening?"

Billy watched her reaction on spotting the tears rolling down Tom's face and her smile turned to consternation as realization dawned.

"She'll send mi to the workhouse if yer close down. She's told mi so. She heard about it in the post-office. She canna stand the sight of me, mi own sister, what am I to do, Missus?"

Bess groaned. "I really don't know Tom, I wish I did."

Tom, a quiet chap and a bit simple, was described by some as 'nine-pence to the shilling'. Billy remembered back to that freezing cold day years ago, when he had first discovered him, covered in snow, sitting on the wall outside the church. From that moment on Tom found a safe haven and was welcomed into the inn whenever he turned up. Tom's income was made up from any odd job he could find, so Billy gave him the easy things to do and fed and watered him in exchange. When trade had been better he had slipped him the odd shilling, but lately they had been few and far between.

Billy put his arm around Tom's shoulders, "Come on now, and sit yer sen down. We'll sort summat out."

Tom looked at Bess with star-struck eyes. She was the only woman, apart from his mother, ever to show him kindness and when he drank in excess of two pints, he proclaimed to anyone who would listen about how wonderful she was. "An angel from Heaven," he would call her.

"Would you like some meatloaf?" asked Bess, knowing that if anything could assuage Tom's grief, it would be food. "I made it fresh this morning and I have some gooseberry chutney to go with it."

Billy put the jug under the tap to find that the warm air had increased the fermentation of the hedgerow brew and it frothed and spilled all over the floor.

"Flippin' stuff!" railed Billy, "hang on a minute Tom, I'll have to clean it up."

Bess brought in the food. "I'll see to that." She tutted, fussing over them both as they settled at a table.

"'How did yer get on at Jess's yesterday? Did yer see Ada?" Tom asked, as he spread the butter on his bread.

"We did indeed," Billy expounded settling back in his chair, "our Jess is very comfortable. The house is grand. They have a shiny, black front door with a proper knocker and a black paling all around the front," Billy shook his head, "but I do find it odd they don't 'ave a back garden."

Tom stopped eating, mouth and eyes wide open. "No garden? Get off!"

"It's true," Bess explained, "they live right in the middle of the city and have just a back yard with a lavatory and a wash-house."

"Where do they grow the 'taters then?"

"The house is close to the shops and market, so they buy them."

Tom was confused, but the conversation was brought to an abrupt halt by the unexpected arrival of John Booton, accompanied by the dominoes team. Bess quickly removed all signs of food and set the place to rights.

Billy jumped up to do his business. "Good evening, gentlemen." He was dreading the inevitable.

The men removed their hats, mostly settling around the oblong table in the dominoes' corner. Billy watched as John, together with Sam the sexton, leaned on the counter, lighting their pipes from the candle flame. Bess returned directly, carrying a second lamp.

As expected, John Booton assumed the role of spokesman. "Now Billy, there's talk o you folk leavin' the pub."

As if in a dream, Billy watched as Bess stepped into the inglenook, gently guiding the lit spill towards the kindling. The paper and sticks began to crackle as flames licked the sides of the black iron fire-basket. He let out a long deep sigh, recalling the moment at the wedding when his speech had evaporated, and experienced a feeling of sweet relief that at last it was out in the open.

"That's right, John. I canna make it pay, and Farmer Wragg wants to buy it. He's going to close it down and convert it into two dwellings. He'll make more money that way, I dare say."

"I see," John pondered for a moment, "but if he's turning it into cottages, can yer not stay and live in one of em?"

"I suppose we could, but they'll want us out while they do the work."

At that precise moment a familiar, but totally unexpected, voice was heard. "That's not a problem, Father. I'll look after you."

Billy and Bess's son George walked in through the front door to stand in the middle of the room, dressed in army uniform, haversack on his back and hat still on his head. "You can come and live wi me. I have an house in Portsmouth."

Billy's mouth fell open. Added to the astonishment at seeing his firstborn suddenly appear from out of the blue, this fairy tale was something he could hardly bear to listen to, certainly not in public and Billy was mortified.

"There's plenty a room, there's no reason why not." George took some coins from his pocket, "And I'll have a jar, please.

George had never before paid for his ale. Ignoring the money, Billy turned to fill a jug from the barrel, whilst at the same time throwing his son a disapproving look. The beer overflowed again and Billy sent a whistle of annoyance through his front teeth. "We'll talk about it later," he growled, face red with embarrassment.

Bess put her arms around their son and planted a kiss on his cheek. "You're a good lad, our George and it's lovely to see you, but it's early days yet. We only just know about it ourselves and please, take off your hat."

"Where you come from, then, George?" enquired John Booton.

"Jersey. It's an island, you know."

"Is that right? So, what's yer regiment?" asked Sam.

George put his shoulders back and proudly recited, "3rd Battalion Leicestershire Regiment, 17th foot."

"Oh yes, and what rank do you hold then?"

George pointed to his stripes, "I'm a Corporal Sergeant, I am."

"Is that good?" enquired Tom.

Sam spoke for him, "Sounds good to me!"

By the time the dominoes team had shaken George's hand and slapped him heartily on the back, Billy had regained some of his composure. It was Tom who saved the day. "Tell em about your Jess's house, Billy. He reckons they don't have a garden."

"Is that right?" asked Sam, tearing his eyes from the Manchester Guardian.

Bess was quick to explain. "Yes, it is right. They don't need one. They're close to shops and the market. The vegetables are cheap enough, but they do have a new pan-lavatory which the council empties every week and they have a separate parlour. It's all very grand."

The men gazed in wonder at her words. "The council empties it? How much does that cost?" asked Sam.

"Nowt," Billy took over, "it's included in the rates."

"What rates?"

Billy sighed in frustration, he had enough problems with the ale frothing everywhere, without having to answer tedious questions. "A charge that property owners have to pay the council to cover drainage and street lightin' and such."

The response was almost unanimous. "Street lightin'?"

"You should see it," John Booton expounded his expert knowledge to the crowd, "they have it in the towns so yer can see to walk the streets at night. They have it in Leicester, cities can be dangerous places."

"How does that work then?" asked Tom, thoroughly confused and a bit annoyed at having to wait for a reply whilst John Booton took snuff from a tiny heap on the back of his hand, first up one nostril and then up the other.

He shook his head and dusted the surplus from his jacket sleeve, before turning his attention once more to Tom. "A man from the council comes along at dusk and lights 'em. Yer must have heard o the lamp lighter.

Tom scratched his head. "Are they coal, these lights?"

"No, yer daft bugger, they're gas lamps," retorted John Booton, who was hardly ever heard to utter a swear word, "they're stuck on top of a pole."

Billy, finding the situation too daft to laugh at, paused to listen as Sam enquired about Ada. Sam had a son about the same age, and at one point thought the two might make a match of it.

"Has our Ada already left, Mother?" asked George.

"Yes son, she went last week." Turning back to the men, she answered Sam's question. "She's doing fine. They're working her hard, though. Do you know, last Monday she did the washing and she helped with the ironing, as well as baking bread every day? Imagine, there's only Ada and the lady, and they have two young farm-hands staying there as well as their own two children. That's a lot of work with all them sheets and pillow cases."

"And how's the cooking going?"

Bess glowed with pride. "They have a really big bread oven and a griddle, properly built in like in the big houses and there are two coppers. She's learning to make all sorts of different breads. Mrs Ludlam sent some over for us."

Bess saw some of the men begin to salivate at the thought. "Shall I make some supper?" she asked.

"Aye," answered Billy, "and can yer spare some more o yer meatloaf?" He asked of Bess, before turning to the team to explain." I were just getting the taste on it when yer all came in. There's no reason why we canna share it." Billy cleared a space and the counter was set with bread, cheese, meatloaf and a good selection of chutneys. Bess pulled the cork from a fresh pot of pickled onions.

"That looks good," enthused George, licking his lips.

"We're going to miss this. I know not of any other landlords who look after their customers the way you

The Late Elephant

two do." John Booton, who Billy had always thought didn't particularly like him, was getting quite morose.

"Does Ada know about yer leaving?" enquired Sam, putting the paper to one side.

"Aye and she were really good about it, only I'm not sure the light of day has properly dawned yet. I just hope that when it does she can handle it." Billy turned away to light his pipe.

"She's a sensible gel that one, she'll understand alright." Sam puffed on his pipe and folded the newspaper to cogitate along with the rest of the company.

Bess contemplated the conversation so far. "She went very quiet. I think hearing about the move was a bit of a shock. I think it's going to take her some time to get used to the idea."

As the throng silently mulled on the situation, Billy absorbed the scene before him, one of candle-light and the magic of companionship. The crunching of Bess' pickled onions, together with the spitting of the logs on the fire, were, for just a few brief moments, the only sounds occupying the space. He would miss this. He glanced around. The tap-room looked grand. Bess cared for the inn with pride. The chairs and tables shone, with not a smear of ale or food anywhere. Every night, after the place had cleared, she would open the windows and set about cleaning the floors. She even scrubbed the brush handles. Said she didn't fancy touching them next morning, unless they were clean.

Billy's ears pricked up on hearing the grocer hold forth. "Dear, dear, we're going to 'ave to walk all the way to The Crown or The Spade Tree, for a game o' dominoes. Do yer think they'll let us keep our own team?" John Booton was looking most concerned.

"I dunno," was Tom's comment, "what do yer think Billy?"

"Per'aps one or two of yer could go and sound em out afore we finally close the doors." He thought for a moment. "Yer know, if yer do it well yer could negotiate some good terms for the team. Try the Belper."

"That's a bloomin' good idea," agreed Sam.

All eyes turned as John Thomas walked in. "Sorry I'm late, we had to wait for the train. Mrs Thomas was not happy. She's had to keep mi dinner hot and the mutton stew had almost flippin' dried up before I got back." He had swapped his black silk top-hat for a cloth cap, which he now removed and hung on the hat-stand, before smoothing his hair, and reaching out for his ale and a newspaper.

"I know not about your missus, but mine has a bone to pick next time she sees yer," Sam the sexton complained.

John Thomas lifted his ale to his lips and saw half of it off before answering. "Why, what's upset her?" He already had the paper open, his eyes eagerly scanning the pages.

"She reckons yer drove by that fast the other day, it nearly took the end of her nose off."

The proprietor of the Newton Nethercôte Stage Coach Company lowered his tabloid to peer sternly at the sexton. "Aye, perhaps I did take the bend too fast. We were most likely between railway-stations and if one of them trains was late, we would be making up time. If the post and these papers don't get delivered on time," he stopped here to rustle the pages of the one he was holding, "I don't flippin' get paid. It's as simple as that." He folded up the newspaper, placed it under his arm and crossed to the fireplace. He lowered a spill into the flames to light his pipe.

Sam, with hackles raised said, "Don't get yer hair off wi' me, I'm only telling yer what she said."

John Thomas puffed on his pipe and turned towards the counter. "Now then Billy, what's this I hear about yer closing down?"

§

Bess blew out the candle and climbed up into the bed, with Billy facing away from her, wide awake and looking towards the window. As the curtains wafted to and fro in the breeze, she wrapped herself around him, holding him tightly to her.

"Billy Elverson, I can understand how you must feel, but we have each other and four wonderful grown up children and more importantly Jarvis who still needs rearing."

"I know." He took her hand, raising it to his lips, but did not turn towards her

"Come on, Billy, don't fret so."

He gave a half-hearted chuckle, but stayed put. "Fancy our Jess telling me I shouldn't have spent so much money on the weddin'. What did she expect me to do?"

"How do you think she feels and William? Try to look at it from their point of view. They're only trying to help." She sighed, still holding him tightly.

"I know that, but it takes some swallowing when yer daughter and her husband feel they have to offer yer money," Billy gritted his teeth, "and as for our George, well, I were thunderstruck when he walked in. I could have flippin' well hit him." Bess tightened her hold as his anger grew. "Fancy saying all that in front o the blokes. He has about as much gumption as that washstand. And I tell yer what, Missus, if he owns an house, then my name's Lord Nelson.'"

Bess giggled. "Your face was a picture, but he was hurt at your reaction. You'd better explain in the morning. I know it was embarrassing, but he only wants to help. If none of them offered help, then Billy Elverson, you would have a problem. They'd do anything for you."

After the briefest of cogitations Billy turned over. "Yer know Bess, when I dared to court that pretty little housemaid from the big house, I never imagined that she would turn out to be such a wonderful woman."

"What made you ask her to marry you then?"

Billy put his arms around her. "Well, I just fancied a bit a posh. It were the way yer spoke, all ladylike."

"Is that all? Suppose I start talking like you then?"

Billy tightened his hold. "No, it wouldn't sound right coming from you."

They lay for a while in silence.

"What are you thinking?" she asked.

"I were wondering how long it'll be afore yer say it."

Bess could almost feel the smile playing on his lips. "And stop complaining!" She replied, before tutting at him.

All that could be heard was a loud guffaw, but Bess smiled secretly to herself, relieved that some normality had returned and her husband had found comfort.

Chapter 11

The Sale

Bess was cooking breakfast when she heard the clanking of measures against the bucket. The milkman was late as usual on Wednesdays, it being egg delivery day. She picked up a jug and took it to the door. The farmer stood with the bucket at his feet and the ladle in his hand.

"A quart please, Mr Marsh and a pound of best butter."

He touched his cap. "Mornin', Mrs Elverson." Lingering for a second before handing back the jug, he stuttered a little, "s-sorry to hear that yer leaving. Not that I'm a customer mind, but it'll be a shame to see the place close."

"Thank you, Mr Marsh. Times are a changing I'm afraid, and we have to change with them."

George ambled down the stairs. "Mornin', Mr Marsh." He yawned, scratched his head and after filling a cup with tea, carried it out into the garden.

"Mornin' George. Good to see yer back. I have some beestings Missus, I know Mr Elverson is partial."

Bess was delighted. "Good, I'll have a quart of them as well then," thinking it would be enough for two good pies. Now that George was home, she would need to double up. "Will you be stopping for a cup of tea?"

"No Missus, not today, I'm already late. Best get back. Mrs Marsh will have mi breakfast ready, but I'm much obliged for the offer."

Billy, with Jarvis close on his heels, walked through the door as soon as the milk-cart had departed. "I suppose he knows as well?"

"He does," replied Bess, "but he's brought some beestings, so you'll have a pie for dinner, and after breakfast you can bring in the bath. Our George could do with a soak. You can also explain why you were so short with him last night."

He grinned. "Yer might just as well have said, 'and stop complaining'."

Bess threw him a look of irritation and tutted. "So stop complaining! The worst is over. Anyway, how are you feeling today?"

"As a matter of fact, I've been doing something useful. I've made a list of all the things we can sell." He passed across the house-keeping book. "Look, I thought we could hold a sale here and tomorrow I'm going to visit all the pubs and shops and ask em to put up a notice."

"That's a wonderful idea," said Bess.

He expounded further. "I'll sell the horse and trap separate and the pigs. I think they'll make a better price."

Bess lifted Jarvis onto the chair. "Can we not take the pigs with us, wherever we end up?"

"No. I'll feel safer with some money behind us."

Bess could feel the excitement begin to mount. "I could do some baking and we could offer refreshments. Will the sale last all day do you think, because if it does, we could supply dinner and tea?" She paused for a moment, eyes sparkling. "Decide when you want to do it, and I'll start making the posters." She set about opening drawers and cupboards, collecting scissors and cardboard stored carefully away, for just such an occasion as this.

Billy leaned back on his chair, with a smile on his lips. He just knew his Bess wouldn't let him down. "What day do yer think is best?"

Bess was adamant. "It's market day in Measham on Fridays and in Ashby on Thursdays, so I reckon Wednesday. Folk will not come on market day."

"So are we are agreed on that? It's to happen a week from now?" Billy put the spill to his pipe, looking much more confident.

Bess sat for a while turning it round in her mind. "Do you have enough ale for all those people for a whole day?"

"Aye, I think so. We can brew more hedgerow beer, and make sure we have enough." He paused briefly to light his pipe. "Perhaps it's as well our George has come home, he can help."

"Good," sighed Bess, grateful that her husband had found a way forward.

"Is breakfast ready?" A voice from the doorway interrupted.

"Yes, it is son, come and sit down. When you've eaten, your father will bring in the bath and you can get yourself clean."

George nodded in agreement, not daring to do anything else.

"And you can borrow my scissors to trim your moustache."

§

Mr Choice, the auctioneer, brought down his gavel on a more than generous offer for the third and last sow. His gamble had paid off, and the stock fetched well over the odds. Reading the mood of the crowd correctly and unexpectedly adding the livestock right at the end of the sale, he had managed to secure a better than expected return. William jumped to his feet to shake Billy's hand and, turning to the auctioneer, thanked him profusely. "I cannot believe how you kept the momentum going Sir, right through the day. You are a master of your trade."

The man smiled in response to the compliment. "Thank you, Mr Chamberlain, you are most kind."

"Kindness has nothing to do with it. How would you feel about selling tanned hides this way? Do you think it would work?" William awaited the reply with bated breath.

"If you mean will you get more money from them, it's difficult to say. It depends on so many things, like who turns up, and how much they want what you are selling." He turned a quizzical eye towards William. "If it's the right price you're looking for, then you'll get that eventually by waiting for a buyer, but if you offer it for sale by auction, then you could be lucky or you could lose. It really is the luck of the draw." He took a large cigar from his inside pocket, bit off the end and discharged it into the spittoon. Looking around for a light, he realized there was no fire in the inn, on account of the hot weather, so he turned back to William. "The thing is, once the bidding has started you can't withdraw the lot without gaining for yourself a bad reputation and hardly anyone will attend the next one. Word soon gets around. Do you understand what I am saying?"

"I do Sir," nodded William, "but you had the bidders in the palm of your hand today. You manipulated them beautifully."

"Yes, but only because they allowed it. These people respect Billy and paid the price to help him along and even at that they were getting a bargain. You don't always see this type of clientele at a sale. However, think on what I've said. If you should decide to go to auction, please come and see me. I'm sure we can come to some arrangement. Now, if you'll excuse me young man, I'm about to see if Mrs Elverson has another of her delicious pies left, and perhaps she will show me some means of lighting my cigar. I really do crave a smoke."

"Here, Sir," said William walking behind the counter, "a box of matches, I'm sure Billy won't mind."

§

Bess stood at the sink in the scullery, taking comfort from the apparent success of the sale. She tackled the washing up, ears cocked for the sound of Napoleon's departing steps. She paused for a moment and overheard Billy arranging to deliver both the horse and the trap in a few days' time. Mr Marsh had bought them both, lock stock and barrel, so the trap and horse hadn't needed to be separated. At least she had some good news for Ada. She would be pleased to know that the horse wouldn't be far away. Bess recalled Ada's reaction to the news of them leaving the Elephant and was aware that some of that dejection was due to her daughter being soft on Duncan. She had a yen for him. It was obvious by the way her eyes lit up on hearing his name. Bess wondered what her reaction would be when she discovered he was walking out with Bella Bishop.

Jess bustled in with yet another tray full of dirty pots to be washed, then took up the tea-towel to begin drying. "It sounds as if you've done well, Mother, everything seems to have sold."

"I do hope so. Your father was depending on today."

Mr Choice put his head round the door. "My dear lady, do you by any chance have one of your delicious meat pies left?"

"No, Sir, I am afraid not, but I can offer you a bacon sandwich." Bess knew how helpful this man had been, but she was most tired and the smoke from his cigar was making her cough. Her back was aching fit to break and she just wished that he and everyone else would go home and leave her in peace.

"Thank you, but no, dear lady. Cook will have supper ready when I return home. It's gluttony I am afraid, I simply cannot resist your pies."

"It is indeed most kind of you to say so, Sir." Bess's wish was granted. He went on his way. It was then she noticed the lateness of the hour and discovered how hungry she was. She carried in a pan of new potatoes, the first of the season and the skins had practically floated off. She placed them on the hob and stoked up the fire.

"Yer not starting again are you, Mother?" bellowed the voice of her eldest son.

"Yes, unless you can do without your dinner. Anyway, I've a couple of rabbit pies on the thrawl, already cooked from yesterday. The potatoes won't take long to boil and there's some chutney left. Well, if your father hasn't sold it all that is."

They were still laughing together, Bess, Mary and George, when Billy joined them, face aglow with relief.

"What a day! It couldn't a gone better if I'd planned it. I canna get over Mr Choice. What a gentleman!"

"I was surprised Mr Marsh bought the horse and trap Billy, I didn't realise he was that well off," observed Bess.

"Reckons his horse is too old now to pull a full float. Says it makes him late with the deliveries."

Billy called out for William and Jess to join them. Taking the money out of the tin, he placed it before them on the table. "Now, I want to say thank yer for helping. Today has been hard work, and I want to share some of this with yer."

§

"This rabbit pie is really tasty, Mother," said George, wiping his mouth with the back of his hand.

"Good," replied Bess, deliberately placing a napkin in front of him, vowing that his table-manners had all but disappeared since he left home. He could at least make an effort in front of William.

No sooner had she tutted, when a loud banging and shouting was heard, coming from the direction of the tap-room. Billy, weary from his long day, moaned in protest but put his plate of half-eaten food on the side of the range to keep warm and made his way to see what all the fuss was about. Bess followed to find the dominoes team assembled in full force, most of the members worse for wear. Sam was the first to speak, hardly able to form his words. "We've just bin down The Spade Tree and the Crown to negotiate, like you said."

He began to sway, but John Booton, who always stayed sober, managed to steady him.

Sam words were slurred. "I canna remember what we deshided, can you John?" His eyes rolled.

Billy's mouth opened in disbelief. "You mean yer've spent all day in here and then yer've been drinkin' in both The Spade Tree and the Crown? Are yer flippin' off yer heads?"

Sam tittered and with a little encouragement from John Booton, sank down, hitting the chair with a plonk. "That's right, Billy!" He burped. "John, what were deshided?"

John looked at him with a certain amount of disdain. "Yer slurring yer words, Samuel. Lillian is going to be very cross."

Billy immediately registered the possible results of this comment. He took Sam's arm, prizing him back up onto his feet. "I do appreciate yer support lads, but in all fairness to yer missuses yer'd better get back home now, else they'll be coming over here to sort me out."

As the team turned to leave, a lad from the village ran in, breathless and visibly struggling for words.

"Sit yer sen down lad and get yer breath. What's up?" John Booton pulled up a chair.

The boy looked around for a sight of Billy. "Master Elverson, Fred Smith has just passed away, so his cottage will be coming empty. Mi mam said to come and tell yer."

Billy put a hand on the young man's shoulder. "I'm sorry to hear that, lad, but tell yer mam thanks for thinking of me. I'll go to Upper Fields in the morning and see the farmer."

"Perhaps you should go now, Father," suggested George.

Billy turned again to the lad. "When did he die, son?"

"About half an hour ago, Master Elverson. Mi mam were there. She said I should come and tell yer straight away."

Billy pondered for a moment. "I think I'll leave him to get cold afore I go after his home. I'll deal with it tomorrow." He thanked the boy, and after fumbling in his pocket, handed him a florin. "Give that to yer mam and tell her to treat yer."

Bess returned to the living room to find her rabbit pie and potatoes quite cold. However, she was not about to let a little thing like that spoil the moment, and despite her sympathies with the Smith family, secretly thanked God for his bounteousness.

§

Jess was up, dressed and doing well before either her husband or her parents. Moses had escaped outside and the cat swaggered in, mewing impatiently for food and wrapping itself around her legs until she poured milk into his tin bowl. The fire soon began to crackle, with the promise of a pot of tea emanating from the kettle.

Jess felt the pull of The Late Elephant and was eager to recapture precious memories. This was a moment to be shared with no-one. She moved her hand over the table-top, stroking its uneven surface. A myriad of half-forgotten scenes passed through her mind, reflections of her whole life-time. She recalled the evening when Ada was born, the rag-doll Grandma had given her, holding Jarvis for the first time. Many of the people involved in her life had been at the sale and she held their faces to her heart like a prayer.

Sounds from above signalled that Father was out of bed, so she smoothed the table-cloth and fetched bread from the pantry, slicing it ready to fry. She placed cups and saucers onto the tray, together with the slop-basin and sugar bowl, then brought in a jug of milk from the thrawl in the pantry.

Jess was anxious that William begin the day with a good meal. It would be late before he arrived home and it wasn't unknown for him to go without a bite until the evening, sometimes resulting in indigestion. There was a dish of cold potatoes from last night, and together with bacon, eggs and fried bread, they'd make an ample breakfast.

Billy nodded on his way to the lavatory, pausing on the way back to wash his hands in the scullery, before taking his place beside the fire. "I want yer to accept some of this money, our Jess. It's only right that yer should, considering the effort yer've put in over these past few days."

"For goodness sake, Father, when does a body have to be paid for helping out parents? I thought we made it clear last night that none of us are going to take it." She bustled around, pouring Billy his tea. "William would never forgive me and really Father, we don't need it. Put it towards Ada's keep."

The conversation was cut short by the arrival of Bess and Jarvis, and the moment was gone. Billy reached for his jacket. "I'm off to Upper Fields Farm to see about the cottage. I'll have mi breakfast when I get back. Put yer hands together and ask the Almighty to smile down on us."

William took his place at the table, just as Billy departed. "Good morning," was all he had chance to say. Jess broached the subject which was upper-most in all their minds. "I've been wondering about Ada. She was more upset on Sunday than she let on. William says she hardly spoke a word to him on the way to the coach."

"Yes, I'm aware of that and I've written a letter. She should have it by now." Bess's face showed her concern. "There's little we can do for the moment, except allow her time to settle at Glenfield, so I just said how lovely it was to see her and that we'd let her know how things progressed."

William looked thoughtful. "I could call in and tell her how well the sale has gone. What do you think?"

Bess answered sharply. "No! I would rather you leave it to me. I'll correspond regularly, once or twice a week. I think that would be better." She paused. "When we're settled, I'll send for her. It'll put her mind at rest. If Billy's visit this morning is successful, I'll write immediately."

William looked at her somewhat quizzically, "As you wish."

Jess, along with the rest of the family, felt that William hadn't allowed her sister enough time to absorb the news, before launching into his speech about it all being for the best, yet at the same time, he had helped out. The situation had to be dealt with and it was obvious that Father was unable to deliver the words. It had been a difficult moment.

"This is for me to sort by letter." Mother had her mind made up. "I know our Ada, she can go off in a minute, but when she's thought about it, she'll want to come home and see for herself that all is well. She's a good girl."

Jess nodded. "I agree Mother, she'll come round. I've never known Ada to sulk, but then again, it's a heavy load for her to come to terms with, losing both her home and her horse. We all know how attached she is to Napoleon." Jess paused, hoping her husband would offer a reprieve for the horse, but he didn't raise an eye from his plate. Jess didn't feel able to ask him directly for help and she knew Father would probably not have the funds to keep the animal in feed, so there was little hope. She looked over at Mother and shrugged her shoulders, resigned to the situation. George took his place at the table.

"Good morning, George. How's life in the army?" As William moved up to make room, George blushed. "Very well, ta, but I've something to tell you."

There was a silence. Jess sensed a modicum of anxiety in the air.

"I've met a young lady."

"Have yer now," came a gruff voice from the doorway. Billy had returned, "and who might that be?"

"Oh, Father, did you get the house?" All eyes turned to Billy.

"Yes, and we can move in as soon as we like after Fred's stuff is out. The rent starts a week on Monday, so by then they should have him buried."

The Late Elephant

Jess, jumping to her feet, wrapped her arms around both her parents. Billy took his seat at the head of the table, with a smile on his face, looking triumphantly up at Bess, as she placed the tea-cup and saucer before him. "Well done, Billy. I told you the Lord would smile on us."

"So come on then, tell us about yer young lady." There was a definite lilt to Billy's voice. "Where's she from? Not Timbuktu, I hope."

"It's no matter if she is," retorted Bess, "she'll be welcome here!"

"She lives in Portsmouth. I told you the night I came home that I had an house there. Well, it is not exactly mine. Nelly shares it with three of her friends. Well, a room that is, but folk are always coming and going, so it wouldn't be difficult to find you a place."

A look passed between Bess and Billy, but Jess saw that, rather than spoil the moment, Billy redirected the subject.

"So, what sort of a name is Nelly?"

"It's Eleanor, really, but the girls call her Nelly."

"Who are these girls, the ones who share a room with her?" Billy looked directly at his son, almost afraid to hear what was to come next.

George was undaunted and enthusiastically launched into his tale. "They work at the New Theatre Royal. It's ever so posh."

Only the occasional clatter of cutlery disturbed the tension. Billy scratched his side whiskers "What exactly do they do at this theatre?"

"They're actresses. Sometimes they sing, you know like Mrs Booton does at the church concert, except they're prettier than her, especially Nelly. She has a lovely voice, Father."

Jess giggled, wondering what John Booton would have made of that last remark. She noted the sparkle in her brother's eyes and was glad when Father stayed gentle with him. Our George is in love, she thought.

"When are we going to see her?"

Before George could answer, William interrupted. "How did you manage to meet her in Portsmouth when you're posted on the island of Jersey?"

"She came over with the troupe. They were attached to a travelling theatre, while the alterations were being made to the Theatre Royal." His voice trailed off, unsure now of his family's thoughts on the matter.

William stood up. "We must make a move Jess, the stage will be here soon, but as an afterthought, he turned back to shake hands with his brother-in-law.

"We look forward to meeting her, George."

Jess was thrilled to hear the words, having feared that William was again about to put his foot in it with another one of her siblings.

Chapter 12

Harvest

"Hey, steady on," laughed Ada, protecting her eyes from bits and pieces showering down from the apple tree. "Ouch! Ben, give over," she yelled as an apple landed on her head.

"I've got to shake it, Ada, cos the ladder's not long enough to reach the ones at the top." Ben handed down another good hand-full of Bramleys, which she carefully placed in the basket.

Onions lay strewn all around them, drying in the sunshine. The grass in the orchard had turned a straw-like colour and been trampled almost flat. It looked untidy and scruffy, and fluffy seeds from dandelions filled the air and floated up Ada's nose. Leaves were beginning to change colour but the afternoon sun, low in the sky, was still powerful.

Eli had not been replaced. Mr Ludlam determined they could manage until next year, so with help from casual labourers, the corn harvest had been carted and stacked and much of the threshing completed.

Ben jumped down from the ladder. He leaned forwards and gently removed a dead leaf from Ada's hair. She smiled back at him, and followed him into the scullery where he duly deposited the basket. Mrs Ludlam stood at the table laden with vegetables and fruit and, together with Missy, was peeling and chopping onions for the chutney, eyes streaming in the process. Ada joined her.

"The best way to stop your eyes watering is to breathe only through your mouth," suggested Mrs Ludlam, "pretend you have a cold." Ada tried this, but as soon as she began to speak, the salt stung her eyes as the tears ran down her cheeks.

"Put a clothes peg on your nose," suggested Missy, her face reflecting the seriousness of her advice.

"Where did you hear that?" enquired her mother.

"At school! The gypsies are camped just behind the playground, and the woman calls at houses in the village to sell her pegs. She carries them in a basket."

"I hope she calls here, so we won't have to spread the sheets over the hedge to dry."

Ada's eyes smarted and streamed so much, she could hardly distinguish the figure walking through the doorway.

"Now I know the summer is over. The smell of chutney always announces the onset of cold weather, not that it's cold in here, mind." Mr Ludlam placed his newspaper on the dresser, before removing his jacket and rolling up his sleeves. "I've just spoken to the rector. He was in the post office. He says to remind you that the church is to be decorated on Saturday afternoon for the Harvest Festival. He said to tell you they will begin around two o'clock."

His wife responded immediately. "We haven't forgotten. The girls have been cutting out covers for the tops of the jars. We could do with some more twine to tie them, if you have any left over from the shucking."

He pulled a coil from his jacket pocket and placed it on the table. "It might need a wash." He also pulled out a letter and handed it to Ada. "The girl in the post office asked me to give you this."

"Thank you, Sir." Ada moved aside her apron, pushing the envelope into the pocket of her dress.

"I understand that the gypsies are here, parked behind the school." He turned to his daughter. "Make sure you stay with the other children on your way home and don't speak to strangers. You don't know who you can trust."

"Yes, Father. Do you think Eli has run away to join the gypsies?"

"That's a possibility, how clever of you for thinking it." He glanced briefly at his wife and sat down before asking his daughter, "Why did you say that?"

"Because I didn't trust him."

"Why not?"

The girl shrugged her shoulders, "I didn't like him," and concentrated on peeling a large Bramley apple.

"Did he say anything or do anything which I should know about?"

"He didn't clean his teeth for one thing, and he smelt awful, but you never told him off like you would me."

"Happen you're right, daughter. Happen I should have been stricter with him."

§

The thorns on the blackberry hedge dug into Ada's flesh as she leaned forwards on tip-toe, using the hook of a walking stick to pull towards her the branches bearing the biggest and juiciest clusters of fruit. She was looking around for the next patch, when she heard the unmistakable crunch of a twig. Panic gripped her. She must be at least half a mile from the house, alone and unprotected. She held tightly to the stick, determined to act, should she need to.

Relief flooded her face on seeing Ben climb over the stile. "It's alright, it's only me." He held the stick while she stripped the berries from the branch. "I've come to bring up the cows. I didn't mean to startle you."

"I thought it was Eli."

"Don't worry about 'im, you'll not be seeing 'im again."

"Don't you think so? I wonder sometimes if he might come back."

"Well don't! He's gone for good."

"How can you be so sure?"

"Because cowards like him don't come back for more of what I gave him." Ben looked down at her, bashfulness forgotten for a moment. "I'm sorry you're still frightened."

"I'm not most of the time, but I hadn't realized I'd come so far from the house, and Missy said earlier that she wondered if he had joined the gypsies, so you see, he was already on my mind." Ada offered the basket. "Here, have some."

He sat down beside her and took a handful of blackberries. "These are lovely. It's almost a shame to cook them."

Ada laughed. "You'll not say that when you're eating the pie." She turned her face towards the sun. "Where are your parents, Ben?"

"I don't know. I was brought up in the workhouse. Mr Ludlam took me out when I was eleven. I've worked for him ever since."

"I'm so sorry! I shouldn't have asked."

"It's not a secret. I'm surprised Mrs Ludlam didn't tell you." Ben lay down on the grass stretching out his long legs. "This is different, lying in the sun chewing blackberries."

Ada laughed. "We'll get shot if anybody sees us."

"I suppose you're right," but he made no immediate move to go. Instead he lay with hands behind his head, eyes closed against the sun, chewing on a blade of grass. In the next field, a frustrated herd of milking cows was making its presence felt.

Ada began to giggle. "Just listen to them. I bet your Buttercup is furious with you."

Ben did eventually stir but it was with reluctance.

"I'm most grateful for your stopping Eli. You do know that, don't you?"

"Of course I do, but I would have done it for anybody, so don't feel beholden."

"If there's anything I can do to repay you, I will."

"Well, there is something, actually. Will you teach me to read?"

Ada could hardly believe her ears. "Of course I will, I'll be delighted. We can begin tonight after dinner."

"No, not in front of the family, I would feel daft."
"Where do you suggest?"

"I'm not sure. They wouldn't take kindly to you coming up to my room, but Mrs Ludlam might let us go into the bakery. What do you think?"

"I'll ask her."

"I can read a bit, but only small words. I want to be able to read the newspapers and understand what's going on in the world." He grinned, seemingly happier and more contented than he had been of late. Ada wondered if he too was appreciating the absence of Eli.

"If you can read short words, you'll soon get the hang of it. What about writing?"

"Well, yes, I suppose. Do you mind?"

"Of course not."

He turned towards the lower meadow.

"Ben, you're covered in blackberry juice, all over your chin." He grinned at her, wiped his mouth with the back of his hand and took off in the direction of the herd. Twenty or so cows were now gathered by the gate, stating their annoyance at being kept waiting. Their mooing becoming more hysterical than ever on a sighting of Ben.

"Alright, Buttercup, that's enough!"

Chuckling and at the same time feeling pleased that she could do something to square things with Ben, Ada pulled out the latest letter from her Mother and read it again.

Dearest Ada,

On Sunday week we are to visit Jess. She and William would like you to join us. This time you will be able to enjoy your dinner without any bad news. I do worry about you and wonder how you are really managing. You don't write much about your feelings and I would like to see for myself.

It occurs to me that your mandolin is still at Albion Street, so you will be able to take it back with you.

We are to celebrate our Harvest Festival at St. Peter's on Sunday. This will be the first time we haven't attended together. It's only one of many things I know, but somehow Harvest and Christmas are special, and you used to enjoy them both.

Please write and say you will come to Jess's. We have settled well into Hill House, and I would like you to see it one day soon. Jarvis sends you a kiss, and we all send our kind regards.

Your loving Mother and Father Elverson

§

Mrs Ludlam was pouring tea. "Those look lovely, Ada."

"Did you get scratched?" enquired Missy.

"Not too badly, look." She gave the child a hug. "What did you do at school today?"

"We collected leaves and put them in a book to dry." She raised her eyes to Ada. "We could gather some later if you like and make a picture."

Her mother intervened. "Ada hasn't time for that just now. She's only just come in from the field. Ada, come and have a drink of tea, before we set about jamming these, it'll be another job done."

Ada gave a brief and wistful thought to her moment in the sunshine. Missy joyfully accepted her mother's suggestion that, if she had nothing better to do than collect dead leaves, she may as well go to the orchard and start gathering the pears. She had taken Allen with her.

Once the children were out of ear-shot, she enquired after Ada's news. "What did your mother say in her letter? Are they all well?"

"Yes. They've invited me to Albion Street a week on Sunday."

"Good, of course you must go. Catch the earlier stage, then you'll not be holding up dinner." Mrs Ludlam noticed the reluctance. "Do you not want to go?"

"I do, because I would like to see Jarvis and Mother and Father".

"You're still angry with Mr Chamberlain."

"Yes, and then what happened with Eli has left me frightened. I thought he'd come back this afternoon. It scared me to death, but it was Ben come to bring up the cows."

"Perhaps you should stay nearer the farm, at least until the gypsies leave."

"Next Saturday is the Harvest Supper. I thought you may need me here to help with the extra work."

"That's not a problem, the church women will be here on the day and they usually help to clear up afterwards. The biggest work load will be after they come to kill the pigs. That's to be done on Tuesday, giving us the rest of the week to see to the meat.

"I think you should go to your sister's. Once you've broken the ice things will be easier, although I can well understand your feelings. Try not to bear grudges. A lot of men are outspoken, but I do believe Mr Chamberlain genuinely wants to help. He thinks the world of you."

Ada gave a wry smile. "I know you're right."

"Good, well that's settled then. Come on now, let's put these blackberries on to boil, then you can take a pot with you, and show them all how good you are at making jam."

Ada took a last sip from the cup, deliberating on how to best approach Ben's request.

"I need to ask a favour."

§

Ada carried a jug over to the cowshed. Ben and Mr Ludlam were crouched on the milking stools, rhythmically squeezing. Steam rose as the liquid made contact with the chilly air of the milking parlour, making a hissing-sound as it squirted into the metal buckets. The beasts stood patiently, swishing their tails against unwelcome flies. Ada watched as they stamped their hooves onto the hard stone floor, as if encouraging the herdsman to quicken his pace. She felt sorry for them, having to carry around such heavy udders, it couldn't be pleasant, yet she found the smell of the animals somehow comforting.

"Here Ada," called Ben, "how much do you need?"

"A quart will do for now, enough to make custard for the pie." She hid behind the rear end of a cow and mouthed to Ben, "She said yes." Then she pointed to the master, and mouthed, "She will ask him."

"What's in the pie?" A voice resonated around the cold, dank walls.

"Apple and elderberry, Sir," Ada called back as she came out of hiding and crossed to where the two men sat.

"My favourite, good girl!"

She shared a knowing grin with Ben as he let go of the teats to pour the milk from his bucket into the jug. His hands, seemingly too large and cumbersome, dealt with the task without spilling a drop. "Here you are," he said on handing to her, "this here's from Buttercup. She gives the best milk."

Not quite knowing if he was serious, Ada picked her way between the cow-pats. Half-way cross the farm-yard, William rode through the gate. Ada was determined not to show animosity.

"Good evening sister-in-law." He dismounted.

"Good evening William. I hope you are well." She quickened her step, not sure how to handle this unexpected meeting. "How's Jess?"

"Very well and so are your parents. Have you received the letter from your mother, asking you to join us on Sunday week?"

"Yes, thank you." She felt awkward.

William untied a sack-bag from his saddle. "I've brought your mandolin. We thought you'd be missing it."

Mrs Ludlam waved from the window, and called out, "Good afternoon, Mr Chamberlain. Mr Ludlam is still milking, but come into the house and take a cup of tea before you go across.

"What's in the bag?" she enquired, but before Ada could explain, William replied, "It's her mandolin, she plays really well."

"Mandolin? Really? Oh, Ada, you must play for us, we can have a sing-song. Wait until I tell Mr Ludlam."

Ada nodded somewhat reluctantly. It had been months since she'd played and was in dire need of practice, but she so wanted to teach Ben to read, she was willing to agree to almost anything.

§

It was as though Heaven had waited until the harvest was complete, before sending the rain. It was indeed every farmer's dream to wait until the crop was safely gathered in before inclement weather commenced. However, for days now, it had fallen in a steady but continuous downpour and God's excellent timing was quickly overlooked.

Despite the discomfort of having to wear galoshes and carry the umbrella, Ada loved the change of seasons and breathed in the damp, heady smells of autumn. Vibrant colours of chrysanthemums and Michaelmas-daisies filled every nook and cranny of the church. The deep stone window-sills were decorated with marrows and pumpkins. Vegetables and fruits of every possible description, all arranged in colourful groups, glowed beneath the light from hanging lamps and candles, in contrast to the greyness of outside.

Mrs Ludlam had proudly positioned a large, flat, unleavened loaf, in the shape of a sheaf of corn, on the altar. It was her centre-piece and had taken hours to fashion. Earthen-ware jars of jams and pickles, all labelled and bearing frilly hats, were arranged in groups on a table in front of the pulpit. She had placed a basket, lined with ears of barley and filled with large brown eggs, next to them. There was even a bunch of black grapes from the conservatory at Glenfield Frith Hall.

Ada and Ben sat right at the end of the family pew, nearest the wall, with the children in the middle and Mr and Mrs Ludlam next to the aisle. The door at the end was pulled to and fastened, and Ada felt most honoured to be included. She glanced to the back of the church where servants from many a household sat, whilst their employers settled either in the family pews or on one of the benches at the very front.

The door opened and a whisper fluttered around the worshippers. As a hush descended the sound of rain was heard through the open door, pelting down onto the stones. There was a definite change of mood and Ada saw that Mr and Mrs Ellis had arrived. People craned their necks to see what Mrs Ellis was wearing. Usually, when Ada delivered bread to The Hall, she saw the housekeeper. This was the first time she had been close enough to get a good look at the Ellis family. When they passed through Glenfield in their coach, it was usually at too fast a speed to see much at all. As they walked along the aisle, past where the Ludlam's sat, Ada heard the rustle of silk skirts. They didn't take a side-pew, however, but sat in the middle, in the very front row, blocking Ada's view of both the chancel and the choir.

It gave a perfect opportunity for Ada to take particular note of the hat Mrs Ellis was wearing. She promptly dismissed it, however, with its pheasant feathers and harsh lines.

The group didn't acknowledge anyone on their way through and Ada noted that they were not nearly as approachable as Charles and his family. Ada made a mental note to ask Charles how exactly they were related.

It was disappointing that, because of the position of the Ludlam box, the altar was completely out of sight to Ada, but nevertheless, it was a most prestigious place to sit and Ada felt important. Ben shuffled beside her, but a sideways glance showed that he was leafing through the hymn book to find the first hymn. Ada concluded that he could at least count. She had to put a strategy together on how to teach him to read, but was still waiting to hear if Mr Ludlam agreed.

Ada rose to her feet as the organ spilled out the introduction to the processional hymn and felt that she belonged. Her place was here at Glenfield and she gave thanks to Almighty God, opening her heart to the words and music of one of her favourite hymns:-

"Come, ye thankful people come,

Raise the song of Harvest Home."

One week from today she would visit Jess and William and make everything right with the family. It would be one less problem lurking in back of her mind.

§

"I'll not read from the Bible tonight," announced Mr Ludlam, "seeing as we've only just returned from Church."

His wife agreed. "Perhaps Ada will play her mandolin after supper. It would make a nice change to sing to music."

Ada cringed on hearing this suggestion. "I'm a bit rusty, I haven't played in ages and will have to use the plectrum. My fingers are sore from plaiting the onion swags. I'd forgotten how hard that was."

Immediately Mr Ludlam turned to her. "Talking about those onion swags, Ada, I can't help but look at them. In spite of your sore fingers, you've made a really good job. They look well hanging from the beams."

Mr Ludlam didn't often give compliments and appeared more relaxed than Ada had seen him for some time, and she decided it must be because of the excellent harvest. "There's something special about this time of year." He said, settling into his chair, contentment softening his face.

"Why not play for us now? It's ages yet before supper. We'll not mind if you make some mistakes, you're among friends, after all." Mrs Ludlam smiled at her encouragingly. "Go on Ada, go upstairs and fetch your mandolin."

She perched for a minute or two on her bed to tune up and practice a few cords, and by the time she had returned to the parlour, Mr Ludlam had opened a bottle of elderberry wine. His wife collected glasses from the dresser cupboard and carried them on a tray, through to the parlour. He poked the fire and added a couple of logs, before removing the cork and pouring the deep claret liquid into the most beautiful glasses Ada had ever set eyes upon. "These are lovely," she commented, "and so delicate."

"They belonged to my Mother," said Mrs Ludlam, taking a sip and settling Allen on the rug with a few toys.

With her heart in her mouth, Ada opened a book of sacred tunes, propping it up on a cushion at one end of the sofa. She chose a children's hymn which she knew Missy sang at school. After an initial false beginning and a giggle or two, the words of the hymn:-

"There's a friend for little children above the bright blue sky," echoed clearly. Ada nodded her head, indicating when to begin and the miller and his wife nodded proudly as their daughter performed.

The last verse was sung by all of them, even Ben letting rip with his full baritone voice. Ada relaxed, the ice now broken, and began to enjoy her evening, appreciating once more how wonderful it was to make music. In any case, they were making so much noise when they all sang together that you could hardly notice when she did make a mistake.

"Will you play at the Harvest Supper next week?" enquired Missy.

Immediately and before Ada was able to react, Mrs Ludlam intervened. "Goodness, child, don't frighten her to death. No, she will not. Your father has arranged for Isaac to come with his brothers, like they do every year."

Chapter 13

A Letter

It was Friday and Ada had completed the deliveries and collected the bread-money, but today, instead of returning to the house, she held onto the reins, bracing herself as Homer negotiated the corner leading into Mill Lane. With a smile on her face and with three shillings and ninepence-worth of tips jangling in her skirt pocket, Ada approached Fullbrook and The Mill.

The wheel was still. Except for the burbling of the mill-race the building stood in silence. This she had not anticipated. Nevertheless her hands shook with excitement as she tied Homer to the hitching post. She stood in awe in front of the building. White strands of flour had escaped to create lacy patterns around the door-frame and the large metal ring felt cold in her hands. Holding it with both hands she twisted it. The heavy door groaned on its hinges as it swung inwards.

Ada stepped inside and looked up into the vast space. Two mezzanine floors, one set above the other and both supported by hefty props, protruded from the walls and it seemed that the space continued on and upwards forever. Everything was coated in a fine, undisturbed layer of white dust, resembling a light sprinkling of snow. Even coats and hats hanging from hooks on the wall bore the look of newly dusted bread, while cob-webs, woven in places too high to reach, festooned like fine crochet. It was a ghostly scene.

The fusty smell of mould from past grindings permeated the air, causing Ada's taste buds to explode on recognising the raw taste of yeast and whole grains. A tiny mouse scuttled across the floor, raising a fine trace of powder in its wake.

"Ada, I didn't hear you come in." She jumped almost out of her skin as Ben clattered down the narrow and somewhat rickety stairs, taking them two at a time. His voice echoed spookily, his large hands disturbing the powder from the hand-rail, lifting it in clouds. On finally reaching the stone floor, Ben added his footprints to those of the mouse, and the magic of the moment was gone. Despite wearing a straw hat, which blended perfectly with his millers' smock, Ben's bushy ginger eye-brows were loaded with dust. Ada suppressed a giggle, thinking he only needed a piece of straw sticking out of his mouth, to complete the picture.

"What can I do for you?"

Ada was so enthusiastic at what she was about to see, she could hardly form the words. "We're baking ready for the harvest supper and Mrs Ludlam needs more flour, and I do so want to see the wheel turning. Are you not going to make it work? I'm most eager to see what happens."

Ben laughed. "We've been cleaning the stones, but I'll start it again directly."

She watched as he removed a sack bag which had filled from a spout extending down from above. Ada needed to see the upper floors. The thought of huge mill-stones sitting just above her head was so exciting, she was thrilled almost to bursting, but she had no choice but to contain herself until Ben, after tying the sack and adding it to an assortment near the door, replaced it with an empty one. He turned towards her with a wink. "Are you prepared for this?"

She watched with baited breath as he walked over to a lever hanging on the wall, about five feet from the ground. It looked like the hand of a giant clock and was obviously heavy and difficult to budge. He called upstairs, "Are you ready, up there?"

"Indeed I am." Mr Ludlam's voice was almost lost in the vast space.

It took all Ben's strength to move the wooden blade, his face contorting with the effort. As the apparatus began to function, Ada heard water begin to rush and the groaning of timber as the wheel turned. She was torn between a desire to run outside and see the water cascading and a need to climb the shaky stairs. She chose to follow Ben up to the top of the first set of steps, willing the structure not to give way beneath her. She stepped onto a platform, pausing in wonder before the huge mechanical fusion of metal cogs and stone circles. They all worked together, noisily protesting, creating a surge of power which was gathering momentum.

Mr Ludlam stood over the far side, closely scrutinizing the performance of the apparatus. He looked across and nodded, his fedora coated as usual and as the air began to fill with tiny fragments, Ada began to understand the enormity of the risks threatening the lungs of those employed in this occupation, and why Mr Ludlam chose to wear a hat with a large brim. Skipper stood on full alert, tongue hanging out and panting with excitement, giving the odd bark of apprehension as the wheels grunted and ground. Ben looked down at them from the floor above. He was pouring grain from a sack-bag into the hopper. Ada noticed the string tied around the bottoms of his trousers to stop the rats. She looked around to if there were any in sight.

As the huge stones increased their speed, Ben darted down the stairs once more, holding her by the shoulders as he squeezed past on his way to check the filled bags. The whole building seemed to have absorbed the energy of the wheel, and together with the magnitude of sound, it caused the structure to tremble from top to bottom, and the metal fixings of the stairs to vibrate against the wall.

Despite her adulation at the sheer strength of the apparatus, Ada was alarmed, both by the juddering and the dust-filled atmosphere. Hanging onto the rail for dear life, she lost her need to explore further. Instead of progressing to the highest level, she retraced her steps, holding tightly to the thin handrail, finally making it to the bottom and gratefully followed Ben out into the fresh clean air of the open fields and Fullbrook.

Ben appeared at the door, manoeuvring a hand-cart loaded with small, over-stuffed white bags. He deftly lifted them onto the trap. After the third load was safely deposited, he grinned at her and removed his hat, slapping it against his thigh, sending clouds of flour and husks into the air. He wiped his brow with the back of his hand, and looked down at her. "That's all done." His eyes held hers, and she felt her heart miss a beat. "Now I have something to tell you. Mr Ludlam has given permission for us to use the bakery in the evenings, so you can teach me to read."

"Oh, Ben, that is good news. If nothing else it means he trusts me. I've had nightmares in case he believes I behaved badly."

"I've put him right on that score, Ada, and anyway, he's not daft, he knows who was at fault."

Ada frowned, "Mind you, I'm not sure when we'll find the time. Every evening seems to be taken up with something. Perhaps when the harvest supper is over?"

Ben laughed. "There's no rush. In the meantime, don't forget to dust yourself down before you go into the house."

As he helped her up onto the seat, Ada reflected on how she liked the feel of her hand in his. It was safe and reliable and wonderfully, absolutely wholesome, but was it enough? She took up the reins and smiled her thanks. Ben gave Homer a pat on the buttocks and without needing to look back, Ada knew he had lingered to watch as the trap trundled along the lane.

§

Alfred Ludlam closed the umbrella and, anxious to find shelter, reached for the door knob. Constant rain had caused the post office door to swell, leaving him with little choice but to apply his shoulder. As the heavy portal swung from its frame, he was jettisoned forwards into the office, the clattering of boots on the wet slippery floor-boards, together with the jangling of the bell, clearly announcing his arrival. Having regained his balance, but still somewhat flustered, he bid the young woman behind the counter, "Good day."

"Morning, Mr Ludlam. Come for a newspaper, have yer? There's post as well." She lifted a letter from one of the pigeon holes behind her, and whilst fluttering her eye-lashes and pursing her lips, she simpered, "Will that be all, Sir?"

He handed her two-pence for the paper. "Yes, thank you. Goodbye." Embarrassed by her inappropriate behaviour, he declined to doff his hat and prepared to struggle again with the door, when he noticed the addressee on the envelope. It read:-

Mr Eli Turner
Mill House
Glenfield
Nr. Leicester

Mr Ludlam reluctantly and with a sense of impending doom, turned back. "Is the postmaster in? I need a word."

Percy Grummet appeared from behind a chenille curtain, monocle firmly placed over one eye. Whilst straightening his back and squaring his shoulders, in order to make the most of his five feet one and a half inches, he cordially greeted his customer. "Good morning, Mr Ludlam, Sir. What can I do for you?"

Mr Ludlam looked sternly down at him. "It's a personal matter. Is there somewhere we can speak in private?"

A gaggle of customers had entered the shop and, along with the young woman, were showing obvious interest.

"Follow me, Sir."

Alfred Ludlam removed his hat and dipped his head, before passing under the curtain, nodding to the people bending over a large trestle table, sorting the letters into piles. Settled in the back-room, Alfred Ludlam quietly explained.

Percy took the envelope and turned it over, scrutinizing the writing, "Do you have his new address?"

"No." Mr Ludlam cleared his throat. "He just took off. I thought he may have gone to visit his sister but as this has a Lincolnshire post-mark, I can only assume it is either from her or from Eli's mother."

"I seem to remember there have been other letters?"

"As far as I am aware there has been just one from his mother, informing him that his sister was delivered of a boy child." Alfred Ludlam was wondering what Percy was playing at. He knew exactly what correspondence went in and out of his establishment. Everyone knew what a gossip he was, and what was worse, the talking had ceased from the other side of the curtain, along with the shuffling of envelopes.

"Did he actually give you that news?" The postmaster stretched his mouth into a semblance of a smile, but Alfred saw that it did not reach his eyes. Percy rocked back and forth on his heels, signifying what Mr Ludlam recognized as a man enjoying power.

"No!" replied Alfred. "I read the letter to him. He's unable read, you see." He was acutely aware that the postmaster was finding the situation somewhat entertaining and had known all along that Eli couldn't read. As was to be expected, Eli's sudden absence had already given rise to gossip. Mr Ludlam sighed.

"I thought as much." Percy was still playing games. "In that case you are quite within your rights to open it."

The miller, looking pensive, made no move to do so.

"Would you prefer me to do it? One of us has to, if only to return it to sender."

After due deliberation, Mr Ludlam nodded, and Percy took a paper knife and carefully slit along the top crease of the envelope,

The letter read:-

Dear Eli,

I shall be returning home a week on Monday. The stage should reach Glenfield in the middle of the afternoon. Please go to the cottage in the morning and light a fire.

It is costing me to have this written, so I hope you are well and I will see you then.
Your Mother.

There was no address.

"Leave it with me," replied Mr Ludlam, and with a somewhat frustrated sigh, pushed the envelope into his pocket, "and thank you for your assistance."

He walked past the prying eyes and back into the street, feeling both bewildered and irritated at Percy's outlandish behaviour. He couldn't understand for the life of him why the man couldn't be straightforward and say what he thought, instead of playing games. He also knew full well that Eli's unexpected disappearance would be common knowledge in Glenfield by the morrow. Alfred Ludlam felt angry and it was not a feeling with which he was comfortable.

The rain having ceased, he made straight for the Alms Houses, berating himself for not thinking of it before. It was the obvious place for Eli to go. On approaching the place however, it became clear that the front-door hadn't been opened for some considerable time. Spiders' webs hung intact, highlighted by silvery dew and decorated with a collection of dead leaves and insects. He cautiously placed a foot on the overgrown border beneath the front window, trying not to damage a hollyhock still in the throes of flowering. On peering through the glass, however, the room appeared undisturbed. He felt a hand grab his shoulder at the same time as he heard the words, "Can I help you?"

He jumped back. "Oh yes, probably. I'm looking for Eli Turner. Have you seen him by any chance? I wondered if he'd come back here."

The warden assured him that to his knowledge, Eli hadn't been there and he would have been informed had it been the case. The man was obviously puzzled. "I thought he was living with you."

"No, he left a couple of months back. I am not sure exactly when."

The warden removed his hat and scratched his head. "Well Mr Ludlam, he aint bin here, but if he does turn up I'll let yer know."

"Thank you Sir. Do you have a key for the cottage?"

"I do, but it's more than my job's worth to let yer in."

"Oh no, I'm not asking you to do that, but I have this letter, look, from Mrs Turner, she's asking Eli to light a fire. Perhaps you could do that for her?"

On reading the letter, the warden commented, "So, Dolly doesn't know where he is then?"

"It's beginning to look that way."

The warden shook his head. "He's a worry to her. He'll come to a sticky end, that one."

Alfred's mouth tightened, all ears now, as the man continued. "Mind you, lads like him often come up smelling o roses. You never can tell. Perhaps he's gone to make his fortune."

"Will you see to the fire, then?" Mr Ludlam persisted.

"Aye, I'll see to it."

§

"Alright Ada, yer can start now." The assassin's voice echoed menacingly in the still, dim light of the pre-dawn. The noise of two shots fired in the darkness, still rang in her ears. Ada had always felt a rapour with pigs and although she was quite aware that it was a necessary procedure, somehow couldn't quite come to terms with their moment of slaughter.

Tying the rough tapes of the oiled-cloth pinafore around her middle, she struggled to lift the bundle of knives and the bucket brimming with hot water, and drag them outside to where two trestle tables were placed beneath the scullery window. On each one lay the still warm carcass of a dead sow. Ada ladled the water from her bucket over the nearest one and began to scrape the hairs from the leathery pink skin. She began at the rear end, avoiding having to look into its eyes and at the hole where the bullet had passed through the poor creature's brain.

The butchers sat on their wooden trolley, sharing a tot of whiskey with Mr Ludlam. Ada was surprised to see the bottle of whisky. The master hardly ever consumed alcohol, certainly not on a week-day, but apparently it was the custom. She also noted they only consumed one glassful each.

"So, what happened to young Eli, then? I've heard tell he's done a runner." The question hung in the yard like a carbuncle. Ada paused for a split second and thanked the Lord God Almighty that she had her back to the men. Her cheeks must be the colour of Chinese lanterns.

Mr Ludlam coughed, discernibly caught unawares. "Well, yes, I suppose you could say that. Certainly he has left us."

Ada wanted to rescue him, but there were no words to help him out of this dilemma. She crossed her fingers, and left him to it.

"Did yer just find his bed empty, or did he tell yer he was leaving?"

Ada turned abruptly on hearing this and accidently knocked the knives from the table and just for a moment the clatter of metal on cobbles helped to block out the voices. She worked quickly, the sooner these men were off the premises the better. She struggled to reach the fattest parts and despite the pinafore, her sleeves were sodden and streaked with blood. She beckoned for them to turn the bodies.

"My word Ada, yer've worked up a sweat. Yer cheeks are all aglow." The man laughed, but Ada stood her ground.

"I need to finish before the sun has a chance to shine over this side of the farmhouse."

"Ah, that yer do." The man took his eyes from her and did as he was bid.

As well as rescuing the Master, the joints of pork needed to be safely inside the larder, away from flies and any damage that prolonged warmth could do to the meat. Short of a thunder storm, the weather couldn't be much worse for dealing with pork.

Once done, the men took over and Ada was only too happy to leave them to their butchering. It would give them something to think about, other than the whereabouts of Eli Turner.

Mrs Ludlam was in the bakery, with both coppers lit and the water at a rolling boil. Before they attempted to bake the bread, the internal parts of the animals must be dealt with. There were chitterlings to soak and the scratchings would need to go in the bread oven after the bake. Ada's favourite job at the killing was making brawn.

"Come on, we'll have something to eat before they start bringing in the meat." Ada followed Mrs Ludlam into the living-room. Tea was ready in the pot, so all Ada had to do was pour it.

"They've been asking about Eli."

"What?"

"Yes, either Mr Grummet at the post-office or the warden at the Alms Houses must have said something."

"Both of them I shouldn't wonder." Mrs Ludlam shook her head, but carried on preparing breakfast.

Ada helped herself to a toasted tea-cake spread with butter and honey. She was ravenous and it was swiftly consumed. The second one took a little longer and Ada was able to relax and relish the sweetness of the dried fruit, the melted butter squeezing out onto her chin, but as she reached out for a third the men walked in carrying one of the carcasses, gutted and without a head or feet. They manoeuvred the animal around the table and through the larder door, hanging it from a hook in the farthest corner.

"It'll be alright there until Saturday," Mr Ludlam said, "just keep the door closed as much as possible, to stop the flies and keep checking it hasn't been blown on by a blue-bottle. The last thing we need is maggots in the roast pork. The rector would never forgive us."

The three men settled around the table and Ada, thankful to be leaving the scene of gossip, picked up a huge basket containing certain animal parts. A familiar pink snout poked out from beneath a bunch of cloven hooves.

Ada bent over the copper, allowing the steam to encase her and a saturating film to form globules all over her face. She loved the smell. The head, hocks and trotters were cooking inside, together with a good helping of beef and fresh sage, a few of pounds of onions and a good pinch of whole peppercorns.

The heat was building in the bread oven. Somehow the slaughter had interfered with Ada's balance of thought and she was unable to gain the usual sense of peace from the kneading.

Eventually, with the first batch in place, she turned back to the copper. She ladled the contents into a puncheon before tearing the flesh away from the bones, ready to chop. She managed to fill four moulds, and using plates as covers, placed them on the cold surface of the thrawl with weights on top. By tomorrow morning, they would be pressed, the juice having jelled, and they would be ready to cut into slices and eat with a pinch of salt, good chutney and a chunk of freshly baked bread. In spite of herself Ada salivated. There was nothing quite like a slice of good brawn.

By the time Mrs Ludlam returned from the bread delivery, Ada had two pork joints deposited in the meat-safe and the sides of bacon already infused with saltpetre and wrapped in muslin, ready to hang from the larder beams.

"Whoever does the deliveries tomorrow can take a couple of these hams to the butchers. We'll have them smoked. It'll make a nice change. Leave the faggots for tomorrow as well, Ada, we'll roast a joint of belly pork for tonight's dinner. We'll stuff it with sage and onions and some apricots. It's beautiful, rolled and carved really thinly, one of Mr Ludlam's favourites."

Chapter 14

A Sighting

Mrs Culyer, the butcher's wife, burst into a fit of giggling. "Do you remember the year afore last, when Mrs Pepper mislaid her husband and found him fast asleep next to a sheep? She didn't speak to him for a month. He reckoned it was the most peaceful time of his married life he could remember."

Despite her hands being sore from the saltpetre, Ada was in her element. She hadn't felt this degree of excitement since Jess's wedding, and she had a new ribbon for her hair. In the middle of the yard menfolk took it in turns to rotate the spit. Smells of roasting pig had been taunting appetites for most of the day and the atmosphere was already one of festivity. Ada stood for a moment, watching as the turner dipped a ladle into the trough beneath, taking the time to baste the carcass, causing flames to leap up all around.

The rain had held off for the last couple of days, allowing the farm-yard to dry. Ben's efforts with the yard brush and shovel had paid off and the whole area was clean and tidy. Using a piece of slate he was marking out a game of hop-scotch for the children and Mr Ludlam had made some whips to go with the tops that Missy sometimes played with. Allen was trying to help and Ada was impressed to see how patient Mr Ludlam was with his son.

A constant stream of women walked to and fro from the farm-house to the barn, depositing food on trestle tables. Hilarity was the order of the day, the ladies being delighted at escaping their daily rituals. Ada was arranging the dishes, when a young woman approached. "Will Eli be here tonight?" she enquired.

Ada was lost for words and caution warned her to keep a still tongue. She could see that everyone within ear-shot had stopped, but the answer was instantly supplied by Mrs Ludlam. "He no longer works here!" Her voice was clipped and discouraged any further discussion. She turned to Ada. "You and Ben have made a grand job of the barn Ada, the bunting looks really festive." With that she tossed her head and left. The helpers hurriedly turned away, making more of an effort to occupy themselves, than was absolutely necessary.

Despite the young woman being scruffy and unkempt, Ada felt sorry for her. She was obviously crestfallen, but being unable to furnish her with any further information, Ada continued with her task as though the question has never been asked.

§

Ada looked longingly at her bridesmaid's dress but it wasn't at all suitable for the occasion. However, she couldn't resist slipping it on. The result wasn't quite as expected. She had filled out so much that her nipples showed clearly through the delicate fabric. She needed to purchase a corset.

Her best Sunday dress lay ready. Ada had sewn rows of braiding down the front of the bodice to cover the tears. It had actually improved the look. Having arranged her hair, she pinched her cheeks to give her face colour and picked up her shawl, before tripping back down the stairs.

The smell of sage and crackling pork had infused Ada's bedroom and she was hungry. The farmhouse looked strange with no chairs in sight. Everything capable of being sat on had been utilized for the festival. She was the last person to leave the house and music drew her towards the barn.

A crowd had already begun to form around the spit. Children were playing hide-and-seek and as she grew nearer, she saw how cheerful the barn looked, illuminated by hurricane-lamps. Ada paused just long enough to smooth the excess softening butter into her hands.

Isaac and his sons were positioned on a trailer at the far end of the barn. Two fiddled zealously, one was bashing a tambourine, held high above his head, whilst the third one played the spoons. Isaac stamped his foot heavily on the boards to keep time, with his concertina opening and closing to the beat. He made a comical figure with his bowler hat tipped just a little too far forwards and his trousers several inches too short, flapping around his legs. An overzealous farmhand shouted up to him, "Yer wants ter tie the string round yer trousers to stop 'em from flappin'. Yer'll have the rats up 'em."

Some revellers were already dancing a reel and Ada saw Ben standing with the girl from the post-office. Mr Ludlam called out, "Ada, come and have some punch," but Ben, with cup in hand was already walking towards her.

"Much obliged I'm sure, Ben." Ada took the drink. "You're looking very smart." He was wearing a white shirt with black trousers and a grey waistcoat, but not the ones he usually wore for church. She wondered if he had bought them especially. She took a sip, looking up at him over the rim of her cup. She felt herself blush and was startled by her reaction.

Ben looked down at her, cheeks aglow and with a lop-sided grin on his face. Ada blushed and turned her gaze to check if people were watching. Her eyes inadvertently met those of Percy Grummet from the post-office with his wife sitting beside him and Ada recognised a similar look in his eyes to that of Eli's.

§

"You're looking well, daughter." Billy's face was flushed and his eyes sparkled on seeing his favourite child. She was looking a lot better than she had the last time they all sat around the table at Albion Street.

"I am well, and I've so much to tell you all. I went inside the mill for the first time last week. It wasn't at all what I expected. In fact it was quite frightening."

"Your mother wouldn't let me take you inside Clock Mill. She thought it too dangerous for young undeveloped lungs. She reckoned yer could catch yer death in there."

William filled their glasses with cider, a firkin of which he had acquired on one of his business trips. The whole family raised their glasses to welcome Nelly into the family, for George had assured them that she was the only girl for him and he intended to marry her, although he didn't say when that would be.

"Talking about Clock Mill," Billy continued, "they've installed a steam engine to drive the stones when the water levels are low. Flippin' good idea that."

"Expensive though," said George.

William sharpened the knife before carving the pork, whilst Father told the tale. Ada laughed with them at hearing about the sale-day and the darts team having imbibed a little too liberally, but at the same time she felt some regret at not having shared the experience. Jarvis sat in the chair next to her and she helped him tuck his napkin into his shirt collar.

In response to her mother's questions, Ada was more than happy to reply. "Everyone is most kind to me. We all work hard, even Missy does her chores and everyone is considerate and respectful. It's almost like being at home."

"But what are they like, Ada. Are they like us?"

Ada laughed. "No, Father, not at all. Mr Ludlam is very proper. He never says words like flipping and flopping, in fact he doesn't ever seem to get angry." She turned towards her brother-in-law. "Would you agree with that, William?"

He shrugged, waiting for her to continue.

"He always wears a collar and tie, even at work in the fields and Mrs Ludlam is tall and graceful. Actually, she's ever so slightly taller than him." Again she waited for a comment, but none was proffered. "They are very kind people and they always say Grace before a meal." No-one commented on this either.

After the draughty stage coach ride, walking into Jess's front room had been like walking into Heaven and Ada had been overjoyed on seeing George sitting on the sofa with a young lady by his side. George's girl seemed overwhelmed by the gathering and said little. Ada looked across the table, into the green eyes of the auburn-haired girl with the pretty face and lovely smile, and felt her shyness.

"Mother, have you settled in alright at Hill House? I'm longing to hear all about it."

"I'm hoping you can come and see us before too long. It's so much smaller than The Elephant. I'll have time on my hands once everywhere is straight, especially after Jarvis starts to school."

William changed the subject. "How was the Harvest Supper?"

"Very good, thank you."

"And what about the cooking, are you learning anything new?" Billy seemed anxious to discover if his investment was paying off.

"Most certainly, Father. As before, I've brought some bread and scones for you to try, and we've been making jam and chutney."

"And is it as good as your mother's?"

"Leave her be, Billy," interrupted Bess, "you can judge for yourself when we get home."

Ada noisily crunched on a piece of crackling, remembering back to the night before, when she had sat next to Ben and enjoyed a hot pork and sausage sandwich.

William commented on the gravy which he found particularly tasty. Jess was eager to point out she had taken a tip from her sister, and added a pinch of sugar.

"Sugar? In the gravy? What is that supposed to do?"

"It brings out the flavour of the meat," answered Ada, feeling quite superior. "I learned that in my very first week."

"Do you do all the cooking our Ada, how does it work?" asked Father.

"On Tuesday we killed two sows, and I made the brawn and the chitterlings and the scratchings."

"But you already know how to do that."

"Yes indeed Father, but I also learned how to make a pork-pie."

"Did you bring some of that for us to try?" There was only the shortest of pauses before Billy yelled "Ouch!" obviously having received a kick under the table for his remark, and everyone except he and his wife laughed heartily.

"What's been happening in Swepstone?" asked Ada, not really expecting much of a reply, but feeling it was time for a change of subject.

"Yes, as a matter of fact, we do have something to tell yer." It was Billy who offered the news, whilst still rubbing his shin. "And yer'll never, in a million years, guess what it is." He sat back in his chair, as was his way, giving his words the usual space to make an impact.

"Well, go on then, Father, don't keep me in suspense."

"Tom has gone to live with Mrs Scarlett."

Ada was shocked. "Never!"

"It's true," endorsed Bess, "mind you, it only occurred last week. We've yet to see how it works out."

"What prompted that?"

"Well, as yer know, his sister made his life a misery. In truth they couldn't stand the sight of each other, and one day he were walking past Mrs Scarlett's cottage on his way up to us, when she walked out, bold as brass and invited him in. She suggested he move in with her, said she could do with a man about the place to do jobs. It seems that she's suffering from the screws, and finds it difficult to clean the lavvy and see to the garden." Billy chuckled.

"Well," said Ada, "I hope it works out. Tom is a good man."

"She refers to him as the lodger," said Bess. "Mrs Scarlet means well. It's only when she gets her dander up, that folk have to watch out. Perhaps I should have a quiet word with Tom."

"Yer'll do nowt o the sort, Bess," cut in Billy. "Let him deal wi it. Tom's not as daft as yer think."

Jess turned to Nelly who was sitting patiently, hardly saying a word. "Tell us about yourself dear, George says you work in the theatre."

The girl's face became alive. "Yes, I do," she nodded, causing her auburn curls to bob around her face. Ada thought she had never before seen eyes as green.

George encouraged her. "Tell em about the famous people you've met."

Nellie brimmed with pride. "Sarah Bernhardt and Henry Irving. They've both performed there."

"So you're famous then!" Ada was impressed.

"No, not really. I sometimes dance in the chorus, but when there are no parts for us, we help with painting the scenery and I make some of the costumes."

"She made the blouse and skirt she's wearing," George announced. There was mutual appreciation from all quarters, even Billy nodded his approval. "And you should see the tablecloths she's crocheted and her embroidery. She's very gifted." George glowed with pride.

"Who taught you to crochet?" asked Bess.

"Nuns. The Sisters' of Mercy, to be exact. They visited us regularly for a while. I think they wanted to convert us to Catholicism, but when they realised most of us had already been baptized, they stopped coming. Well, I think that's why they stopped coming."

There was a lull in the conversation.

Jess placed a large apple pie on the table and beside it a jug of custard. She cut a piece for George first and he set about demolishing it immediately.

"You'll have to get Mother to show you how to make pastry," he said to Nelly. There was an immediate intake of breath. The women glanced at each other, while the men kept their heads down, not quite sure what was to come next.

"You can't make pastry?" asked Bess.

"No, I can't cook much at all. Mother died giving birth to me, so there's been no-one to teach me."

"You poor child!" Bess almost shouted the words. "Who brought you up then?"

"Father, until he died. I was thirteen then and was already helping at the theatre. The girls took me in."

"Well, I'm sure between us, we can show you how to cook a proper dinner. It's not difficult."

THE LATE ELEPHANT

"How do you eat, if you don't cook?" asked Jarvis.

Usually, following a question such as this, someone would have told him not to be rude, or nosey or whatever, but each family member was just as eager to hear the reply as was the small boy who had asked the question, so they all stayed as still and quiet as church mice.

Nelly laughed. "We go to the pie shop. There's one right next door to the theatre. That's what most people do who live in town, except if you are very rich of course.

"Mr Boughton, who owns the New Theatre Royal, has a big house with servants. Some of us went there once when his wife held a soirée."

Jarvis sat with his big blue eyes open wide like saucers. "What's that?"

"It's a social evening. A party held at someone's home. They have entertainment and supper." Nelly looked directly at Jarvis. "They didn't serve pie and mash there. They had joints of roast meat and whole salmon with all manner of different dishes. Then afterwards we all danced and sang. It went on late into the night." Nelly picked up her fan and began wafting. Ada could see her eyes sparkling and wondered, for just a moment, if a look of wistfulness had hovered.

The account, however, had prompted eyes to widen and eyebrows to rise and a certain expectation filled the air. As it happened, the subject of food was not, as yet, exhausted and Jarvis was still curious.

"What sort of pies do they sell at the pie shop?"

"All sorts. I like eel pie best. Mind you, they do lamb with mint, beef and onions, chicken with thyme and parsley and you can have them all with mash and liquor." Nelly paused, speculating on what the next question would be, but this time Billy beat him to it.

"What's this liquor exactly?"

Nelly was prepared. "It's a sauce made from the water which the meat or fish is cooked in, with some milk added. You mix in corn-flour and butter, if you can afford it, and a spoon full of vinegar. You see, I know how to make that. It goes lovely with the pie and mash."

Ada said, "I've never heard of it, Nelly, but it certainly sounds good, you'll have to make it for us."

Before Nelly could respond further, Bess enquired, "I expect you would find it dull, living in Swepstone?"

Nelly looked at George and her eyes filled with admiration. "Oh no! Not with George there."

Ada stifled a giggle.

William said, "So Ada, tell us about the Harvest Supper."

Ada put down her spoon, making no effort to hide the smile. "I did so enjoy it. I danced almost every dance." She blushed.

"Oh yes, and with anyone in particular?"

"No-one in particular. We all sang at the end. You should have heard us giving rise to 'Widdecombe Fair'. It was a splendid evening."

"That reminds me," said Bess, reaching into her skirt pocket, "this came for you."

Ada took the envelope and at a glance saw that it was from Charles, and she blushed, particularly on seeing William grinning.

Chapter 15

The Black Maria

Ada was the last passenger to alight from the coach. Inside her bag was the corset which Jess had given her and she was impatient to try it on. She waited for the stage to continue on towards Kirby Muxloe, before crossing the road. Breath from the horses floated into the chill night air and Ada pulled the shawl tightly around her shoulders as she walked quickly out of the square.

She wondered how Ben was feeling and smiled on recalling the previous night and how they had danced together. There had been a few other partners, but Ben had hardly left her side. She felt a warm safe feeling, knowing he was around to protect her and it was probably just as well that he had taken a little too much strong drink. She had found him behind the barn being heartily sick, but had tip-toed away, saving him the indignity of discovery. Fortunately it had been towards the end of the revelry and, due to their only being moonlight to see by, no-one had appeared to notice Ben's pallor.

There had been a couple of times when his hand had lingered just a little too long in hers and she had to admit that if they had been alone together under the stars, things may have developed somewhat. However, Eli's assault was still fresh in her mind. Ada shuddered as the memory returned and those dreadful moments when she had felt so helpless. At the merest glimpse of a red spotted kerchief, her knees turned to jelly. An incomprehensible surge of emotion resulted in her feeling guilty about feeling an attraction towards Ben and wondered what Mr Ludlam would make of it if he could read her thoughts.

She quickened her step. The moon was high and bright, giving ample light for walking, but somehow the darker corners behind walls and bushes took on ominous proportions. A shiver ran down her spine. On closing the five-barred gate behind her, she saw that the back-door was open and the light from a lamp framed a figure, as Mrs Ludlam stood waiting.

"There you are, Ada."

"Thank you. You needn't have worried, I'm quite safe."

The family, including Ben, was already gathered around the supper-table. On taking her place beneath the pool of light cast by the hanging lamp, Ada lowered her head to say Grace. She wrapped both hands around the large china teacup, luxuriating in the warmth and took comfort in being safe and sound once more.

Ada glanced towards Ben and saw that his colour was up. He was concentrating on the food, painstakingly cutting his ham and moving the potato salad around on his plate. Ada wondered if his stomach was still feeling the effects of his overindulgence.

Turning to her mistress, she enthused, "I did so enjoy last night. Have you managed to clear the barn?"

"Oh yes," said Mrs Ludlam, "don't worry about that. Ben and Mr Ludlam helped to bring the last few things across and Missy gave a hand with the washing-up. I'm surprised your legs didn't fall off Ada, I don't think you sat a dance out all night."

Ada was cheered to see the grin on Ben's face, pleased that he was oblivious to the fact that she had witnessed him in embarrassing circumstances. He half lifted his eyes to steal a quick glance at her.

Alfred Ludlam carved a slice from the ham, dropping it onto her plate. "How was your visit?"

"It was wonderful, thank you Sir." Ada's eyes lit up and her words spilled out. "My brother George was there and his lady-friend, Nelly. She seems really nice."

"And how are your parents since the move?"

"Mother seems quite settled in the cottage and Father was on form, reporting on the sale-day at the Elephant." She paused, recalling Mother's happy demeanour. "I think they're going to be alright. The cottage is called Hill House, but it's not nearly as grand as it sounds. Father has begun work at Upper Fields, for the farmer who owns it."

"So you're familiar with the property then?" enquired Mr Ludlam.

"I know which house it is, but I've never been inside. It stands at the top of the hill, on the right, going out of the village towards Heather and looks directly back down the lane. Apparently it has a living room and a parlour, as well as a scullery, of course and there are three good-sized bedrooms."

"And what about land? Does it have a garden?"

"I'm not sure, but I suppose it must have, because Father was talking about buying some more pigs and a few chickens, once spring is here." She giggled. "He's purchased a goat to keep the grass down." Ada picked up her knife and fork.

"You should go and see for yourself. How easy will it be to get there?" Mrs Ludlam had mentioned this before.

"I'll have to take the train to Ashby, and check with Mother if Mr Thomas runs the stage in the afternoon. I'll have to give it some thought. It's a long way to walk from Ashby to Swepstone, especially with heavy bags."

Mrs Ludlam was not prepared to leave it at that. "Would you like to go for Christmas? I feel sure we could manage. What do you think Mr Ludlam?"

Ada held her breath, but the look of horror on the miller's face soon dispelled any hopes she may have in that direction. "I don't deem it at all possible, my dear. Think back to last year. We didn't finish the deliveries until well into the afternoon of Christmas Eve. I don't wish to detain you here unduly, Ada, but it is our busiest time."

Ada hadn't really believed there would be any chance of going home for Christmas, but she had, just for one sweet, fleeting moment, allowed herself to become more than a little excited by the thought of being in St. Peter's Church on Christmas morning and seeing Duncan again. There was to be no Christmas kiss, it seemed.

Ada was becoming ill at ease. Ever since she'd arrived, Mr Ludlam had been shuffling around on his chair, as he did when he was about to do something with which he was not comfortable. It was a trait of his and suddenly Ada felt the usual warning hairs standing up on the back of her neck.

Sure enough, he coughed a little nervously and began. "Now we are all back together, there's something very serious I need to discuss with you." He removed a letter from the inner pocket of his jacket. "This is a letter, addressed to Eli. I shall read it to you."

Ada sent an involuntary glance towards Ben, an action which she instantly regretted, as Mr Ludlam was watching her over the top of his spectacles. As Ada's blush deepened an uneasy silence crept over them all, and he read.

Ada was the first to comment. "So where do you think he is, Sir?"

"I don't know. He's not at his mother's cottage and he's obviously not at his sister's house and as he is not here either, I've run out of suggestions." He turned to Ben. "Have you any idea where he might have gone?"

"No Sir." Ben's eyes stayed focused on his plate, as did everyone else's, in fear and dread of what was to follow.

It seemed to Ada that the heat from the lamp had intensified. The smell of fat from the bacon and spices from the marrow chutney seemed to have increased and hung heavily among them.

"I know you are a man of few words Ben, but try to remember if he mentioned anything which would give us a clue to his whereabouts."

Ben shuffled his feet and sighed. "Nothing Sir, he never talked about anywhere else except here and his sister's."

"Did he ever talk of going to sea or joining the army?"

"No, never!" Ben's eyes stayed lowered.

Ada wished the whole thing would go away. No sooner had she resolved one dilemma, than this had resurfaced. At the railway station, while she was seeing off her parents, she had briefly caught sight of someone she thought was Eli, but there was too much of a crowd around her to be sure and so she was in two minds whether or not to mention it.

"You don't get on with him at all, do you Ben?" Mr Ludlam seemed determined to pursue the questions.

"Please, Sir," Ada spoke with conviction, "you can hardly blame Ben. If it hadn't been for him, I would be a fallen woman."

"I understand that, but it bothers me that if he doesn't show up before his mother arrives back in the village, then the police will become involved." After a moment's deliberation he added, "By rights, I should go to the police and report him missing. He is in my care."

Ada's response was swift. "Beg pardon, Sir but he's old enough to look after himself. You can't be his keeper, with respect." She wondered if perhaps she'd overstepped the mark, but was prepared to fight for Ben's honour, regardless of the outcome.

Ben surprised them all, "He only talks about bad things, Sir and it's always about ladies. In fact some of em were married. I don't like it. I find it disrespectful, Sir."

Everyone gasped at this.

Mrs Ludlam saved the moment. "Time will uncover the truth of where he is. One day he'll come whistling into the farmyard again, you wait and see."

"I certainly hope not," cut in her husband, "because in that case he'll be most certainly given his marching orders. After what I've just heard, I might even be tempted to set the dog on him."

Having excused herself, Ada climbed the stairs to her room. She must be extra careful not to stray too far from the house. Eli could be anywhere and she had this uncanny feeling that he was somewhere close by. Sitting on the bed she shivered then realized that she was clutching her bag with the parcel inside untouched.

Ada unrolled the corset and slipped off her dress. She wasn't at all sure how to get into it. She was intrigued by the garment which was held stiffly in shape by long hard bones. Finally, after pulling it up over her pantaloons, Ada manoeuvred the thing into place, struggling to do up the hooks. Pulling the tapes as tight as she could and after much wriggling, Ada stood in front of the mirror. After all the effort, she could see that it was far too big and she despaired. However, turning and titillating, she both enjoyed and appreciated the unexpected reflection of seeing herself as a woman. Until this moment she had been seeking a means of flattening her bosom, but now, as long as she could somehow diminish the too obvious protrusion of her nipples, she was content to allow the swell of her breasts to remain. Tightening her hands around her waist she stood on tip-toes to peer once more through the looking glass, delighted to imagine just how womanly she would look, in a corset of the correct size.

Ada pushed the garment into a draw and as she slipped the soft cotton nightdress over her head she thought of Duncan and wondered what he was doing at this moment.

§

Ada had woken to her dreaded woman's days, and felt more like going back to bed than knocking back. Her head ached and the pains in her abdomen were dragging her down, not to mention her painful breasts. However, she pushed and pulled at the dough, extracting a certain comfort from the familiar feel of the soft, raw mixture as it yielded beneath her touch. She used the moment to order her mind. This morning she was occupied with thoughts of tonight's rabbit pie and of how she would cook it. Mrs Ludlam had different ideas from those of mother, and Ada wondered what would be included in today's tuition.

She jumped, startled at a sudden knocking on the back door. Ada shook the surplus dough from her hands, rubbed them vigorously on her apron and flew into the scullery, eagerly throwing open the back door, excited on thinking it may well be William.

There stood a corpulent lady, tearful and out of breath, clutching a shawl about her shoulders. She was a total stranger, yet Ada instinctively knew that this poor unfortunate woman was the mother of Eli. "Is Mrs Ludlam in, please? I need to see her, or the master, it doesn't matter which."

Ada hesitated, but the woman pushed past her and straight into the bakery. "I'm Dolly Turner. I work here sometimes."

Mrs Ludlam hurried in and put out her arms. "Dolly, hello dear, how are you? How's the baby? Did it all go well?"

The woman burst into a fit of sobbing. "It's our Eli. The warden's told me he's cleared off and nobody knows where he is. I've come to see if he left me a note or anything so as I know where he's gone. Tell me what happened," begged Dolly.

"Let's go into the living room and leave Ada in peace. She has much to do and only a short while to do it in, as you yourself are aware. Come along, Dolly."

Ada hadn't thought about the consequences of Mrs Turner coming back to work. She would have to keep a very tight rein on any conversations and wondered just how much the woman already knew, if anything.

Ada lost concentration and made too many small rolls. The dough had to be reformed which usually meant it wouldn't rise so well. She couldn't imagine working with Eli's Mother. She crossed to the oven, shielding her face with her arms as the door swung open and heat blasted towards her. She raked the cinders to the edge and held the bucket beneath to catch the hot ashes. As the loaves were loaded and pushed into position, the feeling of hopelessness began to grow and the thud from the latches of the door closing seemed to intensify the beating of her heart.

A much needed cup of tea was placed before her on the table. "Here, Ada you must be parched."

Ada raised the cup to her lips. Mrs Ludlam smiled a half smile and, raising her eyebrows, announced, "Dolly is going to come and help us out. She used to work here before you came. As you have obviously realized, she is Eli's mother."

The woman hovered. "I'm pleased to meet yer, duck, but I'll be going now. I'll see yer in the morning." With that she pulled her shawl around her shoulders and left. Ada watched through the window as she picked her way through the cow pats in the yard.

"I had no choice, Ada, but I've told her that you had nothing much at all to do with Eli, other than to meet at mealtimes. After all, it only happened just a week after you started here, and I'll try to make sure you don't have to work together. If you see to the bakery and Dolly deals with the housework, it should work out. It was all getting too much for us anyway, so you needn't be too much in her company. Can you manage that, do you think?"

"As long as I don't have to answer her questions, I'll deal with it."

Mrs Ludlam sighed. "How in heavens name do you explain to a woman her son that has attempted to rape someone?"

Sounds from the scullery announced both the return of the men and the need to cook breakfast. Ada rose to her feet.

"No, no stay where you are. You look unwell. I expect it's the shock. I'll see to breakfast. We can make do with porridge this morning, and there are some oatcakes left. I'll fetch the jam."

§

Slop bucket in hand, on her way to the midden, Ada stopped in her tracks. A black box-like carriage turned into the farmyard and trundled over the cobbles towards the house. The large stocky horse came to a halt, shaking his head as if to rid himself of the steel bit. His eyes rolled wildly and foamy balls of saliva escaped into the air, only to collect on his long gleaming mane.

There were two men inside the vehicle, one a stranger and the other one, wearing a uniform, Ada recognized as police sergeant Kirchin from Chestnut Road. Her heart was beating fit to burst. She threw the contents of the bucket onto the pile and ran, but couldn't find Ben, neither in the cow-sheds nor in the barn. She needed to warn him, but daren't call his name. She even stooped to peer through a hole in the lavatory door, but he wasn't in there either. She had no choice but to return to the house.

Ada cautiously opened the back-door and slipped into the scullery, putting down the bucket as quietly as it was possible to place a metal object onto a hard stone floor. She opened the door into the living room to reveal a daunting rear-view of the two officers. The stale smell of tobacco oozed from their clothes. She looked around, satisfying herself that Ben was not present, and squeezed past them on her way to the hall door. Once out of sight, she flew up the stairs to peer from the window, but still Ben was nowhere to be seen. Within minutes she was summoned.

"We are here to investigate the apparent disappearance of Eli Turner." Both officers faced her, both of them large in height and girth. The one speaking was the stranger. He wore a cape which made him look huge and a pork-pie hat sat on his head. Ada thought how rude it was for a gentleman to keep his hat on whilst inside someone's house. He had a thick black moustache, which hung low at the sides of his mouth. It looked false, as if someone has stuck it into place. Both officers were turned towards her, their eyes boring into hers. She was intimidated and felt herself shrink away from them.

A long pause hovered until the sergeant leaned forwards about to speak, but the back door swung open and Ben strode in. He looked towards Mr Ludlam for guidance. "Beg pardon, Sir, but I were in the lower meadow when I saw em arrive in the cart." He turned to the officers. "Have you found him, where is he?" His fists were clenched and his eyes like those of a rabbit in a trap.

"Alright Ben," Mr Ludlam spoke sharply, "come in and sit down. The police officers are having a few words with Ada."

They turned back towards her, the uniformed officer continuing with the questioning. "Do you know where Eli Turner is living?"

"No Sir," answered Ada, unflinching.

The moustache took over. "I want you all to think very carefully. It may be that we're dealing with a serious crime, so it is most important that you tell us anything you know about the missing man." He raised his eyebrows, which were equally as black and shiny as the growth on his upper lip. "If we can't find any evidence of his whereabouts we'll have no choice but to treat this case as suspected murder."

"He's not dead, I saw him," Ada blurted out, her face turning to crimson, "he was at the railway station in Leicester." She glanced across at Mr Ludlam, before continuing. Hardly able to believe what she was saying, the words fairly tumbled from her mouth. "The platform was crowded and so I couldn't see where he went."

She felt again the panic on seeing the red-spotted kerchief around the neck of the tall dark-haired young man, but there had been no time to check that it was in fact him and she had not felt inclined to lessen the distance between them. The truth of the matter was that, at the time, her head had been too full of the harvest supper and Ben.

"What were you doing at the railway station?" The moustache enquired.

"Seeing my mother and father off, the last time we visited my sister. She lives in town."

"You didn't mention seeing him before," Mr Ludlam remarked.

"No Sir, it slipped my mind. There had been so much going on, what with saying goodbye to my family and the harvest supper." She lowered her eyes, cheeks burning, feeling Ben's eyes on her.

Mr Ludlam's voice rolled through the room. "Are you quite sure it was Eli who you saw?"

The words filled the space and Ada could hear a pounding in her head. She stayed stubbornly resolute, smothering the questionability of her sighting. Even the honesty emanating from this God-fearing, upright man whom Ada trusted completely, was not enough to change her response. She had, at all costs, to protect Ben.

"Yes Sir, I am quite sure."

"Very well, gentleman, there is your answer."

Chapter 16

Christmas

A bitter north wind was blowing, taking anything and everything in its path, but there was still one last Christmas order lying homeless in the trap. Ada had placed her shawl over her head, squashing her hat, anything to protect against the cold. She steered the horse into the inn yard, appreciating a modicum of shelter from the wind. If it snowed tonight, there would be drifts by morning. She tied Homer to the post nearest to the inn's back door and braced herself.

The air inside was choking. Not only was it thick with fumes from pipe tobacco, but huge clouds of black smoke were gusting out from the inglenook chimney. The Landlord looked across at Ada and ceased his pumping, setting the huge bellows aside. His attempts at stemming the backdraught had been unsuccessful.

"Good, you've brought the Christmas order!"

Ada made no move to go back outside to collect it, but instead walked over to where he knelt on the stone hearth and held out a crisp new brown envelope, thinking that, taking into account the dirt on his fingers, it wouldn't be spotless for long.

"Here's your bill, Mr Dennis, I'll just wait while you settle it, then I'll bring in the bread."

Even on his knees, the landlord's eyes were almost on a level with hers. They faced each other, the big red-haired man and the small girl with her hand outstretched and a defiant gleam in her eye.

Ada suffered a sudden feeling of unease. She looked around, but once assured that Eli was not among the motley band of drinkers, nodded at the sea of expectant faces all turned towards her, waiting with interest for the next move. She glanced with disgust at the ceiling and walls, covered in dark brown tobacco stains. Mother and Father would ever have allowed the Elephant to reach such a state, and she wondered how clean would be the hands that sliced the bread.

The landlord climbed somewhat awkwardly to his feet and took the envelope, tearing it open as he sauntered over to the money draw. He selected various coins. Ada took them from him and counted them.

"Thank you Sir, I'll fetch your bread." There was no Christmas tip included in the payment.

Ada struggled to manoeuvre the large wicker tray through the doorway. The young woman from the harvest supper, the one who had enquired after Eli stood watching, loitering, as if to speak. She stopped in her tracks at a bellowing from the landlord. "Wife, are you there? Go and help the girl with the bread." He sneered, "The flibbertigibbet looks as if she'll struggle to carry it on her own." A snigger went around the room, but the customers soon lost interest and returned to their business. Ada would have liked to confront him and ask, who did he think he was, calling her names, but she was feeling distinctly vulnerable, surrounded by him and his motley clientele, so swallowed her pride and continued with her task.

The woman's cleavage showed well below her neckline and her hair was untidy. She looked as if a good scrub in the bath-tub was long overdue. She hovered, turning to Ada, but the voice from the bar roared forth once more, "It's taking you long enough. What are you doing, making it?" The woman lowered her eyes and laughed, showing a row of uneven, yellowing teeth, but she took hold of one end of the bread tray.

Ada was more than a little relieved on hearing the inn's back door close behind her. At last she was finished and it was Christmas Eve. The wind had dropped. All along the road blinds were being pulled and lamps lit, and having successfully manoeuvred Homer through the farm gate, she pulled to a standstill.

There was a holly-wreath hanging on the back door of Mill House. Ben strode across from the cow-shed, a sack-bag clutched around his shoulders. He called out to her as she reached up for the empty baskets, "I'll see to those. Go and warm yourself, its fit to freeze you out here. We've been wondering how you were doing."

"Ta, Ben," uttered a grateful Ada.

She smelled the sweet aroma of roasting chestnuts just seconds before registering the smiling faces around the table and the sprigs of holly strewn on the dressers and ledged on top of pictures. Ada began to feel as if Christmas had arrived.

Pulling off her mittens, she made straight for the fire and, leaning over the guard, stretched out her hands. The coins in her pocket moved against her thigh. Those were hers to keep, but she eased the leather strap from around her neck and handed the money bag to Mrs Ludlam. "It's all there. Even the people at the public house have settled their bill."

"Oh, well done, Ada," chorused the Ludlams. Ada was so grateful that her day's work was over, she couldn't be bothered to explain her triumph and how she'd stood her ground against the landlord. She finally moved away from the fire and removed the shawl, taking her place at the table where Missy was trying to teach Allen how to make a paper chain.

The tea warmed Ada. "Has Dolly gone home?" she asked.

"Yes, Mr Ludlam thinks it will snow, so we let her go early. It's quite a step up to the alms houses and I didn't want to have to ask you to take her in the trap. It's better if you're not alone with her."

"She'll be back here tomorrow, though?" asked Ada.

"Yes. She'll come back home with us after church and have her Christmas dinner here."

Ada looked around. "The room does look festive. It's been a good year for holly berries."

"It's just started to snow," called Ben from the scullery, his head just visible around the door."

He held a hand up to his ear as he tip-toed across the floor in just his stocking feet, and said, "Listen, everyone!"

Through the door came the sounds of the church choir:-

"It came upon a midnight clear, that glorious song of old, with angels bending near the earth to touch their harps of gold."

Mrs Ludlam jumped up and flung open the back door, before returning to place a plate of mince-pies and a dish of peeled chestnuts on the table, whilst her husband searched for the corkscrew and opened a large grey-hen full of elderberry wine.

§

Ada pulled back the drapes from the window. Dawn was breaking, but there was enough light for her to see the whole world blanketed in snow. She could almost feel it, cold and soft between her fingers. Wrapping the shawl around her shoulders she stepped out into the corridor. From there she had a perfect view of the church tower with its conical top rising sternly from a white counterpane.

Already candles and lamps could be seen peeping from windows. Two sets of footprints crossed the yard to the cowshed and light from the hurricane lamp spilled out onto the snow, making it sparkle like silver. Ada wondered if the cows would sense the importance of today.

She shivered and went back into her room to light a candle. Despite the room being above the bakery, it was now freezing cold. Back at the Elephant, she would have dressed downstairs in front of the living room fire, along with the rest of the family.

There was a goose to cook and a plum pudding sitting in its basin, waiting for the big saucepan to be filled with boiling water from the kettle. It wouldn't steam itself, so Ada hurriedly pulled on her Sunday dress and splashed her face with cold water. Holding the flannel with both hands, she wiped the sleep from her

THE LATE ELEPHANT

face, pausing to think of home and whether or not Jarvis would be awake and anxious to see what was in his Christmas stocking.

The house was quiet. Ada saw that Mr Ludlam had already made up the fire in the living room. Two stockings still hung undisturbed from the mantle-shelf and Ada set the kettle to boil, bringing in the milk jug and butter from the larder and setting out the cups and saucers.

There would be no cooking of breakfast today. Ada had no idea who it was that decided women had enough to do to cook dinner on Christmas day, without the added workload of breakfast, but Ada felt they deserved some sort of beatitude. Cold ham, together with Ada's second attempt at a pork pie, sat ready on the thrawl. It was wonderful not having to dash into the bakery and light the fire in the bread-oven and Ada relaxed, eager to begin.

On hearing the first foot-fall from the top step of the staircase, Ada opened the hall door to call out, "Merry Christmas."

"Merry Christmas to you too, Ada," called back Mrs Ludlam, "is the kettle on?"

"Not only is it on, but the tea is mashed and poured."

A cold draught caused the door to swing open as the men returned from milking and at the same time a clattering could be heared from upstairs, announced the impending arrival of Missy and Allen. Mrs Ludlam followed in hot pursuit and lifted down the stockings, to hand them to the children, before announcing, "Good! In that case, I'll fetch the rum from the pantry. We always take a drop of rum in our tea on Christmas morning, isn't that so, Mr Ludlam?"

Chapter 17

Fullbrook 1892

"Oh, there you are. I didn't realize you were home." Bess stood over Billy whilst he milked the goat. "I need to speak to you."

Without pausing to look up he asked, "What about?"

Bess shivered against the cold of a March morning. "Now we're settled, I've agreed to go down to The Manor, just in the mornings, and give Mrs Stevenson a hand."

The silence hung between them like a stone wall. Bess could have cut the atmosphere with a knife.

"What yer mean is that yer've been and flippin' asked for a job as a skivvy." He paused just long enough for his face to turn scarlet. Then he yelled at her. "I'll not have a wife o mine reduce herself to a char-woman, when there's no flippin' need. I can provide well enough for us. When do yer ever floppin' go without? Aye, answer me that."

The terrified goat jumped and kicked the bucket. Billy caught it before it went over, slamming it back in place on the brick floor of the shed.

THE LATE ELEPHANT

Bess stayed outwardly calm, even though she was shaken at his passionate objection. "Of course you provide well, it's nowt to do with that. I need the company. You're out all day in the fields and Jarvis spends most of his time round at Violet's. The silence is beginning to drive me mad."

Billy tried replacing the bucket, but the nanny-goat backed away, baying at him in fear. Bess tried again. "It's not hard work and I'll be home just after mid-day, in plenty of time to see to the doings here. It's only three mornings, just to keep the silver and the brasses cleaned and maybe do a bit of cooking."

Billy stood up, stool in one hand and bucket in the other. "Leave me be, woman." Without even a glance, he walked back towards the cottage. He paused, just long enough to incline his head and hiss out the words, "You disappoint me."

Bess was shaken. She hadn't anticipated this level of anger. She found the milking bucket in the sink and the stool back in its corner. Billy was sitting by the fire in the living room, lighting his pipe, his back turned towards her. Bess tutted.

"And stop flippin' well tutting at me," he shouted.

A knock on the door and John Booton's voice called out. "Are yer there, Mrs Elverson?"

"Coming, Mr Booton."

"There yer are, Mrs Elverson," he said, handing Bess a letter, "I thought yer would want to read it straight away. It's from your Ada, I'll bet a pound to a penny."

Bess took the letter from him. "Yes, I dare say it is. I'll have to find the glass before I can read it."

"Come on in John and have a bevvy."

Bess could feel Billy's hot breath on the back of her neck. He stepped past her, offering a hand to his friend. "Good on yer to bring it all the way up the hill."

Bess smiled. "Go and show him the hens, Billy, I'll pour the beer."

The two disappeared into the garden, comparing notes on rearing livestock. Bess took refuge in the cupboard, removing tankards and opening the cake tin, knowing full well that the arrival of the postmaster had saved the day. Hopefully Billy would soon be over his strop and then perhaps he would see that a few shillings a week extra would make all the difference, especially if George and Nelly were to wed. As Nelly didn't have any family, they could both end up back at Swepstone. Bess wanted George out of the army and safely home again and as she had taken a shine to his young lady, was looking forward to teaching her to cook.

Bess filled the tankards from the barrel in the scullery, but before delivering them to the top of the garden, she filled the sink with cold water and immersed the bucket containing the goat's milk. The lady at The Hall would be sending a lad to collect it shortly, and it needed to be cool and fresh for the baby.

§

Ada had spent the first half-hour in the bakery with Ben. He had turned out to be an able student. She left him to complete a composition before joining the family around the table. She slid The Girls' Own Annual over the chenille cloth, guiding it in the direction of her mistress. "Pardon me, Ma'am, but I would like to make this. It would be a lovely Mothering Sunday gift. Do you think I'll be able to manage it?"

Mrs Ludlam moved her magnifying glass from the accounts book to study the pattern of a short cape. "I don't see why not. It appears fairly simple, it's just a circle. Are you good at sewing?"

Ada grinned. "Afraid not, although we did learn to sew at school and like you say, it seems simple enough, except for the scalloping around the edges."

"I can help with that. We could draw round something, a saucer, perhaps. Sewing is not my best subject either. Needles have a mind of their own, I find."

Ada caught sight of Mr Ludlam, a grin playing about his lips, before disappearing once more behind his newspaper. His wife noticed and colour crept into her cheeks. She laughed. "Mr Ludlam does have the odd grumble when my darning goes haywire and the lump in his sock makes a worse impression on his foot than the hole I've tried to repair."

He laughed heartily. "Well my dear, you can't be good at everything and as your cooking skills are legendary, I feel you can be forgiven." He jumped up, hitting his head on the lamp, which had been lowered to give optimum illumination to those usefully employed around the table. Rubbing his head, he walked around to where Ada's book lay and stood between the two women, studying the pattern. He leaned down to look more closely, spectacles balancing precariously. "You'll manage that between you. I'll calculate the circle and make a pattern from an old newspaper, if you like." Turning to his wife, he added, "We could do with a visit from the scissor-grinder."

"Yes," she replied, "I was thinking that only the other day. He hasn't been round for a while."

She turned back towards Ada. "What fabric will you use?"

"I thought velvet would look smart."

Mrs Ludlam pondered. "You're right it would, but a good quality woollen material would be warmer. I have an old cloak upstairs, it's made of cashmere. There should be enough there to make a lining and if you interline with something else fairly substantial, it will protect her from the cold."

Ada pledged to make a visit to the haberdashers in the village.

§

Dear Mother and Father,

I am writing to tell you that I shall be arriving on Saturday afternoon, whenever the stage leaves Ashby for Swepstone. Jess and William will arrive on Sunday in time for dinner and will stay overnight. William is needed at the tan-yard on Monday, but Jess and I will catch the train from Ashby.

I can't tell you how I am looking forward to seeing you both.

I am sorry I'll miss George and Nelly and am thrilled at the news. It looks and sounds serious. We'll discuss it on Sunday. Don't go to the trouble of making bread, I will bring some with me.

I would like to visit Grandma Elverson if that is possible. Perhaps Father and I could walk to Measham after Church on Sunday. We could be back before dinner.

Your loving daughter,

Ada

§

The bitter waft of a March wind brushed Ada's bared arms as she pegged the wet sheets onto the clothes-line. Dolly was at home nursing a feverish chill, and Ada was dealing with the extra chores. Her hands were so cold she could hardly feel their soreness. However, Mothering Sunday was only days away and she refused to allow anything to distract her from the excitement. She could hardly wait to see the family again and with luck, a sighting of Duncan.

The cape was ready. Night after night, she had spent stitching beneath the oil lamp. In the end she'd taken Mrs Ludlam's advice and selected good-quality black worsted, lined it with cashmere and used flannel for the inter-facing. It would protect Mother's shoulders from the chill and the layers had given just enough thickness to make it suitable for quilting. Ada was thrilled with it. When she spread it flat out on the table, it looked like a black sea-shell. It was finished off with plaited velvet ties and a small stand-up collar, perfect for church.

The weak glow of a winter sun was fast melting the snow. Ada deliberated on how quickly Monday mornings came around. There actually seemed to be more of those than any other days in the week. Some late snowdrops were still in bloom and catkins jiggled playfully from the hedges. If one looked closely enough, just the merest hint of pale green shoots were visible on the long slender boughs of the willow. She could hear the water. Fullbrook was living up to its name, cavorting at high speed through the valley, carrying along all manner of rural detritus. Twigs, dead leaves, birds' nests, anything which hadn't the strength to resist were carried towards the weir.

Her observations were interrupted by the furious barking of the dog. There was certainly urgency in the animal's yelping. She watched Mr Ludlam race across the field, closely followed by Ben.

Mrs Ludlam came out to see what all the fuss was about. "What a pandemonium. That dog gets so over-excited. I hope it isn't just a rabbit he is trying to put out. Mr Ludlam will not be well pleased."

The commotion was coming from the other side of the mill, just a few yards downstream. Ada shaded her eyes from the sun, hanging low in the sky. "There's a lot of shouting going on, but it's too far away to hear what they're saying." She spotted Ben hurtling back towards them, and knew when he broke through the hedge, instead of using the road, that something serious was afoot. He certainly needed to come back in a hurry, perhaps one of the cows had wandered too close to the edge and was stuck in the mud.

Ben was winded by the time he reached the house and bent almost double, his face ashen. He gasped, "We've found Eli! In the brook! Mr Ludlam says can we have something to cover him?"

"Did you say Eli?" asked Mrs Ludlam, tentatively. "Is he alright?"

Ben straightened up and looked at Ada. "He's dead.

It's horrible. He's been in there for some time."

"Are you sure it's Eli?" blurted out Ada, unable to believe it.

"Yes, he's wearing the red scarf, and his boots with the black laces." Ben fell to his knees, gasping. "Please, fetch a blanket."

Mrs Ludlam flew into action, running hell-for-leather towards the house, while Ada comforted Ben. She put an arm around him. "Take your time. That must have been a terrible shock," she said, giving his shoulders a squeeze. "It'll be sorted out now and don't worry, I won't let them do anything bad to you." He turned his eyes towards her, about to speak, but Mrs Ludlam came out carrying the blanket and his words remained unsaid. Ben climbed to his feet, leaving Ada to watch as he headed back down the hill, slipping and sliding over the wet grass, back towards Fullbrook.

Mr Ludlam left Ben to keep guard over the body whilst he headed for the post office to send a telegraph message to the police. Ada knew the moment of truth was imminent. She closed her eyes and prayed to God. Among her supplications she gave thanks that Eli's mother hadn't been present to witness this.

The women, with shawls clutched around their shoulders, waited outside for the black horse-drawn hearse to arrive. It seemed to take for ever, but it didn't seem right to close the door on a dead man.

§

For two days and nights the rains fell. It was so unrelenting that Ada didn't even attempt a visit to the post office in order to post her letters. In fact, she didn't have the heart to write any, let alone post them. She had only managed the briefest of notes to her mother and father, saying how much she was looking forward to her visit and Mr Ludlam would post that for her when he collected his newspaper.

Eventually, after hours of worry, the same two policemen returned and Ada became fuelled with determination that Ben would stay a free man. They sat at the table and Ada busied herself making tea and offering round pastries. The officers announced that an autopsy had been carried out on Eli's body. Mrs Ludlam explained to Ada what that actually meant. Ada's stomach began to churn at the thought. As usual, the presence of the policemen dominated the space, thrusting the gathering into a depressive gloom. Ada was pleased to see that they had both removed their hats. However, moustache set his on the table next to the teapot. Despite sending the tea-strainer flying onto the floor, he didn't reposition it and it was, therefore, in the way of Ada pouring the tea. The officer in uniform had a red mark all the way round his forehead, where his helmet had sat. Ada thought how uncomfortable it must be for him.

The dimensions of the room appeared to decrease in size and she was finding it difficult to breathe. It had been two full days of waiting and wondering and the tension had built. Mr Ludlam entered with Ben, who stood, as usual, with fists clenched and head bowed. Ada thought he looked like a man condemned.

The moustache, with the hair on his head just as dark and thick as that on his face, slurped half the contents of the tea-cup, before wiping away the surplus with the back of his hand. "I've come with some disturbing news." His voice boomed out, filling the suffocating stillness with trepidation. "We're treating Eli Turner's death as murder." He paused for effect and Ada froze as she watched the officer scan the faces of each member of the household, before first turning towards Ben. "Now then young man, I want you to tell me everything you know about the activities of the deceased."

Ada's eyes were glued to Ben's face, but his only reaction was to tighten his lips even closer. "I don't know anything, Sir."

"I understand, from your employer here, that you and Eli shared, not only employment, but a room. Is that true?"

"Yes Sir." Ben still didn't move, apart from a muscle just under his left eye, which gave an intermittent twitch.

"Do you mean to tell me that he did not discuss his comings and goings with you?"

"No Sir."

The officer persisted. "Apparently, he was given to bragging about certain exploits, some concerning ladies. I find it hard to believe that he would waste an opportunity to tell you about them."

At last Ben raised his head just enough to send a searing glance towards his interrogator. "He bragged about having been with women, mostly married, but I didn't believe the half of it and I didn't know any of em. I can't speak about folk I don't know."

After a brief smoothing of his moustache, the officer resumed. "I understand that, but it will help us if you can shed further light on the situation."

"Look, officer," Mr Ludlam challenged, "Ben is not one to speak ill of people and I think it wrong to try to force him. After all, it would be 'hearsay', surely and that's not allowed in court, or so I believe."

"Indeed!" The Moustache stood up, stretching his shoulders back, taking full advantage of his size and looked sternly back at Mr Ludlam. Ada thought how tired he looked and wondered just exactly what his work would entail, when faced with a situation like this. Then, turning abruptly, towards her, he said, "And you, young lady. Is there anything you would like to tell us?"

Ada's eyes flashed backwards and forwards between them. "No, Sir." She answered abruptly.

"Did he pay you attention, a good looking girl like you? Was he sweet on you, young lady?"

Ada froze to the spot. "I didn't like him particularly, so I kept away from him."

"Is that so?"

"Yes, Sir." Her knees were threatening to give way. She couldn't stand much more, but concentrated on keeping her chin down, although the marks had faded long ago.

Mr Ludlam said, "Ada had only been with us for a week when Eli disappeared. She hardly knew him at all."

"Very well!" After sharing a knowing look and a nod, the two officers rose abruptly to their feet and after replacing their hats, the senior officer announced, "I ask you to think long and hard in case there's anything you've forgotten. The Sergeant here lives close by, so you can inform him, should you think of something, and I would appreciate it if you will all stay within easy reach of the farm. I may need to contact you again."

He cast his eyes around the circle, and Ada felt her heart skip a beat. "Please, Sir, I'm to visit my family next week."

"Where is your home?"

THE LATE ELEPHANT

"Swepstone Sir, it's near Ashby-de-la-Zouch, and it's Mothering Sunday."

"I'm quite aware of what day it is, but I ask you again to stay here for the time being. I may need to speak with you urgently." He stood looking straight at Ada and her eyes opened wide and her disappointment grew, as she heard the words, "I'm not at all sure you understand the seriousness of this matter, Miss. A man has been murdered!"

The door closed behind them.

"Ada." Mr Ludlam pulled an envelope from his inside pocket. "This came for you yesterday, with all the fuss I forgot to give it to you."

It was a letter from home. Ada took it from his hand and, without bothering to look for a knife, tore the envelope open, hungry for news from home, desperate for anything which would give her comfort. The letter read:-

Dear Ada,

I am very sorry to tell you that Grandma Elverson passed peacefully away on Friday night. She died in her sleep but appeared most comfortable.

I know this will be a shock for you, but she was ninety two years old, and had lived a good life. She would have been the first one to tell you that.

Father and I don't see the need for you to come all this way to the funeral and know that you will hold her in your thoughts, as we do you. When you come to us next week, we will go together and put some flowers on her grave.

Much love and best wishes,

From Mother and Father Elverson.

§

Ada cringed under the eyes of the postmaster, as he appraised her body from beneath lidded eyes, his mouth visibly salivating. She shuddered and escaped out onto the road. Ada walked away, gratefully inhaling the smell of clean, fresh earth after the downpour. She had sent the cape to Swepstone by parcel post, together with a postal order for five shillings and a letter blaming the change of plan on a sudden and unexpected occurrence. She simply couldn't put into words what had happened.

The rain had stopped and as she drew nearer the square, a ray of sunshine broke through the clouds, warming the puddles, as Grandma would have said. Ada felt a sudden yearning for a hug from Grandma. She recalled the smell of coffee and moth-balls and wondered if she was indeed walking beside her.

There was no possibility of seeing either her family or Duncan in the foreseeable future. With all of that, plus missing Grandma's funeral and being cheated out of the Mothering Sunday roast dinner, there wasn't much to feel happy about. She would have to make the most of giving Mrs Ludlam the scarf she had purchased from a shop in the village and although she truly admired her mistress, it simply could not compare with going home. Ada was suffering a headache, something to which she wasn't prone, but the constant pressure had been too much. Conversation had all but dried up at Mill House with no-one inclined to talk just for the sake of it.

Ada crossed the road, closing the shop door behind her, struggling to collapse the umbrella. Even a visit to Mr Heames couldn't managed to bring a smile to Ada's lips, so after only spending one shilling and sixpence on a new tin of toothpaste and being too despondent to respond to grocer's polite chatter, she hastily withdrew.

The rain had stopped for the moment and Ada crossed the road, trying to avoid the piles of sludge brought along by the torrents of rain and made her way back to Mill House. She wondered why William hadn't called, particularly since Grandma's death. It wasn't like him not to come and explain and tell her about the funeral. She wondered if he was aware of Eli's murder. It had been reported in the Leicester Mercury, so she supposed he must know.

What concerned her most was the possibility of Ben being arrested. If it did happen, she would be compelled to go to court and tell the story of Eli's attack and how Ben rescued her. She broke out into a cold sweat every time she thought about it, but the prospect wouldn't go away. She imagined herself giving evidence, facing a huge courtroom full of people, mostly men and strangers and her stomach began to churn.

Ada imagined Ben in the dock. He wouldn't stand a chance against his inquisitors. She walked along the street into Kirby Road with a heavy heart. There were two carriages parked on the road outside the church and the rain began to fall once more. The horses stood, looking as dejected as Ada felt. There was obviously a wedding in progress as white ribbons were in evidence on the horses bridles, but they were sadly flattened and dripping.

It started to rain and again Ada struggled with the umbrella, but on finally managing to unfasten it, she saw the church door open and the wedding couple sprint to the waiting vehicle. The bride was holding onto her hat and the groom tried to shield her by holding a newspaper over her head. Ada noted the bride's fashionable blue outfit with a hat, piled high with satin flowers, and thought how stylish it looked.

Despite the dreariness of the weather, the couple laughed and waved to her as she stood back, allowing them to pass. The rest of the party was equally merry and Ada grinned back and wished them well. It seemed that, despite her anguish, life was going on just the same as always, leaving her behind, cold, wet and forsaken, so she decided to return to the bakery and set about cleaning the cutlery. It was one of the most boring jobs on earth, but an excellent way to deal with frustration.

§

Dearest Ada,

You must be devastated at missing both Grandma's funeral and Mothering Sunday. Mother was most upset to think of you unable to share either family occasion, but she was thrilled with the cape. How clever of you, I didn't realize you were so good at sewing.

Mother is working for Mrs Stevenson at The Manor. It is just three mornings a week. Father is not happy about it. You know how he prides himself at being a good provider, but Mother has stuck to her guns and is enjoying the company.

William has been unable to visit you at Mill House, as he spends more and more time doing business with the automobile gentlemen from Coventry, so I thought a word or two from me, explaining the latest doings would be welcome.

The funeral went well. It was at Measham Church, of course, and Grandma is laid to rest in the churchyard there. You will be able to visit when next you are in Swepstone, and you know in your heart that she would understand your position.

Mother tells me that the young curate has left, and Rev. Townend is once more back in sole charge. I think they were sorry to see him go, he was a pleasant fellow.

Now, dear sister, I have something really special to share with you. I am in the family way. We are to have a baby, the expected arrival some six months from now. William is so excited, he can hardly contain himself. I am pleased, of course, but feel nauseous most of the time, and can go to sleep at the drop of a hat.

William has arranged for a woman to come and help in the house. She attends to the washing on a Monday and returns on a Tuesday to iron it. It is a great relief.

If we have a girl, I would like to call her Elizabeth after Mother. If it is a boy, we can't agree on a name. I would like to call him after his father, but William says there are already too many Williams in the family, so we shall have to wait and see. I miss you, Ada, do try to come and see us soon, and we will go together into Leicester to visit the shops. I love the big stores, Marshall and Snelgrove in particular, and I think you would too. It is a much nicer experience if there is someone to share it with, and I want you to see the owls. They nest in Victoria Park, which is quite close by, and they fly around at night. It's a beautiful sight.

The next thing is a little delicate, but I can't help but mention the murder at Glenfield. It read, in the Leicester Mercury, that the victim worked as a mill-hand and lived at Mill House, and if this is correct, then you must know him. William thinks he must be the son of a lady we met on the train going to Skegness. He says there are two young men working there but doesn't know which one he is. I so hope this has not caused you and Mr and Mrs Ludlam any particular worry, although you must be upset if you knew him. I hope for all your sakes that it is resolved soon.

Your loving sister,
Jess x

§

Mothering Sunday had come and gone, and although they had all put on a brave face and been more polite to each other than ever, it had been a bitter disappointment to Ada.

Mr and Mrs Ludlam went together to Dolly's house to break the news, but there had as yet been no further word from the police.

This morning Ada had received two letters, one from Mother and one from Jess. It turned out that William was still spending much of his time in Coventry, discussing the possibilities of supplying the new automobile trade with leather. Ada hadn't seen an automobile and didn't think too much about them. Mr

THE LATE ELEPHANT

Ludlam showed an interest, discussing with Ben details gleaned from articles in the newspaper, but he said they had a long way to go yet, before anyone in Glenfield would witness one driving through the village.

Dolly had returned to work. She had lost her sparkle and was coughing constantly. It was raining cats and dogs again, so Ada had rigged up some lines inside the bakery, and hung the washing there. It meant everyone had to bend their heads to get near to the pantry where the flour was kept, but it was a case of, 'needs must'.

"Oh good girl, Ada." Mrs Ludlam came bustling past. "You've finished cleaning the floor. We'll get straight on making the dough, and later perhaps, some of the washing will be dry enough to iron."

No sooner had the words been uttered, than a banging on the back door resonated throughout. It was the police. Ada heard the voice, "Will you fetch young Ben, please and Mr Ludlam. We need you all together." His voice boomed like a cannon through the house and Ada's heart sank to her boots.

"What's going on Missus, is it about Eli?" Dolly stood at the door, her face as grey as the blanket hanging on the line. Mrs Ludlam looked across at Ada and shrugged. What else could she do but allow her to stay. The three women wiped their hands on their aprons and Ada followed Dolly into the living room, wondering what on earth the poor woman was to hear.

There was no need to go in search of the men. They could already be seen striding towards the house, sack bags over their shoulders against the rain. Ben's eyes looked like those of a scared rabbit, but his jaw remained strong and unyielding. He had been constantly railed by Dolly's questioning about Eli, but had stayed calm, explaining that he and Eli really didn't see that much of each other outside of work. Ada felt so sorry for him. Seeing the look on the faces of the police, Ada thought, this is it, time now for the truth.

Mr Ludlam didn't appear too much in control, his face was thunderous. Ada wondered what he was thinking. Mrs Ludlam ushered the officers inside. Once they'd wiped the rain from their eyes, the senior officer began. "Is there anything else you wish to add regarding the murder of Eli Turner?" He looked firstly at Ben, who shook his head. Just for once, Ada noticed, Ben didn't have his head down, but looked straight in to the eyes of his interrogator. The man asked Ada the same question, she simply replied, "No, Sir."

"Are you sure about that, because the person you saw at the railway station was certainly not Eli Turner. Why did you tell us it was?"

Ada felt the colour flood her cheeks. She looked back at him in horror, "I was sure it was, Sir. He had a red kerchief just like the one Eli wore."

Everyone's eyes were on her. Ada's bottom lip began to tremble.

The officer seemed to contemplate what to say next, smoothing down his moustache before continuing, "Very well, I have come out of courtesy to inform you of a serious development."

He took his eyes from Ada and addressed the whole assembly. Ada pushed a lock of hair back under her mob-cap, rubbed her poor sore hands together and waited with baited breath, expecting the worst. She glanced across at Dolly and noticed her pallor.

"I feel it expedient to inform you that, earlier today, we arrested a man for the murder of Eli Turner."

There were audible gasps.

"You did?" gulped Ada.

The officer addressed Dolly, who had buried her face in her pinafore. Ada could see her shoulders shaking with silent sobs. The policeman placed a hand on her shoulder. "I'm sorry that you have to hear this, but the truth has to be told. Apparently the deceased had been keeping company with a married woman. The husband discovered them together and took his revenge."

He turned to Ben. "You must have known about this affair. I was hoping that you would name the woman involved."

Ben stayed resolute. "I'm sorry, but he mentioned that many, I can't remember. In the end it went in at one ear and out of the other." He glanced at Dolly, but although she had lowered the pinafore, her eyes remained glued to the floor and Ada could see a tear rolling down her cheek.

Ada sank down onto a stool and put her head in her hands. Mrs Ludlam gave her a reassuring squeeze and crossed the room to Dolly. At last the nightmare was over.

"How do you know it was this man, inspector?" queried Mr Ludlam.

"He's admitted it. We have a signed confession." He turned back to Ben. "So you won't be needed to give evidence."

Mrs Ludlam laid a hand on Dolly's shoulder. "It's alright, Missus," Dolly said, "I know he liked the ladies. I told him many a time, he'd get into trouble." She let out a sob. "But I never thought it would end like this." She blew loudly into a large handkerchief and asked, "Who was it who did it? Was it the chap from the pub down the road?"

"Yes, it was. Why, do you know him?"

"No, I don't know him at all, but I heard the gossip, yer know, that his wife were sweet on our Eli."

Ada stood with her mouth open, dumbfounded, hardly able to believe her ears. She watched in shock as the officers replaced their hats and the sergeant fastened his chin-strap. It was only when the vehicle trundled across the farm yard and out of the gate that she dare take look across at the other equally astounded faces and admit to herself that she had been face to face with Eli's killer.

Soon, she thought, very soon now, I will go home.

Chapter 18

Master Henry 1894

"Now, Ada," began Mrs Ludlam, "you've come to the end of your apprenticeship. When you first came to us I promised in your debentures, to teach you how to bake bread and how to make pastries and cakes, so after your time was served you would be a competent baker and a plain pastry cook. I have also endeavoured to instruct you in the basics of all other aspects of cooking, from main meals to puddings and any other knowledge I had to offer. You never know what the future may hold. You may need, at some point, to take up another position." She paused, and Ada nodded, anxious for her employer to continue. "I personally need to be certain that you are satisfied with your training."

"Oh, goodness me yes. Thank you, Ma'am," replied Ada, "you've done that and more. I've found my time here most satisfactory."

Mrs Ludlam nodded. "Good. It's what your father wanted and it's what we agreed. Now, Mr Ludlam and I thought eight shillings a week wages is fair, payable every three months, as we do with Ben."

Ada immersed herself in the moment. At only eighteen years old and taking into account that her board and lodgings were free, she was earning as much as some grown men.

Her face lit up. "That's most generous. I'll be able to send home to pay Father back."

"That's exactly what Mr Ludlam said you would do." She poured the tea.

"There's something else I keep meaning to talk to you about. In the linen room there's a trunk full of clothes. I can't vouch for the condition, but we can go through them if you like and you can take whatever you want. Shall we do it now?"

Ada couldn't believe her luck. "Yes please."

"Don't get too excited in case you don't like them. They came from the cook at The Gynsills. She was having a turn-out and asked if they would be of any use to me, so I told her yes. I could see no point in refusing. She said some of them belonged to her mistress, so they'll be good quality."

On the way upstairs, Mrs Ludlam asked, "How do you feel about staying on here with us? I wondered if you may want to spread your wings, now that you've qualified."

"Oh no, Ma'am, I love being here, it's like being at home. I miss my family, of course, but there's Allen and Missy and they're like family now." As a second thought, she added, "And you too, Ma'am, if you don't mind my saying so."

Sarah Ludlam patted Ada's arm. "I'm pleased you feel that way, but it'll not be long now before you find a nice young man and want to be married. What we should be doing is collecting things for your bottom drawer."

THE LATE ELEPHANT

Ada felt the colour rise to her cheeks as they dragged the trunk out onto the landing. "Look," said Mrs Ludlam handing a jacket to Ada, "this should fit you."

Ada tried it on, running into her bedroom to look at herself through the dressing table mirror. It fitted. There was a black hat with a brim, trimmed with a black ribbon. It was plain and simple and a little worn, but Ada liked it.

"Here, put this on." Mrs Ludlam passed over a straw boater. "That does look smart. Now," she said, struggling to her feet, rubbing her knee as she did so, "I think it's time I put the kettle on. You carry on looking."

Ada didn't like to say so, but she really didn't like the boater.

Back in the living room, Mrs Ludlam broached another subject. "I didn't mean to shock you earlier, mentioning marriage, but I just thought that perhaps you and Ben might make a match. He's certainly very fond of you."

Ada was uncomfortable with the conversation, not knowing quite how to change it, but this last remark brought forth a sharp answer. "Oh no, I could never marry Ben, Ma'am, it would be like marrying my brother. I mean, he's a good friend and I'll never forget how he rescued me, but I couldn't marry him. Do you see?"

"Yes of course, but have you never had a sweetheart? What about the letters from Charles?"

"Oh dear me, no! He tried to kiss me once. I was so vexed. Had it not been for the fact it was my sister's wedding day, I would most probably have hit him."

Mrs Ludlam put her head back and laughed uproariously at this. Ada set her eyes on the pattern of the cups and saucers on the table and watched closely as Mrs Ludlam poured the tea, but her thoughts were far away and she recalled Duncan's face and the special tingle she experienced when they were together. It enveloped her and she was overcome with a desperate need to share her memories.

"There was someone I did like very much." As soon as the words had escaped, Ada felt uneasy with them.

"Do you want to tell me about him?" The voice was gentle.

Ada's eyes took on a glow as she recalled their sharing breakfast on the morning of Jess's wedding. "He's much older than me, a friend of William's. I don't think he will ever take me seriously. He teases me, like Ben teases Missy."

"Age shouldn't make a difference. Mr Ludlam is ten years older than me."

Ada was surprised to hear this and it dawned on her that in fact it may be possible for her and Duncan to be together, now she was almost eighteen years old.

"I'm amazed to hear there's such a gap between you and Mr Ludlam. No-one would know you were older than him."

"It doesn't matter if they do because age is irrelevant in such matters. I tell you Ada don't ever give yourself to anyone who you don't truly love. Marriage brings its own tensions, especially when the babies arrive. It's then you need the support and understanding. I couldn't have survived it with anyone other than Alfred."

"You do seem most agreeable together." Ada sighed. "Mother and Father are the same. It must be wonderful, but if I can't be with Duncan, perhaps I will never feel that way about anyone else."

The Late Elephant

"Oh yes, you will and when it happens there'll be no doubts at all. You will know in your heart. If you're unsure, just imagine how you'll feel when he reaches out for you in bed, first thing in the morning." She sighed. "Don't let Eli and his bad behaviour destroy your life. Not all men are like him."

Ada bared her heart. "I still have nightmares about that night. If he'd removed my undergarments and exposed me, I don't know how I would ever be able to hold up my head or for that matter face another human being. Fortunately my cries were heard. I'll always be in Ben's debt, but I could never marry him." She wiped away a tear.

"How do you know when someone is telling you the truth? Not that Duncan actually said that much to me, but his behaviour indicated that he was more than just fond of me, yet he was doing the same thing with another, a great deal more, actually. Grandma said to look into his eyes to see the truth. Perhaps I only saw what I wanted to see."

"There are men who simply can't be faithful to just one woman, I'm afraid, but you'll find someone special, just you wait and see, and don't be in too much of a hurry. A good man is worth waiting for."

Mrs Ludlam jumped up. "Goodness gracious, I almost forgot." She walked over to the dresser and pulled a package from the drawer. "This is a gift from my husband and me with our sincere thanks for your hard work."

Ada pulled away the paper to reveal a copy of Miss Eliza Acton's book, 'Cooking for Private Families'. Ada was overjoyed. Sarah Ludlam laid a comforting hand on

Ada's before emptying the dregs into the slop's bowl and refilling the tea-cups.

The ticking of the clock filled the empty space until a piece of coal exploded into the fireplace, almost causing the women to jump from their skins.

"Talking about menfolk, we'd better make a start on dinner, otherwise I can think of two people who are going to be exceedingly grumpy.

"That's something else you should understand. Men are like babies. If they're cantankerous, feed them. It almost always succeeds in putting them in an agreeable frame of mind."

§

The latest contraction dissolved away, allowing some little time for recovery. Jess struggled to recall the occasion when Jarvis was born. Together with George and Ada, she had been taken off to Measham to stay with Grandma Elverson, so she was not present to witness any sounds from her mother. She could vaguely remember a shout coming from the bedroom when Ada arrived. She had only been six years old and her prime concern at the time was to see the baby be taken from the midwife's black bag.

The pain swept through her loins once more. Surely to God, this can't be right. There must be something the woman can do to help. That creature sitting on a chair at the foot of the bed, with eyes barely leaving the four knitting needles from which a grey sock was beginning to take shape, was meant to be helping.

"Can't you do something?" pleaded Jess.

"Afraid not, Mrs Chamberlain, it'll get worse afore it

gets better." Her cold eyes never left her knitting, and Jess despaired at this lack of communication from the grim-faced woman who was her only hope of escape from this purgatory of childbirth.

"Will you fetch my husband, please?" Jess was beside herself.

This time the woman stopped her knitting and looked across with an accusing stare. "Certainly not! This is no place for a man. Birthing is women's work."

Jess let out a yell. She felt as if her body was being torn in two. A rush of water gushed from between her legs, causing her to pull up her knees almost to her chin. The woman had moved. The chair was empty and for one dreadful moment Jess thought she had been abandoned, but gave an audible gasp when she saw her leaning over the bed. Jess felt the woman's hand on her thigh and was thankful that at last she had decided to join in the experience.

"One good push and it'll all be over!"

Jess filled her lungs and with every ounce of energy she could muster, gave it her all. The next thing she felt was a bundle of wet limbs slither from her body, slipping gently down between her thighs. Then silence.

The woman cut something with a large pair of scissors before holding up by the ankles what looked to Jess like a purple, freshly skinned rabbit. The woman slapped the tiny creature on the buttocks. Its mouth opened and a yell, loud enough to compete with that of his mother, announced the arrival of Henry Osman Chamberlain.

As the damp child lay fidgeting in Jess's arms, instinctively searching for her breast, she shed tears and audibly gave thanks to God for her healthy robust son.

After cleaning away the blood and changing the sheets, the woman covered her nakedness with a clean nightgown and called for William to come and meet his son and heir.

§

Ada was thrilled with the big city. It was her first time in Leicester and she was there alone. She had followed instructions and gone to the market. Ada loved the clattering and banging and the shouting from stallholders.

Inside the shopping bag lay the horse shoe, borrowed from the front door. It would make an adequate weapon if needed. William had warned about pick-pockets and her purse was tucked safely away. She would feel the movement on her thigh if anyone dared to try and steal from her.

There wasn't much time to linger, as the evening meal would shortly need attention, but Ada was captivated, enthralled by the busyness of the streets, and not only with traps and carriages to-ing and fro-ing, but with horse-drawn buses. They were such a clever idea, she thought, and William was right to warn her to look both ways before trying to cross the roads.

Barrow boys called out to the crowds and there were flower stalls everywhere. She was bewitched and, wearing her newly acquired jacket and hat, felt quite up to the occasion.

Inspired by a window-display of baby-clothes, Ada went inside, intent on purchasing a bonnet for her nephew. When she saw the lovely quilts and crocheted blankets, she wished she had more money to spend. Jess

THE LATE ELEPHANT

and William had converted the smallest bedroom into a nursery, and Ada wanted to buy something pretty to add to it. Jess had cleaned and polished the wooden cradle they had found in the loft and Ada had stood and rocked the baby, loving him more than she had known it possible to love anyone. The shop displayed cot-sized winceyette sheets which had been chain-stitched all around the edges and long nightdresses trimmed with broidery-anglais.

Ade deliberated on the items, but on counting her money, chose a bonnet as planned. She needed to leave enough money to purchase a bunch of violets for Jess. Ada had noticed her sister was finding it difficult to sit down and hadn't dared to enquire too closely as to what it was like to give birth, but she did feel a compulsion to give her something nice to compensate for the discomfort.

The shop next door sent out delicious aromas of coffee and ham boiled with cloves, smells reminiscent of home and Jess's wedding day and her last visit to Grandma's cottage. The sign over the door read, 'Simpkin and James'.

She was running short of time and the last stop was to the butcher's. William had directed her and in addition to her order of lamb chops, Ada was given a dozen links of venison sausages, freshly made that very morning, as a gift for Mrs Chamberlain.

"I always send my ladies sausages for their confinement. They don't take much cooking, you see, so when you have your hands full, so to speak," he paused here to grin at Ada, "it makes life just that little bit easier." He nodded his head. "And tell her congratulations from me and I trust mother and baby are doing well."

§

A brand new perambulator stood in the front hall, making it difficult to pass, especially with shopping bags, but William came clattering down the stairs, two at a time and with a huge smile on his face. He relieved Ada of her burden, and deposited the shopping on the living room table.

"What do you thing of the baby-carriage? I ordered it this morning and they have just delivered it."

Ada smiled at his enthusiasm. "It's wonderful William, young Henry will love it. Perhaps I can accompany Jess into town, when she is recovered. Maybe, if I ask her ever so nicely, she will allow me to take a turn at pushing?"

Ada placed the violets in a pot and took them upstairs for her sister, together with a glass of lemonade. The baby lay sleeping.

"Thank you Ada. You may pick him up if you like. By the feel of things it's nearly time for a feed."

Ada cradled the baby in her arms. She had never seen anything quite as beautiful or as perfect as this little fellow, who looked so much like his Grandfather Billy.

"Hello, little Henry, I'm your Aunt Ada."

The baby was fast asleep. Ada turned to her sister. "How was it, the birth? Was it as what you expected?"

"It was nothing to worry about. The memory has all but faded and when I look at him and see the pride in William's eyes, I know it was all worthwhile."

The child began to squirm in Ada's arms. He was

waking.

"He needs his napkin changing, Ada. Do you think you can manage that?"

"I'll try."

The huge linen square needed to be folded twice and then was still far too big for the tiny bottom, but between them they managed to secure it, and Ada was relieved to see that the one she had removed was only wet, not actually soiled. She could deal with wet.

Having suckled the baby, her sister was soon sleeping and Ada returned the little one to his crib to make herself useful downstairs. The place was remarkably well-ordered, considering Jess had given birth only two days ago. Apparently the washer-woman was competent and easy-going and had been only too pleased to do extra hours to help out. She had been there when Ada arrived and Ada had been impressed by her smart appearance and friendly manner. They referred to her as Mary, as she had requested.

"What would you like me to do?" Ada enquired of William, before embarking on making a cake and cooking sausages for supper. Mrs Ludlam had agreed to her spending a few days here, and Ada was eager to make the most of it.

Chapter 19

A New Hat 1895

Dearest Ada,

I trust this finds you well.

Your last letter was most amusing, describing Allen falling off the milking stool. I expect he will soon get the hang of it as he grows older. It is good to know that you are happy. Your obvious cheerfulness makes me aware of how much of life I am missing, being away.

At the end of this term, sometime around the end of July, I will have completed my education, and shall return home from Cambridge. Is there a chance that you will be at Swepstone at this time? My brother Henry has arranged for me to take a commission in the army and I am to join the Queen's Rifle Corps.

I would like us to meet before I leave Swepstone. Once my appointment commences, fate and Her Most Royal Majesty's Army will decide where my future will lie. So, this meeting between us will be 'Au Revoir', for some time, I fear, but not, God willing, 'Adieu'.

I await your reply, and remain your devoted friend.

Charles Townend

§

Ada was taken aback when, after dropping the majority of passengers outside the Swan Public House, Mr Thomas drove the coach straight on along the Measham High Street instead of turning for Swepstone. He'd changed the route and as there were still two gentlemen aboard, both obviously clerics, Ada guessed they were destined for Snarestone and her heart began to beat faster on realizing that she was, indeed, to pass by the Tan Yard. She leaned forward in her seat, looking eagerly for a sighting of Duncan. However, crane her neck as she might, there was no sign of him.

The two gentlemen were carrying on a lively discussion about religion, not attempting to include her, thus allowing her to travel undisturbed. Ada felt irritated at the inconvenience, and had no choice but to accept the extra hour on the journey. She settled herself against the window, clutching her precious box and resolving, at an appropriate moment, to approach Mother about news of Duncan.

Ada, on arrival at Ashby station, had found herself with almost an hour to wait for the stage coach, so despite the bitterly cold wind, she had deposited her luggage with the clerk and walked to Market Street to do some important shopping. Tomorrow George and Nelly were to be married, so she had purchased a new hat from the second hand stall on the market. Ada gave the box-lid a pat, she was extremely proud of what nestled inside. The black hat from Mrs Ludlam's trunk was too dull to be worn to a wedding, so Ada had invested in a soft-brimmed grey felt with a trim of black and grey roses. It was fashionable and blended very well with the jacket from the Gynsills' trunk. She had also splashed out on a matching silk handkerchief.

She had purchased a wedding gift for George and Nelly plus a little something for Charles. It had cost her almost all of her money, including the remains of Grandma Elverson's pouch. However, it was worth it and Ada felt her heart flutter at the thought of seeing Duncan in church.

Her thoughts went back to Glenfield and Missy, who had been designated to carry out Ada's duties for the weekend. She would be leaving school soon and intended to become a teacher. Mr Ludlam had arranged for her to assist at the school at Glenfield, working with the younger children. It wasn't yet clear where she would eventually go to study, but it was likely to be some distance away. Ada would miss her and wondered how she was coping and if she had managed to finish the knocking back on time.

The Blacksmith's shop in Snarestone was busy as usual and a few late drinkers spilled out from The Globe, but apart from that and some children playing in the road, the village was quiet. The coach stopped outside Snarestone post office, where Mr Thomas handed down the last of the passengers. She was now alone and on the last leg of her journey.

The Late Elephant

They set off again, and on looking to her left, Ada caught sight of a familiar figure.

It was Duncan! It was! It was him! He was outside one of the cottages set back from the road and was digging the garden. She banged on the window and waved frantically. She looked around for some means of attracting his attention when she saw a young woman opening the front door of the cottage and calling to him. Ada couldn't hear the words, but she recognized the person. It was Bella Bishop. She was with child. As she raised her hand to peer at the passing coach, a flash of gold reflected from Bella's left hand. Ada pulled back, lest they should see her. Her heart was pounding fit to burst as the shock and horror enveloped her.

At last they reached the crossroads. It was a great relief to feel the lurch as the horses came to a halt outside the school. All Ada wanted to do was to throw herself into the arms of her father and weep.

No sooner had the coach disappeared towards Newton Burgoland, than a commotion was heard coming from one of the cottages opposite. A young boy, somewhere around early teens, sped out through the garden gate, followed by a person whom Ada assumed was his mother, but who was obviously no match for his speed.

The woman was waving a rolling-pin and shouting, "Come back here you little sod. Wait 'till your father hears about this." The rest was lost to the wind, as they took off through the newly planted school hedge and away across the fields

Father shook his head and muttered, "Those Forresters again. She keeps having more and more children, and she can't control any of 'em."

Several small faces were squashed up close to the window-panes downstairs and Ada wondered who if anyone was in charge of them while their mother was rampaging over the fields. The ruckus had helped raise her spirits somewhat, and as they began the walk home, she turned her attentions towards her brother. Her heart wasn't in it, but she felt duty bound to show some interest. After all, it wasn't their fault she had so stupidly harboured feelings for Duncan.

"You have grown, Jarvis, you'll soon be as tall as me and your hair has darkened. It's almost the colour of Father's."

He giggled and hunched up his shoulders against the wind. "I've joined the Church choir. I'm to sing a solo tomorrow." His face beamed.

"Well done. Do you enjoy it?"

"Aye, he does, don't yer son?" joined in Billy, "he has a good voice, and it'll not be breaking for a while yet, so the choir-master is making the most of it."

Ada's heart weighed heavily, but as they passed the church, she felt a sense of comfort. With a backdrop of dark sky and scudding clouds, the huge building sat like a dowager duchess, with the village grouped around, like Grandma used to be with her family. It seemed to Ada as though it was protecting them all and she had the strangest feeling that the grey stones sighed and smiled at her, while the leaded windows opened and closed like the all-seeing eyes of God.

On reaching the lane end, Ada felt a great urge to turn left towards The Late Elephant and resume her life from where she had left off, but instead she bent her body against the wind and clutched the box with one hand and her hat with the other, and struggled up the hill.

§

A fire crackled in the parlour grate, accentuating the aromas of black-lead mingled with lavender and furniture polish and a familiar bark invaded the peaceful scene, as Moses dashed in from outside, his whole body wagging along with his tail. Ada looked around, taking in familiar belongings in unfamiliar surroundings.

"I see you have Grandma Elverson's grandmother-clock. It looks well hanging there!"

Bess laughed. "Wait until the hour, when both clocks chime together. I'll ask your father to disable one or other of them when he comes back in."

"The house looks lovely, Mother. The chaise longue might have grown there, and look, Grandma's pictures, I'm so pleased you kept them, they were her pride and joy."

The print of a mature Queen Victoria gazed down upon them. It was a large sepia composition in a heavy frame and its stern presence dominated the area. There was a colourful print of a young girl with copious amounts of curly hair, holding a rose and an equally colourful picture of a kitten playing with ribbons.

"Do you have the Measham tea-pot?"

"No, my brother took that. It was all he asked for, so I could hardly disagree." She walked over to a small table in the corner. "I've kept these for you, if you want them, your Grandma's hymn book and psalter. They both have full scores, because as you know, she sang contralto."

Ada took them, tears suddenly overflowing. Bess put an arm around her daughter's shoulders and with a sigh, led her towards the living room. A most welcome and familiar smell of freshly baked lamb and potato pies enveloped them. Ada would have recognized that smell anywhere.

"Come and sit whilst I lay the table and tell me you news."

"I do miss Grandma. I feel so awful because I didn't attend her funeral. It must have been horrible for you having to remove her things from the cottage."

"It comes to us all in the end Ada, and your father and I have tried to make sure that the things she loved most are in safe hands. She was a good friend to me. I don't know how I would have managed without her when all of you came along, and I know she would be most content in the knowledge that you are taking good care of her books. Grandma had a soft spot for you."

It was on her mind to enquire about Duncan, but footsteps could be heard and Ada was thrilled to see Nelly descending the staircase.

"Nelly, how are you? Where's George?"

"He's staying with Sam's family. You know, his son Samuel who was at school with George."

"Of course, I didn't think, we can't have you two under the same roof, until after the nuptials." Ada thought Nelly looked a little awkward with this remark, and wondered what the sleeping arrangements had been in Portsmouth. It wouldn't matter much after tomorrow. Mind you, she thought, Mrs Scarlet wouldn't be gossiping about Nelly, considering she Tom unchaperoned under her roof.

"I think I'm in your bedroom, Ada, but you can share with me tonight if you like." She grinned, "It might be a bit crowded tomorrow night."

"I thought you could manage on the sofa, Ada," said her mother, "do you mind?" Before Ada was able to answer, Bess continued, "Call your father and Jarvis please, we need to get dinner over. I've filled the copper for the bath. Can't have the bride going to church mucky, now can we?"

§

Ada lay on the sofa in the parlour. She could smell the softening butter and thought of the Elephant and Jess's wedding day. Ada was envious of the glow emanating from Nelly but at the same time she did not begrudge her. Ada sighed. The wedding dress was hanging on the back of the bedroom door in Nelly's room and the garter and petticoats placed on the chair ready for tomorrow. Ada had put her ungainly parcel on the living room table, along with other gifts. Inside was a mixing bowl and rolling pin. It had been difficult to wrap.

Ada watched the last few flames in the fireplace as they fizzed to a temporary flame, only to flicker and die. I'm like that, she thought, glowing at just a mention of Duncan and then sinking into gloom. This will be the second wedding spoilt by sadness because of his behaviour. It wasn't really his fault. Ada was aware that the only person who could stop this incessant suffering was herself. She wondered if, had it not been for that invasive kiss, perhaps she wouldn't have felt so passionately for him.

She pulled the patchwork quilt up to her chin and immersed herself in the smell of Grandma. Mrs Ludlam's words came to mind, "Don't be in too much of a hurry. A good man is worth waiting for." There was one thing certain. She would not contemplate marriage to anyone unless she felt about them the way she did for Duncan.

§

Ada, resplendent in her new hat, sat next to Charles in the trap on their way to Ashby to have tea. Mother was right, it did seem a long way to go, but it was such a lovely day. The wind had dropped, the sun was shining and Charles looked so handsome in his uniform. He was a far cry from the gauche schoolboy she had last seen and he now sported a magnificent moustache, waxed and twisted to curl up at the ends. She felt quite important, sat next to him.

"It's so good to see you Ada. I can't believe how you've grown up all of a sudden. It almost seems as if you've become a different person. Until you smile, that is. I'd know those brown eyes anywhere." He turned to glance at her, "And may I say how utterly delightful you look?"

"Thank you, Charles, and may I say how much I like the moustache?"

"You may indeed. However, I don't have a choice, its regulation."

"Yes, so I understand."

The Late Elephant

"I was sorry to hear about the death of your grandmother. I trust your father has recovered from the shock. It must be a terrible thing to lose one's mother."

Charles steered the horse out of Swepstone, taking the Measham Road. "My word the Elephant does look different with a tiled roof."

"Yes," said Ada, "but the thatch needed attention. It leaked during a thunderstorm and they are so expensive to renew. I don't expect Farmer Wragg thought it viable."

"How did the wedding go?"

Ada smiled, "It went very well, thank you. My new sister-in-law looked stunning in the gown. She didn't wear a veil, but put her hair up and secured it with the most beautiful tortoiseshell comb. Apparently one of her actress friends sent it as a wedding gift."

"Yes, I've heard what a beauty she is."

Ada looked at him in amazement, "Have you? Who told you that?"

"Oh, just village gossip, my dear. Well, you wouldn't want me to say otherwise, now would you? Who gave her away? I understand she's an orphan."

"Jack gave her away and Mary sat in the front pew where her mother would have been." Ada's face beamed, "And you should have seen Hannah, she's only five you know, and she was attending. Mary took the bouquet, and Hannah stood and turned full circle in the aisle, looking up at every one. It was most amusing. She almost stole the show".

They rode out of the tunnel of trees and headed towards the colliery. "The wheels are still today. It being Sunday, I suppose," said Charles, "I love to see them turning. It looks so ingenious, somehow. I'll see if they'll let me visit and take a closer look."

They turned into Gibbet Lane and Ada held a hand over her eyes as they passed the post.

Charles laughed, "There's no one hanging in on it, Ada, there's no need to be frightened."

"I know that, it's just the idea of it."

Ada thought back to the wedding when George had enquired about the murder. She felt again the shiver as she had replied, "Not now George, I'll tell you some other time," but on looking round, Ada had seen all eyes turned expectantly towards her. She tried to get away with saying as little as possible, "Yes, it was a terrible situation. The young man worked at the mill, but I didn't really know him. He went missing just a week after I arrived."

"I couldn't believe it when Mother wrote and told me." George had said.

"Did she?" Ada had snapped. "She's never mentioned a word of it to me."

"No, young lady, because I knew you'd tell me when you were good and ready," had been Mother's reply.

Resigned to her fate, Ada had looked back at the expectant faces. There had been no escape. It was a welcome break to be here with Charles and out of the way of questions, although Ada was in fact relieved that at last the subject had been addressed.

Jess had mentioned Duncan's marriage. She said it had taken place only one week before. Jess was horrified at the news and upset that he hadn't asked William to be best man. Ada had shrugged. A child was on the way and Duncan was the father. It would have been almost impossible for him to continue staying in Measham if he had not honoured the consequences of his actions and it was obvious from Bella's size that he had left the decision to marry quite late enough.

The trap turned right at the Five-land-ends cross roads towards Ashby. "I remember coming here with Papa when I was very small and having to stop to pay a toll," said Charles, interrupting Ada's thoughts.

"Do you? I don't remember it, although Father sometimes speaks of it."

They continued on along the road, chattering happily about folk they both knew, lingering over old memories of tennis and windows being broken and carol singing on Christmas Eve and chilblains.

Apart from the beautiful palisaded villas with their tidy front gardens, there was nothing much to see. It was Sunday afternoon and most people were resting after their meal, so Ada wasn't paying too much heed to her surroundings. She was startled when, without a word of warning, they pulled up outside the Royal Hotel. She had expected to visit a tea shop. Charles helped her down and offered his arm. Ada walked up the stone steps and through the huge doors held open by the commissionaire who touched his hat as they walked past.

Once in the foyer she tried not to stare, but it was difficult not to gaze in awe at the sweeping staircase. She was overcome by the magnificence of it all. Charles led her straight ahead towards the dining room, where they were met and welcomed by the maître d'hôte. He seated them at a table by the window looking directly over the bath-grounds, where a cricket match was in progress.

"I'll sit with my back to the window Ada, or I may just be tempted to watch what's going on out there. If I do, it'll take away the whole point of the occasion."

Ada watched with interest as a waiter arrived with a casket filled with ice, inside of which nestled a bottle of wine. He fussed around them, making a huge to-do about removing the bottle and wrapping it in a large white linen napkin, before pouring. It all seemed most professional.

"This," began Charles, as he raised his glass, "is a toast for the future, wherever it may lead us, and a safe return home for us both."

Ada had never in her life tasted anything so perfect, and adored the feel of the bubbles tickling her nose. She leaned forward and moved the napkin away from the label, to read the name, 'Crystal'.

Charles explained. "This wine was bottled in France twenty years ago, in 1876, by Louis Roederer. It's reputed to be the best champagne in the world. The Tsar of Russia drinks it and I rather think the manager stocked it in case the Tsarina visited. She takes the waters at Harrogate, you know. The owners of the Ashby spa were convinced that she would come here instead, as of course it would have meant much less travelling. She didn't of course and it's too late now. Such a pity the Bath House had to close, don't you think?"

Ada had no idea why the Bath house had closed. She was feeling blissfully content and not at all inclined to worry about such issues. "Do you know, Charles, this wine was brewed the year I was born?"

"So it was," he smiled, "a wonderful year, indeed."

THE LATE ELEPHANT

Cheering and clapping from outside prompted a brief turn of the head in order to see what was transpiring, but at that exact moment, as if by some miracle, tea arrived.

"I do hope this is to your liking, Ada. If there's anything else you'd prefer, I'll ask the waiter to see to it."

"Oh no Charles, this looks quite delicious, thank you. You are spoiling me," and she chose the smoked salmon with anchovy cream and caviar.

"I'm spoiling both of us." He sat back whilst the waiter refilled their glasses. They chattered on about her life at Glenfield and his regiment, when they were not occupied eating the sandwiches and selecting a vol-au-vent or two and the odd cheese straw. Ada was particularly taken with the potato and parsnip crisps.

"Are you worried about your future, Charles? I do hope there's no risk of your being sent anywhere dangerous."

"That's something I'll not know until I have completed my training. By the nature of the profession, I dare say that on occasions there'll be a modicum of danger, but I'll write and tell you as soon as I find out, but for now, let us not dwell on such matters."

His face beamed. "Ah, here comes the serious stuff." A plate constructed of three tiers, each laden with tiny chocolate éclairs, vanilla slices and meringues stuffed with strawberries, was placed in the centre of the table.

"There now, do help yourself Ada," he said, handing her a pair of silver tongues.

Charles remained silent for some minutes, obviously anticipating the moment when his taste buds would be titillated by the haute cuisine of the pastry chef. Ada watched as he deliberated before selecting his cakes to carefully place them onto his plate. Then he picked up a fork and delicately approached them with the utmost precision.

She could see that, despite his newfound sophistication, he was still taking life most seriously. However, despite being fascinated by the expression on his face, she couldn't resist sharing the sensation as her teeth crunched into meringue with strawberries, causing a delicious explosion of taste buds.

"When do you leave?" Ada asked.

Charles dabbed both corners of his mouth, and folded his napkin, laying it at the side of his plate. There wasn't even the tiniest smidgen of chocolate in evidence on the fine damask.

"I have to join the regiment the day after tomorrow, so we'll not meet again for some time, I dare say." He pulled a silver watch from his breast pocket and checked the time. "We'll have to be on our way shortly I'm afraid, Mother has guests tonight and I'm expected to attend."

"A farewell party?" asked Ada, raising her eyebrows, knowing full well that she did not qualify in terms of status, to attend such a gathering. His cheeks flushed and she wished she hadn't said anything.

"It's a lovely watch. Is it new?"

"Yes," replied Charles, "a gift from Papa. I was rather touched."

Ada pulled a package from her bag. "This is from me. I'm afraid it's rather meagre compared to the watch."

Her gift was a silver hip-flask. Charles was, just for once, speechless.

THE LATE ELEPHANT

"I thought it would be a comfort if you come across a difficult situation. Then you can take a sip and think of home." Ada was touched on seeing his expression of delight. He seemed quite overcome.

"My dear Ada, how perfectly lovely."

He poured the last of the champagne. "We can't let this to go to waste." They touched glasses one last time.

Charles gave instructions for the trap to be brought round and back in the foyer a maid invited Ada to visit the ladies' room to freshen up before the return journey. Ada was thrilled. There was a white porcelain wash-hand basin with beautiful brass taps and not a pump in sight. On a glass rail attached to the wall hung a starched and pressed white towel. A door, standing slightly open, invited Ada to take a look, so she pushed it with her foot, ever so carefully, not knowing what to expect, and there right in front of her was a modern water toilet. Ada knew what it was, because she had seen a sketch of one in Mr Ludlam's newspaper. Just wait till I tell Mother about this. It was worth coming all this way just to see it, she thought, settling comfortably onto the mahogany seat and anticipating the experience of pulling the chain with the white porcelain handle.

Back on the road once more, Charles chattered endlessly about all and nothing. They had barely left behind the houses in Tamworth Road, when Ada realized she had a problem concentrating. "Charles, stop the trap, I feel quite ill." She struggled to the ground. Charles ran to her side, but she vomited almost immediately and his shiny boots were spattered. Mortified but quite unable to stop, Ada vomited twice more, before she felt anything like herself, but her head was pounding and she felt as if it could explode at any time. Despite feeling so dreadfully ill, she was full of apologies. "Please forgive me, Charles, I am so sorry. It must be something I ate."

"That's alright old girl, you can't help being ill." Stooping, he pulled a handful of dock-leaves from the verge and cleaned his boots.

"Do you think it was the wine? Perhaps a tiny drop too much for you?"

"I have no idea Charles, but please, do hurry. I need to go home to bed."

"That is a pity. I'd rather hoped that, on the way home, you would tell me about the murder."

Chapter 20

Parma Violets 1896

Jess was anxious to put some intimacy back into their relationship. William worked far too hard and the hours were long. He hadn't been so eager for her since their second child had been born, but Edgar was now almost twelve months old and Jess was missing their passionate moments. She had reached out for him a few times, but he had lain snoring beside her. That wouldn't have happened three years ago, before the babies were born.

Jess placed baby Edgar in the perambulator with Henry beside him. Seconds after she began the journey along the cobbled street, the two little ones fell asleep. For weeks now, William had stayed late at work, trying out different ways to colour the leather and tonight they were to be inspected by a man from the automobile company. It may very well be past ten o'clock before William returned home, so Jess thought it would be a nice gesture to take him a hot meal. She had plated some shepherd's pie made from yesterday's roast lamb, with lashings of mint sauce, just the way he liked it. In fact, William preferred it to the roast joint, so he would be thrilled. Jess had wrapped the dish in towels and placed it in the space between her children, hoping their body-heat would help to keep it warm. Instead of coming home late and eating cold meat and pickles, which caused him indigestion, he would take a break and see his sons before bed-time. She was mulling over whether or not it would have been better to have warned him.

The streets were quiet, being too early for city workers to return home and Jess had tried to organise things so that William would have time to eat before his client arrived. She crossed the road, leaving behind the lamp-lit streets for a cul-de-sac just behind Charles Street. The evening had turned warm and William had said that very morning, "maybe they were in for some good weather," and wondered if they were to have an Indian summer.

Jess had recovered well from the birth and was giving some serious thought to asking Ada to come and stay for a couple of days. Her sister hadn't had much time off since she had begun working at The Mill and Jess wanted to give her a treat. They could visit the shops and she would buy Ada a brand new corset. She would mention it to William that very evening, and together they'll plan the outing.

Jess paused to straighten her hat before pushing the pram through the gateway to the warehouse, but stopped abruptly on hearing voices through an open window. It was a man's voice. She stood for a moment, listening, but it certainly didn't belong to William. It must be the man from the automobile company. Now what was she to do? She hadn't enough food to bring an extra plateful and she couldn't give dinner to William without feeding his visitor. Jess felt sure William had said the man didn't arrive until the end of business. There should have been over an hour yet before his visit.

In order to assess the situation, and a little afraid at being discovered, Jess positioned herself just inside the stable. William's horse snorted as she entered, but after a brief glance, turned back to the manger and continued champing the hay. She caught sight of someone through the window and heard a woman's voice. The boys were fast asleep, so she tiptoed over to the building and peeped in.

Rose Finney was there, laughing and screaming out with raucous delight, her ample, over-exposed bosom wobbling like a jelly, looking straight at William. A man came into view, he had a glass in his hand and he too was laughing with Rose, head back and with loud chortles drifting over on the still night air.

William's voice echoed, loud and clear, "Here, the night is young, let me top you up," and the stranger held out his glass for more. "And you Rose?" Her hand shot out greedily, looking up at William as he poured. There was a look of familiarity on her face. Jess couldn't bear to watch any longer. She began to seethe.

"Well, I never did," she whispered. "If I hadn't seen this for myself, I would never have believed it." She ran back to her babies, asking herself searching questions. Why her? Why a dirty smelly woman, when he could have chosen any woman he wanted? He'd admitted giving her the loaves that Mother had sent on their wedding day. Jess had wondered at the time, why he took the trouble to walk all the way up the hill to deliver them, when there were families just as needy, living close by.

She couldn't see any sign of work, just two unruly men drinking what was obviously whiskey with a whoring woman who would never smell like a rose if she soaked in a bath tub for a month. Jess loathed and detested her at that moment. No wonder William had been getting indigestion, if he'd been drinking like that.

She recalled the moment when he asked her to marry him. He had kissed her properly for the first time and although she was thrilled to feel his lips on hers, she had held back, afraid to succumb to his magnetism. She had felt his urgency. His body was taut against hers and on pulling away he gazed so seriously into her eyes. "Jess, you must know that I'm deeply in love with you. Will you do me the honour of becoming my wife?" The memory would stay with her for ever, yet it would seem that William's passion had taken a change of direction.

Jess remembered her first encounter with that odious woman. She had referred to her son as Osmond. That was William's middle name. They decided to employ someone to help with the laundry and he'd grinned while suggesting, "I don't suppose you would consider Mrs Finney?" Jess had thought he was joking. She shuddered, not daring to focus on any one of the scenarios whirling around in her head.

She pushed her babies back towards home, unsure as yet about how to deal with the matter. Angry, hurt and determined he would not get away with it, Jess was determined to put as much space as possible between the disgusting scene and her two small sons.

Duncan was no better. In fact, he was worse. His preference was for young girls. Had it not been for the fact he knew father would have killed him, he would have taken advantage of Ada. He had succeeded in charming her and it had upset Jess to see how manipulative he was. She hadn't dared mention it to William, the two men being so close.

She thought about the woman from the inn at Glenfield who'd been carrying on with Eli, the chap who was murdered. She knew at this moment exactly how her husband had felt when he killed him.

That woman was dirty, so Ada had said, although apparently Eli was worse. Just fancy her going to Mill House and throwing stones at the window to wake him up. She had meant to have him, by all accounts. Surely she must have been aware he was likely to be unfaithful. Apparently, they had no sooner carried his bags down the stairs and into the street, than her husband showed up, having followed her. Had he not done, Eli and the woman would have been miles away.

What was it about unclean women? Jess sighed. I wonder if William will do that with Rose Finney. Well, if it is the case that he wants her, he must go, there was nothing else for it. It's either her or me, Jess thought. This resolve, however, didn't stop the hurting and Jess brushed the tears away with her coat sleeve.

As she sped along the street, an owl swept by, so low in the air she could feel the draught. Strange, she thought, how life just continued on regardless, even though her world had come to an end and her heart was breaking.

§

William was seriously worried about Jess. There had been a definite withdrawal of all things loving. Even on the Monday night when he arrived back home and announced he had completed the deal with Mr Hardy and wouldn't need to be late any more, she hadn't thawed. He felt sure that had something to do with it, but couldn't understand why. He had told her not to worry about a hot meal, but that he could manage on cold meat and pickles just until the deal was done, so she hadn't been inconvenienced too much, but when the shepherds' pie had been put before him he had eaten gratefully, and thanked her.

Several times she had snapped at him over nothing. He had turned towards her in bed but she had deliberately kept her back to him. On enquiring what was wrong, she had shrugged her shoulders, replying, "There's nothing wrong with me." He watched as she sat before him at the table, picking at her food, hardly eating anything and he noticed the dark circles beneath her eyes. At first he had put Jess's change of mood down to woman's-days, expecting her to undergo a change of heart once they were over. However, this had not happened. The woman's-days had come and gone twice and still she was positively hostile. Sitting at the table, having enjoyed one of Jess's rabbit pies, he decided to investigate.

"Jess, are you not feeling well? Is there something wrong? Is it the children, do you need someone to help? We can find someone, I'm sure."

She rose immediately to her feet and began to clear away the dishes, but he noticed her red cheeks and her lips were clamped together.

"Jess," he put his hand over hers and stopped her in full flight. "There is something. I can see it in your eyes. Look at me Jess. Tell me what's bothering you."

She turned her angry eyes towards his. "I wonder if there's anything you should be telling me, husband?" She spat the words at him, her mood becoming more and more defiant.

William's eyes opened in astonishment. "What do you mean?"

They stood, encapsulated within a stare.

"What's that supposed to mean exactly? What is it I am supposed to have done?"

Jess sat back down at the table and began to sob. William moved to her side and tried to hold her, but she was having none of it. Still in the throes of weeping, she shrugged him away. He moved back to his seat and watched silently. Pulling a handkerchief from her sleeve, she wiped her eyes and continued to clear the table.

"Jess, you can't do this." He jumped up again. "You have to tell me what's bothering you." He tried to take her hands, but she pulled away. He grabbed her wrists and forced her towards him. "I shall not let you go until you've told me what it is that's upsetting you. You must know how much I love you, how can you do this to me and to yourself?"

As they faced each other across the table, she spat out the words in an angry deluge, "It's you and that Finney woman. Don't tell me there's nothing going on, I saw you with her at the warehouse. You had been with her when you told me you were working late. You and that other fellow, drinking whiskey and cavorting with her. How could you do such a thing and with a dirty woman like her?"

He let go of her and sat down, the colour draining from his face. The silence was deafening.

His voice was no more than a whisper. "I was with her, but not as you think. Hardy turned up early, in the middle of the afternoon in fact, and we finished the hides sooner than expected. I told you about that, mixing the different colours to see which one he wanted to use on seats for the new automobiles. Jess, this could mean a fortune for us." He paused, before taking a deep breath and continuing. "She was cleaning, like she does every evening, so I offered her a glass, well, I could hardly leave her out."

"Why not?" snapped Jess. "She's just the bloody cleaning woman."

This was a shock to William. He'd never heard Jess swear. "I know this sounds daft, but I think she's my sister."

Jess shouted at him. "What? You *think* she's your sister?" She was furious, fists clenched and ready to fight her corner.

Despite the tension of the moment, William couldn't help but laugh at her indignation. "I know it sounds strange, but my father had a dalliance with a woman up the road and everyone reckons that Rose is a result of that relationship. When we were growing up the other children were really spiteful. They made Rose's life unbearable. I remember her standing in the playground at school, crying her eyes out because someone reckoned she had nits. I saw the muck on her hands and face and I thought, she's my sister, and I felt so sorry for her, I ended up giving one of the lads a black eye.

"I'm sorry Jess, I should have told you, but it's all tied up with the death of my parents and I hate talking about it." He took his eyes away from her and looked down at the tablecloth as he always did when this subject was being discussed. "No one knows exactly what happened that night, but a terrible row took place. They argued about Rose. I remember hearing my mother shouting about the bastard child my father had spawned. I knew who she meant and for the first time it made me realize how Rosie must feel. Her family had very little money and every day she had to pass our house, knowing we had the best, so after the accident I gave her a job at the warehouse and made sure she didn't go hungry. I thought that was the very least I should do."

The silence had lost some of its anger but still weighed heavily. He sat unmoving, with head down. "Father grabbed his coat and walked out of the house, but instead of backing off, Mother followed him. Apparently they went to the warehouse to continue the row. That was the last time I saw either of them alive."

It was Jess who broke the stillness. "She calls her child Osmond."

William raised his eyes to her. "Yes, I know, it was our father's name."

Jess put her hands over her mouth. "I feel awful, ashamed of myself. I am so sorry." Jess walked over to him and he took her tenderly in his arms and rocked her. Still stroking her hair he murmured, "It's alright, Jess, but please, don't ever suspect me in that way. I will never be unfaithful to you, till the day I die. I love you too much."

Despite himself and grateful that at last she didn't look at him with hatred, William couldn't suppress a chuckle. "And you're right, she is dirty. She stinks sometimes, but I can't tell her that, it will simply add to her already low opinion of herself."

"She doesn't seem low on self-esteem to me, the way she wriggles her rear-end when she's walking down the street."

William grinned. "Yes, she is a bit flamboyant, but I'll not be asking her to tea, and in her defence, she made a lovely job of the cleaning, you said so yourself."

§

Ada opened her eyes. Her throat was as dry as a bone and she was confused on noticing sunshine through the curtains. What on earth was she doing in bed in the day time? Her first instinct was to jump out. She tried to pick up her head, but a terrible weight returned it immediately to the pillow. She moaned, clutching the eiderdown, shaking with cold, and with her teeth chattering.

Mrs Ludlam came in, carrying earthenware hot-water-bottles, one under each arm. She set them on the rug and leaned over to wipe Ada's brow with a vinegar-soaked rag. "Do you need the pot?"

Ada nodded, willingly accepting help and with a great effort, climbed out of the bed to squat. After which, greatly relieved, but weak, allowed Mrs Ludlam to sit her in a chair by the window.

"Goodness me, these pillow cases are sodden. You must drink, Ada, put back what the fever has taken out."

Having changed the bed clothes, she handed Ada a glass of barley water and lemon juice. "How do you feel?"

THE LATE ELEPHANT

"I feel poorly, Ma'am, but I'll try to get dressed in a minute."

"You'll do no such thing, you silly girl. You've been really poorly. Doctor thinks it's the influenza and you must rest. You've been like this for three days."

She turned back the eiderdown and indicated for Ada to climb back in. She took the vinegar cloth, folded it long-ways into four and placed it on Ada's forehead, before wrapping the hot water bottles in pieces of old blankets, to sit snuggly either side of her feet.

"Now then, can you eat something, a dish of bread and milk, perhaps? Ben has saved you some milk from Buttercup."

Ada's throbbing head made it almost impossible to smile back. "I would love a drink of tea Ma'am, if it isn't too much trouble."

"Of course it's not, I'll be back directly. Now rest and don't worry about the work. I've sent for someone from the village to help out."

With a smile and a nod of assurance she was gone, leaving Ada alone with her throbbing head and a throat too painful to swallow.

§

"Ada, are you awake?" A timid voice was whispering, but the candle hadn't been lit. Ada could smell that a fire had been burning in the tiny grate and from the sounds of things someone was seeing to it.

A shadowy figure approached the bed. "It's me, Missy I've come to see how you are and to put some wood on the fire. Mother says you must be kept warm and I'm not to open the window, no matter how hot it gets in here."

Ada smiled at the young face. "Thank you, you're most kind."

"Mother says she'll be up in a minute to help you with the chamber-pot. If it's urgent, I could help."

"It is alright, Missy, I think I can manage." Ada squatted down, knowing her legs could let her go at any minute, yet determined not to allow the girl to see her in such a humiliating position. "It's all done, Missy, you can come back in."

Missy lit a candle, placing it on the chest of drawers next to the bed and handed Ada a mug of warm blackberry vinegar. "You've been really poorly. One day you tossed and turned and shouted out things. Mother has been really worried. The doctor came three times and all the raspberry vinegar has gone, Mother said you needed it for the cough."

"I'm sorry, Missy, I'll make you some more when I can, you'll be missing it on your pancakes and I'll pay for the Doctor from my savings."

Footsteps resounded on the wooden floor and Mrs Ludlam entered with a towel thrown over one shoulder and carrying a large jug of hot water.

"You'll do no such thing! The Doctor has been paid, he went off with a cockerel and two bags of flour and now I'm going to give you a bed-bath. You'll feel a lot better for a freshen-up."

Ada managed a smile. She could smell lavender and realised that the headache was almost gone. "What are you doing at home, Missy?"

"It's Queen Victoria's Jubilee celebrations. I'm ever so sorry Ada, but you've missed them."

The Late Elephant

§

Dear Mother and Father,

As William will have informed you, I have been ill, but there is no longer any cause for you to worry as I have been up and walking around for a few days now. I can't quite manage a whole day on my feet, but have been able to help with light jobs such as ironing.

Mrs Ludlam has looked after me very well and Missy has helped. I am so lucky to have such caring employers. I missed Queen Victoria's Jubilee celebrations, and Mrs Ludlam had to find someone from the village to do my work.

I don't know when I shall be able to come and see you again, but I shall come as soon as I am able. I had hoped it would be for my birthday, but I fear that would be too soon.

I am sorry that you haven't been feeling well, Mother. I was too ill to read your letter when it first arrived and hope that you don't catch this awful influenza. I hear people have died of it and am thanking The Lord God Almighty that he has seen fit to spare me.

God bless you all, and keep you safe.
Your loving daughter,
Ada

§

Ada stepped over a pile of hay in the rick-yard, relieved to be back onto cobbles and out of the dust. She had been rummaging around for eggs laid away. The weather had been so hot and dry that the hens hadn't produced enough eggs for the amount of cakes needed. Having shaken out her petticoats and dusted herself down, she picked up the basket and avoiding the cow-pats, proceeded to make her way back to the farmyard, when she felt the voice rather than heard it.

"Ada."

It was a voice as familiar as those of George and Jarvis.

"Yes Ben?"

He took just a couple of strides, in order to stand before her. His hands were behind his back as if he were hiding something. She registered his unfamiliar stance. "Ben, what's amiss?"

"Nothing, Ada, it's just that…" He swung his arm from behind his back and stuck out his hand. Clutched in the large fingers was a bunch of Parma violets.

She looked back at him in amazement.

"Mrs Ludlam said it's your birthday today and I know you wanted to go home at the weekend and couldn't, so these are for you. I thought they'd cheer you up."

Ada stepped forward and took the posy from him. "Ben, thank you. What a kind thing to do. I'm much obliged, I'm sure."

"You look a bit better today, how do you feel?" His face showed tender concern.

"Yes, thank you. Apart from the wretched tiredness, I am recovered." She buried her nose in the violets, they were her mother's favourite flowers and she suffered a pang of nostalgia at not being able to share them. Ben's face was scarlet, but his eyes sparkled as he looked down at her. After a moment of uneasy silence, he muttered,

The Late Elephant

"You look after yourself," turned on his heel and strode back towards the cowshed.

Mr Ludlam stepped through the gate. He saw the basket of eggs, "Well done, Ada, I wonder how many of them will be fresh enough to use?"

"I've shaken them Sir and most of them seem well enough." She saw him raise an eyebrow at the violets, but on remembering something else, he reached into the inside pocket of his jacket and handed her a letter. "This was waiting at the post office."

She tore it open. It was another letter from Mother.

Dear Ada,

I am very pleased to hear you are better and should be pleased to be able to say the same but I cannot say I feel any better and can do nothing, so we think you had better return home on Saturday. I have been looking for the day to come and when your letter came I could have cried. I went to the doctor for the third time on Monday.

Tell Mrs Ludlam I am very sorry to disappoint her and I have tried all I can to manage but I cannot get shut of the pain in my inside. You may leave your box at the station and ask them to give it to Marsh of Swepstone, the milk cart.

No more this time, with best love,

From Father and Mother Elverson.
Don't worry as I hope to get better with help, but I must have someone.

§

Ada went straight to her room and pulled the previous letter from the pile in her drawer. She read it again, remembering that, despite her illness, how delighted she had been on unwrapping the two little pottery kittens.

Dear Ada,

The Sisters are a birthday present from me and I hope you will keep them in memory of me, as perhaps it may be the last one.
Mrs Scarlett brought me a pair so I asked her to get a pair for you. She saved you the box hoping you would like it. I send it now as a token of love for I feel to be getting a little worse for wear.
When people reach 51 they do not always feel well but thank the Lord I can get about and work. At present though, I have aches and pains.
It is just as well I didn't continue to work for Mrs Stevenson after they moved from The Manor to Swepstone House. At least I am not letting her down.
Now I must conclude,
With best love and wishes,

From your Mother.

Perhaps you will find out why I was short with you.

§

Ada understood what Mother was saying, in her roundabout way. Mother had been cross with her, but it had bothered Ada to see Jess so unhappy. She couldn't just sit there and do nothing. All day Jess had sniped at

The Late Elephant

William and he frowned and looked daggers back at her, his mouth set like a vice and his eyes glinting beneath his furrowed eyebrows. What could have gone so wrong? They seemed the perfect couple, with their two little boys, Henry now four and Edgar just turned one. It had happened when the whole family had come together at Albion Street to celebrate the baby's first year with a cake and egg sandwiches and William had criticized Jess about not having cooked his roast beef.

Ada had felt quite justified in standing up for her sister. She had called him selfish, and followed Jess up to the bedroom, trying to calm her, whilst she lay on the bed and sobbed, but Jess was not giving anything away. She just sat up, dried her eyes and said, "Please, Ada, don't take any notice of me, it's just that I get tired with the two boys to deal with. It's not William's fault." With that she insisted on going back down stairs, and they all had to make the best of a most uncomfortable situation. When it was time to catch the stage, Ada didn't want to leave her. She couldn't discuss it with her parents on the way to the railway station, because William went with them. So when Father had tried to explain that Mother was not well, it just became lost among the doings.

Ada had put Mother's strangeness down to her age. Mrs Ludlam was going through a difficult time and had explained about the change of life. Indeed, Ada had watched, mystified, as her mistress stood outside the back door in freezing cold weather, in a desperate bid to stop the sweats. Now, having fully absorbed both letters, Ada was worried. Mother was actually complaining and begging her to return home. She gave the violets a wistful look and proceeded towards Mill

o show Mrs Ludlam the correspondence and to
er bags.

Chapter 21

Grief 1897

"How long have you been like this?" Ada looked down at her mother's pinched face, tinged now with yellow.

Bess looked back through tired eyes, "I don't know, a few months."

"What does the Doctor say?"

"He keeps giving me bottles of medicine, but I don't think it's the right mix. I asked him for a tonic, but he sends the white stuff with bismuth." Bess leaned forwards in her rocking chair, screwing herself up against the pain. "Nelly brought some ginger-root, but it didn't do any good and I tried slippery-elm and that didn't touch me." She put out her hand to Ada. "Thank you so much for coming. I'm sorry to be a bother, but I didn't know what else to do."

"You're not a bother. I'll stay with you until you're better."

"Did you like your birthday present?" Bess straightened her body.

"I love them, thank you Mother. I've placed them on the mantle-shelf in my room."

"They'll be something nice for your bottom drawer." She groaned while holding her hands to her side.

Ada was appalled at her mother's condition, shocked at the amount of weight loss she had suffered. Her colour suggested jaundice which, Ada was almost certain, meant a liver condition. Mrs Ludlam had mentioned how dangerous that could be.

"Shall I make a pot of tea?"

"Not for me, but you'll need to put the dinner on, Father will be back directly."

"Hello, anyone about?" Nelly was through the door. The two young women embraced, neither daring to maintain eye contact for more than a split second, each encapsulated within their own fear, their obvious unease communicating concerns for Bess's health. Bess managed a brief greeting to her daughter-in-law, before closing her eyes, unable to fight the tiredness.

Ada draped a shawl around her mother's shoulders before following Nelly. They sat facing each other across the table in the living room, still unable to make eye-contact. It was Nelly who broke the silence. "She's very poorly."

A tear rolled down Ada's cheek, but she managed a brief answer. "Yes I know," but before wiping her eyes, she asked, "how are they managing?"

"I think your father must be at the end of his savings. He's been fetching two and three bottles of medicine a week and Mother has seen the Doctor three times. It all has to be paid for. George collects it. He goes straight there from the pit. It saves your father the journey. It's a long way to walk and he doesn't like leaving her."

Ada took a sip of her tea, hardly tasting it. "Do you know what's wrong with her?"

THE LATE ELEPHANT

Nelly looked down into her lap, her eyes also full of tears and she nodded. "The doctor has told your father that she's not going to get better. Ada, I am so sorry. I look on her as my mother, the one I never knew. She has been so good to me. I'll do all I can to help."

"When did you know?" asked Ada.

"When she refused to come to the jubilee celebrations. The committee held a tea-party in the school-room and the children had a fancy-dress competition. You know how she loves to see the children, but she flatly refused to go and your father stayed at home with her. She couldn't control the pain, so your father sent for the doctor to visit." Nellie took Ada's hand across the table. "We were really worried when we didn't hear from you. I knew something was wrong. Are you well enough to deal with this? You don't look well."

Ada nodded and began to sob, covering her mouth in an attempt not to make a noise loud enough to waken Mother. The back door opened. It took Billy no more than a moment to assess the situation. He took his daughter in his arms. "Yer know, then?"

"I've told her," said Nelly.

"That's as well."

"George and I both think Jarvis should stay with us. He's too young to witness what will happen."

After her sister-in-law had left, Ada set the table, but neither were hungry. Father picked at his bacon and potatoes, leaving most of it in an ungainly pile on his plate and Ada simply couldn't stomach the thought of food at all. "If you should need help with money Father, I have a little, I can help out."

"Thanks, yer might have to." He allowed his knife and fork to fall, clattering onto the tin plate and left the table abruptly, almost running in his haste to hide the tears. He stumbled to the farthest part of the garden and Ada watched him lean over the fence. She sighed, but knew better than to interrupt his grief.

The door-knocker resounded through the house. Ada went quickly to answer the summons, afraid that Mother would be woken. Mrs Scarlett stood, her face the usual grim mask of discontent. "Oh Mrs Scarlett, please come in. Are you here to see Mother?"

"No, I've called to see you."

"We'll have to go into the living room. Mother's asleep in the parlour and I don't want to waken her." Ada quickly cleared away the plates, uneasy on noticing the woman's eyes darting everywhere.

"I've come to tell yer there's a position vacant as cook for Mrs Stevenson at Swepstone House. Maggie Peters is full-time, but she's with her daughter who's expecting. She only wants somebody to do the dinner in the middle of the day and prepare something ready for tea. She has a woman to do the cleaning, so I thought it might suit yer."

"I am much obliged to you, Mrs Scarlett. I'll go down later." Ada took the boiling kettle from the fire and poured the steaming water over the leaves in the tea-pot. She was most surprised that Mrs Scarlett had blessed her with such a favour. With tea-cup half way to her mouth, the woman explained, "Yer mam has always been good to me. I know as folks round here don't like me, cos I'm too straight John Bull, but if they'd had my cross to bear, perhaps they would be too." She slurped the tea, returning the cup to its place and wiped the back

THE LATE ELEPHANT

of her hand across her mouth. "I'm very fond of yer mam and I'm sorry to hear her plight. If there's anything I can do to help, I will."

"I shall be for ever in your debt, Mrs Scarlett."

"Yer don't look so well yerself. Yer've lost a lot o weight. Are yer sure yer going to be able to handle yer Mother?"

"I'm sure, thank you!" Ada was adamant.

"Have yer been poorly?" The woman persisted.

"Yes, I had the influenza, but am quite recovered. I just need to put back the extra weight, that's all."

The woman stood up and left as abruptly as she had come.

Billy called from the scullery. "What did she want?"

"Oh, hello Father, she says Mrs Stevenson is looking for a part-time cook, someone to tide her over until her woman is back. Apparently she's with her daughter, pending the arrival of her first child."

"Do yer want to do it?"

"I don't see why not. Nelly will stay with Mother while I go, and the money will come in handy."

"Ah, it will," Billy sighed, "I'll go and sit with her for a while." He hesitated, "Are yer sure yer feeling up to this, Ada, yer look a bit peaky to me?"

§

Ada had washed the pans, scrubbed the kitchen table and was folding a clean tea-towel to hang on the rail when Mrs Stevenson walked in.

"That was an excellent meal, Ada. We're very pleased with your cooking, but I was wondering, how is your mother?"

Ada had difficulty in keeping her tears at bay. "She is very poorly, thank you Ma'am. She has a tumour and it's growing fast. You can see it bulging from her side. Sometimes she cries out with pain. It's worse at night for some reason. Last night I begged the Lord to take her. It's more than a body can stand to have to watch her suffer." Tears threatened and Ada turned away, heading towards the back door.

"Ada, wait. Here, take this." She placed a bottle of brandy in Ada's hand, "it'll help to quell the pain."

"Thank you Ma'am, I am indeed obliged to you. I didn't think about strong spirits, Mother doesn't usually partake, but I'll try anything."

"If she's not used to it, then mix it with warm milk and a little sugar, it'll make it more palatable."

Ada trudged along the road to Hill House, the wind blowing through her clothes. The shawl gave little protection against the bitter chill and Ada wished she had worn her jacket. On passing Victoria cottages, Mrs Scarlett came out to have a word. "How is she?"

"Very poorly. We've brought a bed downstairs. She is no longer able to walk, so I sleep next to her, in the chair."

"Come in and have a cup of tea," the woman offered.

"No, thank you, I won't if you don't mind. Mrs Stevenson has given me brandy to help the pain, so I need to get back."

"Let me know if yer need help, I'll gladly sit with her."

Ada felt a brief moment of comfort, until raising her eyes to the house on the hill, knowing what waited inside.

Father opened the door, his face a picture of despair. The sounds coming from the parlour were heartrending. Ada flew to the living room and set a saucepan of goat's milk on the fire, before pulling off her hat and shawl. The smell of the brandy filled the room as she poured it into a white porcelain feeding cup. Raising her mother, light as a feather now, with barely any flesh left on her poor tired bones, Ada put the cup to her mouth.

"Here Mother, take this, it'll help ease your pain."

Bess sipped the liquid, little by little. She pushed the cup away and looked up into Ada's eyes. "You're a good girl, our Ada. You'll look after your father and Jarvis, I know that."

Ada was lost for words. "Mother," was her only reply. It was more an entreaty than an answer.

Bess continued, "You know I'm not going to get better and I need to tell you how much I love you." She stopped, her breathing becoming laboured.

"Don't talk Mother, I know you love us," but Bess interrupted.

"If I don't see our Mary again before I pass on, will you tell her? Will you tell them all how much I have loved them?"

Ada lowered her Mother back down onto the feather pillow. "Of course I will. We all know that and we all love you. You've been the best possible mother."

"And tell them thank you, and remind your father how good we've been together." Bess gave a wan smile and closed her eyes. "Tell him I don't want to leave him."

§

Ada woke abruptly, perturbed to find the day had already begun. She had tossed and turned throughout the night, reliving the echoes of her mother's last agonizing hours, but just before dawn sleep had claimed her, denying her the right to rise early and prepare herself in seclusion for the funeral. Instead she had been forced to manoeuvre around other family members. Once dressed, she positioned the black hat carefully and turned towards the stairs. Nelly held her in a reassuring embrace and Mrs Scarlett nodded, dispensing a look of resignation.

"You should have woken me," Ada said lamely, unable to put any emphasis to her words. She nodded briefly to distant relatives from her mother's family, before noticing that Jess had arrived and was hanging onto William's arm. They looked comfortable with each other, and she assumed they had called a truce.

"We decided the extra sleep would do you good," Father said, giving her hand a squeeze.

The pall-bearers proceeded to the parlour, standing in place now, with boots polished and hats in hand. Ada had nothing to say to anyone and an uneasy silence swathed itself over all those present. Mr Insley from Shackerstone had been at the house two mornings before to take measurements, returning before tea-time with the finished coffin. Supervised by Mrs Scarlett, Ada and Nelly had laid Bess out. They had washed her body. Ada had rejected the shroud, dressing Bess in her best skirt and blouse, the one she wore on Sundays, with Ada's cape around her shoulders to protect her against the cold of the church yard.

The Late Elephant

"I don't care what people usually do, Nelly, I couldn't bear to see anyone else wearing Mother's things. They'll go to rest with her."

The men had helped to lift her inside and they positioned her in front of the fireplace in the parlour.

"Don't," implored Ada, as they began to screw the lid down, "don't shut her away."

Mrs Scarlett led her into the living-room, and held her until she could cry no more. Jarvis ran to her side and cried with her.

Mary, on Father's arm, with Jess and Ada behind, followed the coffin. It looked smaller than ever, outside in the cold winter's day, being carried shoulder high by those who loved her. William had brought along some spare bowler hats and leather gloves and the dark-suited men formed a smart team. Jarvis walked with Mrs Scarlett and Ada turned to assure herself he was bearing up. He looked so grown-up in the hand-me-down suit which used to belong to George, and thanks to Nelly, his hair was parted and trim. As with pecking order on these occasions, it had fallen to Nelly to walk with Mother's brother, uncle Osmond, who lived somewhere in Lancashire, and who Ada couldn't remember having met before.

The bearers carefully navigated the slope of the hill with its rough surface, but once on the flat, they passed Victoria Cottages with an even step. Every window had closed its curtains, as a mark of respect for Bess.

Ada remembered the pile of letters, some as yet unopened, back home on the chiffonier, expressing regret and conveying condolences, and almost all of the people who had sent them were now waiting for the family to arrive. Despite her grief, Ada felt a great pride, as she watched her brother George, her two brothers-in-law and Tom carrying Mother with love, compassion and respect. It was comforting to know she was in safe hands on her last journey.

Saint Peter's Church was full to overflowing. Heads bowed as the villagers stood to receive Bess for the last time. Miss Johnson was playing the same music that Jess had chosen for her wedding and Ada wished she had a hat with a veil to cover her tears. The font stood before her and it crossed Ada's mind that in fact, neither Bess nor her children had been christened there, but at the chapel at Newton Burgoland. As the organ fell silent, the rector led the cortege down the steps, his voice echoing around the stone arches. "I am the resurrection and the life. He who believeth in me will live, even though he dies, saith the Lord."

Having successfully manoeuvred the steps, Ada raised her head, only to look directly into the eyes of Duncan. As their eyes connected, a longing coursed through her body, but the words of the rector brought her swiftly back to the present and the inappropriateness of her feelings.

Standing in the soft candle light surrounding the front pew, still in shock from seeing him, Ada gazed on the small coffin, recalling the moment, just a few days previous, when she had held her dying mother in her arms. As she stood with this thought, Ada experienced a sensation of being gently enclosed by the comforting warmth of her mother's arms. She could smell her. A healing calm descended, to sooth her desolate soul. "Thank you," she whispered through her tears.

The congregation remained standing. The first hymn, a well-known non-conformist composition and a favourite of Bess's, filled the space, uniting members of the congregation in their grief.

"Oh worship the lord in the beauty of holiness
Bow down before him, his glory proclaim.
With gold of obedience and incense of holiness,
Kneel and adore him the Lord is his name.

§

The small cottage was packed with mourners and Sam had to squeeze past the schoolmistress on his way to join the rest of the team. It had been a sorry day for him. He'd dug Bess's grave with tears in his eyes and sadness in his heart and had hidden behind a gravestone whilst they lowered her in. Despite having done the job for the last ten years, he felt the rector's words cut into him.

"We commit thee, Elizabeth Elverson to the ground," and his lip had trembled as he heard, "ashes to ashes and dust to dust," and the sounds of soil as it was sprinkled onto the coffin brought a lump to his throat. It had seemed so final. It's always the best people who go first, he thought. He'd always had a soft spot for Bess, but she had chosen Billy. He didn't harbour any feelings of resentment, it was just the way life went sometimes, although, now and again he wondered what life would have been like with her. Anyhow, he was alright with his own wife. Truth to tell, they didn't spend that much time in each other's company.

Lillian hadn't come. She was chapel and objected to Bess being taken to St. Peter's, a Church of England establishment. She had stood with her mouth clamped in a straight line and her hands on her hips as he set off with his shovel. Still, she would be over it by the time he returned home and there would be a meal on the table, as usual.

The wind had been enough to blow you off your feet. Poor Ada had taken it badly and Sam had given silent thanks to the Almighty that Bess had been lovingly cared for in her last days.

"Samuel, over here." He saw John Booton's hand wave over the motley concoction of hats and bonnets and he battled on towards his group of friends.

"There's no alcohol," John whispered.

"That's as well," replied Sam. "I have to cover her over before I go home. In fact, I've only come as a token of my respect for Billy. I don't know how he's going to manage without her." He took the plate from Ada and a ham sandwich from the dish and as he looked around in hope of a cup of tea, sorrow enveloped him and he knew nothing would ever be the same again.

Most of the guests hadn't lingered. The refreshments hadn't included strong drink, as Bess had been brought up in the Primitive Methodist faith, and as a matter of principle, hadn't partaken. She saw no actual harm in it, which was fortunate, considering her years in The Late Elephant, but the family had agreed that, as a mark of respect, it was not to be offered.

Ada accepted a hug and kind words from Tom as he shook his head. "She'll be sadly missed, yer Mother. She were a good woman with a kind heart, that she were." Tears threatened.

Ada squeezed his arm. "And how are you doing with Mrs Scarlett?"

THE LATE ELEPHANT

"A lot better than wi my sister."

Mrs Scarlet interrupted, "His sister is a member of the Primitive Methodists. She should know better than to behave that way towards her own brother."

"If she'd carried on much longer, I'd have bin pleased to go to the work'ouse, it can't be much worse."

"Dear, dear," muttered Mrs Scarlet. Ada noticed the smile she gave to Tom. It was obvious that the relationship was working, however it was being played.

There was no time to enquire into the Jess and William dilemma and Ada was heartened to see that for today at least they certainly appeared to be back to normal, but she did chance asking William a question. "I saw Duncan in church. I thought he would join us."

"Ah," began William, "he sends his apologies, and will call on you tomorrow, God willing. We have some new clients from the automobile company visiting and as Jess and I need to return home with the boys, Duncan is entertaining them."

Before Ada could take in the information and mull on its emotional implications, a voice cut into the serenity of the gathering. "I thought you would take Elizabeth down to the chapel at Newton Burgoland for the service, seeing as how that was the faith she was brought up with." This remark was made by Bess's brother, as he stood, a sardonic expression on his face and with a cup and saucer in one hand and a piece of Ada's Simnel cake in the other, but Billy was prepared.

"It's too far at this time of year to carry her all the way there just for a service, then have to carry her all the way back again, to bury her. Most of the people who cared for her live here in Swepstone and anyhow, Bess loved St. Peter's. She believed that God could be worshipped anywhere by anyone, not just Primitive Methodists. Your lot don't have the monopoly on God."

An uncomfortable hush hung heavily between the guests and the Jarvis clan left soon afterwards, leaving Billy free to say what was really on his mind.

"That lot make me really mad," Billy exploded, "there he stood, partaking of our hospitality, spouting like he's a bloody lord. He never flippin' cared a jot about his sister while she were alive, didn't agree with her marrying me at all, so what right has he got to come here after she's dead and tell me how to flippin' bury her?"

Tears were looming, but William intervened. "You're absolutely right," he said, "but you gave him his answer, he couldn't argue with that."

Billy wiped his sleeve quickly across his eyes, "Now them buggers have gone, we'll have a real drink."

Ada had the glasses ready and filled them from a bottle of whiskey, which William had brought. Just as well thought Ada, after settling Mr Insley's bill of one pound, eighteen shillings and sixpence for the coffin and buying extra food for the refreshments, it had barely left enough for her train fare back to Glenfield. There was certainly nothing left over for strong drink.

Violet Bentley squeezed through the front door, returning Henry and Edgar back to their parents. "They've had their tea, although I expect an extra slice of Aunt Ada's cake wouldn't go down amiss."

Ada knew that, although Father was under a lot of pressure, he wouldn't swear in front of the boys, and she was grateful, for it was something Mother would not have condoned.

Chapter 22

A Wind of Change 1899

Early spring sunshine flooded the farmyard, and as she breathed it in, Ada experienced a surge of energy. With help from Ben, she had hung the parlour carpet on the washing line, and was now beating it with more zest than was usual. Remembering Grandma Elverson's words, she grinned and thought it must be the sap rising. She chuckled out loud and vowed not to think too seriously about it.

Charles had departed to some far-flung place with his regiment, so he was firmly out of harm's way. She blushed a little on recalling her demise at their outing together, and contemplated his new self-confidence, augmented by the uniform and moustache, and she almost, but not quite, wondered if they could have lived in harmony together.

Duncan was spoken for, and although she had felt a spark between them, on seeing him at Mother's funeral, she doubted that he had. He had visited the following day, as promised and been friendly and respectful, as always, but there had been nothing to give her hope. In fact, she chastised herself for even thinking such a thing, knowing full well that he was already married to someone else, particularly as that same person was carrying their third child. She sighed, but despite her Christian ethics, and pledges to dispel him from her thoughts, her heart missed a beat and the old flood of longing came rushing back.

Missy had secured a place in a young ladies college, studying to become a school teacher. If the truth were known, Ada missed her, and smiled on wondering if she would meet some nice young school teacher who would steal her heart away. Missy would make a good wife and mother.

Despite her single state, she couldn't help but feel joyful on such a lovely day as this, and stopped dead in her tracks on hearing a distant but distinct, "cuckoo."

"Ada!" Ben's voice resonated with a definite note of urgency. "Mr Ludlam has just arrived back from the post office. There's a problem, I think you'd better come."

She dropped the carpet beater and ran for all she was worth. Not Father, she prayed, please, don't let it be Father.

Ada burst into the living room. Mr Ludlam stood, his face devoid of colour. "I'm so sorry to have to tell you this Ada, but there's been a calamity at the colliery in Whitwick and I believe your brother-in-law Jack, works there." He paused, giving her time to absorb the shock. "Do you happen to know which shift he works?"

Ada was rooted to the spot, hardly able to absorb the words. "I don't think so, no. Why, what's happened?"

THE LATE ELEPHANT

"There's a fire underground. Apparently it began in the night. If Jack only works day-shift, then he wouldn't be down there."

Ada sank down onto a chair. "No, he works nights, I remember now. He says it gives him more time to look after his animals. He's saving up to buy more land, so he can farm full-time." Her voice became hysterical, and she burst into tears. "That's terrible," she choked out the words, "to be trapped underground in a fire." Engulfed by panic Ada wrapped both arms around her head, crying out, "Oh, my goodness!" She felt Mrs Ludlam's arms around her shoulders.

"We don't know the full story yet, so try not to take on so."

"Mary will be in a terrible state, and poor Hannah, she just adores her father."

Mr Ludlam coughed. "Ada, shall we pray to God and ask his mercy to console us in this difficult time?"

Ada raised her face to him in horror. "No, I don't think I can do that, I feel too upset, Sir, if you don't mind."

"Very well." He turned on his heel and went back outside, beckoning Ben to follow, but after a moment's hesitation, turned and reached out a letter from his breast pocket. He held it out. "This came. I think it a little too early to be news of the fire."

She tore open the letter.

Dear Ada,

It is with great sadness that I have to inform you that the Reverend Townend has died. He was on holiday with his wife in St. German in Cornwall.

I understand that it was sudden and he did not suffer. Perhaps, under the circumstances, you will wish to contact Master Charles.

Your father seems to be bearing up and both he and Jarvis cope well in the house. I do what I can, but they are both independent.

I trust you are keeping well and am sorry to be the bearer of bad tidings.

Your friend as ever,

Nelly.

Ada felt sick. She sat with her head in her hands. Her mouth was dry and she gratefully drank the tea which was placed before her. She passed the letter to Mrs Ludlam, too upset about Jack to read it out loud. "I don't know what to do," she cried out, "how can I find out what has happened to him?"

Mrs Ludlam scanned the letter and placed it back in the envelope.

"There is nothing at all you can do, except wait for news to come. Perhaps there'll be something in this evening's Leicester Mercury. I'll ask Ben to fetch one later, before the Post Office closes. The papers don't usually arrive there until around half-past-four."

§

The following days were agony. Ada could neither eat nor sleep, and although the newspapers reported the extent of the explosion and the state of the fire, they hadn't as yet, published any names. The death of the

Reverend Townend appeared in the obituaries column of Mr Ludlam's newspaper and Ada cut it out, putting it on one side, intending to write to Charles once she had positive news of Jack.

It was late afternoon and Ada was crossing the yard towards the milking parlour, jug in hand, when William galloped up to the hitching rail, dust rising around the horse in a grimy cloud. Ada stood transfixed as he dismounted and began running towards her. She saw him stumble on the cinders, regain his balance, then open his arms. She clung to him as he gasped for breath, waiting to hear his words. Fearing the worst and breathing in the unfamiliar smells from his jacket, Ada wished fervently that she had not rebuffed Mr Ludlam's offer of a prayer and implored the Almighty that her brother-in-law be unharmed.

"It's alright Ada, Jack is safe."

"Thank the Lord, oh thank the Lord," She pulled away from him, "where was he? I thought he worked nights."

"He does usually." William stepped back, removed his hat and, using his jacket sleeve, wiped the dust and sweat from his brow, "But his mother had a bad turn, and he took the day off to visit her and stayed the night."

"So it was a miracle?"

"It was certainly a stroke of luck."

Ada dared to smile. "Thank you so much for coming all this way to tell me. I've been beside myself."

"I could see that from the look on your face. I'm sorry not to have come before, but I was away when it happened." William took her arm and they made their way towards the farmhouse. "Do you know about the Reverend Townend?"

"Yes, Nelly wrote to me. I haven't given it much thought because of Jack. When Ben called me, I thought Father must be ill. How is he? Have you seen him lately?"

"He's as well as can be expected, considering how much he misses your mother, but he carries on. What choice does he have?"

Ada's heart sank on hearing this. "I felt bad about leaving Nelly with the responsibility. Mother was ill for so long, there weren't any eggs pickled for the winter, no apples put up in the loft and no bacon cured. Father must be spending a fortune at Booton's stores to keep him and Jarvis going."

"I think John Booton has helped out. They've been friends for a long time. Jarvis has his job at the farm and he's been rabbiting and shooting with some of the lads from the village, so they're not going short of food. Jess sends cakes and pastries, when she can and George has been sharing potatoes from his winter camp."

Mrs Ludlam's voice interrupted their discussion. "William, how good to see you. Can I assume that the news is good?" She ushered them both inside and Ada happily set about making the tea.

"I cannot begin to tell you how pleased we are to see you, Ada has been beside herself with worry," but suddenly she bent forwards, clutched her breast and let out a moan.

"Mrs Ludlam! Ma'am, whatever's the matter?" Ada put her arm around her shoulders and wondered if they had become smaller or if she was just imagining it.

THE LATE ELEPHANT

"It's alright it's just indigestion, it'll be gone in a minute."

Ada and William helped her to a chair by the table.

"Sarah!" her husband rushed to her side, "is it that same pain again?"

"It's only indigestion Alfred, just leave me be a minute."

Ada looked at the face, creased into a mask of suffering and recognized the similarity to that of her mother. She sat down and her eyes met those of William. The former sparkle, ignited by the celebration of a life saved, had been extinguished and replaced by distress.

Ben appeared in the doorway. Mr Ludlam spoke sharply. "Ben, go and fetch the doctor. He should be at the surgery. Just keep your eyes open for his trap, in case he's already been called out." He turned to William, "Will you help me carry her upstairs? She needs to be in bed."

The two men formed a seat by clutching each-others' wrists and she sank onto it, allowing herself to be conveyed without protest. They carried her as though she were a small child. Her long slim body seemed to buckle under the strain, yet despite this, she turned her head to speak. "I don't want anyone telling Missy about this, until it's absolutely necessary. Do you understand?"

William returned back down the stairs and made straight for the door. "I'll leave you to it Ada. There's nothing I can do to help."

Once out in the farmyard, he turned to face her, holding his hat in his hands, his face suddenly beaming. "Actually, I have some more news. Jess gave birth to a son yesterday and I had wondered if you would come and stay for a few days, just until she gets back on her feet, but with Mrs Ludlam in this condition, I think I'd better find a nurse instead."

"Oh William, I am so sorry, I didn't even ask about Jess. Did it go well?"

William blushed, his paternal smile filling the day with pride. "Yes, it was much quicker this time, we've called him Walter."

"And is the mid-wife still in attendance?"

"Yes, for the time being and there's always Mary, I just thought it would do both of you good to spend some time together. I know Jess will be disappointed, but you have enough problems here, by the look of things."

The sound of hooves on cinders announced the doctor's arrival in the trap, with Ben sitting beside him.

Ada turned to William. "Give Jess my love. I'll do my best to visit soon."

§

Dear Ada,

Thank you so much for the money you sent for the children. I bought a new pinafore for little Walter, as the old ones are looking a bit grey. He is such a good baby. I can't wait for you to see him, but understand how difficult it must be for you at the moment.

I was shocked to hear William's words, describing Mrs Ludlam's illness. As much as no one wants to fear the worst, it did sound serious.

I want you to know Ada, you are welcome to come to us at any time. I feel that you may be in for a rough passage, and I saw how it took it out of you when Mother died.

There were photographs in the Leicester Mercury of the funeral at Whitwick for the miners who were killed. Two thousand mourners turned up. I hear the streets were blocked. Wasn't that a wonderful thing for people to do? Some comfort for the families. I thank the good Lord every day that Jack is safe.

It was a shock to hear of Reverend Townend's death. He will be sorely missed. According to Duncan, Mr Henry Townend, the rector's son is to follow in his father's footsteps. As he has already taken Holy Orders, it should be a simple matter, and so Swepstone will still have a Reverend Townend. Have you heard from Master Charles lately? I dare say he will inform you.

That seems to be all my news for present, look after yourself and may God bless you, which he surely will.

Your sister, Jess.

§

Ada's heart was breaking just as surely as Alfred Ludlam's as he stuttered, forcing out the words. "I'm sorry, Ada, but you'll have to leave us. I can't carry on with the mill while my wife is suffering so." He sank down at the table and sighed.

"But I can help. I know what to do. I looked after Mother."

"I know you did, but I want to do it myself. I can't leave her, not even for a moment, without worrying in case she needs me. We've always been like that." He took the cup Ada offered and, cradling it in his hands, stared into it as if the answer to his problems lay somewhere within. He raised his eyes to Ada. "Please, please, understand how difficult this is for me. You've been with us for so long, it's like telling one of my own to go away, but you have a family over in Swepstone and your father isn't getting any younger.

"I'll not be able to pay you. I'll need every penny for medication. The doctor is going to supply laudanum and that doesn't come cheap. He tells me it needs careful control of the dosage. I can't pass that responsibility to anyone else, Ada. I have to see to her myself. Do you understand?"

As the weeks passed it broke Ada's heart to see this couple who had been her surrogate family for so long deteriorate at such a pace, but it became obvious that the two of them needed to be alone, to share this last intimacy without interruption or interference. Ada packed her bags ready to leave Glenfield and her beloved mill, on what turned out to be exactly one calendar month before Sarah's death. Ada would like to have stayed to be a comfort for Missy, to whom a letter was now on the way, but it hadn't been her decision to make. Ada had given Allen a hug and told him what a good boy he was, and that he was to help Missy look after his mother and father.

Ben decided to stay on to tend the livestock and keep the farm tidy. He argued that, eventually things would go back to some sort of normality and Mr Ludlam would have to continue farming in order to provide for his children. He himself had nowhere else to go, so it made sense to stay. "When Missy gets her letter, I dare say she'll want to come home," he told Ada, "but until then, cooking can't be so difficult that I can't manage to feed us."

Ada was perturbed at the thought. "Just remember not to have the oven too hot when roasting the meat, and try to baste it a few times, it'll make all the difference, and keep it in the meat safe, else you'll have the flies blow on it."

Ada opened the bedroom door and tiptoed over to where the invalid lay. "I've come to say goodbye." Her bottom lip trembled as she held Mrs Ludlam's hand. "You've been so good to me. I can't find words to express how grateful I am. I shall always remember my days here and how kind you are."

Sarah Ludlam mumbled something incomprehensible. She was under the spell of the laudanum and Ada knew it would be a sin to encroach further, so she closed the door behind her just as carefully as she had opened it and ended a huge part of her life.

It was a bright sunny day. There were pies and fruit tarts on the thrawl and tins full of cakes and pastries. Ben had loaded her bags onto the trap and they were off. She reflected on the first time she had crossed the threshold, to eat beestings' pie and drink milk. She didn't want to leave this place, with all its memories, even though it was to go home to Swepstone to be with Father.

The journey passed almost in silence. They finally reached the railway station, and on handing her down, Ben looked into her eyes, "If I thought you would say yes, I would ask yer to marry me, but yer wouldn't would yer?"

§

Ada ran as fast as she could down Market Street. She had managed to purchase some reasonably priced boots and a couple of yards of good quality cotton for Nelly to make into blouses. She had a heavy bag in each hand and her old boots, with the soles almost worn through, were not providing much protection against the uneven road surface. She hoped the fish she had purchased for supper was still in the brown paper and not passing on its smell to the flour, but there was little she could do about it, as the stage coach was almost ready to leave and time was of the essence.

She stumbled past the last market stalls, only to see John Thomas climb up onto his seat on the top of the coach. Abandoning decorum, she shouted with all her might, "Mr Thomas," and fortunately he heard, but as he raised his hand in acknowledgement, her best hat succumbed to a gust of wind and, despite the hat-pin, took off into the air. Necessity kept her legs in motion, but as both hands were otherwise occupied she suffered the indignity, not only of being seen bare-headed and shouting in the street, but to watch her most treasured possession cart-wheel down the road and straight under the wheels of a passing cab. She was painfully aware that her commotion was being watched by others, but she was desperate to reach the stage coach. A young boy rescued the hat, but there was hardly an inch which was not crushed and covered in horse-dung, so he shrugged his shoulders and tossed it back into the gutter.

§

The Late Elephant

"Did yer get any boots?" called Father, on hearing the front door close behind her.

"Yes. I bought some from Mrs Moore's second-hand stall." She walked into the scullery and removed the fish, before poking the fire and placing the kettle over the coals. She filled a mug from the pump, and gratefully sipped the cool spring-water, returning to the parlour to plump Father's cushions. "I bought your linctus from the apothecary, but you seem a lot better today."

She pulled out the glass stopper and poured some into a spoon. "Father, where have the spectacles come from?" Before he could answer, she tipped the contents into his mouth.

"Ugh, that is strong." He wiped his jacket sleeve across his mouth before answering her. "Nelly found the spectacles in a drawer. Yer mother was lent them by Mrs Scarlett. They belonged to her sister, I think. They really work, here have a look."

Ada balanced them precariously on her nose whilst stretching the wires behind her ears. She picked up Father's newspaper. "Oh yes, that's marvellous, much better than having to rely on the magnifying glass." She turned to him. "Have you been alright without me?"

"Yes, George came round as soon as he came home from work, but I can get to the lavatory by miself now and this morning I managed to wash mi sen. Nelly brought me some rabbit pie for mi dinner. What's happened to yer hat?" he said, peering at her wind-blown hair.

"It blew off and a carriage drove over it." She shrugged her shoulders, no point in worrying about it. "You didn't tell me Simpkin and James have opened a shop in Market Street."

"Have they?"

Ada was on the verge of asking more questions, when she heard Jarvis. She went into the living room to pour him some tea. "What are you doing home at this hour?" She could see from his face that something was amiss.

"I have something to tell you." The words spilled out, but he kept his voice down to almost a whisper. "I'm not working at the farm any longer. I've finished there today and I start at Measham Main on Monday morning."

"Jarvis, you can't do that. You promised Mother you wouldn't go down the pit."

"I know, but I'll earn twice as much money. With you just doing part-time at Mrs Stevenson's and Father being off with the influenza, we need the extra and I want to buy a bicycle, like Frederick Booton and then I can visit Mary and Jess."

He pulled at his braces and twisted his head, exercising his shoulders. "I feel really stiff. I've been laying hedges all day."

"You'll hurt a lot more than that after Monday. I've heard tell there's hardly room to swing a cat in some parts of the pit and you have to stoop because the roof is so low. Most of the miners suffer from neck pains." Seeing the expression on his face she gave up, knowing that, at almost fifteen years old, he must be allowed to choose his own way.

Jarvis changed the subject, something he was good at. "Are you working tomorrow?"

"Yes, so if you're going to be at home, perhaps you'd keep an eye on Father. It'll save George and Nellie. I shall be up and gone before you're even awake."

"I'll need to get some moleskins afore Monday and I need some hob-nails to put in mi boots."

"As long as you're not gone too long, he'll be alright. If you'd told me before I could have brought you some from Ashby."

Jarvis shrugged.

"You'd better go and tell Father your news."

Ada removed her coat, rolled up her sleeves and made a start on the fish pie.

§

Rain was plummeting and Ada could feel it running down her back. She finally reached the top of the hill and instead of entering the parlour to drip all over the carpet, she went round to the scullery door, pulling off her boots. After removing her drenched shawl, she spotted a pair of men's boots standing in the corner. She quickly rubbed her hair with a towel, and after smoothing it back and securing it with pins, peered around the door into the living room. There was no-one in there but voices could be heard in the parlour.

He jumped up, hand outstretched, a huge beaming smile on his face.

"Ben, what are you doing here?"

"Mr Ludlam has moved us into The White House in Heather."

"I don't believe it. It's a wonder somebody hasn't said something, knowing how they gossip in this village." Ada couldn't hide her delight. "He doesn't want a housekeeper, does he?"

"No, I don't think so, Missy is doing the cooking."

"How old is she now?"

"Nineteen, I think."

Ada turned to a grinning Jarvis and a knowing wink from Father. "I hope you've been looking after our guest?"

Ben reassured her. "I've had two cups of tea and very welcome they was too, and a piece of your Victoria sandwich cake. I've missed that taste."

He looked through the window, wiping away the condensation with his sleeve. "The rain has stopped, so I'd best get back. It's good to see you, Ada. Mr Ludlam says you're welcome to come and visit anytime you like."

"Tell him thank you and tell Missy if she needs help I'll come willingly."

Ada saw him off and placed her shawl over the fire guard. Steam began to rise, and she screwed up her nose at the smell of wet wool. Returning post-haste to the parlour, anxious to hear Father's comments, she asked, "Well, Father, what do you think to the Ludlams living just up the road in Heather?"

"I think young Ben would make a very nice son-in-law, that's what I think." Billy puffed on his pipe, a twinkle in his eye as he added, "'Is eyes fairly lit up when he heard yer voice."

Although Ada felt she should put him right on the subject of Ben, she was loath to wipe the smile from his face. It hadn't appeared much since Mother died.

Chapter 23

Long Live the King 1901

Ada had purchased a shoulder of pork for Sunday's dinner, thinking that such an occasion commanded respect. After all, it wasn't every day a country buried a monarch as good as Queen Victoria, while at the same acknowledging a new King.

Ada would have preferred to serve beef like Jess had, with roast potatoes, horseradish sauce and Yorkshire pudding, but the price of a good beef joint was too expensive, so she had settled for pork instead. In any case, it wasn't the season for horseradish and because of poor Mother's demise there were no pots of preserves in the cupboard.

Ada placed a dish of roast potatoes and one of Brussels-sprouts, onto the table and sat down next to George. Father had almost finished carving the meat and she took her plate from him, helping herself to vegetables. She cut carefully and raised her fork. She was hungry. "You missed a good sermon, Father. The rector prayed for King Edward. The anthem was, 'Lead me lord, lead me in they righteousness'. I thought it a good choice for a new King."

George nodded in agreement. "It's a shame you missed it. Being as today is the day of Queen Victoria's funeral, we all had to stand up at the end and say God Save the King."

"Did you now?" said Billy. "I read in the paper they've taken her to St. George's Chapel in Windsor. She'll rest beside her husband in the Great Park. Pity her son doesn't walk in her ways and have the same respect for his wife that his mother and father had for each other."

"The rector spoke well of him, didn't you think so George?" remarked Ada, but before George could get a word in, Billy snapped back.

"Ah, well, happen so, but I don't care what yer say," Billy waved his knife in George and Ada's direction, "Prince Edward is not going to make a popular King. How can he, wi all them rumours about him and his women?"

"You don't know if they're true!" George was adamant. He was a staunch royalist and had worn his uniform proudly.

"Don't be daft, they can't all be wrong and he has that beautiful woman, Princess Alexandra, as his wife. I wonder what she makes of it." Billy stopped to chew, his few remaining teeth sadly inadequate for the purpose.

"They lead very different lives from us, Father," said Ada. "Most of the marriages are arranged, or so I believe."

"Just fancy that," commented Nelly. "Imagine having to marry someone you've never even met."

THE LATE ELEPHANT

"Even so, he married her in the Church of England faith, and he should stand by his vows. I know what yer mother would have said. She didn't at all approve of his doings and as for the old Queen, God rest her soul, well she must be turning in her grave."

"He made Yorkshire pudding popular and you like that well enough," pointed out Ada.

"What?" Father bellowed, "A batter puddin' given by some at the beginning of a meal so the children don't eat too much meat? Where's the splendour in that?" His face was scarlet.

George and Ada shared a knowing look. He'd been like this for a day or two and Ada wondered whatever it could be that had made him so angry.

"When the Rector prayed for him this morning, he promised God that we would all be loyal to the new king." Ada grinned at her Father. "I thought at the time, it's a good thing Father stayed at home, he most probably wouldn't agree with that." Ada giggled.

Billy peered at them all over his spectacles and carried on chewing in silence.

Ada thought it time to change the subject. "Mind you, it was really cold in church. I sat behind our George. His ears were bright blue and just about everybody seemed to be coughing and sneezing. You could see the rector's breath blowing white into the air. "Who was that boy walking with you, Jarvis? I watched you processing to the choir stalls and the poor little thing was shivering under his cassock."

"That was Frederick Forrester. He didn't have a jacket or a scarf or anything."

"Poor little chap, said Ada, "I'll have a look after dinner and see what I can find."

"Yer'll do nowt o the sort," exploded Billy, "yer know how I feel about that family. His mother should be spending her money on clothing her children, instead of frittering it away in Ashby." He paused for a moment, to finish off a mouthful. "Yer know I can't abide waste and John Thomas told me that he dropped her off once, from a trip into Ashby and she had purchased a cabbage from the market. John has a good view over their hedge from the top of his coach, so he shouted down to her, 'Mrs Forrester, I know it's none o my business, but why are yer spending money on cabbages when yer have a garden full of em?' He reckons she looked back at him, a bit vacant like, and said, 'Do I?' He reckons she's never been down to the bottom o their garden. Mind yer, apparently that's where her poor husband goes to get a bit of peace and quiet, not that he spends much at time at home, mind, he's always at work, earning money for her to spend."

Ada looked at George, wondering if the tirade would ever finish.

"Now, she is the sort who will spend out on a joint o beef just because the King eats it, whether they can afford it or not."

Ada hid a grin behind her napkin. "I'll make us a suet pudding tomorrow. That'll help keep us warm." She heaved a sigh of relief that he seemed to have simmered down and felt that perhaps, in future, she would keep her thoughts to herself.

"Have you heard from Master Charles lately, Ada?" asked George.

"No. Not since the death of his father. Charles has gone with the army to foreign parts, you know." She stood up. "I'll fetch the apple tart."

The Late Elephant

§

Easter arrived and for once it was warm and sunny with hardly any breeze. Ada was helping in church, arranging catkins and pussy willows in the two brass vases which stood at either end of the altar. "This is my favourite season," said Ada, "the colours promise sunshine and blue skies. I can almost smell the primroses. Mind you, last year we struggled to sing, it was so cold, do you remember?"

Before Mrs Scarlett could deliver an answer, a ghostly creak echoed through the empty building. On feeling a shiver run down her spine, Ada was much relieved to see the door open and a tall young man make his way down the steps. He was carrying a trug full of white lilies. "Mother has sent these," he said, "she's unable to come herself, as Freddie has croup."

Ada took the flowers, wondering who he was, taking in his blue eyes and tidy suit and the collar and tie. The shirt-collar was a little worn she noticed, as were the cuffs of his shirt, but they were clean and his shoes had been polished. His brown hair was tightly curled and free of pomade. Ada liked this, it gave him the look of a cheeky little boy and in any case, she was not overly keen on well-greased hair, combed flat. As he addressed Mrs Scarlett, Ada thought what a pleasantly spoken young man he was.

"That'll be all then, Ernest," said Mrs Scarlett, her voice harder even than usual, "tell yer mam, thank you." The sound of the door latch clunked into place, announcing that the young man was gone. It was all a bit abrupt and Ada gave Mrs Scarlett a quizzical look, only to be told, "He likes the young ladies a bit too much for my liking."

Ada watched the woman turn and walk away and wondered if there had been a tear threatening and it struck Ada how difficult life must have been for her. The pit accident had been around this time of year and the young man would be of a similar age to that of her sons at the time of their death.

Mrs Scarlet had removed the purple altar-cloth, used during Lent, and was exchanging it for the Easter one. "Ada, give us a hand will you?" They lifted the heavy drape, stretching it out to fit the top of the rectangular table, before allowing it to cascade to the floor. Ada gently stroked it, feeling the white silken cloth beneath her hand, tracing the yellow and gold embroidered thread with her finger and enthused over the cloth of gold inlay which highlighted the petals of the Jacobean flowers. Mrs Scarlett carefully unfolded a long white linen cloth, edged all around with the finest crochet and starched to perfection and placed it on the top. Ada caught her breath, "Mrs Scarlett, this is so beautifully done, you really do have a gift. I wouldn't have the patience."

Satisfied that it was properly centred, they stood back to admire. "Will you be going to the social on Monday?" Ada enquired, as much to make conversation than to extract an answer.

"I shall be helping with the refreshments as usual." The reply was short and sharp, as if Ada should have known better than to ask in the first place.

"I hear some of the ladies are boycotting it, as we're supposed still to be in mourning for the Queen."

Mrs Scarlett looked at Ada as if she had blasphemed. "Cancelling the social won't bring her back and we need the money. Anyway, the King has only decreed mourning for six months. No-one takes these things as seriously as they used to. I remember when the women covered their faces with black veils for at least twelve months. Ridiculous if you ask me."

Ada wondered if she dare ask Mrs Scarlett who the young man was with eyes the colour of delphiniums, but thought better of it, knowing Mrs Scarlett's inclination to gossip, so instead she transferred the catkins and pussy willows into earthen-ware jugs before replacing them with the Easter lilies. The white waxy petals and golden stamens blended perfectly with the altar cloth and Ada pondered further on the young man who had delivered them.

§

The social was over. On leaving the school, he doffed his cap and bowed low before her. "I bid you good evening, Miss Elverson, I have so enjoyed your company. I trust we'll meet again soon." He turned and strolled across the road, disappearing through the gate opposite.

"Oh," exclaimed Ada, still blushing behind her fan, "does he live there, in School Cottages?" Ada's question was met with silence. "Who does he live with, the school teacher or the Forresters?"

George answered. "With the Forresters, of course, don't you recognize him?"

"No."

"Well apparently, according to Jess, on her wedding day he caught the bouquet which was really meant for you."

Ada was aghast. "You can't mean young Ernest? But he's just a boy."

Nelly laughed. "Maybe then, but he's grown up now and he's not so much younger than you."

"But I was at school with William and Alfred. They didn't live next to the school-house then." Ada tossed her head, the light of day beginning to dawn. "Why haven't I come across him in church?"

"Because when his family does attend church, which isn't often, they go to the evening service. You go in the mornings."

"Cheeky monkey! Goodness gracious, whatever next?" Her face was burning. She headed towards home, embarrassment fuelling her flight. Inwardly she was furious with herself for becoming distracted by a mere boy, for that was all it was, a moment of frivolity and nothing more. Whatever could she have been thinking? No wonder his cuffs were frayed, they must be hand-me-downs from his older brothers. So much for her secret imaginings that he may be a young school teacher. She should have made sure before letting herself down like that.

George and Nelly caught up. "What's the hurry, Ada? Haven't you had enough exercise for one night?" asked George, followed by a snigger. She had no answer, and her cheeks puffed up with exasperation. She needed to get out of this village as soon as possible.

"He's not going to be your Prince Charming then?" Nelly teased her.

"Certainly not!"

The Late Elephant

"Hold on, Ada, he's not a bad chap. He works at the pit. He seems alright to me."

At last Ada was back in her bedroom, staring into the mirror, remembering back to when she had sat in the living-room preparing for the social. It was Easter Monday and the Parochial Church Council had organized a celebration in the school-room, hoping to raise money to fund some new hassocks. Nelly had twisted velvet ribbons around Ada's locks and arranged them into a fashionable hairstyle. After the last pin was inserted, she had said, "There you are Ada, fit for a prince."

Ada had laughed. "Some hope of that, in Swepstone."

However, she had attended in good spirits, wearing her best skirt and the cream silk blouse. She had pinned on a brooch which Mother had given her years ago. It was a delicate bunch of violets, fashioned in cheap gilt no doubt, but the flower heads were enamelled in shades of lavender and blue and Ada liked it.

She shivered on recalling the evening, admitting that not only had she succumbed to his guiles, but even worse, she had cavorted and flirted with him in front of the whole village. He had held her hand so tenderly, kissing it after each dance and she had giggled shamelessly. What would they think of her? Ada had convinced herself he was the new school-master, he was so well-spoken and with such charisma. Fancy her not insisting on being properly introduced, before taking his hand for the dance. She had been intoxicated by his charm, there was no use denying it, but it must never happen again. Mrs Scarlett had warned her in Church. "He likes the young ladies a bit too much for my liking."

Just imagine, waking one morning to be just another 'young lady' amongst his list. He must be at least seven years her junior, that would make him around eighteen. He was far too young. No, it simply would not do.

Ada tore the ribbons from her hair and washed her hands and face, determined to remove the smell of him. Once in bed she concentrated on thoughts of Duncan and the way just a mere glimpse of him made her heart flutter. Regretfully, however, her ploy didn't work, so she opened Charles' anthology to read once more those captivating words, 'How do I love thee, let me count the ways', but the young man's face refused to budge and so the anthology was immediately placed back on the table and the candle flame extinguished.

Ada lay with her eyes tightly closed, willing sleep to rescue her.

§

Ada spotted William's horse as soon as she turned the corner into Street End. Despite her impatience to join him however, she was forced to lay the heavy basket on the ground for a moment to rest her arms. She had purchased flour and sugar from Booton's Stores, and they weighed heavily. Father was almost well enough now to return to work and after struggling up the hill with her load, Ada found the two men in the garden, discussing the egg yield and enthusing over a crop of potatoes. After a wave, she put on the kettle. Father and William returned immediately to the house. William's voice held a note of urgency. "Ada, I can't stay long, but I have something to tell you."

They all three sat down at the table. "Very well, go on."

"A position of cook has become vacant in a house at Burley-on-the-Hill."

"Where's that?" She could see William beginning to fidget, taking out his pocket-watch to check the time.

"It's near Oakham, in Rutland, but I've worked out the journey. You will take the train from Ashby and only have to change once. There'll be a coach waiting at Oakham station, to take you to the house."

Ada suffered conflicting thoughts at this abrupt announcement. She certainly needed to escape the village and put a few miles between herself and Swepstone, but she was overcome by a sudden panic. It was similar to the one she suffered on the day of Jess's wedding, when she had contemplated leaving The Late Elephant. "Please, go on."

"There isn't much more except that the housekeeper, Mrs Watson, is eager to meet you. The job is yours if you can leave within the next few days. She's desperate to fill the position."

The silence hovered between them, with Father looking intently at her. Ada picked up the teapot to pour, but put it back down again. "Thank you William, I do need somewhere permanent. Father, are you well enough for me to go? Will you and Jarvis manage?"

"We certainly will. I'll be back at work next week and Jarvis has settled in at the pit. Yer young, yer shouldn't be stuck here at Swepi, well, not without a husband." The twinkle returned. "And if yer'll not accept that nice Ben, then this is a good alternative." Billy guffawed. "And yer won't be sorry to see the back o the goat, I'll be bound."

William jumped to his feet. "Sorry, I can't stop to hear the tale. Today is Thursday, and I'm back to Burley tomorrow to complete a deal with the steward. I suggest you leave on Monday morning, and take the first train to Leicester. Can I tell Mrs Watson that for certain?"

"Yes, you can."

"Good, I shall go to the ticket office on my way home this evening, and purchase your fare. All you have to do is collect it and go on from there."

She turned to ask a question, but William was already at the door. "I must get back." He mounted his chestnut mare and waved his hand.

Ada shouted after him. "Tell Jess and the boys, 'hello' from us. I'd hoped to be with her when the new baby arrives," but he was already steering the horse down the hill. "And thank you, I am much obliged."

Ada turned to Father. "I shall be sorry to leave before Jess has this next child. I wonder how far from Burley, Leicester is? But you're right about one thing, Father, I shall be relieved to put a distance between myself and that goat. If I had to milk her for much longer, I would probably wring her neck."

"And what about Ernest Forrester? Will yer be pleased to see the back of him?"

Ada was thunderstruck.

Billy concentrated on filling his pipe, but before putting a spill to it, he said, "I heard about the social. Apparently he couldn't leave yer alone."

Ada snapped back. "He danced with me and that was all." His words had totally unnerved her. Her cheeks were glowing and she felt guilty and a little frightened as to what was to come.

The Late Elephant

On noisily clearing his throat, he continued. "He danced wi yer for most o the evenin', so I am told. Yer know, Ada, I would hate to think on yer throwing yer sen away on somebody like him. He has a terrible reputation with the women. It's his mother is the problem. Never in all my puff have I ever come across a woman like her. She's a witch. She spends her husband's wages on daft things like having her photograph taken. She's always on the stage-coach going into Ashby. You ask John Thomas if yer don't believe me."

Ada grinned. "You make her sound like Old Mother Hubbard."

Billy laughed, despite his anger. "Remember yer mother's words, Ada. As the hen flappeth her wings, her chickens will do likewise." At this juncture, he pointed the end of his pipe at her. "Mark my words her children don't stand a chance of being anything like decent."

Ada retaliated. "I doubt if Nelly would agree with you. She didn't have a good start, but she's turned out well enough."

"Yes," nodded Billy, "but although she was orphaned, she wasn't badly treated. I've heard tales about how that Forrester woman locks the lads up in an upstairs room and leaves them alone while she goes out, and how they climb out of the windows to escape." He was really angry now. "Fancy anybody flippin' well locking children up and leaving em alone. Suppose they set the house on fire? It gives me the creeps just thinking about it."

Ada sighed, no point in arguing with Father when he was angry. "Well, I can't dance with him if I'm in Rutland, so take comfort in that thought." She turned to put some distance between them and put the kettle on.

"Did yer hear what William said about Duncan?"

Ada returned to the parlour. "Heard what, Father?"

"'Is wife has died in childbirth, delivering their third child."

"When?"

"It can't be long ago, William were only here last week, and he never mentioned it then."

§

Knives, forks and spoons sat in separate piles, waiting to be polished. Ada placed a handful of clean dusters next to them and began what was without doubt one of the most boring tasks of all time. However, it afforded her time to think.

She must visit Duncan. Ada was torn between the need to see him and the awful truth that his wife was not even in her grave. It was certainly too soon to expect a proposal of marriage. She needed time. The situation needed time, but time of course, was something she didn't have.

She sighed, what was she to do? There were so many conflicting emotions turning her inside out, but she couldn't and wouldn't give up this opportunity to at least visit him and see how the land lay. Although it did seem inappropriate under the circumstances, she had to know how he felt about her. If she didn't do it now, she would spend the rest of her life wondering. The real question, however, was what was she to do about the position in Rutland if Duncan did have feelings for her?

Ada looked at the clock. It was half past ten. Father was busy in the garden. She gave the last of the knives a quick rub and plunged them all into a bowl of hot water

THE LATE ELEPHANT

and green soft soap. In less than an hour she was finished, and shortly afterwards, their mid-day meal was on the table.

"It's early today, Ada."

"Yes Father, I've decided to walk into Measham this afternoon. If I'm to leave for Rutland, I'll be needing some things from Mrs Wade."

"What do mean, *if* you leave? William will have bought your ticket by now. Yer hadn't better let him down."

"No, Father, of course not, and you'll be needing balsam from the pharmacist, as you still haven't got rid of your cough." She stared defiantly back at him.

§

Ada approached The Late Elephant. It looked very different. There was no longer a sign hanging from the eaves, and the thatch had been replaced with roof tiles. Children played outside, some climbing in and out of the front downstairs windows. There didn't appear to be a grown-up in attendance. Ada called out, "Hello, you seem to be having a good time."

One of the young boys stopped to look at her. "Yes, Missus."

"Isn't there anyone with you? A grownup?"

"No, mi mam's at the farm, but she'll be back soon wi mi dad. Our Susan's looking after us."

"Oh, that's all right then." There was no older sister in sight, but it was no business of her's.

There was no sign of life coming from The Hall. Ada assumed the family must still be away for the summer. Ada noticed a cart laden with tree trunks and saw that many of the oaks had been felled. She remembered Jarvis saying they were used for pit props and she wondered just how many they would need.

The Gilwiskaw was high and she stopped a moment to rest and watched as it gurgled along towards Newton Nethercôte. The surrounding bog was alive with yellow flags and the bull-rushes were showing their dark brown velvet spikes. Any other time and she would have stood for an hour or more, appreciating the scene, hoping to spot a kingfisher or a heron, but today was different and with much trepidation, she began climbing the hill towards the tunnel of trees leading to Measham Main Colliery.

The question of Ernest Forrester confused her. She daren't allow herself to seriously consider the feelings he invoked in her. Where they had come from goodness only knew, but the whole situation was ludicrous and unreal. She had been in love with Duncan for almost as long as she could remember. He was mature and kind. Jess had been adamant that he would never have married Bella if she hadn't been in the family way, so it stood to reason that if he had a good hardworking woman as is wife, someone who would keep his house clean and cook well for him, things could be different. He would no longer have the need to look further. Ada walked out of the tunnel and into sunlight. She crossed her fingers and quickened her step.

The shop bell jangled and Mrs Wade came out from behind the counter to shake Ada's hand. "Ada, my duck, how nice to see you. Have you heard about Duncan's wife?"

"Yes, Mrs Wade. How is he?"

The Late Elephant

"Oh, he's alright!" She pulled a face. "He's already moved Bella's sister in. A scandal if you ask me. Mind you, they've been carrying on for ages. I've heard tell as how they used to meet down by the canal. Some say that she keeps the house cleaner than Bella and the children are a lot better fed. Even so, I ask you Ada, fancy him carrying on with his own sister-in-law?"

Ada felt sick, but she needed to say something, anything to fill the silence. "I suppose, under the circumstances, it's just as well she is there, certainly for the welfare of the children."

"I suppose so, but she's barely sixteen. He likes em young, that one. Too young in my opinion."

Ada's legs threatened to give way.

"Ada, are you ill? Your colour has just drained from your face." Mrs Wade pulled up a chair. "Here, sit yourself down." Turning, she called to a young shop assistant.

Ada gasped. "Oh dear! I think the walk has worn me out. I'll be alright in a minute."

"You just sit yourself still, there's nothing to rush for." She turned to the shop girl. "Get Miss Ada a glass of water, if you please."

Ada was stunned, but she needed to know more. "What happened to the baby? Did it survive?"

"Yes, it lived, another one for Bella's sister to tend. I wouldn't be surprised if she isn't the next to be in the family way. You'll see in a month or two."

The words withdrew into oblivion as Ada struggled to process them. There was little or no room for manoeuvre, no excuses left to be made, nowhere for Ada's emotions to seek refuge. She was left sitting there with the dark, scruffy, unpalatable truth.

"And you, my duck, what can I do for you?"

Ada forced herself to concentrate. "I need some stockings please, and a new white collar. The ones on my bodices are looking a bit grey."

Mrs Wade placed a tray of lace-trimmed collars onto the counter. "There you are. Is it for something special?"

"Yes," answered Ada. "I have a new position at a house in Rutland. I leave on Monday."

After a few minutes she added, "And when you see Duncan, please say that I'm sorry to hear of his wife's death, and am leaving Swepstone, most probably for good."

The End

Thank you for taking the trouble to read **The Late Elephant**. It is my first attempt at a novel and is intended to be the first of a series entitled, 'Tales from Old Swepi'.

It's loosely based on the life of my grandmother, and although I have used old family names like Booton and Thomas, the characters' escapades are purely figments of my imagination.

I hope you enjoyed the tale.

Janet Scrivens née Forrester

Acknowledgements

To all of you who have helped to collect information for the book, have read parts of or all of it, commented, made suggestions, answered my multitudinous questions or just listened to my going on incessantly but have been too polite to tell me to shut up, thank you:-

My friend Joyce Clarke who, in 2005, introduced me to:-

The Grace Dieu Writers' Circle, without who's members, past and present, this would not have been written,

Friends on Writesmith, in particular Gail Jenny Orbell and Mary Newman,
All friends on Facebook who have been most supportive,
Jane Boyce and fellow members of The Sence Valley Supper Club,
Newton Burgoland and Swepstone Web Page led by Louise Smedley-Hampson,

Linda Abrahams, Tony Gutteridge, Trish and Alan Newbold, John Haynes, Roger Pilgrim, Mick and Hilary Dolphin, The Ludlam family of Cattows Farm, Betty Cawte, David Ramsey, Brenda and Nick Makin, Stefanie Offiler, Raymond Hill, Nancy Deacon, Rosamond Cope, Janice Mee, Susan and Graham Tyers, Susan and Graham Bentley, Audrey Glen, Dorothy and Fred Fell, Rose Glover, Henry and Dorothy Everett, Jill Dearden, Janet Firman, Mick and Pat Brown, Vivienne and David King, Rob Nichol, Maureen Howard, Nigel Rolnis, Lin Bradley, James Turner at Crestline Printers, Ken Hillier, The Ashby Museum, The Ashby Library, The Measham Museum, The Rector of St. Peter's Church, Glenfield and the ladies at the Ibstock Community Café, who brew such delicious coffee.

>
> The Late Mrs Phyllis Evans
> The Late Miss Doreen Cooper
> The Late Mr Ernest Glover

>
> My family:-
> William, Angela, Daniel, Harriet,
> Michael, Leslie, Jamie, Sophie,
> Lucy, Simon, Charlie, Tom
> And Grandma Win

The bibliography:-

The Holy Bible

Modern Cookery for Private Families by Eliza Acton, pub by Quadrille publishing.

Mrs. Beeton's book of Household Management by Mrs. Beeton pub by Oxford University Press.

Up and Down Stairs by Jeremy Musson, pub by John Murray.

At Home by Bill Bryson, pub by Transworld Publishers

Burley on the Hill Mansion by Raymond Hill pub by Janet Kirkwood

The History of Burley on the Hill by Pearl Finch pub Unknown

Life below Stairs by Alison Maloney pub by O'Mara Books

Leicestershire and Rutland-Within Living Memory, by Leic. and Rut W.I.s pub by W.I.s

Writers' and Artists' Year Book 2001 by Jo Herbert pub by A. and C. Black, Publishers

The Victorian Hospital by Lavinia Milton pub by Shire Publications

Chatsworth, the House by Duchess of Devonshire pub by Francis Lincoln Ltd

An Illustrated History of Market Street, Ashby de la Zouch, by Robert Jones, pub by Ashby Museum

Harewood House, Yorkshire by Andrew Esson pub by Raithby Lawrence and Co

The English Bread Book by Eliza Acton pub by General Books, Memphis

Shoes by June Swann pub by B.T. Batsford

Peelers to Panders (A History of Leicestershire Police) by Ben Beasley, pub by Breedon Books

Who do You Think You are? by Nick Barratt pub Harper Collins

Ey up mi duck by Richard Scallins and John Titford pub Countryside Books

How to be a Victorian by Ruth Goodman pub Penguin Books

Leicestershire Water Mills by Norman Ashton pub by N.D. Ashton

Memories of Leicestershire Coalfields by David Bell pub by Countryside Books

Changing Times, My Story by Len Haynes pub by Len Haynes

Ashby de la Zouch, The Spa Town by Ken Hillier, pub by Ashby Museum

Ashby de la Zouch, Past and Present, by Ken Hillier, pub by Ashby Museum

Shire County Guide, Leicestershire by Jeffrey Hopewell pub by Shire Publications

Shoe-making by June Swann pub by Shire Publications

Measham in Focus by Keith Elliott and Jim Salton pub by Leicestershire Libraries

Victorian Britain by Patrick N. Allitt pub by The Great Courses

Reminiscences of Coalville by Denis Baker pub by Norwood Press

Notes on the Leicestershire and Nottingham Railway by Clement E. Stretton pub Unknown

Crochet (A History of the Craft Since 1850) by Pauling Turner pub by Shire Publications

Kelly's Directory

Collins Book of English Verse by Harper Collins

The Girls' own Annual 1898 by

Various hymn books and psalters

Lest We Forget by North West Leicestershire pub Ashby Museum

Printed in Great Britain
by Amazon.co.uk, Ltd.,
Marston Gate.